Return to Prior Park

BOOK 3 IN THE
BELLEVILLE FAMILY SERIES

J MARY MASTERS

First published 2019 by PMA Books, A divn of Peter Masters &
Associates, ABN 72 172 119 877
Unit 111, 1 Halcyon Way, Bli Bli Qld 4560, Australia

 A catalogue record for this
book is available from the
National Library of Australia

ISBN 978-0-9943276-3-5

Cover design: J D Smith Design, UK
www.jdsmith-design.co.uk

www.pmabooks.com
Tel + (61) (0) 488 224 929
Email enquiries@pmabooks.com

Return to Prior Park

BOOK 3 IN THE
BELLEVILLE FAMILY SERIES

J MARY MASTERS

WWW.PMABOOKS.COM

PMA Books

About the author

J Mary Masters (Judith) was born in Rockhampton, Queensland, Australia in the 1950s, the youngest of four children and raised on a cattle property.

For more than twenty years, she was involved in the magazine publishing industry as a senior executive.

Having now given up full time magazine work, Judith is devoting her time to her writing career, with an emphasis on writing for women readers. Her stories feature a mix of town and country settings, drawing heavily on her early life.

She is a member of the Queensland Writers Centre (QWC) and the Australian Society of Authors (ASA).

Judith now lives on Queensland's Sunshine Coast with her husband Peter.

Readers are invited to contact Judith through the following channels.

Website	jmarymasters.com
Twitter	@judithmasters
Blog	judithmasters.wordpress.com
Facebook	www.facebook.com/JudithMMasters
Email	jmarymasters1@gmail.com

Also by J Mary Masters

Julia's Story
(previously published as *The House of Secrets: Julia's Story*)
Book 1 of the Belleville family series

To Love, Honour and Betray
Book 2 of the Belleville family series

To the readers of my first two books in the Belleville family series, thank you for your encouragement, feedback and ongoing interest in the lives of the Belleville family.

To my husband Peter, thank you for your unfailing encouragement and love.

And thank you to my dear sisters Deidre and Beverley for your enthusiasm and support.

Key characters - book 3

AUSTRALIA

BELLEVILLE FAMILY (Prior Park)

Richard Belleville	Elder son of the family
William Belleville	Younger son of the family
Alice Belleville (formerly Fitzroy)	William's wife
Julia Fitzroy (formerly Belleville)	Only daughter, James's wife
Paul Belleville	Richard & Catherine's son
Anthony Belleville	Richard & Catherine's son
Marianne Belleville	William & Alice's daughter
Mrs Duffy	Housekeeper, Prior Park
Charles Brockman	Manager, Prior Park
Alistair McGovern	Francis Belleville's natural son

FITZROY FAMILY (Mayfield Downs)

Amelia Fitzroy	Mother
James Fitzroy	Son
John Fitzroy	James & Julia's son

WARNER FAMILY (Armoobilla)

Tom Warner	Owner of Armoobilla
Jane Warner (formerly Saville)	His wife

OTHERS

Dr Philippe Duval	Surgeon
Pippa Jensen	Julia Belleville's daughter
Edith Henderson	Pippa's Great Aunt
John Bertram	Richard's friend
Dr Robert Clarke	Registrar/Surgeon
Patricia Clarke	His wife
Anita Clarke	His daughter
Karen Clarke	Robert Clarke's niece
David Clarke	Robert Clarke's brother
Deborah Clarke	His wife
Bianca Ferrari	Karen's friend
Ian Dixon	QC
Angela Dixon	His wife
Lucy Dixon	His daughter
Gerald Lester	Owner of Berrima Park
Kate Lester	His wife
Tim Lester, Nancy Lester	His son & daughter

ENGLAND

CAVENDISH FAMILY (Haldon Hall)

Lady Marina Cavendish	Mother, daughter of an Earl
Catherine Cavendish (now Belleville)	Only daughter
Sir Edward Cavendish	Distant cousin to Catherine

Prologue

In December 1957 we left the Belleville family at a crossroads. The family matriarch Elizabeth Belleville is dead, killed by a fire lit maliciously by her late husband Francis's embittered bastard son Alistair McGovern.

The family's grand nineteenth century country home at Prior Park lies in ruins, a smouldering wreck from which nothing can be salvaged.

Unaware of the awful events at Prior Park, Julia, Elizabeth Belleville's only daughter, who has lived her life haunted by the memory of the baby girl she was forced to give up, is unexpectedly confronted by her past in a hotel dining room. In the moment of candour that follows, her marriage to James Fitzroy collapses as she turns back to her first love Philippe Duval and embraces the daughter she had long thought lost to her forever.

Meanwhile, her brother, war hero Richard Belleville, who tried desperately to rescue his mother from the burning house, struggles with the collapse of his marriage to the English aristocrat Catherine Cavendish who has returned to her native England following the death of her father.

Against this backdrop, it is William Belleville, together with his wife Alice, who is left to pick up the pieces at Prior Park but Alice's loyalties are tested with her brother James raging against the duplicity of his estranged wife Julia.

As the Belleville siblings face life without their matriarch amid the horror of what Alistair McGovern has done, they must also look to rebuild their own shattered lives from the rubble.

CHAPTER 1

January 1958

There had been no happy Christmas for the Belleville family and now in the heat of January, Richard Belleville, together with his brother William and his sister Julia, stood silently side by side in front of their mother's grave. Her name – Elizabeth Marianne Belleville - was etched deep into the newly erected white marble headstone. She had been just sixty years old. Beside her grave, the weathered headstone of her long dead husband had begun to lean as the dry ground cracked around it. Richard made a half-hearted attempt to stand it upright.

For each of them, the shock of their mother's death was still raw, coupled as it had been with the loss of their grand home, Prior Park, the burnt remnants of which lay just behind them.

It was William who broke the silence.

'Well, we did what she asked,' he said sadly. 'We buried her alongside our father. If she had known what we knew, would she have wanted that?'

He posed the question, even though he knew that no one could say for sure.

It had been her final fatal decision to rescue a photograph of her late husband from the burning house that had, in the end, cost her life. She had broken from Richard's grasp and flung herself back into the house in a final desperate bid to save the photograph, not knowing the extent of her husband's deception and that his actions, ultimately, had been the real cause of the tragedy.

'It was better that she did not know,' Julia said finally.

The memory of her reconciliation with her mother as she lay dying was something she cherished.

'Perhaps you're right,' Richard said quietly. 'Perhaps you're right. She could at least maintain the charade of a successful marriage right up until the end.'

William turned his head to look at his brother. He was surprised at the unmistakable bitterness in his words.

'I think they had some good times,' William said.

It was as if William felt someone should at least make a pretence of defending their father's reputation.

'I think there was disappointment on both sides,' Julia murmured.

She might well have been speaking about her own failed marriage and both her brothers were keenly aware of it.

She bent down and began to rearrange the flowers they had each brought to honour their mother. It was a futile gesture for they each knew that the flowers would not last in the heat.

After a few minutes they began to move away, but none of them could bring themselves to look at the ruin that lay before them. In parts, the outer walls of the house remained standing but the walls of the dining room and the front porch had collapsed in on themselves into a pile of tangled bricks and burnt timber.

Weeds and grass were already growing up through the broken bricks. It was clear it would not be long before what remained of the house was completely engulfed.

It was William who raised the question.

'Are we just going to leave it like that?' he said, gesturing towards the burnt out ruin.

Richard shrugged his shoulders.

'As we've agreed not to rebuild, what else do you suggest?' he asked.

His own marriage had failed partly because of his wife's unhappiness at Prior Park, so far from the sophisticated society she craved. Their arguments all seemed so futile now that the house was in ruins. Had he been wrong, he wondered, to cling so stubbornly to an idea of home that, in the end, had been reduced to a pile of unrecognisable

3

rubble in just minutes?

'I thought perhaps we should clear the rubble,' William said, ever practical in his approach. 'It could be something of a hazard in years to come.'

'If you like,' Richard said, 'but I'd like to see it stay for a while. Call me sentimental if you like.'

He wasn't ready just yet to obliterate all signs of the house. William turned towards him and nodded his head in agreement.

'That's fine, Richard,' he conceded. 'We'll leave it as it is for the time being but I might get the men to fence it for safety.'

Julia moved ahead of them, not taking part in the conversation, but hoping that the ruins would be left. She had no stake in Prior Park for it had been left to her brothers, but she had loved the house and all it represented. Now, just when she would have revelled in the comfort of being welcomed back home, it was no longer there.

With her mother's death, she had become a wealthy woman but for her the price had been too high. The chance discovery of the daughter her mother had forced her to give up for adoption had changed her life. But it was too late now to erase the bitter memories. She mourned the loss of her mother not only for herself, but for her daughter Pippa who would never know her grandmother.

As Julia headed towards her car, her brothers, deep in conversation, followed. It was William who spoke but it was clear to Julia that her brothers had been discussing her situation quietly between them.

'How is your mother-in-law treating you?' he said, his tone clearly sympathetic.

Amelia Fitzroy had always been very cordial towards William, whom she regarded as an excellent catch for her daughter Alice. On the other hand, she had not warmed to Julia as the wife of her favourite child and only son James. With the revelations of Julia's daughter, born before her marriage, she had been outraged at the duplicity of both mother and daughter in tricking her son into such a marriage.

'It is frosty,' Julia replied. 'We haven't actually had a conversation about any of it. Her only comment was that we must do the right thing by John.'

'And Alice?' William ventured.

He knew full well the depth of Alice's disappointment at being excluded from the secret of Julia's unacknowledged baby. Alice had been Julia's best friend. He had found himself apologising again and again to his wife, as if it had all somehow been his fault.

'I've hardly seen Alice,' Julia lied.

What use was it to tell William that Alice had been very angry with her and that she had responded angrily herself trying to explain why she had not told Alice of her predicament all those years ago.

'And James?' he asked finally.

'I rarely see him,' she said, with a slight shrug of indifference. 'With school in recess, John is staying at home with him at the moment and they seem to be managing without me.'

'A boy in his father's image, I would say,' William said. 'Has he been told about his half-sister?'

Julia nodded even as she tried to hide her surprise that William would ask the question. It was as if, having done nothing to help her when she found herself pregnant and unmarried at nineteen, he suddenly felt an urge to reach out and help her now.

'He has. He didn't say much. I'm not sure he could even understand what it really meant,' she said.

'We would all love to meet her, you know,' he said. 'I've said to Alice she will always be welcome at our home.'

Julia glanced up quickly at her brother, trying to read in his almost expressionless face what lay behind the sudden burst of warm feelings towards her.

'That's very kind of you, William, but are you sure Alice feels the same way?' she asked doubtfully.

In any case it would be at least the end of the year before Alice and William would be able to move into their new home. All of them had been rendered homeless by the catastrophic events that had enveloped them. Alice and William had taken up residence with her mother in town. Both Richard and Julia had sought refuge in the Criterion Hotel as a temporary home.

'Alice will be fine,' he reassured her. 'She's just hurt she wasn't taken into our confidence and sorry we hadn't all been more honest with

James before you married him.'

Julia simply nodded her thanks.

'And have you told Marianne?' she asked. 'If she doesn't know she'll find out from John.'

William smiled at the memory of his daughter's reaction.

'Yes, we told her,' he said. 'She thinks having another girl in the family is a very good idea.'

Julia laughed. Marianne counted three boys among her cousins and clearly felt outnumbered at times.

'How funny life is,' Julia said, 'perhaps they will grow up to be good friends.'

Richard had been standing nearby listening intently to this exchange. Finally, he spoke.

'Well, I'm sorry to say they'll have to put up with terrible gossip if your daughter comes up here to stay,' he said. 'I don't care in the least on my own account but the gossips will have a field day.'

Julia ran her fingers through her blonde hair and thrust her head upwards in a gesture of defiance.

'Well let them, I say,' she said. 'As long as Alice and Marianne are aware of it, and John too of course, I don't think the gossip will concern them at all.'

'I hope that's the case,' Richard thought, but said no more on the topic.

'Is John going to stay living with James?' he asked.

'For the time being he is,' she said. 'At least until I'm settled.'

She did not add that her estranged husband had begun to question the wisdom of them sharing custody of the child. She decided that information could wait for another day.

'And when will that be?' Richard asked for they were both unsure of their sister's plans.

'I don't know to be honest,' she said.

If they were expecting certainty in her response, they were disappointed.

'A lot depends on how things turn out,' she added, without being specific.

It felt to her as if she was being torn between two lives, her old life of which much remained and a possible new life in a new place that meant picking up a relationship after more than fourteen years with a man she had long believed to be dead and with a daughter she did not yet know well.

William could not meet her eyes just then. He bent down to brush an imaginary insect from the leg of his trousers. He had conspired with his mother to intercept Philippe Duval's letters to his sister until they stopped coming. Now, as he stood alongside her listening to the disintegration of her life, he was ashamed of his actions but it had been impossible to go against their mother who had insisted no letters ever reached Julia. Richard, of course, had not been at home.

In quiet moments, William could not help but feel how easy it had been for Richard to say things would have been different if he had not been away overseas.

It was an observation that had not done anything to assuage William's guilt or the perception he was somehow less caring of his sister than his elder brother. It happened less often now but every now and again small pangs of jealously flared when he found himself compared unfavourably with his brother. Richard was taller, better looking, more charming and more polished than he would ever be and a small part of him resented his older brother for it.

Julia did not fail to notice her brother's discomfiture but she did not feel inclined just then to absolve him of the responsibility he shared for having deceived her. She could not erase the knowledge of how her brother and her mother had betrayed her trust so completely. In quiet moments, the extent of their deception troubled her afresh.

William tried to form more words of explanation and apology but failed completely. He was deeply ashamed of what they had done. He realised too late how they had changed the course of his sister's life. It was only luck that had brought her face to face with her former lover and the daughter she had been forced to abandon. He knew he would carry the regret he felt to the grave but he had found it hard to find the right words to ask for his sister's forgiveness. She generously had said they would not speak of it again but still the knowledge of it was a heavy burden for him.

'And you, Richard?' Julia asked.

She was keen to escape further questioning.

'What does the future hold for you and your boys? Have you heard further from Catherine – or her lawyers?'

He gave a half laugh. He made a half-hearted gesture.

'The legal wheels grind on,' he shrugged. 'I simply do what I am asked to do, sign whatever I am asked to sign, agree to whatever I am asked to agree to. By the end of next year or the year after, who knows, I expect our divorce will be finalised.'

He said it as if he were a mere bystander to some arcane process that he barely cared about. In truth he was bitterly disappointed at the failure of his marriage but he could not say so. He knew he was not blameless. He doubted he had tried hard enough to please Catherine but in the end the distance between them had been one of geography and upbringing and nothing could change that.

'And apart from the divorce? What plans for the children? Where are you going to live?' Julia asked, for neither she nor William were privy to his plans for the future.

'I'm taking one day at a time,' he said obliquely. 'Paul is staying on with his school mate in Bowral during the holidays. Because of the fire, of course, and Anthony, no doubt, is becoming a proper little English gentleman. Catherine writes to me with regular reports and has sent a recent photo.'

He drew out his wallet and offered a small black and white photograph for their inspection. It showed a small boy, half smiling, half scowling for the camera against a backdrop of winter snow.

It was William who ventured an opinion on what Richard should do.

'You need to get yourself a house in town,' he said, 'sooner rather than later. Then you can have Paul at least to stay during the school holidays.'

Richard almost laughed out loud as if that was the complete solution to his problems.

'So, a house, yes, I agree,' he said. 'I have been looking. And are you suggesting I get a new wife too to go with the house?'

William reddened at his brother's flippant tone. He'd heard the gossip about his brother and later been rendered speechless when his brother had confessed to it being true, yet he did not want to believe that his brother would actively seek to lure away another man's wife.

William ignored the question, instead bringing them back to reason why they had gathered behind the ruins of the big house at Prior Park. He made one last effort to arrange the bunch of roses he had brought with him.

'I am sure Mother will rest peacefully here,' he said as they all looked at the gravestone one last time.

William was first to move.

'I must get back to town. I have a meeting with the architect who has drawn up some plans for our new house. We're keen to get it underway.'

He hugged his sister briefly and shook his brother by the hand.

Richard and Julia watched him reverse his car and then turn onto the Prior Park driveway. Within minutes the car was lost in a cloud of dust.

Julia turned towards Richard, smiling.

'I think you embarrassed our brother,' Julia said.

Richard laughed at the suggestion.

'I think we've both embarrassed him with our wayward lives,' he said, giving his sister a quick hug.

'Yes, I think his views on life and marriage are very orthodox,' she said.

She did not know the full details of her brother's indiscretions. But she knew, from the experience of her own marriage, how much it hurt to have a husband turn his attentions to another woman.

Yet she had sympathised with Richard. She did not blame her brother entirely. As much as she had liked Catherine, she had never believed the marriage would endure. Julia understood completely how the charms of rural Australia would quickly fade for someone whose upbringing had occurred in a privileged aristocratic world of sophisticated pleasures of which they knew nothing.

Richard managed a smile.

'William thinks everyone should be as certain about their life choices as he is,' he said. 'He is completely happy with Alice and with their daughter. There is no doubt in his mind, no question mark at all about his existence. He thinks everyone else can have a life like that too but it isn't as simple or as straightforward as that, is it?'

Julia was surprised by the question and surprised too by her brother's unexpected revelations.

'No, it isn't always straightforward, is it?' she answered quietly. 'I spent a long time grieving for my lost daughter and my lost love. Now that I have found them both, what do I do next? Is it reasonable to expect we can pick up where we left off? I don't know. I wish I had William's certainty.'

Richard nodded, only too well aware of Julia's dilemma. He did not say so but he faced the same problem. With little effort he knew he could once again draw Jane Warner back to his side but is that what he really wanted? Was he really prepared to offer her marriage? If he did so, it would leave another marriage in tatters.

'That's why I'm in no rush to make decisions, quite frankly,' he said, 'and neither should you be.'

There was a note of brotherly concern in his voice. He was four years her senior and now, as the eldest of them, he felt it his duty to caution his sister.

She laughed at the warning note in his voice.

'So, taking the fatherly line, are you?' she jibed. 'Playing big brother now?'

He laughed in turn.

'No, not really, I was never much good at it,' he replied. 'I never thought I'd have much success in reining in my headstrong sister.'

She hugged him and they laughed together.

'I must go,' she said. 'I promised John I would take him to the afternoon matinee to see some awful cowboy picture.'

Richard held open the door of the car as she slid in behind the steering wheel.

'Drive carefully,' he said. 'One day we'll get a better road out this way but you need to be really careful.'

She hardly needed reminding but smiled at him anyway.

He watched her car disappear, as William's had, in a haze of dust. He was about to turn to walk the short distance to his own car.

Without warning, a savage blow caught him from behind. As he began to fall, he twisted his body around and saw looming above him the grinning face of a madman. Seconds later, Alistair McGovern swung the broken tree branch again this time aiming for Richard's head.

At the last moment, Richard rolled to his right to avoid the blow but he could not avoid it entirely.

The full weight of the broken branch struck him on the side of the head. Blood began to flow as he lost consciousness, the shrill laughter of an evil lunatic ringing in his ears.

CHAPTER 2

January 1958

Alistair McGovern was breathing heavily. He paused, the bloodied stump of the broken tree branch raised above his head, as he prepared to deliver the fatal blow. He was gloating now, talking rapidly, his words incoherent. He felt only contempt for the badly injured man sprawled before him. Every utterance of hate and bile he directed at Richard Belleville went unheard. But that did not matter to him.

He had achieved his first great triumph against the Belleville family only a matter of two months earlier. Now he was about to have a second great moment of triumph. He was about to kill Richard Belleville, the much loved and revered elder son. The much-admired war hero. A man born to wealth and privilege.

He despised everything about Richard Belleville because Richard Belleville was everything he was not. In his deluded mind, he believed he could have been like Richard Belleville if only the Belleville family had accepted him.

He had dreamed of this moment of revenge ever since his arrest. It had been Richard Belleville who had thrown him out of the house when he had come wanting to be friends, to be accepted by the family. It had been Richard Belleville who had turned him away like a mongrel dog.

Well, he had shown them. The house was in ruins, their mother was dead, all at his hands. Now the elder son was about to die in the dust, his head split open, his blood oozing out of his wounds as his life slipped away.

He was summoning his strength for the final blow. He tightened his grip on the stump of broken branch and tensed his muscles for the final assault on his helpless victim.

But Alistair McGovern, so intent on his victim, did not see Charles Brockman.

He did not see Charles bring a rifle to his shoulder in one swift practised action. He did not hear the sharp crack of the rifle as he fired. It was only his eyes that registered the shock of the bullet as it split his forehead open and forced his head to jerk backwards. His crude weapon fell harmlessly from his hands.

Blood began to trickle from the gaping hole left by the single bullet wound. He was dead before he hit the ground.

Charles Brockman wasted no time. He set his rifle down and ran inside the house. He had for years occupied the manager's house at Prior Park. He quickly picked up the telephone and called the local police sergeant who only an hour earlier had alerted him to Alistair McGovern's escape from custody.

When that warning came, he had taken precautions. He had unlocked his rifle cupboard and taken out his favoured .303 rifle, checking it carefully and loading it.

From his house he had noticed the Belleville siblings gather at their mother's graveside but he had chosen not to intrude. Instead he had watched from his verandah.

Later, as he saw first William and then Julia drive away, he had been about to go off to saddle his horse but at the last moment, something, he could not say what, caught his eye.

It was then he saw Alistair McGovern. He tried to shout a warning to Richard but he was too far away. He watched helplessly as the first blow hit Richard across the back. Before he could react, he watched Alistair McGovern strike Richard again.

In an instant, he knew he had one option to save Richard's life and he did not hesitate. He shouldered his rifle, took careful aim, and fired one shot. One lucky shot, he was later heard to say.

One shot and Alistair McGovern lay dead, sprawled in the dust.

Days later, Charles sat quietly beside Richard's hospital bed, his head in his hands, not quite praying, for he was not a religious man, but appealing all the same to a higher power to spare his friend. He did not regard Richard Belleville as his employer. He had known all the family for longer than he cared to remember. He was almost one of them. He regarded them as his own.

Just then, Richard stirred. He had been drifting in and out of consciousness for days.

'Charles,' he said. His voice was just above a whisper. 'What are you doing here? What happened to me?'

Charles moved his chair closer to the bed.

'Don't try and talk now,' he said soothingly. 'That bastard almost did for you.'

Richard's hand tentatively explored the bandages on the side of his head.

'What bastard would that be, Charles? Alistair McGovern?'

He nodded.

'That's right. He broke out of custody and they alerted me, just in case he came sniffing around. They had men out searching for him but they should have known where he would head to.'

Richard grimaced. He tried to move but every part of his upper body ached. The side of his face was covered in ugly bruises.

'I don't remember what happened.' Richard's voice trailed off.

'I saw it all. He came at you with a big solid lump of broken tree branch. He caught you by surprise. I was too far away to help but I had my rifle out of the cupboard luckily.'

Richard tried to smile.

'My lucky day, huh?'

'Your lucky day indeed,' Charles said.

'And only one shot I suppose?'

Even in his semi-conscious state Richard's memory had not failed him. Charles's marksmanship was legendary.

He nodded.

'I had to make sure I felled him with the first shot. I wouldn't have had time for a second one. It was enough.'

Richard closed his eyes, tired out by the effort of conversation, but he seemed to breathe a sigh of relief.

While Alistair McGovern lived, there had always been the slim chance that he would contrive a way to exact further revenge. Now that he was dead, they could all breathe more easily.

Charles too breathed a sigh of relief. He did not want to be seen as a hero. He had killed a man and that was no badge of honour. He had done it only to save his friend. He did not dwell on the sadness of having to kill Francis Belleville's youngest son to save his eldest son. He knew that Francis Belleville could never have foreseen the consequences of his betrayal of his family. There had been aspects of his late friend's character he had never admired but no one could have ever imagined that his actions would result, years later, in such an awful chain of events.

He left the room quietly, satisfied now that Richard was out of danger and would recover. Charles knew he would face police questioning but he had done what he had to do without concern for the consequences.

William seeing Charles coming down the steps at the front of the hospital raised his hand in greeting.

'How is he today?' William asked, dispensing with the normal pleasantries.

'I think he's getting better,' Charles replied. 'He spoke to me for the first time and he made sense.'

It seemed to him as if William had aged suddenly, as if the events of the past few days and of the past few months had worn him down.

'Thank God for that,' William said. 'I was cursing myself for not having been there to help him, but obviously that madman waited until Julia and I had left.'

They had discussed all this before. It had been William whom Charles had contacted as soon as Richard was on his way to hospital. Then there had been the days of acute anxiety for it had not been certain early on that Richard would survive the assault.

But other things had been praying on William's mind too.

'Will they charge you?' he asked.

He was clearly worried about the consequences.

'I don't know yet,' he said. 'It may just get buried, if you know what I mean.'

William nodded. He would use whatever influence he had to make sure that happened but he didn't want to make empty promises to Charles. Instead, he was cautious.

'But if it doesn't,' William said. 'If they decide to charge you, we will hire the best legal team that money can buy, rest assured on that point.'

Charles shuffled his feet. He did not like to be put in such a position but he was grateful for William's offer, although he couldn't find the words to express it.

'You saved my brother's life. We won't ever forget that,' William said, as if he needed to make the point.

'No need to thank me,' he said quietly. 'I did what I had to do. I couldn't let that mongrel do any more damage.'

Some distance away from the front entrance of the hospital and unobserved by William and Charles, Jane Warner sat in her car.

She watched the short exchange between the two men and then waited patiently for William to re-emerge from the hospital and head towards his car. It was not until he had driven away that she walked to the hospital entrance and asked at the reception for directions to Richard's private room. No one asked who she was and she was grateful for that.

She approached his room tentatively. Should she be here? Doubts assailed her. They had not spoken in more than six months but on hearing news of his terrible injuries she was suddenly desperate to see him. The door to his room was slightly ajar so she pushed at the door.

It was only then that she saw Richard's sister Julia sitting on a chair close to his bed. She had been partly obscured by the half open door.

Before Jane could retreat, Julia glanced up expecting to see a nurse or a doctor. Her face registered surprise but she recovered quickly.

'Jane how are you?' she said, quietly motioning her to the vacant chair alongside her.

'Oh, I'm sorry. I didn't know anyone was here,' she said, trying desperately to cover her embarrassment. 'I won't stay but just tell me how he is?'

Julia too felt the awkwardness of the meeting. She had heard only a few shreds of gossip about her brother's dalliance with another woman and most of that had come from her husband James in the bitter spiteful row that had accelerated the collapse of her own marriage. She had defended Richard at the time, not knowing whether in fact it was true or not. Now she knew for certain. It was true. Why else would Jane be visiting by herself, desperate not to meet anyone else at his bedside?

Quietly and without fuss, for Richard was sleeping peacefully, Julia rose from her chair and took Jane by the arm, ushering her out of the room.

'Let's go and find a cup of tea,' Julia said.

Jane let herself be guided along the hospital corridor to a small sitting room. Both of them were relieved to find the room empty. Julia poured tea from a freshly made pot and handed Jane a cup of tea. She noticed how Jane's hands trembled slightly as she took it from her.

They sat down opposite one another in deep padded armchairs. It was Julia broke the silence.

'Richard will recover fully, Jane,' she said. 'Early on we thought the worst but he has done well since he was brought in here.'

She noticed the relief spread across the other woman's face.

'I only heard about it yesterday,' she said. 'It was a garbled story of him being attacked at Prior Park and nearly killed.'

Which does not explain, Julia thought, why you felt compelled to come and visit him as soon as you possibly could.

'Did Tom tell you about it? He probably had it from Charles Brockman,' Julia asked.

Jane shook her head slightly. The movement was almost imperceptible.

'No, he didn't tell me,' she said. 'I heard it from a friend at the Red Cross morning tea. It was the main topic of conversation.'

Julia would have liked to ask if the identity of the perpetrator was part of the conversation but she didn't know how to frame the question. How do you ask someone if they knew it was your bastard half-brother who had tried to kill your beloved elder brother? But they must all know, she thought. They must all know who it was after what happened at Prior Park and her mother's death.

For a minute or two they sat together in awkward silence. It crossed Julia's mind to wonder why Jane's husband Tom hadn't shared the news with her, for he must have known days earlier. It was clearly something that had not been discussed between them. She wondered idly if Tom knew about is wife's interest elsewhere. Could he not bring himself to mention Richard's name to her?

It was Jane who broke the silence.

'You and your family have been through quite a bit lately,' she ventured.

Julia got up and put her teacup down on the table. How to answer that? How much did Jane know? She would certainly know that Julia's marriage had ended. She would know about the very public destruction of Prior Park and its aftermath. But would she know all the terrible secrets that had given rise to these events?

She turned to face Jane, who had remained seated.

'Yes, we've all had a terrible time just lately,' she said, noncommittally.

'I believe the fellow who attacked Richard was killed. Is that right?' she asked. 'Was it the same fellow who was responsible for the attack on the house last year? That's the story I heard.'

'Yes, that's all true, Jane,' Julia said. 'He had escaped from custody. It seems he hated Richard the most so he took the opportunity to attack him.'

Julia quickly realised her mistake. Such an admission could not pass without further explanation.

'So why did he hate Richard so much in particular?' Jane asked, her curiosity peaked just as Julia feared it would be.

'Because….'

Julia paused, wondering how to frame her answer.

'Because it was Richard who threw him out of the house. He physically threw him out of the house the night of our mother's sixtieth birthday party last year.'

There she had said it.

Jane was silent for a few moments as she considered this information. She had heard rumours that the young man had claimed to be

Francis Belleville's bastard son. Julia had all but confirmed it.

'I'm not sure I can ask this but the gossips say ...'

Julia interrupted her.

'The gossips are right on this occasion. He was my father's bastard son. His name you no doubt know from the newspaper reports of him being charged.'

'And he was killed by Charles Brockman, is that right?' she asked.

Julia nodded.

'Yes,' she replied. 'Fortunately, Charles was close at hand otherwise Richard would be dead.'

She did not want to go into the details of exactly what Charles had done. It was enough that she confirm it was Charles who had saved Richard.

'Very lucky indeed,' Jane said.

She got up to place her own cup back on the table.

'I must be going,' she said. 'I only came to see that Richard was OK.'

There were many questions Jane wanted to ask but could not. Had Richard's wife been told of his injuries? Was his marriage really over as she had heard? Was he in the throes of a long-distance divorce?

She had felt increasing bitterness towards him as the months had passed and she had heard nothing from him following their passionate reunion the previous year, conveniently ignoring the letter she had written him to urge him to stay out of her life.

She was sure her own husband had been oblivious to their affair, absorbed as he was in the day to day work on their large cattle property.

'Shall I tell Richard you called to see him?' Julia asked, curious as to how Jane would answer.

Jane hesitated then nodded.

'Yes, tell him I called to see how he was,' she said.

She did not say anything further. She wondered how he would receive the news.

The two women parted at the doorway of the sitting room. Julia watched as Jane walked back towards the entrance of the hospital before she turned to head back to her brother's room to resume her bedside vigil.

Later that day William sat across the dinner table from his wife Alice. His mother-in-law's house in town had become a temporary home for him and his family with the destruction of Prior Park. He missed the comforts of the large house and the domestic order that had been a hallmark of his life. Amelia Fitzroy's house was much smaller than he was used to and he found himself unaccountably irritated by the small inconveniences of it.

On this particular day, there was added tension around the meal table. James, Alice's brother, sat next to Alice. He ate in silence despite his mother's valiant efforts to engage him in conversation. It was obvious to everyone that the failure of his marriage had hurt him deeply. Yet not for a moment had he considered how his own infidelities might have contributed to the failure.

In his mind, hers had been the greater deceit. He had been publicly humiliated, he had told his mother, and he could not forgive her. He did not add how much it had hurt him to realise Julia loved another man more than him. He could not bring himself to admit that he had loved her, in his own way, more than she had loved him.

It was left to Marianne, William and Alice's daughter, to break the uneasy silence that had settled over the dinner table.

'How's Uncle Richard?' she asked, for she was very concerned about her favourite uncle.

She had not been allowed to visit him even though she had argued vehemently she was now old enough to go to the hospital. At eleven years old, she regarded herself as no longer a child. It frustrated her that her parents did not agree.

'He's getting better, love,' her mother answered. 'He spoke for the first time today.'

'When can I go and see him?' she asked.

She was persistent. She had found in the past that with persistence she usually got what she wanted. Her cousin John chimed in too. After all Richard was his uncle too. Whatever Marianne did, John felt he was entitled to do as well, despite being more than a year younger.

'Perhaps tomorrow,' her father said. 'We'll see how things are tomorrow. We don't want to tire him out with too many visitors.'

Both children knew they had to be satisfied with that response.

There was a note of finality in William's voice that did not brook further discussion.

It was then that James looked up from his meal.

'Was it a sheer coincidence that I saw Jane Warner coming out of the hospital as I passed it earlier today?' he asked, his tone masking the malicious intent of the question.

William looked up suddenly. He was not good at dissembling. He remembered his brother's shock confession of the previous year. There was a faint flush spreading across his tanned face.

'No idea,' he mumbled. 'She was probably seeing a doctor there.'

James laughed. It was not a pretty sound. No one took up the thread of the conversation so silence descended once more on the dinner table.

CHAPTER 3

February 1958

Richard Belleville continued to confound his doctors, recovering much faster and more completely than anyone had expected. As he said repeatedly, it was Alice who made him better. Without a home of his own, Alice had prevailed upon her mother to have Richard stay with them while he convalesced. She proved to be an excellent nurse.

While he was still regaining his strength, he had adopted Alice's late father's routine of sitting on the small front verandah and watching the world unfold before him.

Despite his improving health, he was prone to bouts of despondency. The knowledge that Jane Warner had visited him in hospital had only added to his feelings of uncertainty. What had that visit really meant? And what had it meant to him? He did not know so it was John Bertram's unexpected visit that cheered him the most. His long-time friend and wartime navigator found him on the verandah late one morning.

'So, you make a habit of this do you?' he teased, as he mounted the few steps and extended his hand towards Richard.

Richard grasped the proffered hand enthusiastically but was unsure what his friend was alluding to.

'Make a habit of what, John?' he replied, perplexed. 'Not being beaten up, surely?'

'No,' laughed John. 'Moving into someone else's house and having them take care of you while you convalesce. I was thinking back to

Lady Marina Cavendish's warm welcome of the injured hero pilot.'

Even Richard smiled at this, remembering Catherine's mother with gratitude but hardly affection.

'Yes, I hadn't forgotten about that,' he replied. 'In fact I was only thinking about it this morning. I'm sure she regretted having asked me to stay. And she probably regretted you inviting me to tag along that first time we went on leave to Haldon Hall.'

John smiled as he recalled how Lady Marina had accused him of being responsible for her daughter's hasty marriage.

'She did say something to that effect as I recall when you'd got her daughter pregnant and spirited her off to the other side of the world,' he said. 'It was all my fault according to her. I gave her a wide berth for a couple of years after that.'

Richard laughed, for he could readily imagine how Lady Marina would have turned on John, accusing him of responsibility for her daughter's illicit wartime romance.

'So now you are homeless and wifeless,' John said, hoping his flippant tone would not be misconstrued.

He hardly needed Richard's confirmation of the impending divorce. He was a good friend to both of them.

'Yes, I'm homeless for the moment, and wifeless, as you elegantly pointed out.'

It still hurt him more than he cared to admit saying it out loud yet in his more rational moments he knew he had never believed the marriage would last. The differences between their life together in Australia and her privileged upper class life in England had always been there as the great unbridgeable gulf between them.

'You didn't think one last go at reconciliation was worth it?' his friend asked although he suspected he already knew the answer to his own question.

John had been at their wedding, the only one of the family to attend the hurried affair so he felt at liberty to voice his thoughts.

'No, I didn't think it was worth it.'

Richard answered his friend truthfully. He knew the question was well intentioned.

'As a matter of fact, I think my wife has moved on. I think she has her sights set firmly on her next husband. An Australian husband proved to be too big a complication in her changed circumstances.'

John nodded, half smiling at Richard's accurate perception of how life had changed for Catherine.

'I think you're probably right, mate,' he said, his tone as warm and friendly as ever.

He was well aware that Catherine had never been able to settle in Australia and now, with the added responsibility of inheriting her family's estate from her father, there were ever more compelling reasons for her to live permanently in England. Equally, he knew Richard could never settle for the constraints of life as an English gentleman with a wife far more important socially than himself.

The growing importance of Sir Edward Cavendish in Catherine's life had not gone unnoticed by either of them but John kept to himself the other confidences that Catherine had shared with him.

She had told him about her suspicions of Richard's interest in another woman and that Richard had not denied it.

He could not say to Catherine that he sympathised with his long-time friend. He wanted to say, 'well, you did leave him for long periods during your trips back to England' but he did not. He thought that Richard's infidelity was more a symptom of the breakdown than the cause, for the cause went much deeper as they both knew.

It seemed to him that Catherine had used Richard's infidelity as an excuse for the divorce rather than admit her disdain for the provincial society in which she had found herself in Australia and that her preference for her life in England, which she had missed terribly, had been the real reason for the breakup.

'Have you seen Catherine since we last spoke?' Richard asked.

The two men kept in regular contact by telephone but it was John's work flying the Sydney to London route that made it possible for him to meet Catherine from time to time.

'I saw her in London, just before Christmas,' he said. 'We had lunch together. She looked well and she told me Anthony was doing well, although I gathered he is missing you.'

Richard looked surprised.

'Did she say so?' he asked directly. 'She hasn't mentioned it in any of her letters although she did send me a photo of him with her most recent letter.'

John shifted in his chair. He was becoming uncomfortable at the direction of the conversation. He did not want to be the messenger between warring parents in a custody battle. He did not want to have to pick sides.

'Just in passing you know,' John replied. 'It's natural for a boy to ask about his father. But you won't be travelling over there for some time, after what you've been through.'

Richard grimaced.

'No, indeed I won't and it's really only possible for Paul to go in the long school holidays at Christmas time and he can't go without me.'

'Perhaps Catherine can make the trip to Australia, at least to Sydney, and bring Anthony with her,' John suggested.

'I expect she will, possibly later this year,' he said. 'I'm certainly going to suggest it.'

It was then that John Bertram began to understand the problems his good friend faced in the future. His sons needed a home, but would that home be with him in Australia or with Catherine in England? Now that Richard had no home John could see it gave extra impetus to Catherine's belief she should have full custody of the two boys.

'You need to get yourself a home sooner rather than later,' John said.

'I know, I know.' Richard said. 'You're not the first person to tell me that. I'd begun to look seriously for something here in town and then this happened. It's rather set me back.'

John nodded, fully aware now of what Richard faced. He looked up as the screen door leading on to the verandah opened.

It was Alice with the tea tray. She handed John his cup and then fussed over her patient, who greeted her warmly. Richard had begun to realise just how good a choice his brother William had made in choosing Alice to be his wife. There were times Richard secretly envied the domestic bliss his brother enjoyed for he understood now it had eluded him.

It was Saturday and the weather in Sydney had dawned hot and steamy. Pippa Jensen was feeling very frustrated. She paced the small living room of the neat suburban home she shared with her guardian Edith Henderson. In just over a month's time, she would turn fourteen. She was leaving childhood behind, as she reminded Edith daily. And yet nothing more had been resolved about her life and her future although three months had passed since she had met her mother Julia for the first time.

Weekly letters from her mother to which she replied diligently were hardly enough to satisfy her. Her father Philippe wrote from New York almost as often. She had received beautiful Christmas gifts from both of them, as if they were making amends for the Christmases and birthdays they had missed.

What frustrated her was the uncertainty that now pervaded her life. She had continued to live with Aunt Edith but her great aunt's kind reassuring words were beginning to irritate her. Still she did not want to appear ungrateful. She was genuinely fond of Aunt Edith who had willingly offered her a home when she had been turned out of Essex Downs on the death of her adoptive parents.

She watched as her aunt set the table for lunch.

'My father says he will be here at the end of the month to take up his new job,' Pippa said, waving his latest letter in her hand.

'He says I can help him look for a house when he arrives.'

Aunt Edith smiled. She admired the way in which Philippe Duval had taken his daughter to his heart and was prepared to include her in his life. It had been Edith Henderson who had first learnt of his existence and who had made it possible for him to meet Pippa.

'Now if my mother comes down here to live then we will all be together in one happy family,' Pippa added.

To the young teenager, life seemed so simple, so cut and dried, Edith thought. Her parents were in love once and lost each other. Now they could be together. What could possibly stand in their way?

For the umpteenth time, her aunt tried hard, and failed, to dampen her expectations.

'Pippa,' she said, with just a hint of exasperation. 'Your mother is still married to her first husband. Now, she may have told you she is getting a divorce, but that will take years. And she has another, younger child to consider. And it was a long time ago that she and your father were ..'

She hesitated. She did not quite know how to say what she needed to say, but Pippa filled the void.

'You mean it was a long time ago they were lovers,' the girl said unexpectedly.

Her aunt was shocked by her words. She struggled with the idea that Pippa should have knowledge of such things.

'Have you been talking to girls at school about what has happened? About who your real parents are?' she asked for it occurred to her then that Pippa must have taken some girls into her confidence. She was sure the word 'lovers' would not have occurred to Pippa without prompting.

'One or two,' she admitted. 'What's wrong with that?'

Her tone was immediately defensive because she knew she had been warned about talking at school about her real parents.

Edith wanted to explain to the girl that being the orphaned child of a respectable married couple who had died tragically in a road accident was one thing but being the offspring of an illicit wartime romance between an Australian girl and an American soldier was quite another altogether.

She feared Pippa would pay a high price for her naivety. She feared she would be ostracised, not by the girls who would revel in the gossip but by their mothers who would consider Pippa not to be a suitable girl for their daughters to know. She wondered if it would go so far as to her receiving a request to withdraw Pippa from the school. Meriden had been Edith's choice. It was close at hand and she was a friend of the principal. She hoped that would be enough to withstand any pressure from the most outspoken of the mothers who had high hopes for their daughters and who put great importance on the connections they made at school.

'I suppose you told Lucy Dixon? And Anita Clarke? And Nancy Lester?' Edith asked, listing each of the girls she had heard Pippa speak about as being her closest friends.

Edith knew each of the girls to be very well connected. Mentally,

27

she ticked off their family connections: Lucy Dixon's illustrious relative was Chief Justice of the High Court, Anita Clarke's father was a highly regarded surgeon and Nancy Lester's family owned several well-known grazing properties in the central highlands south west of Sydney. Would these girls be happy to continue to be Pippa's friend, once their mothers knew the truth about Pippa's birth, she pondered?

'Yes,' Pippa said defiantly. 'I told them everything. I wanted people to know that I actually have a mother and a father and they shouldn't feel sorry for me. That I'm not really an orphan.'

Edith could see the girl was close to tears but she pressed her for more information.

'I hope you didn't reveal your parents' names?' she said, trying to hide her anxiety.

Philippe had privately canvassed with her the problems that might occur for him if his parentage of an illegitimate daughter became widely known. He had extracted a promise from his daughter to be discreet but could she keep that promise?

It worried him, not because he was ashamed of her, but he knew full well how it might affect his professional standing. He was in a new city among people he did not know. He was not yet a trusted member of the medical fraternity. He was an outsider with an unusual name who was still being viewed with some suspicion, despite his high professional standing.

Edith moved across the room and put her arm around the girl's shoulders. She hoped and prayed Pippa would not pay a heavy price for the trust she had placed in her friends. Only time would tell, Edith thought. Only time would tell.

In another part of Sydney, Paul Francis Belleville, who had celebrated his twelfth birthday just a week earlier, was holding a letter from his father, whom he had not seen in some months, his absence explained by the recent terrible events that Paul could only partly comprehend.

Paul had tried hard to hide his disappointment at neither parent being present to celebrate his birthday just as he had hidden his disappointment at being sent to stay with his good friend Tim Lester's family for the Christmas holidays. Tim's mother had done her best to help him, sympathising with the boy at the loss of his family home and the death of his grandmother not knowing that he also faced the worry of his parents' impending divorce. This information he had kept to himself. The fire that destroyed his home had been reason enough for his need of an alternative home for the holidays and the Lester family had been generous in taking him in.

'Is that a letter from your Dad? How is he?' Tim asked his friend as he came upon him in a secluded part of the school grounds where they were both boarders. Being Saturday, they were free of schoolwork for a few precious hours.

'He's getting better he says,' Paul replied, folding the letter carefully and replacing it in the envelope.

Paul had heard the shocking news of the attack on his father from the headmaster who had spoken with his Uncle William. The extent of Richard's injuries and the reason for the attack had been downplayed so as not to alarm the boy.

'Did they get the bloke who did it?' Tim asked, for that question was upper most in his mind.

'Yes, they did get him,' Paul answered. 'In fact he's dead.'

Tim let out a low whistle. No one of his limited experience had ever been killed by anyone in a fight.

'Did your Dad kill him?' he asked, his eyes widening at the prospect of knowing the son of a man capable of killing an assailant.

'No, he didn't kill him,' Paul explained. 'Our estate manager did. My Dad was knocked out.'

That was as much as Paul knew. He had not been told the reason behind the attack on Prior Park that had killed his grandmother nor the name of the perpetrator. The fact that the same person had attacked his father had been omitted from the account his father had written. He had said only that it was someone with a grudge against the family.

'Wow, how did he kill him?' Tim asked breathlessly. 'Won't your estate manager go to jail?'

There had been too little detail in Paul's description to satisfy him. He knew he was going have to drag each little piece of information out of his friend.

29

The idea of Charles Brockman going to jail for saving his father had not occurred to Paul, who was shocked at the idea, yet he shook his head. It seemed cut and dried to him.

'I don't think so. Dad says he did it to save his life. And I don't know how he killed him,' Paul answered truthfully. 'I expect he hit him hard. Charles is an old man but he is tall and very muscular. There wouldn't be too many men who would get the better of him in a fight.'

In his letter to his son, Richard had carefully omitted the detail of how Charles had ended Alistair McGovern's life with one lucky shot. Time enough, Richard thought, for the boy to know all the details when the story could be told face to face. It was enough now that he should know the bare facts.

There were other things too that Paul Belleville was being shielded from. He was yet to discover that he had a new cousin – a girl – and that his Aunt Julia's marriage was in tatters. He was good mates with his cousin John who was two years younger but Paul's absence at school so far away had meant the two boys now saw each other rarely.

Tim and Paul sat side by side on a low stone wall, looking out towards the harbour. It was a fine hot day and the water glistened. To them, it seemed unfair to be confined to the school grounds on such a day.

'Let's go down to the water,' Tim said. 'No one will miss us for an hour or two.'

Paul readily agreed. Today of all days he needed to be with his friend. He needed something to take his mind off the other letter he had received that week, this time from his mother. He was surprised at her suggestion he travel back to England with her on her next visit to live permanently in England.

'At the moment your father doesn't have a home,' she had written. 'You enjoyed being at Haldon Hall when you were younger ...'

He was confused by the terrible choice he faced. He knew, whichever option he chose, he was going to disappoint one of his parents.

In England he would be reunited with his mother and his younger brother Anthony and that would be something to look forward to, but his heart broke at the prospect of rarely seeing his father and the place he loved most in the world.

He had not seen the pile of rubble that had been his much-loved home at Prior Park. There was no image of the devastation lodged in his mind. In his imagination the grand house was still intact, adding grace and refinement to the bush landscape.

And he remembered how he had been free to roam the country-side for miles beyond the house. It was Belleville land and he assumed, without knowing for sure, that he would one day take ownership of it. That was where his heart belonged. That was where it would always belong.

CHAPTER 4

April 1958

Hopes of fine spring weather looked to be doomed with the cold winds of March continuing unabated at Haldon Hall in the days leading up to Easter.

But Catherine Belleville hardly noticed the weather at all. Inside the house, great log fires gave off their friendly warmth in each of the downstairs rooms.

For most of the morning, she had been in earnest discussions with Maurice Langton, the family solicitor, who secretly enjoyed the prestige of visiting his most important client at her home.

'We have to deal with the death duties soon,' Maurice Langton said, in a flat, matter of fact tone, once they had dispensed with the ordinary day-to-day business of the estate.

'I know,' Catherine answered quickly. 'It seems such a lot of money. Does it mean I will have to sell some assets, do you think?'

She was aware that her father, surprisingly for someone of his background, had managed his financial affairs well but the estate could not escape the burden of taxes resulting from his death.

'I think so,' her solicitor replied cautiously. 'There are several commercial properties in London that would fetch a good price, I believe.'

But she shook her head.

'Are there no other options?' she asked. 'The properties in London are in prime areas and give us very good rental income.'

Since her father's death, she had become aware of the income needed to pay for the lifestyle they enjoyed at Haldon Hall. Selling income-producing assets did not strike her as a good idea.

'You could sell one of the farms here,' he said, despite knowing Catherine's reluctance. The estate's long serving tenant farmers might be turned off the farms if they were sold.

'No, I don't think that's an option either,' she said. 'Are there stocks and shares or cash deposits perhaps?'

She had not yet fully grasped the extent of her father's wealth or how it was held and he had never taken her into his confidence. She had come to her inheritance totally unprepared. Langton consulted his papers, but he did not really need to do so. He had studied all the financial holdings very closely.

'There are some shares, some bonds and some cash holdings but they will never yield the sort of sum we will need,' he said bluntly.

Catherine did not reply immediately. Instead she got up and headed towards the window. Walking about the room gave her time to think. It seemed to her to be a poor choice to be forced to sell good assets to pay death duties. She turned back towards the centre of the room, her face brightening. She resumed her seat opposite Langton.

'What about paintings? We have two very good J M W Turner pieces?'

He smiled, not having previously considered the possibility of valuable pieces of art as a potential source of cash.

'By all means, we could sell them, if you think you can bear to part with them,' he said.

She shrugged. Better to sell the paintings than land or good commercial property, she thought. Her thoughts drifted to her place in Sydney. It too was bringing in income since she had decided to let it out. But to sell it would disappoint her elder son, she knew that.

She wondered then if she had taken notice of some of the conversations she had heard at the dinner table at Prior Park between Richard and his brother William. They had never asked her opinion about their business decisions but she had listened to their discussions all the same with more interest than they had known. Now it was all becoming useful to her.

'I'll think about it,' she said finally. 'How much time do I have to pay?'

He smiled, understanding very well that the settlement of death duties could be delayed.

'I can stall them with a letter so we have time yet,' he said, but he took the opportunity to raise the other urgent matters.

He cleared his throat. These were difficult subjects to broach but it was his duty, as her lawyer, to raise them.

'Your divorce,' he said, uncertain how to frame the question. 'How shall we proceed?'

The discussion was awkward for him. He paled at the prospect of her reputation being shredded by the tabloid press. He hoped there would not be any talk of adultery.

'How nicely you frame the question for such a distasteful matter, Mr Langton,' she retorted.

He nodded his head politely.

'We have already sent documents to your husband to sign to establish the separation, which he has done.'

'Thank you,' she said quickly, without giving him the opportunity to ask more questions.

She suspected, without being certain, that he had heard gossip about her relationship with her distant cousin Edward Cavendish.

'And custody of the children?' he asked quietly. 'Have you and Mr Belleville agreed on an arrangement?'

'There is nothing in writing, Mr Langton,' she said quickly. 'Anthony is to remain here with me for the time being and I now have an inclination to seek custody of Paul too. My husband no longer has a stable home to offer them since Prior Park burnt down.'

Maurice Langton was surprised and somewhat alarmed at this latest suggestion and said so.

'I think, if I am to understand your informal arrangement, your husband believed the older boy would remain in Australia,' he said. 'Have you considered if you start making demands like this he might make the divorce proceedings more difficult for you?'

It was as close as he could come to outright disagreement with her. He thought her husband had been very fair in allowing the younger child to remain with her. But he did not think Richard Belleville would take kindly to both of his sons being brought up on the other side the world. He doubted a court would side with his client but he did not go so far as to say so. He knew Richard Belleville was a wealthy man with the resources to fight a court battle if it came to it. And a war hero. That would raise his standing in the eyes of any judge.

'Well,' she said finally, 'I've written to Paul asking if he wants to come back with me next time I visit and live permanently with me here.'

'I see,' he said. 'Have you written to your husband with the same request?'

'No, I haven't,' she admitted. 'I wanted to see what Paul's reaction is first before I raised it with Richard.'

Langton paused, carefully considering what he should say next.

'Was that entirely fair on the child, Mrs Belleville?' he asked. 'He is only twelve years old after all. It's a tough choice to be asked to make.'

She shrugged her shoulders.

'We will see, I guess,' she said.

'I take it your husband has recovered from the injuries he sustained in the terrible assault?' he asked, deciding not to pursue the question of custody any further.

'Yes,' she said. 'I got a letter from him earlier this week.'

'I haven't told Anthony about it yet,' she added. 'I didn't think a five-year-old would have much understanding of such a dreadful incident.'

'Very wise I'm sure, Mrs Belleville,' he responded. 'And while we're talking about your children, have you considered how you will dispose of the estate in your will? Have you thought any further about it?'

The issue had worried him greatly ever since she had inherited everything from her father but she had continually stalled his efforts to discuss the matter in greater detail. She had two sons but neither of them was English. Would they, in later years, want the burden of running an English estate, he wondered?

'I haven't decided what to do yet, Mr Langton,' she said finally. 'I think that's a matter for another day.'

She looked quickly at her wristwatch and rose from her chair, indicating that the meeting was over. He quickly gathered up his papers and walked with her towards the door.

Just as the butler opened the front door, they were greeted by the noise of a car speeding down the driveway towards the house.

'I assume that's Sir Edward coming to pay a call,' Langton said, looking in the direction of a deep green Jaguar. It's so shiny it must be new, he thought.

'Yes,' said Catherine smiling broadly. 'I've been expecting him. In fact, he's late. He wants to show off his new car. By the look of it, he's just collected it from the showroom.'

As Maurice Langton walked towards his own car, he raised a hand in greeting to the visitor who did likewise as he walked hurriedly towards the house to greet Catherine.

Looking back as he slowed his car to turn out of the driveway onto the main road back to town, Maurice Langton caught sight of a brief warm embrace before Catherine and Edward disappeared into the house. It confirmed the suspicions he already harboured: that Catherine Belleville had already found her next husband. All that remained was for her to become a free woman so she could marry again.

And what then would the future hold for her Australian children, he wondered, if she was to have a child with Sir Edward? A son of the marriage would inherit the baronetcy which her Australian sons could never do. Would the temptation then be to leave all her wealth to such a child to ensure the viability of the estate? Would the Belleville children in those circumstances be better off being brought up by their father in Australia, where they would no doubt inherit his wealth and feel more at home, he mused.

He mulled over the possibilities as he drove away, oblivious to the bitingly cold wind and the rain squall that threatened to turn into a torrential downpour.

In Sydney Good Friday dawned bright and sunny. A slight breeze helped propel the myriad of small sailing boats that had taken to the water. The Manly ferry chugged away from Circular Quay. It was making slow but steady progress across the harbour on its regular route around Middle Head to its destination on the far side of the harbour.

Julia Belleville sat beside her daughter Pippa on a park bench near the harbour's edge. Together they watched the endless activity on the water. Julia had quickly reverted to using her maiden name. The name Fitzroy, she said, belonged to another life.

Aunt Edith came towards them, clutching an ice cream for each of them. She joined mother and daughter on the seat.

'This is going to be my best birthday,' Julia said, as she took the proffered ice cream.

The three of them sat together in silence for some time. Julia's thoughts drifted to the night of her eighteenth birthday party at Prior Park sixteen years earlier. To her, it seemed like a lifetime ago. She had been an innocent then, not knowing what lay ahead of her. It was only a little over a year later she discovered she was pregnant and Philippe had gone, posted away from Australia. She shuddered at the memory of what she had been through.

Pippa was oblivious to the slight tremor but Edith noticed it. Yet she said nothing. She did not want to embarrass Julia. Edith did not know the full story but had pieced together the snippets she had been told. It was enough for her. She sympathised with Julia. She knew how hard it must have been for Julia to give up her daughter. But she sympathised with Julia's mother too. What other choice could she have made, she wondered?

'Are we expecting Philippe to join us?' Edith asked, for she was sure that had been the arrangement.

Julia shook her head slowly. She was beginning to understand the demands on surgeons. Sometimes surgery could not wait until a more convenient time.

'He phoned me at the hotel this morning,' she said. 'He was called in to do an emergency operation. It was a patient who was injured in a traffic accident last night.'

She had already told Pippa, who had expressed her unhappiness at the news.

'Was there no one else available?' Edith asked, surprised, because she had thought Philippe had not expected to be on call over the Easter break.

'Apparently the surgeon who should have done the operation sprained his ankle playing tennis yesterday,' she said.

Edith nodded. A neurosurgeon of Philippe's skill was always in demand, especially for the most traumatic cases. She wondered how many events he had missed and how many dinners he had forgone to save someone's life.

'And when are you going to see the house he has purchased?' Edith asked.

She had not seen it but Philippe had been as good as his word and taken Pippa with him to see a number of prospective houses.

Pippa interrupted before her mother could answer.

'We're going tomorrow,' she said, 'but we can't see inside it, just from the outside, because the sale isn't finalised yet.'

Julia smiled. She felt as if she hardly needed to see it. Pippa had told her a good deal about it, especially about the garden and the very modern kitchen, and the room she imagined would be her bedroom.

'And how long before the sale is finalised?' Edith asked.

Once again, it was Pippa who answered.

'It won't be final until at least the middle of next month,' she said authoritatively.

Julia and Edith exchanged quiet smiles. They both knew Philippe would have no success at all in keeping anything from Pippa in the future. But what was the future? Julia could not say for certain.

She and Philippe had exchanged letters over the intervening months since they had met unexpectedly in Sydney. But so much had happened since that time. Her marriage had collapsed, as she knew it would. Her childhood home Prior Park had burnt down at the hand of a madman and worst of all her mother had died as a result. Then Richard had been attacked and nearly killed. Life had become complicated.

Could she put all that behind her and rekindle her romantic relationship with Philippe? And what about John? If she was to live with Philippe, did that mean she was abandoning her son?

There appeared to be no easy choices. For now, she had to be content to live in the moment.

The three of them began to walk back along the almost empty city streets towards her hotel. This time they would lunch together for the first time in the hotel dining room where she had first seen Pippa with Philippe.

She often thought how easily she might have missed seeing them that day. It was the day on which her life had changed forever yet it was such an unlikely encounter that she hardly believed it was chance alone that had brought them all together.

'And how do you know Dr Duval, Miss Belleville?'

Patricia Clarke asked the question as she guided Julia towards the room where the other female guests were leaving their evening wraps and repairing their makeup. A babble of voices greeted them as the hostess opened the door. Julia was quickly introduced to five or six women, all of whom seemed to be talking at once. They stopped suddenly on being told she was Dr Duval's partner for the evening. Julia could not help but notice how they looked her up and down, 'as if I was some prize exhibit' she later told Philippe.

He did not know it but his arrival at St Vincent's Hospital had not gone unnoticed by the doctors' wives and daughters. His excellent manners, his reputation as a fine surgeon and his status as a single man had all combined to ignite interest in him on his appointment. An invitation to Patricia Clarke's Easter dinner party had been in high demand when it had become known he would attend.

But Philippe had known that Julia would be questioned about their friendship so her story had been agreed between them. He had not needed to tell her to remove her wedding and engagement rings.

She had at first resisted his invitation to accompany him to the dinner party but he had persisted and she had agreed in the end. She had not wanted to disappoint him.

As she walked towards him in the hotel lobby, he had smiled and whispered, 'you look beautiful'.

He could see she had gone to some trouble with her dress. But he could not allay her nervousness completely. He felt her body trembling as he guided her towards the exit.

'It will be fine,' he had whispered reassuringly.

His words echoed in her mind as she answered her hostess's question.

'I met Dr Duval during the war when he was stationed near my home,' she said quickly. 'We met again recently. I was on a visit to Sydney late last year and he was attending a medical conference. We met by accident.'

Patricia Clarke listened intently. Up until Philippe had telephoned to ask if he may bring a friend, there had been no talk of his being attached. In fact, very little was known of his personal life, something she was quick to point out to her husband, who had quickly lost patience with her questions

'That was fortunate indeed,' Patricia Clarke replied.

The other women overheard her remark and noted the slight scepticism in her voice. The faint marks left on Julia's finger by the rings she had discarded had not escaped her notice but she said nothing more on the topic.

The older woman guided Julia down a long corridor towards a brightly lit drawing room. The house was large with a fine view up the harbour from the terrace which could be directly accessed from the drawing room, a fact her hostess did not fail to mention even though it was dark and the night too chilly for open windows.

'Now come through and meet my husband,' Patricia Clarke said. 'You are the only stranger in our midst.'

Dr Robert Clarke turned at the sound of his wife's voice and extended his hand towards Julia. He was not quite so diplomatic as his wife.

'Ah, so you're the mystery girl. All the other single females at the hospital are going to be green with envy,' he declared loudly.

It was a clumsy greeting but fortunately Philippe, who was standing alongside his host, filled the awful silence that followed. He could sense Julia's alarm. He slipped his arm loosely around her waist.

'What a lot of nonsense you talk sometimes, Robert,' Philippe said smoothly. 'I'm a middle-aged man well past my prime. I think the young girls have much better prospects than me.'

He turned towards Julia.

'I'd like you to meet an old friend of mine, Julia Belleville. I knew her family when I was posted here during the war.'

Robert Clarke held onto Julia's hand longer than politeness dictated.

'How do you do, Dr Clarke,' she said quietly.

It's as if I'm back in school at deportment classes, she thought. How many times had they practised those words and then dissolved in giggles? It seemed to her much safer to say very little than to begin to embellish the story of how she and Philippe first met.

She was saved by the hostess who, just at that moment, began to usher her guests into the dining room. She came alongside Julia.

'Don't mind my husband,' she said. 'He can be very tactless at times but he's a fine surgeon.'

Julia smiled but said nothing.

There were twelve guests in all. Philippe, distracted by a question from another guest, did not notice Julia's attention turn towards a number of photographs neatly arranged on the grand piano that stood near the doorway leading out of the drawing room. One photo in particular caught her eye and she could not look away. She had not asked who was in the picture but her hostess took her cue.

'That's my daughter Anita with some of her school chums at Meriden,' she said, picking up the photo for closer scrutiny. She pointed to the girls, one by one, for Julia's benefit.

'That's Lucy Dixon – her great uncle is Chief Justice – and Nancy Lester. Her people have property in the southern highlands. The girl on the right, standing slightly apart, is Pippa Jensen.'

She placed the photograph back on the piano.

'That last girl has a very sad story. She's an orphan but now she's telling the story at school that she's actually the illegitimate daughter of a wartime romance between a young girl and an American soldier and that her parents are still very much alive. All very sordid if you ask me. I've suggested to Anita she should see less of the girl.'

Patricia Clarke continued to chatter but Julia did not hear her. It was all she could do to nod politely. She breathed a sigh of relief as her hostess's attention was demanded elsewhere. She caught Philippe's eye and motioned silently towards the picture.

He looked at it but did not pick it up. He did not want to draw further attention to it. He said nothing but took her hand and slipped her arm through his.

'She does not think Pippa is a fit girl for her daughter to know,' she whispered. 'They are at the same school. I did not know.'

'Neither did I,' Philippe said quietly. 'It never occurred to me to ask about their daughter. Robert has only ever mentioned her once and only then because she was in strife about something.'

For the first time, Julia began to realise how little she knew of her daughter's life and how Pippa might be despised for the circumstances of her birth if it became widely known. Would that even be resolved if she and Philippe married, she wondered? How would they explain a teenage daughter?

Philippe too was beginning to see the problems that might lie ahead. He had always believed his professional standing and qualifications would be the determining factor in his career. But in a conservative hospital environment would they be prepared to look the other way if his personal life became the subject of gossip? He hoped it would not come to that. But in bringing Julia with him to the dinner party he realised too late he had foolishly exposed himself to the very conjecture he had hoped to avoid.

Why had he given up an outstanding career in New York to move to Sydney, they had all asked? No one he met had ever been entirely convinced by his explanation of wanting a new challenge. Yet he offered them no other reason. Now, he might have unwittingly provided that other reason.

For the first time, Julia noticed how tired he looked.

'Are you quite well?' she asked.

The concern in her voice was unmistakable. He smiled at her. The sight of her lifted his mood.

'The surgery yesterday was very difficult and demanding,' he said, 'but successful. And I had a full week of surgery before that.'

She nodded. She knew very little of his work but it did not take much imagination to know the work he did was extremely demanding.

'We must look after you,' she said, just as they were separated by their hostess who was keen to ensure the carefully arranged seating plan at her dinner table was not upset by the unexpected presence of Dr Duval's unknown friend.

'I've put you next to Robert's niece, Karen Clarke,' Patricia Clarke said.

Without taking breath, she spoke quickly to the young woman alongside of whom she had indicated the empty chair for Philippe.

'Karen, this is Dr Philippe Duval, the new surgeon working with your uncle. We must make him feel at home.'

Philippe extended his hand and felt a small cool hand touch his very briefly. He smiled acknowledging the introduction. She smiled at him in return.

'I've heard a lot about you, Dr Duval,' she said, 'and all of it good.'

'I can't believe all the reports would have been favourable,' he said, returning her friendly banter.

'Oh, but they were, Dr Duval, they were,' she said, disputing his attempts to make light of his reputation. Her voice, raised to emphasise the point, could be heard along the length of the table.

Julia, seated towards the end of the table, watched the exchange with just a small pang of anxiety.

Karen Clarke was, she calculated, at least five years younger than her. Her face, framed by a mass of auburn hair, was turned towards Philippe. Julia's gaze moved to her dress, which was elegant and clearly expensive. She wore a diamond clasp on each shoulder. Julia never doubted the diamonds were real. Karen's hand, she noticed, rested lightly on Philippe's arm in playful rebuke of his refusal to believe everything she had heard of him was positive.

Dr Jules Hamilton, who sat alongside Julia, followed her gaze.

'That's Karen Clarke,' he said without prompting. 'On the lookout for a husband I believe. She was due to marry one of the Fairholm boys but she called it off before the big day, so she's back on the market. Looks like she might have Duval in her sights. If that's the case, he won't have any chance of escape.'

Julia heard all this in stony silence.

Dr Jules Hamilton, totally unaware of Julia's interest, shrugged his shoulders at her silence and instead attacked the entrée of prawns that had just been placed before him with gusto.

43

CHAPTER 5

May 1958

Richard Belleville was now fully recovered from the murderous attack that had almost claimed his life. His doctors had finally agreed he was fit to travel although he had argued with them months earlier that he was well enough.

'They're too cautious' he had complained to his brother William repeatedly when they had scuppered his plans to visit his son Paul in Sydney. Now, finally, he had been given a clean bill of health.

It was a fine late autumn day and he was standing beside his brother William. They were watching the foundations being laid for William and Alice's new house, just a few hundred yards from where their once grand home lay in ruins.

'How long will it take to build?' Richard asked.

William raised his hand to his eyes to cut out the glare as he took in every detail of the work going on in front of him.

'Probably three to four months,' he said. 'At least it's winter time and we shouldn't have any rain delays.'

Richard then turned to look at the ruin. It disturbed him anew every time he saw it. He blamed himself for his mother's death. How many times had he relived the horror of her dash back into the burning house to rescue a photo of her husband, their father, not knowing it was his actions that lay at the heart of the tragedy.

'At least it's quicker than rebuilding the big house would have been,' he said, nodding in the direction of the pile of rubble that lay undisturbed. 'That would have taken years.'

William nodded. Rebuilding it had never seemed sensible to him. 'And you're settling into your new house?' he asked.

He was relieved Richard had finally bought a house. He approved of its situation in the hills above the town where at least there might be a breeze on a hot summer's day and no risk of flooding. The house was large and enveloped on three sides by the classic Queensland verandah. The gardens were lush and well established.

'Yes, I'm settling in, although it seemed very odd at first being by myself,' he said. 'And I have nothing that isn't new. I think that's hardest to accept. It's all gone.'

'Except your medals. If you remember I insisted we put them in the bank vault along with the important papers,' William said, having privately congratulated himself a number of times for his wisdom in keeping the important family papers safe.

'Yes, I know, and I will leave it there,' Richard said. 'I need nothing to remind me of the war. Those memories are best left behind.'

William did not understand his brother's reluctance to acknowledge his bravery.

'And your new housekeeper and gardener are working out alright?' William asked. He could not imagine Richard doing these things for himself.

'Yes, I have a married couple who look after things but they don't live in,' he said, not for the first time recalling wistfully the glory days of Prior Park when they were all together. 'Not quite up to Mrs Duffy's standard but they will do.'

William smiled. He at least was able to look forward to Mrs Duffy taking charge of his household again. Even in the smaller house he was building, he wanted Alice to have the benefit of a housekeeper.

They turned away from the ruin of their old home and headed towards their cars. There was no evidence now of where exactly Richard had been attacked, except that it had been close to the gravestone that marked their mother's grave.

'Any news from the police as to whether they will charge Charles?' Richard asked, assuming that William would be the one to know.

It was then they heard footsteps behind them. Charles had not been home when they arrived so they had not expected to see him.

'I think I can answer that question,' Charles said, as he came up to them. 'I finally heard yesterday and they won't lay any charges, which is a relief.'

Richard clasped Charles's hand. It was the best news he had received in months.

'You did me a great service, Charles,' he said. 'I wouldn't be standing here if it wasn't for you.'

Charles brushed his thanks aside.

'I think you've already told me that often enough, Richard,' he said, half laughing to hide his embarrassment.

He did not enjoy being feted and thanked. He did not want Richard to feel he was in his debt. William was silent. What pressure the Belleville family lawyers were able to bring, he did not know and would not ask. It was enough that Charles would not face any charges.

'And your sister?' asked Charles. 'What's become of your sister?'

'She hasn't told us very much about what she plans to do,' Richard said. 'I did ask her if she wanted to stay with me, but she decided to rent a house in town for a short time. She seems to spend half of her time in Sydney. John spends most of his time with James or with his grandmother.'

Charles nodded, saying he was not surprised at the news.

But it was William who ventured an opinion.

'Perhaps she is still uncertain as to what the future holds,' he said. 'Alice says it's by no means certain they'll resume their relationship when Julia is divorced. There's been a lot of water under the bridge, I suppose.'

No one spoke his name but they all knew William was referring to Philippe Duval, the man both Richard and William continued to regard as their sister's seducer. And no one spoke Pippa's name. Their sister had so far sidestepped any opportunity to introduce her daughter to her extended family, as if she wanted that part of her life to be separate from the life she had so far lived.

'Well, one thing's for sure,' Charles said. 'James Fitzroy isn't letting the grass grow under his feet.'

Both Richard and William spoke in unison.

'What do you mean?'

'Just that I saw him yesterday in his car heading towards the coast, probably for the weekend. He had a very attractive young lady sitting alongside him.'

'Who was it?' Richard asked, although he was hardly curious about James's activities now that he was in the throes of divorcing their sister.

'I didn't know her,' Charles said, 'but it did look very much as if his broken heart has healed.'

The hint of sarcasm in Charles's tone did not escape them. William shrugged. Like Richard, he was barely interested in his brother-in-law's romantic life.

'I'll be out tomorrow, Charles, to discuss what cattle we'll send off to the saleyards,' William said.

The cattle business had now become William's sole responsibility. While Richard loved the bush, it was his brother who had made a success of their cattle interests with the new cattle breeds that had been introduced to Prior Park.

'I'll come too,' said Richard, without invitation. 'It's time I got on a horse again after so much inactivity.'

Charles nodded.

'Your horse will be pretty frisky so you'll have to be careful,' he said with just a note of caution. The animal had not been ridden at all for months.

'And I'll warn Mrs Duffy to expect you both for lunch.'

William laughed.

'You won't have your own housekeeper for too much longer, Charles. Remember she's coming back to work for me and Alice in the new house.'

With that William threw his hat into the back seat of his car and jumped into the driver's seat. He knew he was already late for lunch and his mother-in-law, not to mention his wife, would be far from pleased.

Richard lingered. There was no such urgency for him.

'Have you heard anything of the Warners lately?' he asked.

Well, that was a question out of the blue, thought Charles, although he did not say so.

47

'Not a lot except that the young fella has left his school days behind him and is now helping his father full time,' Charles said, knowing full well that this was not the information Richard was seeking.

'He'd be a good help, I'm sure,' Richard said, for want of something more meaningful to say.

'Yes, particularly as Tom Warner bought the adjoining paddock late last year, so they have increased their holding quite a bit.'

Richard was surprised at the news. He thought William would have been keen to buy any local land that came up for sale but he hadn't mentioned it.

'Any other neighbouring properties up for sale?' Richard said, wondering if, by not living at Prior Park, they were missing opportunities.

'Only the part of the Fitzroy holding that went to James's Aunt Margaret when she married,' Charles said finally.

He had wondered if he should alert William and Richard to the fact that it was for sale.

'I guess they want to retire,' Richard said, 'and they have no children to take over from them. But I don't see James wanting his aunt to give us the chance to buy it. Surely he will be looking at it himself.'

'Yes, I would think he'd want to add it to Mayfield Downs to bring it back to its original size,' Charles said. 'Otherwise he would have mentioned it to William surely.'

Richard laughed.

'I don't think James is in the mood to do us any favours after the way our sister treated him.'

But Charles was having none of it. Julia had long been his favourite.

'I think maybe your mother was to blame for that really although I shouldn't speak ill of the dead,' Charles said. 'And if you knew the rumours I'd heard about James Fitzroy during his marriage to Julia, you might begin to feel that he got what he deserved.'

He could see the shock on Richard's face. He could see that Richard hadn't known about James's reputation.

'I didn't know,' Richard said. 'Of course, William and I had our suspicions but I'd never seen him about with other girls. Perhaps he was careful to keep out of our way. And he always seemed to care for Julia.'

'Oh, he cared for her alright,' Charles said. 'But he just couldn't bring himself to be faithful to one woman.'

It was then Charles realised he had probably gone too far. He noticed Richard turn away from him ever so slightly.

'Sorry, mate,' Charles said. 'I wasn't meaning to ..'

His words trailed off. He didn't know what else to say. His silence betrayed his knowledge of Richard's own behaviour, which he had privately condemned.

'It's alright,' Richard said. 'Really, it's alright.'

He turned back towards Charles. Perhaps now was the time to tell his friend what had happened so many years before, not to absolve himself but at least to provide an explanation of his actions.

'I know you know about Jane Warner,' Richard said. 'But what you probably don't know is that she was the girl I was going to marry when I came back from the war.'

He could see by the look on his face that Charles had not known about his early romance.

'We were secretly engaged when I left to go into training,' He said. 'That was what caused the big row with my parents. My mother did not think her an appropriate bride for me. Then she married Tom Warner while I was overseas. And I married Catherine.'

It took some time for Charles to absorb all that Richard was telling him. Finally, he spoke.

'I remember now. It was a pretty quick wedding to Tom Warner,' Charles recalled. 'We were all surprised when we heard. No one from the district was invited. I thought at the time it was a mismatch.'

Richard nodded. He decided then to tell Charles the whole story.

'She told me last year she thought she was pregnant so when Tom Warner took an interest in her, she accepted him,' he said.

'I take that to mean she thought she was having your baby?' Charles felt he had to ask the obvious question. 'And she couldn't take the risk of being pregnant and you not being here to marry her?'

He wanted to be sure he understood what Richard was telling him.

'That's right,' he admitted. 'As it turned out, she wasn't pregnant or maybe she miscarried, I don't know. But her son is definitely her husband's child, not mine.'

Charles was stunned by Richard's sudden need to tell him the story after so many years but he gave a half laugh all the same.

'Even I can do basic arithmetic, mate,' he said. 'She must have written to you to tell you while you were away.'

Richard nodded, remembering how her simple letter had delivered the devastating news.

'She did and I was devastated,' he said quietly.

'And then you met Catherine,' Charles said, wondering if his romance with Catherine had been on the rebound.

'Yes, and then I met Catherine,' he said.

'I remember your mother didn't believe the telegram when you said you were bringing your wife home with you,' Charles said, recalling the uproar in the house immediately before his return.

'I didn't quite know how to tell her that I'd had to marry Catherine,' he said. 'I thought I'd let them figure that out for themselves when the baby arrived.'

Charles laughed, remembering the shock in the household.

'I think your mother turned a blind eye to that little problem,' he said. 'I know she was happy that Catherine was from a good family. She wouldn't have been so generous towards Jane.'

Richard smiled wistfully, remembering the harsh words that had been said at the time he'd announced his plan to marry Jane.

'No, you're right, Charles,' he said. 'She wouldn't have been so generous towards Jane but I think she would have come around in time.'

He felt he'd said more than enough for one day. He trusted Charles in the same way he trusted William but William was not someone who encouraged confidences.

Charles was temporarily at a loss for words. What could he say? What advice or consolation could he offer his friend? He knew Richard had briefly rekindled his romance with Jane Warner the previous year. He had been alarmed at his accidental discovery of their secret relationship. He wanted to ask, but could not, if Richard was still involved with her. Part of him though was relieved to know that Richard, whom he loved like a son, was not the casual philanderer he knew James Fitzroy to be. He had never believed that of him so he was relieved to know the truth.

50

The two men parted. Charles began to head back towards his house while Richard walked the short distance to his car.

'I'll see you tomorrow,' Richard called back over his shoulder. 'I'm looking forward to a gallop across the paddocks.'

Charles waved and watched as he drove away. He fervently hoped that Richard would find happiness again. He couldn't help wondering though if that happiness might come at the expense of someone else's marriage.

It was just a week later that Richard walked across the tarmac at Sydney airport, making the long overdue visit to his elder son Paul. This time he was not alone. His sister Julia followed closely behind him. She had finally yielded to his insistence that he meet her daughter so the pair travelled south together.

It was a cool day that looked likely to descend into showery weather. With rain threatening, the two of them walked quickly to the airport terminal. Once inside, it was left to Richard to collect their luggage while Julia searched the faces in the crowded terminal for Philippe.

'Were you being picked up?' he asked.

It had not occurred to him until that moment that she might have expected Philippe to meet her.

'Only if Philippe is available and he doesn't always know when that will be,' she said, turning back towards Richard. 'I don't see him so let's get a taxi to the hotel.'

With their bags safely stowed, they settled into the back seat to be driven to the hotel. Both of them had stayed at the Australia Hotel previously so the half hour drive was no longer a novelty.

'When are you going to get Paul from school?' Julia asked.

They had not discussed any plans for the visit beyond travelling together.

'The term ends tomorrow,' Richard said, 'so I plan to pick him up after school. He says he can't wait until Saturday. He can stay with me at the hotel for a few days. I've got some business to do and then I'm taking him home for a week or so.'

Julia looked out the window at the darkening sky. The weather they had left behind was bright and sunny.

'He hasn't been back, has he, since the fire?'

Richard shook his head.

'No, he hasn't,' he said, the concern in his voice evident, 'but he has to face it some time. I can't keep denying him that opportunity. And I need him to see he has a new home.'

It was this last observation that caused Julia to flinch. She could not settle to the idea of buying herself a house. If she bought a house in Springfield, it pointed to her preference for her old life. If she settled in Sydney, she felt as if she would be cut off from her former life completely, abandoning her son and the rest of her family. Another question too remained unanswered. What would her relationship with Philippe be after her divorce? She could not honestly answer that question yet.

As the hotel porter extracted their luggage from the taxi, Richard paid the fare and then followed his sister into the foyer.

He noticed she used the name Miss Belleville as she checked in. He heard the clank of the room key in her hand. He then stepped up to the desk and gave his name. He waited patiently for a few minutes as they checked his reservation. The receptionist finally turned back to him but did not offer him a room key.

'Sir, Mrs Belleville checked in this morning,' he said. 'Your wife will have the key to the suite, room 602.'

Richard responded immediately. He assumed there had been a mistake.

'I'm sorry, there's been some mistake, my wife is not with me,' he said, in an even measured tone.

The hotel receptionist looked puzzled.

'Sir, she arrived from London this morning. On the Qantas flight I believe,' he said. 'Although I must admit when she checked in, she was surprised the reservation was in the name of Mr Belleville and not Mrs Belleville.'

'We assumed it was just a small mistake, sir,' he added.

Julia observed all this and saw the shock on Richard's face. There had been no plans, as far as he knew, for Catherine to visit Sydney during the May school holidays. His first thought was for his younger son.

'Did she have a small boy with her?' he asked.

Suddenly, he was desperate to know. If Anthony was with her, he could look forward to a reunion with both his sons for the first time in many months.

'Yes sir,' he said, 'she did. A small boy of about five I would think. A very proper little English gent he'll be when he grows up.'

Richard couldn't help but smile at this description. Had they really changed Anthony so much from the small tearaway who had endeared himself to everyone at Prior Park, he wondered.

'Shall I call Mrs Belleville's room and let her know you are coming up, sir?' the receptionist asked, uncertain how to proceed. He could see for himself the information had been totally unexpected.

Richard shook his head. He had not planned on having to expose his marital woes in so public a place but he had no option.

'My wife and I are separated,' he said quietly. 'I would appreciate my own suite, if you wouldn't mind.'

The man's face reddened. He was flustered by this unexpected development.

'By all means, sir,' he said. 'I'm sorry if we embarrassed you.'

He handed Richard the key to a suite on the fifth floor.

'Mrs Belleville is in 602 you say?'

'She is, sir,' he answered quietly. 'You can call room to room, which may be best.'

Together Julia and Richard headed towards the hotel lift.

'I take it you didn't know that Catherine was planning to visit?' Julia asked her brother in a quiet voice.

He shook his head.

'No, I didn't,' he said, 'but perhaps it is opportune.'

Julia nodded, understanding the delicacy of the situation. She was surprised Catherine had failed to inform Richard of her plans. It crossed her mind that the question of who would have custody of Paul might be at the heart of Catherine's subterfuge. If so, it had failed spectacularly, Julia thought.

Chapter 6

May 1958

Catherine was startled by the piercing sound of the telephone ringing on the bedside table. She had sought the comfort of sleep immediately on checking in after the long journey from London.

She picked up the telephone cautiously and answered hesitantly. There was silence from the other end for some moments before Richard spoke.

'Hello, Catherine,' he said. 'You're the last person I expected to meet in Sydney.'

She was shocked into silence for a few moments. What could she say now to justify not telling him of her planned trip?

'Richard,' she said finally, 'what are you doing in Sydney? How are you? I didn't think you'd be able to travel yet after the assault?'

He gave a half laugh. It was not a reassuring sound nor was it meant to be.

'So that's your excuse for bringing our younger son to Australia and coming to visit our elder son without telling me,' he said, his voice rising in barely suppressed anger.

'You didn't think I'd be well enough to travel,' he said mockingly.

He knew it was a hastily cobbled together excuse.

She wanted to say 'no, it's not an excuse' but it sounded such a pathetic justification she said nothing.

'You made that decision all by yourself, without consulting me,' he said.

He controlled his anger with great difficulty.

'It just so happens I got the all clear from the doctors and decided to come to Sydney myself to bring Paul back home for the school holidays, otherwise he could have come back with Julia.'

This news surprised Catherine. And then it all fell into place. Richard had written to her about what he had discovered about his sister, the daughter she had been forced to give up for adoption during the war and her discovery of the child and the child's father in Sydney. Which would explain, she thought, why Julia would visit Sydney at this time of the year especially.

'How did you know I was here? she asked. 'Does Julia know I'm here?'

Richard had calmed down just a little but the memory of his embarrassment at the check in desk was still raw.

'Well I had a conversation at the reception desk downstairs explaining that I would want a different room from my wife and why, because they had given you the room intended for me,' he said.

'And, yes,' he added. 'Julia was an interested observer to this embarrassing conversation with the hotel clerk.'

Catherine was sitting on the edge of the bed, her back to the doorway of her bedroom. Just then, she heard movement and a small insistent voice. She turned to see Anthony running towards her.

'Mummy, is that Daddy on the phone? Can I talk to him?'

She held the phone out to him. His face lit up at the mere sound of his father's voice. After a few moments, he hung up the phone.

'Daddy's coming to see us now,' Anthony said, in high excitement. 'Now, right now?'.

There was nothing she could do to stall the visit. She got up quickly and rushed to the mirror, thrusting her stockinged feet into her shoes as she did so. 'Thank God I didn't bother to undress,' she thought.

All she had time to do was drag a comb through her hair and refresh her lipstick before her young son opened the door to his father.

His squeals of delight echoed down the corridor of the hotel as he threw himself into his father's arms.

Catherine's presence in Sydney added a new dimension to Julia's plans for the week. Within an hour of arrival she too had been reunited with

Catherine and Anthony. She was delighted to see her young nephew again. Anthony was equally delighted to see his aunt, throwing his arms around her neck and talking excitedly about so many things she could make sense of none of it.

But there was a sense of reserve between the two women that had not previously existed. Julia blamed Catherine for her brother's current unhappiness. Catherine, having come to understand what Julia had been through and the subsequent collapse of her marriage, was sympathetic without knowing quite how to convey those sentiments to the younger woman.

An awkward silence prevailed among the three of them for some minutes as they sat together drinking tea in the hotel lounge. It was Anthony, intent on creating pale sludge out of his bowl of ice cream, who lightened the mood. Instead of scolding him, they all laughed at his efforts.

Julia had not confided her plans to her brother. Now she was faced with the necessity of extricating herself from the family group. She put her cup down on the table in front of her.

'I'm afraid I must go and change,' she said. 'I'm being picked up at seven o'clock to go to dinner.'

Both Richard and Catherine noted the careful omission of a name. It was time, Richard decided, to put an end to the charade of secrecy surrounding his sister's visits to Sydney.

'I assume your date is Philippe?' he said bluntly.

Julia stood up. Was this the time to be defensive about her relationship with Pippa's father. She took a deep breath.

'Yes, of course it's with Philippe,' she said as if there was no irregularity about their relationship.

'Don't you think it would be a good chance for me to meet him?' Richard asked, his tone having softened.

'You mean meet him again, don't you?' Julia said.

She had not forgotten Philippe's recounting of his efforts to find their baby daughter in Goulburn after the war and his chance meeting with Richard.

'He told you about that, I guess?'

It was a statement of fact rather than a question.

'He did,' Julia said. 'He told me everything and it broke my heart.'

Richard moved then to put his arm around his sister.

'I didn't know anything about him,' he said, as he watched her fight back the tears. 'And I can't undo the past. I simply can't undo the past.'

Catherine watched with a mixture of admiration for her estranged husband and sadness that she too had not been aware of Julia's turmoil during all the years she had spent as Richard's wife at Prior Park.

'You should have said something,' Catherine said. 'Why didn't you make a clean breast of it before you married James?'

Julia laughed. It was a short sharp unhappy sound.

'You remember my mother,' she said. 'With the best will in the world, it wasn't possible to go against her. She insisted my baby was to be forgotten so I could get on with life and marry a serial philanderer.'

Catherine was not entirely shocked at this revelation about James. It was Richard who spoke then.

'I didn't know about his reputation but I've since heard about it and I was shocked,' he said.

Julia looked at her brother, who had resumed his seat. She shrugged her shoulders.

'It doesn't matter now,' she said. 'I'm never going back to him.'

'And Philippe? Is there a future for you there?'

It was Catherine rather than Richard who asked the question.

'I hope so,' she said, 'but my divorce is still some way off so I'm not making plans until I'm a free woman.'

It occurred to her then that Catherine might well be in the same position.

'I think I should meet Philippe for a drink before you go out,' Richard said. 'It would seem churlish of me not to meet him.'

After a moment, Julia nodded her agreement. Richard had never attempted to lecture her. The two had become closer in recent times.

'I promise to be on my best behaviour,' he said, smiling. 'I promise I won't play big brother and grill him about his intentions.'

She smiled at his lame attempt at humour. Up until now, she had been happy to keep the two parts of her life separate but now it had suddenly become impossible.

'And your daughter?' Catherine asked. 'When are you seeing her?'

Julia turned towards Catherine. It was the question Richard had avoided.

'It's the last day of school tomorrow for the term so I've offered to take Pippa shopping on Saturday morning,' she said. 'She's told me, in every letter, she needs new clothes and shoes so I've promised we will have several hours to ourselves.'

It was Catherine now who was thinking ahead. She understood at some stage her sons would need to meet their unknown cousin, although Anthony, who was still intent on his bowl of ice cream, was paying no attention to the conversation.

'It would be a good opportunity for the boys to meet her,' Catherine said.

Julia hesitated. She knew Catherine was right but it was still complicated.

'And Philippe?' she asked. 'We have to consider his position at the hospital. Last time I was here I went to dinner with him at a colleague's house and we discovered his daughter is a friend of our daughter.'

'Oh dear,' Catherine said, sympathetically. 'That would have been awkward but that won't affect my children meeting him surely?'

'No, you're right,' Julia conceded, 'I'm worrying about nothing so we should plan something for Saturday afternoon. I can't imagine boys wanting to tag along with us shopping.'

They all laughed at this prospect and agreed it was unlikely the boys would be happy with the prospect of being dragged from shop to shop.

'Until later then,' Julia said.

Catherine and Richard watched as she walked out of the guest lounge and headed towards the lift. When she was out of sight, Catherine turned to Richard.

'I admire your sister,' she said. 'She's had a lot to cope with and she's done it with great dignity.'

She could see it pained Richard to think of the pressure that had been brought to bear on his sister while he had been serving overseas. He knew that he alone could have been the one to stand up to their mother and protect her. He had long been acknowledged as Elizabeth Belleville's favourite child. But he could only lament his absence. He could not change the past.

'Can you imagine just how badly I felt when it all came out?' he said. 'My mother had many good qualities but she was a tyrant in some ways, and probably most of all with my sister. Julia certainly deserves some happiness now and I'll do all I can to help her.'

'I just hope it doesn't all end badly,' he added.

Catherine smiled. He could just as well have been making that observation about their own situation.

'Me too,' she said. 'I certainly hope it doesn't all end badly.'

Richard looked at her, catching the unspoken meaning of her words but he was hardly prepared for her next admission.

'I have to tell you, otherwise Paul will,' she said, 'that I wrote to him asking if he would like to come back to England and live with me. I thought with what happened at Prior Park, perhaps there was now no home for him with you.'

He was suddenly very angry but he held it in check.

'So, not only did you not tell me you were coming to visit him and bringing our younger son with you,' he snapped back, 'you planned to kidnap him and take him back to England with you?'

She looked startled at his accusation.

'I wasn't going to kidnap him,' she said, her voice barely controlled. 'I was going to ask him if that's what he wanted. I wrote to him in advance so he could have a think about it. Did he want to live with me or with you? I posed a simple question to him.'

But Richard was almost too angry to hear what she was telling him.

'We had an agreement, I thought,' he said, trying desperately to be calm. 'We agreed Paul would stay on here in Sydney at school. He's doing well as you know. And Anthony could stay with you for the time being. So what's this sudden change? What's it all about?'

She shrugged.

'It seemed to me, with Prior Park gone, you had no settled home for Paul,' she said. 'It was different when you all lived together at Prior Park. Alice always looked after the boys so well. But now you are by yourself I assume?'

She had added the question almost as an afterthought. He had not said so but she assumed he was living alone. Their divorce was far from final.

'Yes, I live by myself,' he said, 'but I have a housekeeper. And William and Alice are building a new house on Prior Park, big enough to have me and the boys whenever we want to stay there.'

Catherine listened to him without interruption. She had always known the problems they would face in sharing custody of their children. But she was beginning to understand what it meant to have a child on the other side of the world. She wanted to see Paul grow up and to share the final years of his boyhood. She wanted him to go to school in England so the two boys could at least be together in the school holidays.

'I miss him dreadfully,' she said. 'I know he was away at school anyway but he was within reach and I could see him every holidays when I lived with you or on a long weekend, if I really wanted to. I miss him and I'd really like him to go to school in England so I can see more of him.'

Richard's tone softened. He could see Catherine was genuinely upset by their argument.

'And me?' he asked. 'You don't think I'd miss my two boys dreadfully if they go to live permanently with you in England?'

She turned to face him. She didn't want him to think his opinion no longer mattered to her.

'Of course I understand your point of view,' she said. 'You must know I really agonised over it all. Agonised over writing to Paul. It wasn't a capricious spur-of-the-moment impulse.'

He let out a long deep sigh. It was all happening exactly as he feared it would. He knew each of them had a legitimate argument but that didn't make finding a solution any easier. Finally, he said what was upper most in his mind.

'I really want the boys to grow up with their cousins,' Richard said finally. 'I want them to consider Prior Park as their place. They'll inherit my share of it and the rest of the family's interests when I'm gone. They need to love the place as I do.'

She could see he was determined not to give in to her. She was cautious. She did not want their relationship to degenerate into angry recriminations. She did not want their divorce proceedings to stall. She had told no one but she had promised to marry Edward Cavendish as soon as she was free to do so.

'Let's not argue about it,' she said, her tone conciliatory now. 'Why don't we just leave things the way they are for this year and see what happens. Perhaps you can bring Paul over to England for Christmas?'

Richard breathed a sigh of relief. He knew in a court of law he would have a strong hand, but so would she as their mother. Far better for them to agree between them.

And despite their differences, there was a lingering trace of affection between them. She was still the beautiful young woman he had married. If anything she had grown more attractive with maturity. He felt the old familiar stirring of attraction. He wondered if she felt it too?

They had paid very little attention to Anthony during their tense discussion. As they both stood up to leave the lounge, he was nowhere to be seen. Catherine looked around frantically.

'Where's Anthony?' she asked, her voice rising anxiously. 'He was here a moment ago.'

It was then Richard spotted him. He pointed towards the doorway. Anthony was in deep conversation with a waiter who had been on the verge of delivering a very elaborate ice cream sundae to a table nearby.

They both laughed.

'Don't be surprised if there's a knock on the door of your suite and a waiter arrives with another ice cream sundae,' Richard said. 'Only this time it will be much fancier than the plain bowl of ice cream he's just eaten.'

Catherine walked towards him, holding out her hand.

'He is rather used to getting whatever he wants,' she said, aware that her younger son, without the competing demands of his sibling, had monopolised her attention and that of his grandmother. He was rarely if ever refused anything.

It was early evening and the rumble of peak hour traffic had finally subsided outside the hotel. The rain which had fallen intermittently all day had eventually cleared. The night air was already chilly.

Philippe parked his car near the hotel entrance. He was if anything a little early. He had spent the afternoon in a meeting at the hospital which he found more tiring than operating. He was impatient with meetings that did nothing much more, he thought, than waste time. His forte lay in the practice of surgery and teaching the next generation of surgeons, he would often say, not in the administration of hospitals. He wondered though how he would explain to Julia that he would have to attend a hospital fundraising gala dinner on the next evening. He had deliberately overlooked the invitation but it had been made clear to him he was expected to attend.

Caught off guard and wanting to make amends for his faux pas, he had agreed to escort Karen Clarke but he was left to wonder just whose idea it had been. He doubted it had originated with her uncle Robert Clarke who had made the suggestion. Since their meeting at the dinner to which he had escorted Julia, he had managed to avoid his colleague's niece but invitations to dinners and cocktail parties at which she was likely to be present had become suspiciously frequent.

Perhaps, he decided, it would be better not to tell Julia, at least about his partner for the evening. It would be easier to say he was engaged on hospital business that he could not avoid.

As he entered the hotel, he paused and looked around for Julia. Instead he noticed a man he thought he recognised. Sitting by himself in the foyer, Richard had been keeping a steady eye on the front entrance to the hotel. He immediately recognised the man he had met, briefly, years before. He walked towards him, his hand extended.

'Dr Duval,' Richard said. 'We meet again.'

The two men shook hands. For once, Philippe was lost for words.

'Let's go through to the bar and have a drink together,' Richard said, indicating the way through to the cocktail bar.

'Julia, is she alright?'

That had been his first thought. That something was wrong with Julia. It was one explanation for Richard's presence.

'Julia will join us shortly,' Richard said, 'but I wanted a chance to have a word with you myself.'

'Of course, I realise now, you have a son here at school, don't you?' Philippe said, by way of explaining Richard's presence at the hotel.

'Yes, my older boy Paul is at school here which is why I came down,' he replied. 'Julia might have told you about the attack on me in January which is why I haven't been down this year.'

'Yes, I remember. She did tell me,' Philippe said. His professional interest was piqued. 'I hope there's no lasting impairment. You were lucky to survive it, she said.'

Philippe wondered just how good the treatment had been in a provincial hospital for the severe head injuries Julia had described.

'I'm fine now, no problems,' he replied. 'I assume Julia told you the whole story.'

'Yes, a terrible business,' he said without being more specific.

He wasn't sure just which part of the horrendous events of the past six months Richard was referring to. He had been very aware of just how much Julia had been through in that time. Philippe was treading carefully.

'You would know that your sister has taken a while to get over the loss of her mother and the tragedy that unfolded while she was down here in Sydney,' he said finally.

'Yes, there's been a lot of turmoil in my sister's life in the past year,' Richard said, 'and not all of her own making.'

'Indeed,' Philippe replied cautiously.

He was uncertain exactly what Richard meant.

'I wanted to say how sorry I am at how my family treated you,' Richard said, his words sounding almost formal.

'There's nothing you could have done about it, Richard,' Philippe said. 'It's in the past.'

He knew Richard's apology was a genuine attempt to repair the damage of the past.

'But I want you to know how sorry I am,' Richard persisted. 'If I had been there, I would have intervened. I would not have let my mother do what she did.'

Philippe was moved by Richard's words but he did not want to drag up the past. Yet Richard seemed determined to say what he felt had to be said. If he left it, he thought, he might never have another chance to say 'sorry' to the man his family had wronged.

'You see William was too young and did not have any natural

authority in the family,' he added. 'He could do nothing but act as an accomplice.'

He knew his brother had acted badly too but he did not want to lay the blame on William. William had been no match for their mother and Richard knew it.

'Thank you but there is no need to apologise,' Philippe said. 'What was done cannot be undone. We can only be glad that we have the opportunity to make a better future for our daughter. You at least will get to meet her since you are here.'

He took a sip of the drink that had been placed in front of him. He had been quite unprepared for the conversation and for once he felt at a disadvantage.

'I'm looking forward to meeting Pippa,' Richard said. 'We've arranged with Julia for all of us to meet on Saturday afternoon. My wife Catherine is here from England with Anthony and Paul will be out of school so it's a chance not to be missed.'

For the first time, Philippe began to see his daughter in the context of an extended family. He had not thought beyond his own relationship with his daughter and Julia's relationship with her. He had been an only child, as had his mother. He had never known his father. He had no extended family of relatives. Now he realised, through Julia, Pippa had aunts and uncles and cousins. If they accepted her, as Julia insisted they would, she would feel as if she belonged. But would he be the outsider?

He spotted Julia making her way through the crowded bar and beckoned to her. Both men stood as she sat down at the table. A waiter was by her side almost immediately.

'A cocktail, ma'am?' he asked, awaiting her order.

'Whatever you suggest,' she said.

The sight of Richard and Philippe enjoying a drink together and chatting as if they were old friends raised her spirits.

'And what have you two been talking about in my absence?' she asked flippantly.

'Introducing your daughter to her family,' Richard said. 'It's long overdue.'

She smiled. She couldn't wait to tell Pippa.

CHAPTER 7

May 1958

Pippa had been waiting in the foyer of the hotel for at least a quarter of an hour before she was rewarded by the sight of her mother stepping out of the hotel lift.

Julia immediately hugged the girl and then regarded her at arm's length.

'My goodness you've grown,' Julia said. 'And it's only a matter of weeks since I last saw you.'

It was the perfect opening for Pippa.

'That's why I need new clothes,' she said, as if she still expected to have to convince her mother of it.

But Julia was fully prepared for the shopping trip and the two set off towards the city centre a short walk from the hotel.

Before long Pippa was surrounded by new clothes to try on for her mother's approval. It was the first time the two had shopped together. For Julia it revived memories of shopping with her own mother and their inevitable clashes over what was considered suitable for a young girl.

After little more than an hour, they were already weighed down with shopping bags.

'I think we might have to take these bags back to my hotel,' Julia said, 'before we buy anything else.'

She laughed. It had been a long time since she had so much fun. But Pippa had other ideas.

'We could go downstairs to the new milk bar,' she said. 'All the girls at school have been talking about it and I'm the only one who hasn't been there.'

Those few words should have acted as a warning signal to Julia but they did not. She had never worried about meeting anyone she knew in the city because she had spent very little time there except for her teenage schooldays so she agreed to Pippa's request. Together they headed to the rear of the store and stepped into the lift to head to the basement.

It was too late as she and Pippa stepped out of the lift. There was no way they could avoid meeting Patricia Clarke and her daughter Anita, who immediately greeted Pippa in a friendly way before catching her mother's eye. It was clear her mother was silently repeating her warning to her daughter to distance herself from Pippa. Karen Clarke, immaculately dressed in the latest fashion, was a few steps behind them.

'Hello Miss Belleville,' Patricia Clarke said while looking first at Julia and then at Pippa, 'I did not know you were in town. I think you know my niece Karen but I don't think you've met my daughter Anita.'

There was no escaping the encounter. Julia's only thought was to keep Philippe's name from being mentioned. It was something she must do at all costs.

'How do you do, Anita,' Julia said, smiling at the girl, who was suddenly tight lipped and sullen.

'Very well thank you, Miss Belleville,' the girl replied.

Before Julia could think how to fill the void, Patricia Clarke spoke again.

'I see you're acquainted with Pippa Jensen then?' she said, her tone almost an accusation or, if not an accusation, then a demand for an explanation.

Julia knew Patricia Clarke wanted desperately to say, 'why didn't you mention you knew Pippa when I showed you the photo of the girls?' but she did not. The encounter was no longer quite so friendly.

Julia stared back at her. Was there any way to avoid the truth? Could she claim to be someone other than Pippa's mother? She banished the thought almost before it had formed in her mind. She knew to deny her daughter would destroy the fragile bond between the two of them and that was more important to Julia than anything else. She could walk away from these people and never see them again without a second thought.

'Please don't make the connection between Pippa and Philippe,' she prayed silently.

She took a deep breath before replying. She knew she owed Patricia Clarke an explanation.

'I'm sorry I did not get a chance to tell you that evening at your home,' she said. 'The fact is Pippa is my daughter.'

There was a fleeting look, not quite of horror, perhaps distaste, Julia thought, on Patricia Clarke's face.

'Oh, I see,' she said as if it was the most commonplace of revelations but the telltale signs of her disdain were evident in the set of her mouth and the ever so slight backward step she took, as if she wanted to distance herself from the undesirable woman in front of her. She began to understand there might be some truth in the girl's fanciful story about her real parents.

'If you must know, I had Pippa when I was only nineteen,' Julia said quietly.

There was a large part of the story she was about to omit.

'She stays here in Sydney with her great aunt so she can attend school.'

It was fortunate for Julia that Patricia Clarke was not a curious woman. The woman accepted the explanation which she was too polite to question. Besides she had already filled in the parts of the story Julia had omitted, guessing that Sydney was far enough away from Julia's home town to hide her illegitimate daughter from the local gossips. Philippe's name had not been mentioned.

'Well, we must be going,' she said. 'Karen still has not yet settled on a frock for the gala evening and that is tonight, so we must press on.'

Karen, who had been only half listening to the exchange, recognised in Julia a powerful rival for the attentions of the charming American surgeon who had so far resisted her overtures. She could not resist a parting shot.

'I'm so looking forward to this evening,' she said, her voice louder than necessary to make sure Julia heard her.

'Dr Duval has asked me to accompany him to the annual fundraising ball. It should be such fun. He's such a charming man. I'm sure I'm half in love with him already.'

Julia sensed that Pippa, who had remained silent throughout the encounter, was about to speak. She slipped her arm through hers and exerted some warning pressure. She spoke quickly.

'I'm sure you'll enjoy it immensely,' Julia said, as she guided Pippa towards the café, whispering to her to say nothing.

Julia knew exactly what Karen Clarke had hoped to achieve but for now she was simply relieved that no one had begun to suspect the nature of the connection between her and Philippe and Pippa.

As soon as they were safe from being overhead, Pippa voiced her opinion. It was all Julia could do to calm her down.

'Why is my father taking her to a ball and not you?' she demanded.

'My darling, I expect he has his reasons,' Julia replied. 'It may be that he was coerced into the arrangement.'

The idea had certainly occurred to Julia. She hoped that was the explanation.

'What does that mean?'

'Well, that it wasn't his idea but he had to go along with it,' she replied, trying to calm the girl down.

Pippa was unconvinced.

'I'll ask him when we see him this afternoon,' she said.

She could see Pippa was determined to hear her father's explanation. The question remained in Julia's mind too despite her reassurances to Pippa. Why had Philippe not told her?

Later that afternoon, Richard and Julia stood together at the entrance to the hotel and waved good-bye to Philippe and Pippa.

Catherine had already taken her two boys up to her suite. She was sure they had brought the smells and dirt of the zoo back with them and she was anxious to get them cleaned up.

'Your daughter is so much like you were at that age,' Richard said as he turned to head back into the hotel. 'Very headstrong and determined.'

She laughed at the unflattering description knowing full well he was teasing her. He had always felt very protective towards her.

'They all seemed to get on together,' she said.

Richard nodded.

'Yes, I noticed Paul particularly was very taken by his new cousin,' he said. 'Seeing us all together again really meant a lot to him, I think. I know he hates being away at school.'

Julia slipped her arm through her brother's.

'Let's go and have a drink,' she said. 'We've still got plenty of time to shower and change before dinner.'

Richard did not need much persuasion. He had enjoyed the afternoon which would have been complete had William, Alice and Marianne been present. There was the remembered pleasure of rare times in the past when they had ventured out together as a family. He missed those times.

They sat down at a low table near the doorway, away from the growing hubbub of conversation. Before long, a glass of cold beer appeared in front of him and he took a long draught. Julia sipped her cocktail cautiously. She had discovered from experience that the sweet concoctions were deceptively intoxicating.

'I take it Paul's relieved that you and Catherine have come to an agreement about him continuing to live in Australia, so he doesn't have to make a terrible choice between his parents?' Julia said, aware that it had been the topic of a tense conversation between Paul and his parents.

'Yes, he is relieved,' Richard said. 'Very relieved. In fact, I've half a mind actually to ask him if he wants to complete his education at home.'

Julia was surprised at this suggestion. She thought it likely that Catherine had agreed to Paul continuing his schooling in Sydney. How she would react to him shifting schools was quite another matter.

'Are you going to discuss that with Catherine?' Julia asked, aware that moving Paul back to Springfield would make visits much more difficult for Catherine.

Richard smiled conspiratorially.

'We're due to go to England for Christmas,' he said. 'I might just fail to renew his enrolment. I know the Grammar School at home would take him and it's only a bike ride from my house. Seems perfect and he can spend the weekends out at Prior Park.'

Julia smiled. She was inclined to agree. How could a child develop a love for the place he would one day inherit if he didn't have the opportunity to grow to love it as a child? She and her brothers had all endured their later schooling away from Prior Park but each of them had always been desperate to return home. What neither of them knew was that Paul's heart already belonged to Prior Park.

'By the way I noticed you having quite a long conversation with Philippe,' Richard said, as he downed the remains of his beer and signalled for another. 'What was that about?'

She smiled at how cleverly he had turned the conversation back to her.

'You don't miss much, do you?' she said.

He laughed.

'Not much, no,' he admitted. 'I could see Philippe was a bit wrong-footed, whatever it was you were discussing.'

She sighed.

'Life gets more complicated than it should be sometimes,' she said. 'When I was shopping with Pippa this morning, we ran into a woman I'd met at the dinner party Philippe took me to last time I was here. She's the wife of his colleague Dr Clarke.'

She paused, wondering how much to tell Richard, but only the full story made any sense.

'When I was at her home, I spotted a photo of four schoolgirls – her daughter Anita, two other girls Nancy Lester and Lucy Dixon, and Pippa. When she saw I was interested, she told me who was in the photo and that Pippa, who they knew to be an orphan, had been telling stories at school about who her real parents were.'

Richard listened in silence.

'I didn't take the opportunity then to tell her I was Pippa's mother so when I ran into her with Pippa this morning, I had no choice. I couldn't deny who I was, but I had to keep Philippe's name out of it.'

Richard interrupted the story.

'And so you admitted to her that you are Pippa's mother?' he asked.

He was beginning to understand the awkwardness of the chance encounter.

'I had to,' Julia said. 'Pippa was with me and Anita, who was with her mother, recognised Pippa of course. And to make matters worse, Karen Clarke, Dr Clarke's niece, was with them. Patricia Clarke had deliberately seated Karen Clarke next to Philippe at dinner that evening. The plan was obvious.'

Richard laughed. His imagination had filled in the blanks in Julia's story.

'So, I take it this Karen Clarke is on the lookout for a husband and a newly arrived highly-regarded American neurosurgeon could be just the thing?' he joked.

'That looks like their plan,' she said, grimacing.

'And she isn't ugly, I take it?' he asked, as an afterthought.

'No, she isn't ugly, quite the opposite in fact,' Julia said. 'She's rich too apparently. The heiress to a fortune. And she's younger than me.'

Richard was inclined to dismiss his sister's concerns. As far as he had observed, Philippe had eyes for no one but Julia.

'But there's more I take it?'

'He's escorting Karen Clarke to the hospital's gala charity ball tonight,' she said, 'but I didn't get that information from him. He had said only that he had hospital business to attend to tonight so I wouldn't be seeing him.'

'So if he didn't tell you, who did?' Richard asked, perplexed.

Julia paused. How much did she really need to tell her brother? But then again, he was likely to be sympathetic to her concerns. She pressed on.

'This morning, when Pippa and I ran into them, it was the last thing Karen Clarke said as we parted,' Julia explained. 'It was so gloating.'

Julia paraphrased Karen Clarke's parting words for Richard's benefit.

'She said, "Dr Duval's escorting me to the gala ball tonight. He's such a charming man. I'm sure I'm half in love with him already."…'

For a moment Richard was speechless. And then he laughed, a hearty full-throated laugh.

'My darling sister,' he said finally. 'Philippe will never fall for a catty woman like that. I bet he's had hundreds of eligible women set their caps at him over the years. He's no greenhorn.'

Julia was forced to laugh too at her brother's description of Karen Clarke.

'You don't think he'll be tempted?' she asked.

'Oh, he might be tempted if she's as beautiful as you say she is,' Richard said. 'After all, he is a man, but his good sense will prevail.'

'He has been married you know,' she said, as if to indicate he hadn't always been immune to the charms of other women.

'But it didn't last, did it?' Richard said. 'His wife's not here with him. He's divorced, isn't he?'

Julia nodded.

'But he should have told me he was taking her to the gala,' Julia insisted.

'Maybe so, but he didn't expect you to find out, did he?' Richard said, springing to Philippe's defence. 'I bet he was coerced into it. Am I right?'

'That's what he said,' Julia conceded. 'He said he couldn't get out of the obligation.'

Richard had finished his second beer and looked at his watch.

'I'm going to get changed now,' he said. 'Are you coming down to have dinner with us? Can you stand the noisy boys?'

She laughed.

'You've forgotten,' she said, 'I've got my own noisy boy at home.'

'Of course, I haven't forgotten,' Richard said, 'and when is he going to meet his sister?'

Julia let out a long slow sigh. Introducing Pippa to her son John meant dealing with James and she was not yet prepared for that conversation.

'Perhaps at Christmas time,' Julia said. 'I need to let James calm down a bit before I take Pippa home with me.'

'Well, if it's any consolation, Charles Brockman says he's dating another woman so maybe he'll have moved on and be more reasonable.'

'I hope so, for Pippa's sake,' she said. 'If not, he may poison John against his sister and that I wouldn't stand for.'

'Neither would I, my dear sister,' he said. 'Neither would I.'

She knew then that Richard was prepared to go to any lengths to make amends for the great wrong her family had done her.

Philippe eased his car into the late afternoon traffic. He looked at his watch. He hoped the traffic would lighten as they reached the outskirts of the city centre. He did not want to be late but he had to drive his daughter home. Pippa noticed the quick glance at his watch.

'Did you enjoy the day, my dear?' he asked, surprised at how unusually quiet she was.

She was normally full of chatter whenever he was driving her home from an outing.

'Yes,' she said, without elaboration. Then she blurted out what was on her mind.

'You're in a hurry I suppose because you have to take that lady to a ball?' she said.

He glanced at her quickly before returning his attention to the road. Julia had warned him that Pippa had been upset by the revelation.

'Yes, that's right, Pippa,' he said calmly. 'I have to partner Dr Clarke's niece at the ball, as a favour to him.'

Pippa laughed.

'That's what Mum said, you were coerced into it,' she retorted, barely satisfied with his answer. 'You shouldn't be taking any other lady out but Mum.'

He smiled to himself. He was getting a ticking off from his daughter.

'When you're older, you will understand,' he said, hoping that would satisfy her.

'That's what everyone says, when you're older,' she replied. 'But I'm nearly fifteen. I'm not a child.'

He laughed. Her fourteenth birthday had been just two months ago so he knew she was stretching the truth just a little.

'But on a serious note,' he said, 'you must not mention my name to anyone. You must not tell people I'm your father. Promise me?'

It seemed a cruel request but Philippe knew it was in all their interests. It had never occurred to him that his world and hers might intersect. He had felt so sure his private life would remain just that: private. Now he worried that if it became widely known he had fathered a child out of wedlock it was very likely the hospital would find a reason to cancel his appointment.

'I won't,' she said, 'although Mrs Clarke and Anita already know who my real mother is.'

He had been very concerned when Julia had told him of the encounter. He was relieved and a little surprised that Patricia Clarke had not made the connection to him.

'That was unfortunate,' he said, 'but it couldn't be helped. You must try and understand. Their knowing who your mother is does not matter so much providing there is no link to me as your father, because of my job.'

He glanced sideways at her. She looked very hurt and upset.

'The people I work with wouldn't understand me having a young daughter and not being married,' he said, trying desperately to explain to her in a way she would understand.

'If you talk about the day out today to any of your schoolfriends,' he added, 'do not mention I was there too. You can talk about your uncle and aunt and your cousins because they are all related to your mother.'

'So it's alright to talk about Mum?' she asked.

'Yes, remember your mother now uses her maiden name. People won't know that she is married and has a son,' he said, trying to help her understand their predicament. 'It's best not to mention you have a half-brother.'

The girl nodded. It seemed unnecessarily complicated but she agreed to do what her father asked. But there was one question to which she desperately wanted to know the answer.

'When her divorce comes through will you ask her to marry you?'

She had somehow always assumed it would happen but now she wanted to hear it first hand from her father.

He hesitated. What should he say? He and Julia had agreed to take things slowly. They both knew Pippa would be grown up and independent of them in a few years' time. She would no longer be the child who needed their protection. If they were to marry, it would have to be for their own reasons, because they loved each other, not because of the guilt they carried about their child.

'We'll see,' he said. 'Your mother and I have been separated for many years. Our first thoughts were for you, not each other, when we met again.'

'But now that you have met again you must get married,' she said finally.

He smiled. To Pippa, it all seemed very simple but to him and Julia, it was far more complicated. It meant too that he would have to commit to living his life in Australia.

He could not ask Julia to move to America and leave behind her son or rob Pippa of her extended family. All this he knew. He knew too that some part of him held back from wanting to make the final irrevocable commitment.

CHAPTER 8

August 1958

Julia sat on the verandah of her rented home in Springfield. She was enjoying the winter sunshine. It was quiet. There was very little traffic in the street. In the months since her separation from her husband she had come to relish the sheer pleasure of being able to please herself what she did.

The squeak of the unoiled hinge on the front gate announced a visitor. She looked up from the letter she was reading to see her brother Richard heading towards her.

'All alone, I see,' he said, by way of greeting.

'Yes, all alone and loving it,' she answered, 'except for your house-keeper.'

Between them, they shared a housekeeper and a gardener. Neither of them had been brought up to do the mundane work involved in running a household, even a small one.

'And young John?' he asked, knowing he would be at school anyway.

She smiled.

'John actually prefers to stay with his grandmother during the week,' she said. 'I think he likes the way she spoils him and he likes having Marianne for company.'

'He comes over after school most days for a visit but he'll be going out to stay with his father most of next week during the school holidays.'

Richard nodded towards the letter she was holding. It was not a private letter judging by what he could see.

'Not bad news, I hope,' he said.

He thought his sister was frowning over the contents.

'No, not bad news really,' she said, 'only I didn't realise it would take so long for me to divorce James.'

Richard sat down in the chair opposite her. She held out the letter from her solicitor and he read it through before handing it back to her.

'By that advice,' Richard said, 'it'll be more than two years before you will be a free woman again. Does Philippe know this?'

'He does,' she said. 'I think though in some ways it's good because we can't rush into anything.'

Richard sat back in his chair. He too faced the same problem but for Julia there was Pippa to consider.

'You do realise your daughter could be seventeen years old before you are free to marry her father,' Richard pointed out. 'If she was the only reason you were contemplating it, I'd think again.'

Julia smiled at him.

'You're beginning to sound like sensible William,' she said. 'At nineteen I wouldn't have hesitated but yearning for someone for so long and then being in a position where you can fulfil your dream is a curious feeling.'

Richard understood her dilemma only too well. He too had revisited an old love only to find it was impossible to recapture the heady days of that first love.

'And you're in the happy position not many women find themselves in of being able to support yourself, thanks to your mother, or grandmother should I say,' he ventured, 'so you aren't forced to remarry.'

She knew he was right. She was grateful for the wealth her mother had left her but still in so many ways she felt adrift as if, in losing the anchor of Prior Park and her mother not to mention her marriage, she had become untethered.

'Is that from Philippe?' Richard asked, nodding towards the other letter that sat on the small table between them.

'Yes,' she said. 'He wants to know if I am coming down during the holidays.'

'And are you?' Richard asked.

'Yes I plan to, for a few days,' she said. 'But Pippa wrote and said she was invited to go to Bowral with one of her school friends for the first week and I thought it was a good idea for her to accept the invitation.'

'After the kerfuffle with Dr Clarke's wife back in May you mean?'

'Yes, I was worried the girls would drop her so I'm pleased they haven't,' Julia said. 'Apparently it's the girl called Nancy who really leads the group. It's her place she's going to. Anita Clarke is going and Lucy Dixon. All the girls pictured alongside Pippa in the photograph I mentioned.'

'That's probably going to make Philippe feel a bit nervous,' Richard said.

Julia nodded. Philippe had raised his concerns with her. They both knew the promise Pippa made not to reveal his identity would be hard for her to keep.

'I asked him if he wanted me to stop Pippa from going,' Julia said. 'He said no but I could tell he was concerned. He said it was important for Pippa to have these friendships and he simply had to have confidence in her that she wouldn't mention his name.'

'How often does he see Pippa?' Richard asked, out of idle curiosity.

'Usually once a week, mostly on a Sunday,' she said, 'but he's become more careful about where he takes her. Or he has lunch with her and her aunt. Mrs Henderson is very understanding of the situation.'

He and Julia spoke quietly, aware that the housekeeper Mrs Freestone would enjoy spreading any gossip she heard. They could hear her moving around in the kitchen.

'Are you going down to Sydney for any part of the holidays?' Julia asked.

'No, Paul's going to come home for the second week,' Richard said. 'He has an invitation to stay for a week with his friend Tim. He wants to go. They have a great cattle property he told me and they go fishing too.'

78

'At least he will see some progress at Prior Park when he comes home with William and Alice's new house now complete,' Julia said.

They were both well aware that Paul had yet to see the ruins of Prior Park. In his memory he held only the grand mansion, fully intact, that had been his home for all his life.

'Yes, with Catherine arriving unexpectedly in May with Anthony,' he said, 'it wasn't possible to bring Paul back with me.'

'And has Anthony settled down since she got back to England?'

'I think so,' he said. 'Bit of a tearaway, isn't he?'

Julia shook her head at this description.

'No more than most boys his age,' she said. 'But you must worry that he is going to be more English than Australian.'

'I do,' Richard said, 'but I'm not entirely sure what I can do about it.'

'But if he doesn't get to spend any time at Prior Park ...?' Julia didn't quite know how to frame the question.

'What you mean is, when I'm gone, how interested will he be in running Prior Park and the Belleville business interests if he hasn't been brought up with them?' he said.

'Well, yes,' she said. 'I don't think you realise how close you and William are and how important it is in the decision-making.'

It was out of character for his sister to comment in such a way but he had noticed how she had matured in the past year. He had to remind himself constantly she was no longer a teenager.

'Well, I'm not in my grave yet,' he said laughing, 'and Anthony isn't quite six so I think we have time, don't you?'

'Of course, I only meant that it's a pity the two boys aren't growing up together,' she said, 'like you and William did.'

'I agree with you,' he said. 'It's not something I planned for. The other difference is in the age gap between them. William and I are much closer in age.'

'Anyway, I must go,' he said. 'I'm off to Brisbane tomorrow. I've got some business to attend to.'

They had almost never discussed business between them. It was only since taking over her mother's trust fund that she was now being called upon to make decisions about investments.

'Belleville business?' she asked.

'Yes, we've been sitting on a pile of cash for a while and I have to look at what we might invest in,' he said, surprised at her question.

'I take it William looks after the cattle side of the business?'

'Yes, he does and he does it very well,' Richard said, giving his brother rare praise.

'I'm told James has negotiated a price to buy back his Aunt Margaret's property,' Julia said. 'He was always keen to get it back. His father was quite upset it had been given to Margaret in the first place.'

'Old Jack was a pretty tough customer,' Richard said, 'but I think his sister was entitled to it. James is lucky they have no children but he won't like having to stump up the cash for what he thinks is his anyway.'

'Don't feel too sorry for him,' Julia said, 'I think he's getting it at family rates. After all he would have inherited it anyway. But his aunt and uncle do need something to live on in retirement. He's not as hard as his father.'

He was surprised at his sister's defence of her estranged husband, but perhaps she was simply being fair to him, he thought.

'I'm pleased to hear that,' Richard said. He did not dislike James Fitzroy, far from it, but he had noticed a natural tension in their relationship since the revelations about Julia had emerged.

'Talking of business,' Julia said as her brother prepared to leave, 'do you have any investment recommendations?'

He paused. He did not know how to answer that question truthfully. He and William were themselves unsure. To advise his sister might be to take her down an entirely unwise path.

'If I were you I'd look carefully at what our mother had done in the past,' he said finally. 'She was far more astute than our father. Look at the history of what she invested in. That will be your best indicator and talk to her advisors.'

She nodded. It was sound advice. She was not going to be rash. But this new responsibility set her apart from the other women she met who were all totally consumed by their domestic lives.

Was she interested in the latest cake decorating tips, they asked? No, she wasn't. Did she sew her own clothes? No, she didn't. Did she knit? No. Or crochet perhaps? No, not that either.

The questions were invariably asked until they exhausted the list of domestic crafts she might have perfected. They asked about her son and she replied. They did not ask about her husband because they knew she was separated. They could not ask about Pippa because they did not know about her.

Instead she began to confide in Alice again. She was confident Alice would not share their conversations with her brother despite his promptings to his sister to share any titbit of gossip about his estranged wife.

Had Julia mentioned Nancy Lester by name to her brother and the fact she lived on a property in Bowral, alarm bells might have rung for both of them. Instead it was Philippe who found himself facing a barrage of awkward questions only a day after the children had all returned to their homes.

It was not much after nine o'clock in the morning when Robert Clarke strode into Philippe's office and closed the door. Philippe looked up. He had been studying the case notes of a patient he was to operate on the next day and his mind was elsewhere. He did not at first notice the angry look on Robert Clarke's face or detect the suppressed rage in his demeanour.

'Duval,' he said brusquely, without bothering with any preliminary greetings, 'how do I put this? Basically, you've deceived us all. You've made fools of us all.'

Philippe was alarmed. He had no idea what Robert Clarke was referring to. His first thought was that his colleague was suggesting his qualifications were not what he had claimed them to be. It was a ridiculous notion that could be easily disproved by the university he had attended and by the hospital appointments he had held.

He could see the agitation in the man sitting across the desk from him. He put the file of case notes back down on the desk.

'What's this you say?' Philippe said, keeping his voice as calm as possible. 'You think I've deceived you? In what way do you think I've deceived you?'

Robert Clarke stood up and began to pace the room. It was not a large office so after a few strides he turned on his heel and retraced his steps back to the centre of the room.

'My daughter Anita got home late yesterday from staying with the Lesters in Bowral,' he said.

His voice was measured; the words deliberate. That hint was enough for Philippe to know what was coming but he said nothing.

'Nancy Lester's brother Tim also had friends staying,' he continued. 'One of them was a lad named Paul Belleville.'

Philippe groaned inwardly. It was all going to come out now.

'This young boy recognised one of the girls his sister Nancy had invited as Pippa Jensen,' he said. 'As it turns out, she and Paul are cousins because his father Richard Belleville and Pippa's mother Julia are brother and sister. As I recall you brought Julia Belleville along to the dinner party at our house back at Easter. No doubt she told you my wife and daughter met her and Pippa shopping a month or so later.'

Philippe said nothing. He wanted to hear from Robert Clarke what he knew. It was possible there were parts of the story he did not know or perhaps was simply guessing at.

'This young boy also had something interesting to say about who Pippa's father was although my daughter says Pippa tried in vain to silence him,' Robert Clarke said.

His anger, which had briefly subsided, was rising again.

'According to my daughter young Mr Belleville's exact words were that Pippa's father was a top American surgeon called Dr Duval.'

There was silence in the room. Philippe could hear the ticking of the large clock that hung on his office wall. He heard the footsteps of hospital staff going backwards and forwards along the hallway outside his office. Finally, he spoke.

'He's right and you are right,' Philippe said. 'I have deceived you. Not deliberately or maliciously but I have deceived you. I expected to keep that aspect of my private life private.'

How much should he tell his colleague? How much was he really entitled to know? Before he could go on, Robert Clarke shot more questions at him.

'So why did you not do the right thing and marry Miss Belleville and give the child your name?' he asked. 'I can't imagine her family were very pleased.'

Philippe pushed his chair back. He was really in no mood to tell the whole sorry story but he could see no way around it. And so he began.

Robert Clarke did not interrupt until he had finished telling the story, ending with a description of the chance meeting with Julia the previous year and their joint decision to involve themselves in Pippa's life.

'And you say that Miss Belleville is really Mrs Fitzroy and that she has a son with her husband?' he asked. 'Are she and her husband still together?'

Philippe shook his head. Robert Clarke's questions were beginning to verge on the tawdry.

'No, Julia's marriage did not survive the revelations,' he said simply. 'Her husband was with her when we met by accident in Sydney.'

Robert Clarke, uncharacteristically, let out a low whistle. Even he could not fail to understand the awkwardness of the encounter.

'If you must know, Julia is in the midst of divorcing her husband but these things take quite some time to achieve,' Philippe said.

His colleague nodded, fully aware that divorce could take years to finalise.

'And are you going to marry her then?' he asked.

Robert Clarke put this question as if there was really no option. It may be years too late but it was clear he believed Philippe was honour bound to remove the stain of illegitimacy from his daughter's name.

Philippe did not answer his question directly. Memories of his own illegitimate birth surfaced briefly.

'I think that's between me and Julia, don't you?' he said.

Robert Clarke shrugged. It was not the answer he expected but in any case he realised Philippe could not marry Pippa's mother yet so there was no easy fix as far as he was concerned.

'I will have to take this matter to the board,' he said finally. 'I have to tell you though they may not take this news very well.'

Philippe had been prepared for that.

'If you want me to resign, I will resign today,' he said.

But Robert Clarke was torn between the scandal that was about to be unleashed, for he knew that's how the board would see it, and his desire to keep a highly skilled and much sought after surgeon on his staff.

'Let's wait until they ask for your resignation,' Robert Clarke said. 'Say nothing to anyone. I've asked my wife not to mention it to the other wives and I've told my daughter not to mention it when she goes back to school. Her other friends who were there don't have fathers in the medical profession fortunately.'

He paused as he opened the door to leave.

'My niece Karen is going to be disappointed by this scandal,' he said. 'I think she's come to regard you as a friend.'

Philippe nodded but said nothing.

At the very time Philippe was revealing everything to Dr Clarke, Julia was listening carefully to the same story, except it was Edith Henderson who was relaying it.

On first hearing Mrs Henderson's voice on the other end of the line, Julia had immediately assumed something awful had happened to her daughter. She was shocked to discover what Edith Henderson had to tell her.

'Pippa arrived home in a dreadful state from her week away yesterday afternoon,' she told Julia. 'I thought at first she'd had a serious falling out with her friends. But then I finally discovered the truth.'

'Go on, Mrs Henderson,' Julia said.

She still had not quite grasped the thread of the older woman's story.

'Your nephew Paul Belleville was a guest of Nancy Lester's brother Tim and he obviously identified Pippa as his cousin,' Edith Henderson said.

Julia listened carefully.

'Then he told them his Aunt Julia was Pippa's mother,' she said. 'Apparently he was then challenged on the identity of Pippa's father because they assumed he wouldn't know because Pippa said she didn't know.'

The older woman took a breath.

'You're telling me he named Philippe?' Julia stammered.

'That's right,' she said. 'He did. Apparently, he said her father was a top American surgeon working in Sydney and his name was Dr Duval.'

Edith Henderson heard the quick intake of breath as Julia registered the shock of what she had just heard.

'But he only met Philippe once,' she said, trying to think back. 'It was that Saturday afternoon in May when we took all the children to the zoo.'

'I know,' Edith Henderson said. 'No one thought to tell him to keep Philippe's identity a secret.'

'No indeed,' Julia said. 'No one could have imagined that Richard's son would be mixing with girls from Pippa's school, that his best friend would turn out to be a brother to one of her best friends.

There was silence for several moments while they both considered the significance of what had occurred. Finally, Edith Henderson spoke again.

'I said to Pippa I would call you this morning,' she said. 'She's very anxious that she isn't blamed for letting out the big secret.'

'Of course not,' Julia said. 'Let me talk to her.'

After a few moments, her daughter spoke.

'I tried to stop Paul telling,' she said, 'but he wouldn't pay attention to me. But I feel it's all my fault.'

Julia could hear Pippa's sobbing.

'My darling girl,' she said. 'It isn't your fault. Try and be calm. I will speak to your father to warn him.'

She hoped her reassurances would calm her down.

'Everything will be alright,' she added.

With that she rang off. She began to search through her purse for Philippe's telephone number at the hospital but before she could find it, her telephone rang again. This time, she recognised Philippe's voice at the other end. Before he could say much, she interrupted.

'I've heard from Mrs Henderson,' she said. 'I know young Paul was staying at the same house as Pippa and he blurted out about you being Pippa's father.'

Philippe sighed.

'You can imagine the conversation I had with Robert Clarke this morning,' he said. 'He was livid, talking about a scandal although it's hardly that.'

'I'm so sorry,' she said. 'Is there anything I can do? What action do they plan to take?'

'Dr Clarke said he would put it before the board next week,' Philippe said. 'It may all blow over. It probably depends on how highly they value my work, to be honest. I did say I thought my private life was my own affair.'

'Did he agree with that?' Julia asked.

'Up to a point I think,' Philippe said.

'Don't blame Pippa – or Paul,' she said. 'Paul wouldn't have done it maliciously.'

'No, of course not,' he replied. 'In fact, I think I was wrong not to be honest about Pippa in the first place.'

'I've just spoken to her on the phone,' Julia said. 'She's very upset. I think she feels she's let you down.'

'I'd never think that,' he said. 'I'll talk to her when I finish work this afternoon.'

With that, he hung up.

Julia sat on the low seat beside the telephone for some time. A feeling of helplessness engulfed her for there was nothing she could do to help Philippe.

Chapter 9

September 1958

For the past month, Philippe had sensed a storm cloud hanging over his professional life but there had been no summons forthcoming for him to appear before the hospital board. If he was a little distracted in his work no one noticed or at least if they did, they did not comment. In his few conversations with Robert Clarke the subject was not raised so he let it lie.

Despite his reassurances, his daughter continued to blame herself. After all, as he pointed out repeatedly, it had been her cousin Paul who had exposed his secret, not her, but whatever he said seemed to fall on deaf ears.

It was late in the afternoon of what had been a fine spring day. Earlier, he had performed a particularly difficult but ultimately successful operation on a patient with a brain tumour. The patient was now resting comfortably in post-operative care and he had written up the last of the case notes.

Satisfied with his day's work, he pushed his chair back and stood up. He slipped off his white hospital coat, hung it up and reached for his suit coat. He shrugged it on. By habit more than necessity, he grabbed his hospital bag and reached for the light switch near the door.

A gloved hand reached the light switch a second before his. He was momentarily startled.

'My dear Dr Duval, you look as though you need a distraction. And a drink.'

The voice was light and teasing. Flirtatious even.

He quickly regained his composure. Karen Clarke's sudden appearance was not altogether unwelcome. He found no particular joy in returning home each evening to a lonely house. He was in need of company, even though he would not have admitted it.

'My uncle said you might need cheering up,' she said, maintaining the lightness of her tone. 'I've been away otherwise I'd have been to see you sooner.'

He had assumed the reason he had not seen her in the past month was because of the revelations concerning his illegitimate daughter. He had not considered the possibility there was a simpler explanation.

He closed the door of his office and they walked down the hospital corridor together. She had slipped her arm through his but he did not mind. One or two of the nurses at the front reception looked up and exchanged glances as they watched the pair walk out through the front door. Their expressions said it all. What chance did they have with the most eligible doctor in the hospital when he'd been claimed by the wealthy young niece of the senior registrar?

'May I ask where we are going?' Philippe said, as she guided him away from his car towards hers, which she had parked in her uncle's parking space.

'You'll see,' she said, as she unlocked the door for her bemused passenger and walked around to the driver's side.

The engine of the powerful Mercedes roared into life. With the practised skill of an expert driver, she reversed the car out of the parking space and into the late afternoon traffic.

For a few minutes she concentrated all her attention on driving. Philippe noticed how effortlessly she changed gear and how expertly she handled the dense traffic.

'You drive very well,' he said.

She laughed.

'So, you think all women drive badly, do you?' she countered.

'No, of course not,' he said, 'but I would say you've had special training?'

She glanced sideways at him but her attention was quickly back on the traffic that edged its way along the street ahead of them.

'It was a condition my father placed on me getting this particular car,' she said. 'He has a number of car dealerships so I could have my pick really, but he insisted I took lessons with the top driver in his racing car team when I chose this car. That all happened six months ago on a slightly older model.'

Philippe was impressed. He had not imagined she would take anything seriously. It seemed he had wrongly pigeonholed her as self indulgent and frivolous.

'I take it you haven't had this car for very long?'

He'd noticed the pristine condition of the luxury interior.

'No, I haven't,' she said. 'It's my birthday present in fact.'

'Which was when?' he asked, somewhat ungallantly.

'Today,' she said, as she slipped the car into a higher gear. The traffic had begun to thin out as they headed east following the main road that skirted the southern side of the harbour.

'Happy birthday for today,' he said. He was guessing her age but she looked no more than late twenties. 'Are we heading out to celebrate?'

It was the only explanation for her sudden appearance at his office.

'Yes,' she said, still concentrating hard on her driving. 'We're nearly there.'

He wondered where 'there' was. They had passed through Double Bay and Rose Bay. He was now in unfamiliar territory. He had not yet become familiar with Sydney's eastern suburbs.

'Where's there exactly?' he asked.

Heading away from the city and the known nightspots, he thought it seemed highly likely they were headed to a private house. She slowed the car to turn off the main through road and then executed a tight left hand turn down towards the harbour at Vaucluse.

Philippe noticed the quality of the houses, all brightly lit in the early evening.

'I want you to meet my parents,' she said, unexpectedly. 'They are hosting a cocktail party tonight for my birthday. I thought it would be fun to kidnap you and bring you along.'

He was a little taken aback by her idea of fun.

'A straightforward invitation would have sufficed,' he said, a little tersely.

He was concerned how his presence might be misinterpreted by her parents.

'And I should probably be in black tie,' he added.

But she waved away that objection.

'You'll blend in beautifully,' she said. 'There'll only be thirty or so guests. Just a small gathering.'

'No doubt your uncle and aunt will be there,' he said, mindful of the big unresolved issue that had caused him so much anxiety.

'Oh, yes,' she said, smiling conspiratorially. 'And you're about to find out the big debt of gratitude you owe me.'

He was suddenly alert. What was she talking about? What could she have done for him that he should suddenly become so much in her debt? She eased the car into the driveway of a large impressive house that dominated its neighbours. The garage door stood open. There was space for three cars but only one space was vacant so she edged her car carefully into the available space. As the engine died, she turned to him.

'About a month ago, I called into the hospital to see my uncle before I went to Italy for a holiday,' she said, without preamble.

'He'd just come from your office and he was absolutely beside himself.'

Philippe knew what was coming then but he remained silent.

'He told me about your little secret,' she said, smiling slightly. 'He said he was sure the hospital board would demand your resignation once they knew and he said he had no choice but to tell them.'

Philippe could not then remain silent. He had to know if she knew the full story.

'Did he tell you the full story?' he asked, quietly.

She laughed.

'Oh, yes, he told me the story about just how naughty our Dr Duval had been in his youth,' she said. 'Keeping secrets about illegitimate children you've fathered doesn't really work, does it?'

He protested. She made him sound as if he was some kind of unscrupulous libertine.

'I only have one child,' he said in an effort to defend his actions. 'And I assume your uncle told you I didn't know about the child until years after the war and then it was too late to do the right thing.'

It was important to him that he not be cast as a heartless seducer. She nodded, smiling at his earnestness.

'Don't worry,' she said. 'I'm not a naïve schoolgirl. And nor do I think you would not have done the right thing had you been around at the time.'

He was relieved. He did not relish the prospect of his reputation being torn to shreds. He had seen his own mother's reputation suffer because of him, her illegitimate son. He had wanted his own life to be beyond reproach to repay her faith in him. But it hadn't quite worked out that way.

'I've been expecting a letter any day from the board demanding my resignation,' he said. 'I'm surprised they haven't acted on it so far.'

Now it was her turn to spring a surprise.

'Oh, that won't be coming any time soon, I assure you,' she said, confidently. 'My father is a considerable benefactor of the hospital. I am his only child. It would not please me to see you sacked so I insisted he have a quiet word with his brother to persuade the board to turn a blind eye to your little secret.'

He could not believe what he was hearing.

'Your father was prepared to do that?' he said. 'He doesn't even know me.'

She smiled.

'Well, it's about time we remedied that, don't you think?' she said as she slid out from behind the steering wheel.

He helped her close the garage door and together they walked up the stone steps leading to the front door. Away to his right he could see the last light of the day shimmering on the darkening harbour. In the far distance the harbour bridge was still clearly visible in all its grandeur despite the failing light.

She opened the front door and ushered him in. The entrance hallway and the rooms beyond were ablaze with lights.

David Clarke met them at the door. He was a larger man and because of it, he cut a much more impressive figure than his younger brother Robert. He hugged and kissed his daughter warmly and then extended his hand towards Philippe.

'How do you do, Dr Duval,' he said as he enveloped Philippe's hand in his. 'I've heard a lot about you and most of it's good. My daughter is a big fan of yours, it seems.'

He smiled as he said it. Philippe groaned inwardly but he was saved from further conversation by the arrival of Karen's mother Deborah who chided her daughter gently for being late to her own party and greeted Philippe absentmindedly.

Within a few minutes of their arrival, Karen had been surrounded by well-wishers, all eager to wish her a happy birthday so Philippe was suddenly left alone. He did not expect to know anyone at the party apart from her aunt and uncle, but he could not see either of them, so he wandered through the living room to the terrace. He welcomed the cool night air rising up from the harbour.

It was now almost too dark to make out any landmarks but he realised the house occupied one of the prime locations in the har-bourside suburb. He wondered idly if the house had been a family home handed down to an eldest son. It certainly looked as if it had occupied the waterfront block for a number of years.

Lost in his own reverie, he did not hear Robert Clarke approach so he was momentarily startled by his voice.

'Beautiful location isn't it?' he said to Philippe. 'It's a magnificent view on a fine sunny day.'

'It is indeed a beautiful location,' Philippe replied.

He was glad of a neutral topic of conversation. 'Was this a family home for you and your brother?'

Robert nodded slightly.

'Yes, it was,' he said. 'We were brought up here. The house is about sixty years old. It was left to my brother after our parents died.'

Philippe turned his back on the view as he spoke. He had detected a hint of wistfulness in the other man's voice.

'Do I suspect that was a blow to you?' Philippe asked.

'Perhaps,' he admitted. 'But I shouldn't say that. I was compensated in other ways. My home at Woollahra belonged to my mother's family so that came to me. But this was always the jewel in the crown, so to speak.'

Just then the noise from the main group of partygoers clustered around Karen seem to grow suddenly louder. Robert Clarke followed the direction of Philippe's gaze. Karen was doing her best to fend off the attentions of an over friendly guest.

'Perhaps you should go and rescue her,' Robert Clarke suggested. Philippe laughed.

'She does not seem to me to be the type of girl who needs rescuing,' he replied. 'I would think if anything that young man will be in need of rescuing if he pesters her too much more.'

They both laughed.

'She's quite a handful, I must admit,' Robert Clarke said. 'But she's certainly exerted herself in your interests.'

They noticed the over eager suitor was now on the edge of the group, having been gently but firmly pushed away.

'She told me this evening,' Philippe said. 'Obviously it was the first I knew about it but how do you feel about it? I'm sorry if her intervention has put you in a difficult position.'

Robert Clarke waved away his concerns.

'Don't be worried about that,' he said. 'The board would be far more concerned if they thought my brother was going to withdraw his generous annual support for the hospital foundation. That's my protection.'

'But you didn't think to tell me about it?' Philippe asked. 'I've been very anxious this past month, wondering what was going to happen but hearing nothing from you. I thought it strange that nothing had happened because there was a board meeting two weeks ago.'

Robert Clarke shrugged.

'I didn't quite know how to tell you what had transpired or why,' he said. 'I thought I'd just let it go. You know, as they say, let sleeping dogs lie.'

Philippe nodded, aware that his colleague was keen to change the subject.

'Well, let's agree then not to mention it further,' Philippe said, 'except of course that I have to find some way to thank your niece and her father.'

'A word of advice, Philippe,' the older man said. 'Karen is a very headstrong and spoiled young lady. She seems to have taken a particular shine to you but if your interest, shall we say, lies elsewhere, I wouldn't encourage her too much.'

Philippe was amused by the warning.

'Thanks for the advice,' he said, 'but I rather think the age difference between us might be enough to dampen her enthusiasm.'

'I wouldn't be too sure of that,' Robert Clarke said.

Just then, she looked up and caught Philippe's eye. She pushed her way through the crowd that had surrounded her.

'What are you doing hiding away here in the half dark,' she said. 'You and my uncle have all day to talk about hospital things. Come and meet my friends.'

He allowed himself to be ushered into the brightly lit room.

Several days had elapsed since the birthday party. Philippe was troubled by what he saw as his complete failure to show his gratitude to Karen for her timely invention on his behalf but the prospect of becoming more deeply involved with her concerned him. Would she accept his friendship only? Would she expect more? Was he in danger of wanting it to be more than friendship?

Despite his misgivings, he picked up the telephone and dialled her number. He recognised her father's voice on the other end of the line.

'Mr Clarke,' he said, 'it's Philippe Duval here. I'm calling to speak with your daughter.'

'Ah, Dr Duval,' he replied. 'She's out I'm afraid. Shopping probably or visiting friends, not sure which.'

Philippe was preparing to end the conversation.

'Well, perhaps you would let her know that I telephoned,' he said politely.

There was a pause at the other end of the line. David Clarke let out a deep sigh.

'I will tell her, Duval,' he said finally. 'I will tell her but as her father, can I say it might be better if you stayed out of her life.'

Philippe had been quite unprepared for this request. Before he could reply, David Clarke went on.

'My daughter is an impressionable young woman,' he said. 'I think she fancies she's in love with you. But for one or two reasons I can think of immediately, I don't think you'd be a suitable match for my daughter.'

Her father's tone was very businesslike. Philippe sensed he was not accustomed to having his authority challenged nor did he want to listen to counter arguments. He had assumed without really knowing for sure what Philippe's intentions were.

'I understand your point of view entirely,' Philippe said in reply, uncertain how to explain his motivation, but he pressed on.

'I'm aware that I owe you and your daughter a debt of gratitude,' he said. 'I feel I should at least show my appreciation.'

David Clarke let out another sigh. It was clear he was impatient with this notion.

'She got me to intervene on your behalf with my brother. That's true,' he said. 'I did it to please her, not with the intention of making you my son-in-law.'

He paused. Philippe sensed he had more he wanted to say so he remained silent on the other end of the line.

'I did it too because we can't afford to let a good surgeon like you leave the hospital,' he said. 'We lost a son, Karen's older brother Michael, to a botched operation to remove a benign tumour near his spinal column. With a better surgeon, I believe the outcome might have been different. I would not have lost my only son.'

Philippe was beginning to understand that Karen had more than one reason for her intervention.

'I'm so sorry to hear that,' Philippe said. 'I did not know about your loss.'

It was useless to say that such operations were extremely difficult and that satisfactory outcomes were rare. If David Clarke had convinced himself a more qualified surgeon would have done better, there was no way Philippe would be able to change his mind.

'Be nice to her, by all means,' David Clarke said, relenting a little. 'Take her out to dinner and dancing. She likes that. But remember I'd rather she settle on someone more suitable. No offence meant because I like you but a divorced man with an illegitimate daughter and someone probably fifteen years her senior is not the type of man I consider suitable for my daughter. Neither does my wife. I want someone more Karen's age and preferably from our circle of friends. Do we understand each other, Duval?'

Philippe replied, his tone very even, knowing that David Clarke was simply protecting his daughter, the only child he had left.

'We understand each other, Mr Clarke,' he said and rang off.

Chapter 10

December 1958

It was a hot day at Prior Park. The cloudless sky held no promise of much needed rain. The dry vegetation crackled underfoot as Richard, followed by his son Paul, headed down the shallow incline away from William and Alice's newly completed home to inspect the ruins of the grand house that had once dominated the landscape.

Their shoes were dusty after just a few steps. It was Paul's first full day at home for the long summer holidays but it was not his first look at the ruins. He had been shocked into silence seeing it all for the first time during the previous holidays. Now he knew what to expect but it shocked him anew. How could someone hate his family, especially his father, so much they would do this?

They stood side by side surveying the derelict ruin; Richard remembering the happy times when they had all been together under the one roof; Paul remembering the pleasure of growing up with his cousin Marianne and his grandmother and aunt and uncle. It had seemed perfect. He was happy, despite his mother's absence. Why had someone ruined it all so maliciously?

They moved then to Elizabeth Belleville's graveside. Paul carefully placed the vase of roses his Aunt Alice had given him in front of the gravestone and stood back. He had been a favourite of his grandmother and he missed her terribly.

'It's almost a year to the day,' Richard said, as he rested his arm lightly on his son's shoulder.

The boy nodded. So much had happened in a year. Losing Prior Park and his grandmother had been the worst thing of all. Before that, his parents had separated and his brother Anthony now lived permanently in England with his mother whom he rarely saw. No one had told him if this was permanent or if his parents were now divorced. Father and son turned to walk back towards the house but Paul stopped his father.

'Where were you attacked?' he asked.

Richard paused. It was time Paul knew the whole story. He pointed to a spot a few yards away from the gravestone.

'I was just farewelling your Uncle William and Aunt Julia,' he said slowly.

The memory was painful. He still suffered occasional headaches.

'He must have been hiding behind that big gum tree there which meant I had my back to him.'

Paul followed the direction he was pointing.

'You didn't see him at all?'

Richard shook his head.

'I didn't see him,' he said, 'and I didn't hear him. I just felt the sharp blow across my shoulders. And then he hit me again. I just managed to roll away so that the second blow missed most of my head. But it knocked me out for a while.'

Paul tried to imagine it but he was struggling. His father was tall, athletic and strong. He had never thought anyone would be able to overpower him.

'Was he taller than you?' he asked. To Paul, it seemed the only explanation.

'No, far from it,' he said. 'He was a good bit shorter than me – more like your Uncle William. If he had been as tall as me, he probably would have killed me with the first blow.'

He could see his son taking in this information, starting to understand how it was that someone got the better of his father.

'And Mr Brockman got him you told me,' he said. 'But how? Was he close by?'

Richard breathed deeply. He did not want his son to start repeating the story but he deserved to know the truth.

'I owe my life to Charles Brockman,' he said simply. 'He was standing on the verandah of his house and he shot him.'

Richard was pointing to Charles's house that stood quite a distance away. It was a small house dwarfed now by its new neighbour.

'Wow, what a shot,' Paul said, his admiration for Charles's marksmanship clearly evident.

'Yes, it was quite a shot,' Richard said. 'Charles has always been good with a rifle and fortunately he'd been warned about Alistair McGovern so he had the gun out of his rifle cupboard just in case.'

Richard knew instinctively what the next question would be. He had so far shielded his children from the awful knowledge of just who Alistair McGovern was and why he hated them so much.

Paul listened in silence as his father related the full story. He left nothing out. As he finished, he put his arm around his son.

'We must forget about it all now,' he said. 'It's better that you don't tell anyone about how Charles killed Alistair McGovern or just who he was. That knowledge belongs to the family. Just us. We're the only ones who need to know.'

Paul nodded. Suddenly he felt he was no longer a child. He was being entrusted with grown up matters and with family secrets.

'Does Marianne know?' he asked.

'I don't think so but I will make sure her mother or father tell her the full story,' Richard said. 'It would be better coming from them.'

'And Anthony?'

Richard smiled. He was touched that Paul was concerned for his younger brother but the boy was only six years old.

'I think Anthony's a bit young yet to be told,' he said, 'so when we go to England next week, you must not tell him. All he knows is that I was injured but I recovered.'

'And what about John?'

'I don't know,' he said, 'I'll have to ask Aunt Julia. I haven't seen young John for a while.'

Paul heaved a big sigh. Life was all so complicated now.

'She might still be cross with me about Pippa and revealing who Pippa's father is,' he said. 'Is that another family secret I shouldn't talk about?'

Richard laughed this time. It seemed there were nothing but secrets to talk about and to keep within the family.

'I think she's forgiven you, but you can't talk about that either, except within the family,' Richard said.

Then he remembered and added a note of caution.

'Don't talk about it in front of your Uncle James or John,' he added. 'John knows about Pippa but hasn't met her yet and Uncle James, of course, is very unhappy about what happened.'

But that's a story for another day, thought Richard.

They had almost reached the verandah of Alice and William's new home. Just as William had promised, there was plenty of room to accommodate Richard and his sons. Richard warmed to the familiar sight of Mrs Duffy, the Prior Park housekeeper, who now managed the new home with the same level of authority she had exercised in the old home.

'Mr Richard,' she said, greeting him warmly. 'I was just putting out tea for the everyone.'

She handed him a cup of steaming brown liquid. She was back where she belonged, taking care of the Belleville family, even if it was a much smaller family.

'Thank you, Mrs Duffy,' he said.

She eyed Paul up and down, noting that he was growing and likely to become at least as tall as his father.

'And tea for you, Master Paul?' she asked.

He nodded and took the cup from her.

Alice and Marianne appeared, followed by William, who had spent a good hour going over the cattle sale reports.

Mrs Duffy was busy doling out tea and slicing cake.

Richard lounged against the verandah rail. Paul stood alongside him and followed the direction of his gaze.

They were both drawn irrevocably to the pile of rubble that had been their grand home. After a few moments, Paul asked the question that had been troubling him.

'Why didn't you and Uncle William rebuild the house,' he said.

Richard did not answer immediately. It was William who provided the answer.

'We thought it best to start a new chapter,' he said. 'Your grand-mother lived in a very formal way. I wasn't sure we all wanted to live that way now. Your aunt and I wanted to be more relaxed in the way we lived.'

It seemed a reasonable explanation to William. He did not say he did not want to perpetuate the memories of their father's betrayal, for that had hurt him deeply, more deeply than anyone imagined.

Years after the encounter, he could still see in his mind's eye Muriel McGovern in the neat suburban home in Brisbane, her schoolboy son, in William's own image, swinging open the gate on his way home from school and the later taunt that his father had found true happi-ness in that small world of which he, his brother, his sister and his mother had never been a part.

Paul accepted his uncle's explanation. He did not know that other deeper issues lay behind the decision. He turned quietly to his father.

'When I'm in charge,' he said, 'I'm going to rebuild it.'

Richard smiled but said nothing. He knew from experience just how quickly the ambitions of a twelve-year-old could change. He did not say either that both Anthony and Marianne would have to agree.

That's a battle for the future, he thought. When William and I are gone, they will have to decide what to do.

It was two days before Christmas. Haldon Hall was more colourful than it had ever been with Christmas decorations festooning the hall-way and the stairwell. Anthony had helped decorate the large Christ-mas tree that now dominated the library.

It was getting on for three o'clock in the afternoon. Light snow had begun to fall. It settled briefly on the shrubs and trees, before melting away into nothing. Snow still excited him but he was more excited still by the imminent arrival of his father and his brother.

He was standing on a chair so he could look out of the front win-dow. It gave him a good view of the driveway. He wanted to be the first to spot the taxi that would deliver them to the front door in time for dinner.

Catherine was nervously pacing the library. Her mother Lady Marina tolerated her daughter's restlessness for some time before finally suggesting she sit down instead of wearing out the carpet.

'And when are you expecting Edward?' her mother asked, as if she did not know.

Catherine ignored her question but they both knew the source of Catherine's anxiety. Richard, the man soon to be her ex-husband, was about to meet the man who would replace him. She did not know how the meeting would go. Was it wise for them to be under the one roof for several days, she wondered?

'You said you'd asked John Bertram too,' her mother said, unable to remember now whether he was coming to visit.

'Yes, Mother,' she said, with a hint of exasperation. 'As I told you yesterday, I have asked him and he is coming tomorrow for two days. I thought Richard would be pleased to see him.'

Lady Marina said she most certainly could not remember having been told otherwise she would not have asked the question. Conversation threatened to get heated between the two women, so Catherine changed the subject.

'You'll find Paul much grown now,' she said. 'He'll be thirteen next February.'

Her mother smiled. Paul had always been a favourite with her.

'I remember when you brought him home for his first birthday. He looked so adorable as a baby.'

Catherine smiled too. He had certainly captured hearts when he was born. Now he was growing older, she wondered what lay ahead of him.

'Are you going to raise the prospect with Richard again of his coming to live with us here?' Lady Marina asked. 'It would be good for Anthony to have his brother with him.'

Catherine sighed. It was difficult to get her mother to accept the fact that her boys were Australians and their father did not relish the idea of them being brought up in England.

'I think Richard and I have already settled that question,' she said.

Her mother decided to change tack.

'Does Richard know about Edward?' she asked bluntly.

Catherine shook her head, alarmed then that her mother might say the wrong thing.

'I haven't told him outright,' she replied. 'After all, we are not yet divorced. But I'm sure he's put two and two together.'

She did not hear her mother's reply. All she heard was the shriek of delight from her younger son as he raced to the front door and flung it open, beating the butler to the task by some margin.

He ran down the front steps of the house and flung himself at his father who scooped him up in his arms and swung him around, oblivious to the snow that was now falling quite heavily.

Catherine, not all that far behind Anthony, swept her elder son into a warm embrace. For just a moment, it was like they had been before. The four of them. All together as a family.

Richard finally relinquished his young son who had so much to tell him the words ran into each other and were completely unintelligible. Richard looked at Catherine and then hugged her briefly. He relished the simple pleasure of them all being together as a family. Perhaps for one last time.

Next morning, they woke to see shallow snowdrifts that had formed against the house. Overnight, the landscape had become mostly white with small patches of green poking through. It was cold and frosty but that was not enough to deter two young boys.

Paul and Anthony burst through the front doors and into the garden, kicking snow as they went and then fashioning handfuls of snow into balls to throw at one another amidst bursts of high-pitched shrieking.

Their father, concerned they would be hurt and Paul would be too strong for his much younger brother, followed shortly afterwards and copped a torrent of snowballs that burst harmlessly as they hit his overcoat.

He looked up at the sky. It threatened more of the same. Despite the warm coat and scarf, he shivered and called the boys to come back into the warmth. How many visits had he made to England during his marriage to Catherine, he wondered, yet he had never become accustomed to the cold damp frosty winters? It was only ever a matter of days before he longed for the deep blue of the Australian sky and the heat of the summer sun.

In England the sunless winter sky produced a melancholy he could not easily shake. But he did not want to dampen the boys' high spirits so he did his best to hide his sombre mood. It was Christmas Eve after all.

'Did Mama tell you the village children are coming this afternoon for the Christmas tree?' Anthony said, as he paused in his attempts to gain the advantage of his older brother in the snow fight.

Richard was slightly taken aback. He wondered when his young son had learned to replace the familiar 'mum' with the unfamiliar 'mama'? Lady Marina's doing, he had no doubt.

And the village children? He never could quite come to terms with the suffocating snobbery he encountered each time he came to England. He worried his young son was observing the class distinctions up close from his privileged position as the son of the owner of the big house. Perhaps those things had once existed in Australia, Richard thought, but they hadn't survived the hard back-breaking work of building a new nation when men and women from all ranks had stood shoulder to shoulder and where the only measure of people was their ability.

He wondered idly what many of Catherine's English friends would make of his family's deep friendship with a man whose mother, a Darumbal woman, could point to ancestors who had trodden the land for thousands of years before European settlement. He owed that man his life. He regarded him as an equal but here Charles Brockman would be forced to use the tradesman's entrance and be consigned to the servants' hall. Richard shook his head to clear his thoughts.

'No,' he said. 'She didn't tell me about it. What happens when the children come? How many do we expect?'

Anthony strode on through the snow in search of his brother who had completely outwitted him.

'I think there are about a dozen children,' he said. 'Mama said it's only the children twelve and under but they come with their parents and get a small present and a piece of cake.'

This was all news to Richard. He could not remember this happening previously or Catherine ever having mentioned it. He turned as a voice behind him filled in the details.

'It's a tradition we used to adhere to when I was a child,' Catherine said, as she came up to stand alongside him.

'Mother thought it would be a good idea to revive it. She thought it would give the local people a chance to get to know me.'

Richard nodded. Catherine had been back in England for well over a year and without a husband. He surmised this fact had been the source of much gossip.

'Which village exactly?' asked Richard.

There were one or two villages several miles away but he thought there would be at least forty children if they were included.

'Oh, it's not really village children,' she said. 'It's the children of the tenant farmers and there are three houses of farm workers near the church, plus the local rector who has an eleven-year-old daughter. I hope you'll help me entertain them.'

He shrugged, happy to help, but concerned all the same.

'Won't that just lead to awkward questions about when I'll be relocating from Australia?' Richard asked.

He did not want to fuel the gossips or have to answer awkward questions. It was Catherine's turn to shrug her shoulders.

'I'm not worried about that,' she said. 'All these families rely on me for their living. I know from experience they are always anxious to please.'

She caught Anthony by the hand and began to head towards the front door, despite the child's protests.

'I'm sure the children will enjoy it too,' she said, almost as an after-thought.

Richard followed with Paul alongside him. Richard put his arm around his son's shoulders.

'Looks like we have to make ourselves presentable,' Richard said.

Paul looked up at his father.

'Bloody cold, isn't it?' he said unexpectedly.

He expected a stern talking to for the bad language but his father only laughed.

'You're right there, son,' he said. 'It's not a place I want to spend much time, especially during the winter months.'

'Me either,' Paul said. 'It's wonderful to see Mum and Anthony but

I can't wait to get back home to ride my new mare. And maybe we can go fishing? John's going to show me a really good waterhole on their place.'

He smiled, reassured by his son's preference for Prior Park.

'It's just a shame Anthony won't be with us,' Paul added. 'He'll miss out on all the fun.'

'When he's older,' Richard said, 'I'll make sure he spends some time with us at Prior Park, then you boys can do all those things together.'

'That would be good, Dad,' he said. 'With him so far away, it doesn't feel as though I have a brother. And maybe we can invite Tim Lester up too.'

Richard nodded. He certainly owed the Lester family a debt of gratitude he was keen to repay. More so since the uproar over his son's exposure of Philippe Duval as Pippa Jensen's father. He made a mental note to ask Julia if there had been any fall out from it because there had been dire predictions at the time and Paul had been, in his opinion, unfairly blamed.

A storm in a teacup, he thought, just as he had predicted at the time.

CHAPTER 11

December 1958

On the other side of the world it was already Christmas Day. Pippa Jensen lay in a single bed in an unfamiliar room. Across the room in a bed very similar to her own, her cousin Marianne lay fast asleep. But Pippa was too excited to sleep. The home she had been welcomed into reminded her of the homestead at Essex Downs. The smells of the countryside were not unfamiliar either, although there were no sheep to be seen anywhere and no shearing shed.

It had been a dizzying day.

She had flown on an aeroplane for the very first time, accompanied by Aunt Edith, who had also been invited.

Every moment since her arrival was seared in her memory. Her mother waving to her as she stepped off the plane, the quick drive around the town and the short stop at her mother's rented house before the hour long drive through the countryside to Prior Park.

She had never seen the grand home that had once dominated the landscape but she could not help but notice the look of sadness that came across her mother's face as she pointed out the ruins as they drove past and headed towards the new home several hundred yards away.

She struggled to believe just how much her life had changed in just over eighteen months. From the devastation of losing her adoptive parents to the discovery of her real parents and now the chance to meet her extended family, it was almost all too much. In the midst of it all, there was the lingering grief for her adoptive mother Anne, who had loved her unconditionally as if she had been her own child. It was a bond that would never be broken.

She drifted off to sleep in a tumble of thoughts to be woken hours later by the warm sun streaming in through the window and her cousin shaking her gently.

'It's time to get up,' Marianne said. 'We have to get ready for breakfast and then we will open our presents.'

Pippa found Marianne's excitement infectious. She had never shared Christmas Day with another child. She had always been the only one.

The two girls giggled together as they dressed quickly and headed towards the kitchen. She knew instantly that she and Marianne would be good friends. Marianne was an only child and the rest of her cousins were boys, who, according to her, had strange interests such as fishing and stuff.

To have a sister had been an unfulfilled dream. To have a girl cousin was the next best thing.

By lunchtime, a small mountain of Christmas wrapping had been despatched to the incinerator although careful watch was kept to make sure no sparks escaped. No one wanted to start a bushfire accidentally on Christmas Day.

The dining room, rarely used when it was just William, Alice and Marianne, was festooned with Christmas decorations and the table boasted the best china and silverware.

But everything was new. All the fine china, all the hallmarked silverware, everything had been lost in the fire. It was almost, as William had said, as if they were a family without memories. A family without a past.

Still, he sat proudly at the head of the table in his new home while Mrs Duffy, helped by Alice and Marianne, brought the food to the table.

Charles Brockman took the chair that William indicated next to him.

'We're missing Richard and his boys,' William said, as he passed the dish of roast vegetables to Charles. 'They should be here with us.'

'And what about your sister's boy John?' Charles asked, noting his absence.

The tension between his sister and her estranged husband had shown no sign of easing, particularly with her decision to bring her illegitimate daughter home to Prior Park for Christmas.

'John and his father are having Christmas lunch with Amelia,' William said. 'I expect they'll call in on the way home.'

Charles smiled and caught William's eye.

'That's going to be a tense visit,' he said quietly, 'depending on what type of mood James is in.'

William nodded.

'I've thought of that but what can I do?' he replied. 'If he gets difficult, we'll just have to handle it.'

Charles looked across the table to where Pippa was deep in conversation with Marianne. It immediately brought back memories of Julia as a young girl. She had been a favourite of his and he had been alarmed at what had happened to her. He felt he had failed her.

In his eyes, she had been a naïve young girl who'd been taken advantage of by a much more experienced man and no one would ever convince him otherwise. If he had warned her parents, it all might have been avoided. But life was full of useless regrets. He could see the young girl's fragility through her bright cheery nature. If James Fitzroy sought to upset her, he would have me to answer to, thought Charles.

It was late afternoon. Christmas lunch had long been cleared away. Pippa had taken her turn at wiping up the dishes and helping her cousin stack them in the cupboard. Alice looked on with approval. She thought it likely that Edith Henderson had been responsible for the girl's good manners and willingness to help, rather than Julia, who had never been required to help in the kitchen.

Julia, too, was gratified by Pippa's good behaviour. She turned to Edith Henderson, who was also looking to be helpful. She was not a woman used to having others do her domestic chores.

'You've done a good job with Pippa,' Julia said to her quietly.

The older woman smiled, secretly pleased at the praise. Up until now, it had been as if no one had noticed the contribution she had made to the girl's upbringing.

'Well, I thought she should learn some domestic skills,' she said. 'My niece Anne had not worried about it. They had a cook at Essex Downs who cooked for the family and the men. And a housekeeper too. Much the same as you would have had growing up.'

It occurred to Julia then that she knew very little of her daughter's early life. There had been little opportunity to talk to Edith Henderson privately.

'I thought that might have been the case,' Julia said. 'Do you know she still carries a photo of Anne Jensen everywhere she goes?'

Was Julia jealous of a dead woman, Edith wondered?

'That doesn't surprise me,' she said. 'She was very attached to Anne. Not so to Anne's husband Harry. He was a hard, unfeeling man. I think my niece only married him for financial security. But you mustn't feel upset by the photo. I think you have to accept her first mother, if I may call her that, will always have a special place in Pippa's heart.'

Julia nodded, aware that she had missed those important years when a mother bonds irrevocably with her child.

'You're right,' she said, acknowledging the good sense Edith was speaking. 'I shouldn't be upset by it. It's very understandable in fact.'

The two women walked together out of the kitchen and made their way on to the wide front verandah. This private conversation was an opportunity for Edith too to ask what the future might hold.

'While we're talking of Pippa,' she said quietly, 'what thoughts do you have for the future?'

It was an obliquely framed question, deliberately so. She did not feel she could ask directly if Julia and Philippe were going to marry once her divorce became final. There had been no suggestion that Pippa would live anywhere else but with her, despite her father having bought his own house in Sydney.

Julia was unprepared for the question, but she knew Edith Henderson deserved an honest answer.

'It will still be some time before my divorce is finalised,' Julia said. 'Until that time I'm not really thinking about what's next for me. And we're so grateful to you for the stability and the good home you've given Pippa, we don't think there's any reason to change that, if you're happy with the arrangement.'

Edith Henderson smiled, privately pleased to hear Julia say she had no plans to remove Pippa from her care. She had become genuinely fond of the girl and taking care of her had given her life real purpose.

'Thank you,' she said to Julia. 'I'm delighted you feel that way. I think stability is everything in a child's life. With Philippe's hours at the hospital, it would not work out at all well for her to live with her father. With me, she comes home from school and we talk about her day while we have tea. She tells me what's happened at school and all the gossip.'

They laughed together. Gossip seemed to be a big part of life at a girls' school.

'I hear lots of gossip about the Clarkes, for example,' she said. 'Apparently Dr Clarke may be a highly respected surgeon and very important in the hospital but his wife rules the roost at home, so Pippa tells me.'

This titbit did not surprise Julia in the least. Her memory of Patricia Clarke matched perfectly with the gossip Pippa had relayed to her great aunt.

Just then, Julia caught sight of a car turning into the Prior Park driveway. She turned to Edith.

'This looks like my estranged husband and my son John if I'm not mistaken,' she said.

Edith noticed Julia tense, in anticipation of the awkward encounter to come.

'Perhaps I should make myself scarce,' Edith said, already rising from her chair.

But Julia shook her head.

'He's more likely to behave himself in the presence of a stranger,' she said.

So Edith sank back into the cane armchair. Out of the corner of her eye, she noticed William walk directly to the front steps followed by Alice. A reception committee, she thought, intent on diffusing any difficulties.

Pippa had noticed the advancing car too and came to sit close by her mother.

James Fitzroy brought his car to an abrupt halt in a cloud of dust. His son John was out of the car almost before it had stopped to greet his mother. After a quick hug, he pulled back from her and stood shyly by her chair.

At ten years old he was four years younger than Pippa. He was small for his age, despite the expectation that he would eventually overtake his father in height. But in his looks, there was almost nothing of Julia. He had the same smile, the same dark eyes and thick dark hair that had rendered his father irresistible to almost any woman he attempted to charm.

'John, this is your sister, Pippa,' Julia said, encouragingly.

Before anyone else could speak, James interrupted, correcting Julia.

'Half-sister, son. I'm not her father.'

His words were blunt, intended to wound.

The encounter was every bit as awkward as Julia feared it would be. Just below the surface the simmering anger of her estranged husband was barely contained.

In the silence that followed, the two children eyed one another but there was no ready offer of friendship from either of them. Marianne, sensing the tension but not understanding it fully, intervened.

'Pippa and I are going to the pictures on Saturday afternoon,' she said. 'Do you want to come?'

John looked to his father for guidance.

'Can I, Dad?' he asked.

'If you want to, son,' James replied, but it was clear his approval had been given under sufferance.

John sensed his father's mood and then declined.

It was at this point that Edith Henderson decided to act. She extended her hand to James and he shook it out of politeness rather than interest.

'It's very good of you to call in, Mr Fitzroy,' Edith said. 'I've looked after Pippa since her adoptive parents died early last year. Anne Jensen was my niece, my only sister's daughter. It was a terrible time. Pippa was thrown out of her home by the nephew who inherited it. We had no idea then how things would turn out. It must have been a terrible shock for you but I have to say I'm very pleased Pippa found her real mother and now her half-brother.'

She was careful to be specific. She did not want to give him the opportunity to correct the relationship of Pippa and John yet again.

'I know you've paid a big price personally for what has happened,' Edith added.

There was silence among those gathered on the verandah. It was as if no one was game to breathe as if the very act of breathing might set off an unpredictable reaction.

James, surprised by the elderly woman's intervention, was momentarily wrong footed.

'You're right, Mrs Henderson,' he said finally. 'I paid a big price for it. My marriage. Many times, I'd wished the girl had never found her mother and I could have continued my life in ignorance of my wife's affair.'

He nodded towards Pippa who stood beside her mother's chair. Julia had put a protective arm around her.

'But it's too late now. We can't go back. We can't undo the past.'

He turned towards his son.

'See you later, son,' he said abruptly. 'Your Aunt Alice will drop you home when you're ready.'

He did not look in Julia's direction. He picked up his hat and with that he was gone.

As they watched the departing car head out towards the main road, Charles Brockman who had been sitting almost unobserved at the far end of the verandah got up and walked across to William and Alice. He knew Alice in particular had been very concerned about how her brother would react to Julia having Pippa with her.

'Well,' Charles observed, 'that probably went about as well as we all expected.'

William turned to him. There was a sense of relief in his voice.

'I'm pleased that's over,' William said. 'James will have to get over it sometime.'

It was Alice then who voiced her opinion.

'For all my brother's faults,' she said, 'I know he did love Julia. He's really hurt by it all.'

She had said it softly. She did not want her voice to carry the full length of the verandah to where Julia and the children and Mrs Henderson remained sitting.

Charles was not convinced but he admired Alice's loyalty towards her brother. He would have expected nothing less.

'How long are they staying?' Charles asked, nodding towards Pippa and Edith Henderson.

'They go home on Monday,' William said. 'Julia thought a short visit was probably best at this stage.'

'Young John seems to be firmly in his father's orbit,' Charles said, having observed the child looking towards his father, rather than his mother, for guidance.

'I think with my sister away so much and not having a settled home that's been a natural outcome,' he said. 'And if she were to marry Duval, there's no way James would let his son be brought up in that household which would be in Sydney anyway.'

'Life's certainly become more complicated for your sister,' Charles observed.

It occurred to him, but he did not say it out loud, that she might actually be preferring the freedom of her life as it now was. He doubted William, whose views were predictably orthodox, would have agreed with him but he could see how Julia had, if not flourished, then at least matured into a woman who could make her own decisions. She was no longer required to defer to a mother or a husband. Charles imagined such freedom might be something she would be reluctant to give up.

That Christmas, awkward situations were not confined to Prior Park. Delayed by the unexpectedly heavy snowfall, Edward Cavendish had abandoned his plans to drive his highly unsuitable Jaguar sports car on the short but hazardous drive to Haldon Hall. He had opted instead for the new Land Rover he had acquired for the farm work at Grantham Manor.

He arrived at Haldon Hall, with his mother Louise, just in time for

Christmas lunch.

Richard, standing alongside his friend John Bertram in the drawing room, watched from the window as the car pulled up as close as possible to the front door. It was the vehicle that attracted their attention to begin with.

'So, what's that?' Richard asked, gesturing towards the unfamiliar vehicle.

'That, my dear friend, is a four-wheel drive car,' John replied. 'And I would hazard a guess and say that's the new model that's just been released this year.'

Richard was impressed by his friend's knowledge. John had always been more interested in new technology and mechanical innovations than he was.

'It certainly looks more suitable for the conditions here than an ordinary car,' Richard observed, as he watched Edward climb out of the driver's seat and then hurry to the passenger side to help his mother.

He watched with interest as Catherine greeted her guests. He was looking especially hard at how she greeted Edward. She had assumed Richard would be watching so she was careful to keep Edward at arm's length.

Paul, who had been sent on an errand by his grandmother to fetch her special knee blanket from upstairs, returned to watch proceedings alongside his father.

'Wow, Anthony's keen on that bloke,' Paul said. 'Who is he?'

It was John Bertram who supplied the answer.

'That man,' he said, 'is now Sir Anthony Cavendish. He's a distant cousin of your mother but because he's a man, he inherited your grandfather's title when he died.'

Paul took all this information on board. Presumably it would make sense one day because it didn't now but it hardly concerned him. What did concern him was why his young brother was greeting this man so warmly in a way that should have been reserved for their own father.

'Anthony seems to like him a lot,' Paul said. 'He must visit here often for Anthony to know him so well.'

John looked at Richard. Out of the mouths of babes, he wanted to say but he did not. He judged that now was not the moment for a light-hearted comment.

It was Richard who spoke. He felt his son deserved an honest answer. He was tired of secrets. There had been enough of those.

'I think that's the man your mother is going to marry when our divorce is finalised,' Richard told his son.

'Oh, I see,' was all he received by way of reply.

He could see the boy was unhappy with his answer. It had not occurred to Richard that Paul had secretly nursed the false hope that his parents would get back together. He patted his son's shoulder in a small gesture of reassurance.

They all turned as the door to the drawing room opened. Moments later, introductions were being made. Richard greeted Louise Cavendish, Edward's mother, and then Edward. For the first time in his life, Richard was at a loss as to what to say.

Standing before him, Edward Cavendish was every inch the polished diplomat. His suit was immaculately cut. His boyish face had not yet descended into middle age. Every aspect of his bearing was a silent reminder of his aristocratic heritage. He belongs, thought Richard. And Catherine belongs in this world, not mine. And this is the man my wife now prefers. He felt he'd been kicked. The hurt he felt was almost physical.

Edward Cavendish's voice finally reached him through this private reverie.

'It's very good to meet you,' Edward said. 'I imagine you're finding the weather difficult. We often get quite a bit of snow in these parts.'

The weather. What else would an Englishman talk about, Richard thought. It was John Bertram who came to the rescue.

'It's a bugger for flying,' he said as he shook Edward's hand. 'Ice on the wings can be catastrophic. I really hate taking off in snow and ice. Give me a sunny day and a light breeze any time.'

Good old John, Richard thought. To my rescue again.

Richard downed the half-finished glass of whisky he was holding and gladly accepted a refill. The temptation to smash Edward Cavendish's smooth smiling face had almost proved overwhelming.

Instead, the conversation had moved on seamlessly. Catherine's drawing room had been spared.

'I won't come again,' Richard vowed to himself.

He spoke quietly to John Bertram.

'Thanks, mate, you saved me from making a fool of myself.'

John shook his head. He didn't think Richard would ever make a fool of himself. He admired his friend above all others.

'No worries, mate,' he said casually. 'I don't like the bloke either if it's any consolation.'

Richard smiled. Thank goodness for John Bertram, he thought.

CHAPTER 12

December 1958

Christmas Day in Sydney had dawned fine and sunny. Soft clouds drifted across the blue sky as the morning wore on. It was a warm day but not blisteringly hot.

For Philippe it was not the first Christmas he had spent in Australia but during the war the celebrations had been very muted. He felt a pang of nostalgia for the Christmas lights of New York and the traditional white Christmas that so fitted the season. How would it ever feel right, he wondered, to celebrate Christmas in the middle of summer?

He made himself a leisurely breakfast. Unless an emergency occurred, he would not be needed at the hospital until the following Monday. He wondered how his daughter was being welcomed among Julia's family. He hoped the visit was going well but he knew it was beyond his power to influence the outcome.

In quiet moments he thought about the future. He would never regret having found his daughter but he wondered if Julia struggled, as he did, to really connect with her. He worried that the bond of parental love was hard to establish across the chasm of lost years.

He looked at his watch. It was time to clear away his breakfast dishes and get ready. He calculated the drive to Vaucluse would take him half an hour.

Somehow, without really knowing exactly how, he had drifted into a friendship with Karen Clarke who had insisted he not spend Christmas alone. He had no plausible excuse to decline her invitation to Christmas lunch at her parents' home, so he accepted gracefully.

Since her birthday party in September, he had taken her to dinner and partnered her several times including to a friend's engagement party. But he had felt very much an outsider among her friends who were at least a decade younger than him and he had told her so. You must find yourself an eligible young man your own age, he had told her often. She had only laughed at this suggestion. But they are so dull and boring, she had said, and they talk only about themselves.

There was so little traffic on the road he arrived early. He pulled up in the street and parked opposite the Clarke house. In the bright daylight he took the time to look at the magnificent homes that fronted the short street, all of which had varying views of the harbour.

These are the types of homes my mother would have cleaned, he thought. Places she would never have been welcomed as an equal. He thought she would be quietly pleased he was now able to move effortlessly in these circles, not because of wealth, but because of his professional standing. No one had asked about his family. They were satisfied with his oblique reply that he had been brought up on Long Island. America was too far away for them to know or care about his family background. They were satisfied to judge him by his standing as an eminent surgeon and not by his family background.

He was locking his car and preparing to walk across the road just as another car pulled in behind him.

Anita Clarke was first out of the car, followed by her mother Patricia, who greeted him frostily.

'Merry Christmas, Dr Duval, she said, before indicating the girl alongside her. 'This is my daughter Anita.'

She did not say 'this is my daughter who is a friend of your daughter Pippa', which she might easily have done.

But Philippe was not surprised. Knowing Patricia Clarke, he knew there was no way the woman would willingly acknowledge the existence of his illegitimate child. He had been relieved to hear from Pippa that Nancy Lester had insisted she not be dropped from their group. He had smiled when Pippa told him. He wondered if it was his daughter's first lesson in the importance of having someone who would champion your cause. He tried to explain it but he wasn't sure she understood what he was trying to say.

The girl half smiled at him before her mother hustled her away. He could see she was well aware of who he was. He simply said 'hello' and moved on to greet his colleague Robert Clarke, who had the good grace to appear slightly embarrassed by his wife's unfriendly attitude.

The group walked across the road together towards the house, the two men falling in behind the mother and daughter.

'Did you let the hospital know where you would be?' he asked Philippe.

Robert Clarke was really never off duty. He knew neither of them were officially on call but he was fond of saying 'you never know when we'll be needed'. Philippe suspected it added to his sense of importance, but there were times, he conceded, that surgeons were needed at very short notice.

'Yes, I did, Robert,' he said. 'Hopefully it will be a quiet time and we will have our Christmas in peace.'

'I hope so too,' his colleague replied, 'but you never know.'

As they were about to mount the stairs to the front door, he put his hand lightly on Philippe's arm in a restraining gesture.

'Just before we go in,' he said, 'there's something I want to tell you.'

Philippe stopped abruptly while Patricia Clarke and her daughter continued on ahead of them. He wondered fleetingly what he was about to hear. If it was to do with the revelations of months before, he thought it was incredibly bad timing. Philippe turned towards the older man with a look of enquiry.

'My brother thinks you're getting too friendly with his daughter,' Robert Clarke said bluntly and without preamble.

Given that months before Patricia Clarke had deliberately put Karen alongside him at dinner, he knew it was his personal life that had rendered him unsuitable but that was nothing new. He recalled David Clarke's warning to him on the telephone. Karen's father had listed his objections to Philippe, all of which made sense, even to him. In David Clarke's position, he would have said much the same. What had suddenly caused him to revive his concerns, Philippe wondered?

'You know we are just friends, Robert' Philippe said warily. 'I keep telling her to find someone her own age.'

'Good advice, I'm sure,' Robert replied.

He found the whole subject distasteful but he did not want Philippe to be caught unawares by any quiet chat his brother might demand.

'Did you know my brother's been looking into your family background?' Robert asked.

He bent his head close to Philippe's. His voice was almost a whisper.

'I think he'd hoped for a well-established Long Island family but that's not what he found, is it?'

Philippe greeted this news with a mixture of shock and outrage. How dare someone investigate his private life in such a manner and on such a flimsy pretext. He tried to remain calm.

'What business is it of his who my family is?' Philippe said, unwilling to answer directly or to lend credence to anything David Clarke's investigations might have found.

'He has no right to do that,' Philippe said, 'and I will tell him that.'

But once again Robert put a restraining hand on his arm.

'Don't be too hasty,' he said. 'Even though he doesn't sit on the board of the hospital, David is very influential.'

But this was too much for Philippe. Remaining silent would be impossible if David Clarke confronted him about his family background.

'Why would he bother with me?' he asked perplexed.

'Because he thinks there's a good chance you are going to propose to his daughter and he wants to know everything about you before that happens,' Robert said.

Philippe shook his head in bewilderment. This was all beginning to sound slightly crazy. He wondered if Karen had been complicit in this or if she was ignorant of her father's deviousness. He hoped it was the latter.

'I've never given Karen any indication I'm going to propose to her,' he said. 'That idea is a figment of his imagination – or hers.'

Robert shook his head, trying desperately to get Philippe to see the problem from his brother's point of view.

'Figment of his imagination or not, my brother thinks it's a real possibility,' Robert said. 'But you didn't answer my original question? I take it you understand what he found out?'

They had begun to walk up the stairs, but Philippe stopped again.

'So you want me to confirm what you already know, is that it?' he snapped.

Robert Clarke could not mistake the anger in his voice but he pressed for an answer all the same. Philippe sighed. Even now it was painful to repeat the story. He understood more than ever the hardship his unmarried mother had faced raising a child alone.

'I'm the illegitimate product of a liaison between my mother, the daughter of a gardener to one of the big houses on Long Island, and the heir to that estate, who was too weak to go against the family and marry my mother. My mother never actually confirmed my father's identity, but in later years I put two and two together.'

Robert nodded as he listened. Part of him was sorry he'd pushed Philippe so hard to confirm the story. But part of him was not sorry. He thought it explained so much about his younger colleague including why he had been so keen to track down his own illegitimate daughter and be part of her life. He saw then that Philippe knew what it was like not to be wanted by his own father. Because of it, his sympathies would always lie with the unwanted children.

'That's what he told me,' Robert said after he had heard Philippe out. 'Knowing all that as a child must have been tough.'

'It was,' Philippe conceded. 'It was tough. My mother did her best in every way she could.'

But he could see Robert had not finished.

'I'm afraid there's more he found out that surprised him,' he said, trying hard to frame the words in such a way as not to cause offence. He plunged on.

'My brother told me that somewhere in your lineage there is some, shall we say, dark blood.'

Philippe could not believe what he was hearing. This was as close to a racist slur as he had ever heard.

'What!'

He was on the point of exploding but he was caught between his natural instinct for politeness and his growing sense of outrage. What else could he do but answer the stupid question?

'If you must know, my mother, through her grandfather, has some Creole blood,' he said with icy politeness, 'but I might just as easily point to my father's English ancestry or my grandmother's French family to explain my breeding.'

Despite the insult and the way he felt, he chose his words carefully. In him it had been more his name than his appearance that had spoken of exotic antecedents. In Italy, he would pass for Italian; in Spain, he would pass for Spanish; in France, he would be claimed as one of their own. It would only be his rusty American-accented French that would let him down.

'Thank you for confirming it,' Robert said, his voice conveying an unspoken apology. He was well aware he had overstepped the bounds of propriety.

He put his hand on Philippe's shoulder in a gesture of rapprochement. Philippe was tempted to shrug it away but he did not. He heard him out.

'My brother was seeing it all in the worst possible light,' he said. 'But I don't blame him entirely. Karen will inherit everything he has built up and he doesn't want it to go to some gold-digging adventurer. Since he lost his son, he's been quite paranoid about it. Did Karen tell you about her brother?'

This sudden change of direction in the conversation caught Philippe off guard.

He nodded.

'I know about that,' he said. 'Your brother told me about losing his son when I tried to thank him for convincing you not to tell the board about my private life. It must have been very hard for the family.'

Robert was thoughtful for a moment. He looked at the ground. It was clearly a difficult topic to discuss.

'Let me tell you, it was very hard,' he said finally, 'especially as I had recommended the surgeon for the operation. But as you and I know, even the most gifted surgeons get it wrong from time to time. There would have been times when both you and I would have had outcomes for patients we'd thought would have been much better than they turned out to be. But that was no consolation to David and Deborah. Or Karen.'

Philippe nodded, only too well aware what it was like to deliver bad news to a patient's family

'I can imagine,' Philippe said. 'To deliver bad news to parents is a surgeon's worst nightmare. We can do everything right but sometimes a small slip or something we hadn't foreseen means a successful operation suddenly turns into an unsuccessful one. That's what I try and impress on the students. Not to think they're God or to be blasé about a procedure they might have done fifty, a hundred times. That's when mistakes happen.'

Robert smiled. They were on safe ground now, talking about a topic of common interest.

'That, Dr Duval,' he said, 'is why I will always move heaven and earth to keep you at my hospital to teach the next generation of surgeons.'

With that they walked together up the remaining stairs to be greeted by Karen who had been waiting patiently for them for some minutes.

To Philippe, lunch seemed to go on interminably. He was grateful to be spared the necessity of making polite conversation with Patricia Clarke.

He had been seated between Karen and her best friend Bianca Ferrari whom he had met once or twice before. It was clear from her heavily accented English that English was not her first language. He decided to risk embarassment with his rudimentary Italian.

'È bello vederti di nuovo. Ti stai godendo il pasto?'

She laughed, amused by his attempt at her native language.

'Vuoi migliorare il tuo italiano, amico mio?'

He laughed along with her, only certain that she had called him 'my friend'. He reverted to English.

'I have a long way to go I'm afraid,' he said. 'I learnt a few phrases when I was a student at medical school. One of my classmates was Italian.'

She smiled.

'What I asked you was if you wanted to improve your Italian?'

Again, she smiled at him, this time urging him to go on with their conversation in Italian but he could not bring to mind any more phrases.

'My Italian needs a lot of work,' he said. 'A lot of work in fact. More than I have time for at the present time.'

She nodded and reached for her glass of wine.

'I understand completely although you certainly look the part,' she said teasingly.

He laughed quietly at her reference to his European looks. It was the second time today his appearance had been commented on, except he thought this time it was meant to be complimentary.

'I'm not sure about Italian blood,' he said, 'but I know there is a family connection to a small village near Grenoble in France.'

'La capitale des alpes,' she said, quickly switching to flawless French.

He answered, relying on half-remembered language lessons.

'Oui, Bianca, tu as raison,' he replied. 'Elle est considérée comme la capitale des Alpes, mais hélas je n'ai jamais visité la ville.'

'I'm impressed,' she said. 'I meet very few truly multilingual people in Australia.'

But he shook his head, not wanting to claim a mastery of languages.

'I need to practice to keep up my French,' he said, 'but sadly there is more Latin than any other language in my life right now.'

Around them, dinner plates were being removed and the dessert course was being brought in.

'I understand,' she said. 'Karen told me about your work alongside her uncle at St Vincent's and that you are considered one of the best surgeons in your field. That is very important work.'

He could see she was impressed by his credentials but he was reluctant to accept such accolades. There were many fine surgeons practising in hospitals throughout Sydney. He did not see any reason why he should be singled out for special mention.

'I do my best,' he said modestly. 'And you? What line of work are you in?'

He knew, unlike her friend Karen whose family did not see the necessity for her to work, she had a career. He remembered she had been missing from some social events on account of her work.

'I'm a fashion buyer for that big department store you pass every time you drive along Elizabeth Street,' she said, testing his knowledge of the city.

'But it's much less important work than yours,' she added.

That was probably true, he thought, but not everyone could be a surgeon. He believed it was important for people to have a pride in whatever they did.

'Yes, of course I know the store,' he replied. 'And I imagine you love your job.'

She was beautifully if simply dressed. Long dark hair framed her face. Her make up, he noticed, was subtle. He thought it was easy to admire such a woman whose effortless elegance seemed so natural.

'Yes, I do love the work,' she said. 'And best of all I get to travel back to Europe every so often. What more could I want?'

He knew there must be more to her story. Europeans had been displaced in great numbers following the defeat of Germany and her allies. Many had made new lives in Australia but still they yearned for the life they had left behind.

Before he could ask, she turned to answer a question from Robert Clarke who was seated on the other side of her. Karen, who had been listening to the last part of the conversation, leaned in towards him.

'I see you've been getting friendly with Bianca,' she said playfully. 'Her parents would never approve of you though because they're Catholic and you are divorced.'

He laughed outright at her precociousness.

'I'm not about to offer marriage to every eligible young woman I speak to,' he said, 'so don't worry on that point.'

'Just protecting you, my dear Philippe,' she said. 'Her parents are on a world cruise at present and her brother is currently in America so she was rather left to her own devices this Christmas. That's why I invited her to join us.'

The explanation was hardly necessary, he thought.

'She seems very nice,' he said. It was such a neutral description.

Karen nodded in agreement.

'Oh, she is very nice and great fun,' she said, 'and her father is a good customer of one of our dealerships.'

Philippe suspected that commerce was never far from her father's mind. It occurred to him to wonder why he did not involve his daughter in his business given that she stood to inherit everything.

'I'm surprised your father doesn't get you involved in his business,' Philippe said, voicing his thoughts aloud.

He was surprised to find that she had been thinking about this too.

'I've broached the subject with him,' she said. 'I think it was losing Michael that made it difficult for him to consider it because Michael was to be the one to take over.'

'And now?' he asked. 'Is he taking your interest seriously?'

He had begun to think she would find life much more satisfying with a real career and a real purpose beyond landing herself a husband that her parents approved of.

'I think he is,' she said. 'I think he'd hoped I would marry someone suitable but he thinks he's waited too long for that to happen. He has this terrible premonition that he's not going to be around for long, so from next year, I'm going to be brought into the business to learn it.'

'And are you looking forward to that?' Philippe asked.

She had never mentioned the possibility previously.

'I am,' she said. 'I've never had a job, and this won't be a job in the true sense. I will be shadowing my father. That's his idea, so I learn about everything that is going on from his perspective and how he makes his decisions.'

Even now, he could detect a new sense of purpose and maturity about her. He realised then he'd completely misjudged her, having labelled her as a frivolous young woman. He knew she would face some prejudice in what would be in all probability a heavily male dominated business environment.

'You'll find that you may encounter some prejudice against you as a woman,' he said. 'I see it all the time among young women doctors who are trying to make their way in the medical profession. The men don't like them trespassing in their territory. Some of them, I'm sorry to say, are bullies.'

'I realise that,' she said. 'I don't think my father would tolerate poor behaviour towards me though.'

'Good on him,' Philippe said. 'I hope for your sake he doesn't.'

'And what wouldn't I tolerate?'

A voice boomed behind them as David Clarke loomed over them, his arm draped over his daughter's chair.

'Karen was just telling me about your plans to take her into your business,' Philippe said.

'Yes, it's probably time she learnt a thing or two about it,' he said.

Then he put a hand on Philippe's shoulder.

'I'd like a quiet word with you before you leave,' he said.

Karen had already turned to speak to her cousin Anita who sat on her right hand side. But she turned back as she heard her father speak.

'What do you want to talk to Philippe about?' she asked, with some alarm.

'Nothing that need trouble you, my dear daughter,' he said. 'Nothing that need trouble you at all.'

CHAPTER 13

January 1959

Julia waved as she spotted her brother and his son emerging from the aircraft that had just come to halt some distance from the airport terminal.

Within a very short time, they were by her side and she hugged each of them in turn, relieved to see them back home after their long journey from England.

'How was it?' she asked as they walked towards the front of the terminal to await the delivery of baggage.

'Cold,' he replied, 'bloody cold. Thank God for some sunshine. And it's such a long way to travel. It will be a while before I submit to that torture again.'

Did he really mean that, she wondered? It would be many years before Anthony would be old enough to travel alone.

'And how was Catherine?' she asked. 'And Anthony?'

They had walked through the small terminal and now stood together under an awning near the vacant space where the baggage trolley would eventually appear.

'Catherine is well, busy with the estate and living the life she was born to,' he said.

His bitterness was almost spent. He had seen her, at close quarters, mistress of the house and the surrounding estate. He could not deny she was thriving and enjoying her life.

'You know, it's odd,' he said, his tone suddenly wistful. 'When we married, I had the feeling she was more enthusiastic about our relationship than I was. I really liked her but I married her because she was pregnant. Then I realised too late the tables had turned.'

Julia could do nothing to ease her brother's disappointment. She thought he was being unusually frank, particularly in front of his young son. She did not ask about Edward Cavendish. Time enough to ask that question, she thought, when Paul was not within earshot, so she turned towards her nephew.

'And what about you, Paul,' she asked lightheartedly. 'Did you enjoy the white Christmas more than your father did?'

'Well, Aunt Julia,' he said, his tone at first serious, 'it was terribly cold, colder than Sydney in the wintertime, but it was fun to run about in the snow. And Mum took us ice skating.'

'And I beat Anthony in the snow fights,' he added proudly.

She smiled.

'You'll miss Anthony now that you're back home,' she said to Paul, but looking instead at his father for a hopeful sign that the boy might be headed back to Australia.

Paul shrugged, knowing it was out of his hands. His father replied.

'He's just turned six so I don't want to upset the arrangements yet,' he said. 'But when he's a bit older I do want him to come and spend some time with us.'

'That would hardly work very well with Paul away in Sydney at school,' she said.

'I'd thought of that,' he replied. 'He's not going back to Sydney to school. I'm going to send him to the local Boys' Grammar School, so he can live with me and ride his bike to school. At least that way he'll be at school with John and will see Marianne too.'

She turned back towards Paul, who was trying but not succeeding to lift a heavy suitcase off the baggage trolley.

'How do you feel about going to school up here?' she asked.

Changing schools was something of a traumatic experience. She remembered her own final years at school in Sydney in a class of girls, none of whom she knew.

He was beaming. The chance to live with his father and be close to Prior Park had answered all his prayers.

'It will be great,' he said. 'I'll miss Tim Lester but Dad has said he can come up to visit. Or I can go down to visit him.'

Julia smiled. The outlook of a child was invariably black and white and based on certainties. She wished her life was so straightforward.

She carried the lightest of the bags as they made their way towards her car. After they had stowed the luggage in the boot, Richard stood for a while looking around him as if he simply wanted to appreciate being back home. His gaze invariably went to the south western horizon looking for any sign of rain. Julia followed his gaze.

'We had some rain last week,' she said, 'but there was much more in the upper Fitzroy catchment.'

He had never known his sister to take quite so much interest in the weather and he said so. She smiled.

'John was out that way with his father looking at some cattle,' she said. 'I was concerned they might get caught up in flood waters.'

He nodded, understanding now why she was able to give such a specific report.

'And how did the Christmas visit go?' he asked, as he settled into the front passenger seat.

She paused in the act of starting the engine and turned towards him.

'It went well, really,' she said with just a hint of doubt in her voice. 'William and Alice, and Marianne too, were very good to Pippa. Charles helped her with riding lessons. She had some lessons as a young child but she was a bit nervous at first. And we went to the beach for a day. And we went to the pictures.'

She listed all the things he expected they would have done.

'And James and John?'

'Well, James hardly acknowledged her presence and unfortunately John took his cue from his father,' she said.

'So your hopes of a meaningful brother-sister relationship are a bit dented, I suspect?'

She grimaced. That part of the trip had not gone as well as she had hoped.

'You know, John is so much like his father even now,' she lamented. 'And I don't really think he understands how he has a sister older than him.'

131

With that, she turned the key in the ignition and pulled the gear stick into reverse.

'There's another piece of news you might be interested in,' she said quietly, hoping that her voice would not reach Paul in the back seat of the car.

'Oh, what would that be?'

'Jane and Tom Warner have split up, according to Alice.'

Julia glanced at him but his face was expressionless.

'When did this happen?' he asked without giving the appearance of any interest at all in the topic.

'Just before Christmas I believe,' Julia replied. 'I think she's staying in town with a friend Miss Pearl who's the local librarian. Alice heard she hopes to resume teaching. She was a governess as you'll recall.'

He smiled, remembering then that his sister did not know the full story.

'I remember,' was all he said.

Julia said nothing more, preferring to concentrate on negotiating the narrow exit from the carpark.

The corridors of the hospital were hot and airless, so Philippe went in search of a breeze in the hospital grounds. Robert Clarke too had gone in search of fresh air and increased his pace to join Philippe whom he had spotted a short distance ahead of him.

'I hear your afternoon surgery's been cancelled because the patient is too ill?' Robert said. It was a question rather than a statement.

'Yes, afraid so,' he said. 'Just a temporary problem but it was too late to bring forward anyone from tomorrow's list.'

Robert shrugged.

'It happens to all of us,' he said. 'Completely out of our control although the hospital hates empty theatres.'

Philippe nodded, acknowledging the truth of what Robert said but totally unconcerned by overzealous hospital administrators. He looked around him.

'Sometimes I wish there were fewer buildings and more greenery,' Philippe said. He loosened his tie and rolled up his shirtsleeves in an effort to cool down.

Robert Clarke nodded as he too loosened his tie.

'Quite frankly, I'd rather be at the cricket,' he said, as beads of perspiration formed across his cheeks. 'Benaud took five wickets in the first innings against the Poms.'

Then he laughed, seeing the look of total confusion on Philippe's face.

'Sorry,' he said sheepishly. 'I keep forgetting you're American and that cricket would be completely puzzling to you.'

Philippe laughed too. He had tried, and failed, to understand the rules of the game which seemed to go on endlessly.

'You're right there,' he said shaking his head in bewilderment. 'I'm afraid cricket's completely beyond me. Actually, I'm not very keen on team sports. I never had the time for them.'

'Me either except to watch a bit of cricket,' Robert agreed. 'I wouldn't risk anything that would damage my hands.'

He held his hands out in front of him, as if inspecting them for damage. Philippe was inclined to agree with him. A surgeon's hands were his lifeblood.

'I think that's wise, Robert,' he said. His own hands were thrust in his pockets as if for protection.

'But you must have a hobby of some kind?'

Robert was curious now. Their conversations to date had been either about work or to do with his private life. Apart from that, he did not know all that much about Philippe.

'I do have a hobby as a matter of fact,' he said. 'I haven't done much since I've been here in Sydney but this weekend I plan to get my camera out and set up my dark room again.'

'Photography's a good interest,' Robert said, with a slight nod of approval. 'You should ask Karen to arrange for you to go out on her father's boat around the harbour. You would get some really great shots then.'

It was Philippe's turn to smile.

'I don't think so,' he said in mock horror. 'I'm trying to stay clear of your brother since our little tête-à-tête after Christmas lunch.'

'Oh God, I'm sorry, I forgot about that.'

He could see Robert was cursing himself for having brought it up.

'There's no need to be sorry,' Philippe said, in an effort to reassure him. 'I told him I'm not romantically involved with his daughter. We are just friends. I don't think he realises she lost her older brother and she was close to him. Maybe I fill that void for her.'

The two men sat down side by side on a garden bench that had seen better days. A slight breeze had begun to stir.

'She was very close to her brother,' Robert said, after a pause. 'I think, looking back, with her father so preoccupied with his business and her mother caught up with her society friends, it was natural for Karen to turn to her brother for companionship. I can see how she might be drawn to you for that reason. But it would be hard to convince her father of it.'

The look on Philippe's face was more eloquent than any reply.

'I take it the quiet chat was as bad as I assumed it would be?'

'It was,' Philippe said, 'and I must say I was grateful for the warning.'

'In your position I would probably have punched him,' Robert said, forgetting for a moment his belief that a surgeon should protect his hands at all costs.

'I thought about it briefly but it would have been terrible for Karen,' he said, 'and not good for my hands. And it would probably have put paid to my career here in Sydney.'

Robert nodded. Philippe was right. It would not have been a solution.

Just as Robert had done earlier, Philippe held his hands in front of him and examined his long elegant fingers. He had learnt unarmed combat in the army, but only out of necessity and then only briefly. He was a healer, not a breaker, of people.

'I'd heard that Karen had some cross words with her father,' Robert said. 'My sister-in-law blamed me and my wife for having introduced you to her. Patricia didn't take a backward step, I'm pleased to say.'

Philippe laughed quietly. He was amused at the idea that anyone would think they could get the better of Robert's wife.

'I don't think your wife would be easy to intimidate,' Philippe said with admirable diplomacy.

'No,' Robert said, 'she isn't. Anyone would be foolish to try really.'

The two men smiled at the prospect. It was the first time they had really conversed man to man.

'For a time there, I thought you might have been interested in Karen,' Robert said, turning side on as he said it to gauge Philippe's reaction. Philippe in turn was cautious in his reply.

'You're right, Robert,' he said. 'I was very attracted to her. In fact, part of me still is but my heart belongs elsewhere.'

'With Miss Belleville I assume?'

Philippe nodded. But to him it was more complicated than that.

'I really like Karen,' he said. 'In the beginning I thought she was just another over privileged over indulged young woman but there's more to her than that.'

Robert was about to interrupt him but he thought better of it and let Philippe continue.

'She deserves an uncomplicated husband, not a divorcee with an illegitimate daughter and someone years older than her,' Philippe said. 'Someone she can build her own family with. I'm past that.'

Robert nodded, understanding and admiring the level of restraint Philippe had exercised. His respect for his younger colleague had grown immeasurably.

'I hope you and my brother did not part on bad terms,' he said. 'I hope my brother understood what you are telling me now.'

Philippe could see Robert was embarrassed that his brother should behave so badly.

'Oh, we parted amicably enough in the end,' Philippe said, 'but he is a hard man to convince so I thought I would stay out of his way. Anyway, Karen has gone away for a couple of weeks with her friend Bianca Ferrari.'

Robert grinned.

'Now there's a duo that could spell trouble for any man,' he declared, in spite of his deep affection for his niece.

Philippe laughed out loud, sharing Robert's assessment of the two young women.

'Perhaps they'll both find husbands while they're away,' he said. 'They've gone off to New Zealand.'

'Oh, no, not a Kiwi, please,' he said, with an exaggerated groan. 'I don't think I could stand the accent.'

Philippe laughed but he did wonder what was so funny about the New Zealand accent compared with the broad Australian twang he heard on a daily basis. He assumed it was just the natural rivalry of two closely-related countries.

'We nearly had Karen to the altar last year but she pulled out three months before the wedding,' Robert said. 'Turns out the bloke was an habitual drunk so that's a good thing.'

Philippe nodded. He'd already heard the story from Karen but he did not let on. Robert looked at his watch and sighed.

'I've got to go,' he said. 'A meeting with the finance committee.'

He pulled a face. He knew Philippe would sympathise. Neither man wanted to be a hospital administrator. Surgery was their business, not finance and administration.

Philippe watched him walk back to the main hospital building and then sat back on the garden bench luxuriating in the rare pleasure of free time.

Following Richard's departure, Catherine was at last able to relax. Having her estranged husband under her roof at Christmas time had proved to be every bit as bad as she had imagined, yet she could not find any reason to criticise his behaviour. It was his mere presence that had created the tension.

She sat alone in her study, watching the flurry of snowflakes drift to the ground outside. It had snowed constantly for a week and it was hard to go much beyond the house, except in Edward's Land Rover which had become almost a permanent fixture in the Haldon Hall driveway through Christmas and New Year and into the first weeks of January.

She heard a sharp knock on the door and looked up as the door opened.

'May I interrupt your work?'

Edward Cavendish had spent much of the morning entertaining six-year-old Anthony who had now been banished to the kitchen for his lunch.

'Thank you for taking care of Anthony this morning,' Catherine said. 'I just needed to deal with some of these matters to do with the estate.'

He sat down in the chair opposite her. He couldn't help but notice the frown on her face.

'Is something the matter?' he asked immediately concerned for anything that might be upsetting her. 'Perhaps I can help?'

She handed him the latest letter from her solicitor.

'Death duties,' she said simply. 'We've been discussing how best to fund them but there's no easy solution.'

He read the letter and let out a low whistle. The figure seemed astronomical. He could understand her concern at the impost on the estate.

'Your father did well to accumulate so many assets,' he said, 'but you are certainly going to pay a price for that now.'

He handed the letter back to her. She in turn tossed the letter on the desk in front of her and sat back in her chair.

'We've earmarked one or two less important assets to sell and we have some cash,' she said, 'but there will still be a shortfall.'

'Would it mean selling some of the land around Haldon Hall?' he asked, trying to mask the concern in his voice.

He thought it would be an extreme measure and one to be avoided at all costs but he waited to hear her reaction.

'No, I don't want to sell any of the farmland because the tenant farmers might be evicted,' she said firmly. 'You might remember I said we had two very good paintings. I'm thinking of letting them go.'

Edward nodded in agreement.

'I've heard it's possible to donate good paintings to the National Gallery and get a credit for their value,' Edward said. 'I could ask if that would help.'

'Would you do that for me?' she asked.

So far, she had never asked him to help her at all but there had been many times when she wished she could hand over some of the more difficult issues.

'Of course, I would. No trouble at all to do it for you, my darling,' he said. 'You only have to ask. I'm at your service.'

She relaxed then. He only ever used terms of endearment when they were alone together. He was very much aware that she was still married to another man. For her part, she welcomed his self-control.

She was a married woman with two young children not a girl in the first flush of passion. And appearances mattered to her. She did not want to think of the staff at Haldon Hall gossiping about them behind their backs.

'You were very well behaved when my husband was here,' she said, with just the hint of a secret smile.

For once he was almost at a loss for words, unsure how to respond, unsure what she expected him to say. Finally, he answered.

'I'm pleased you thought so,' he said. 'If Richard knows about us then I have to say he was the model of restraint. I fully expected to come away with a black eye and bloody nose.'

She laughed at this idea. She too had thought it a possibility.

'I'm pleased you were both so well behaved,' she said, almost as if she was talking about her children.

He smiled. He looked forward to the day when she was free of Richard Belleville but would that ever really be the case, he wondered.

'I take it we'll see something of him in the future until the children are grown up?'

She shrugged. It was something they had hardly discussed at all.

'I expect so, although I plan to go out to Sydney mid-year to see Paul.'

He thought about this for a moment.

'You know it won't be as easy to take Anthony with you when he gets older,' he said. 'The schools here have a hard line policy on unscheduled absences I'm afraid.'

She nodded, well aware of the difficulties she and Richard faced in the coming years. There was no easy answer for parents twelve thousand miles apart who wanted to share custody of their children. She remembered then that it had been Edward who had sought her out.

'When you came in just now, I thought there was something you wanted to see me about?'

He smiled and held up an envelope. She could not see what was so important about it.

'My dear Catherine,' he said, 'I plan to take you away from all the cold and snow for a week of sunshine.'

He had hinted at a surprise days ago. Her mood brightened.

'Where are we going?' she asked.

It was certainly abroad. There was nowhere in England that boasted warm sunshine in January.

'We are going to the Caribbean,' he said. 'To a wonderful place I know in Montego Bay.'

Before she could ask, he added.

'Just the two of us.'

All thoughts of the business matters she had been preoccupied with moments before were brushed aside as she peppered him with questions about their forthcoming trip.

Chapter 14

April 1959

Catherine stood looking out of the window at the street below and beyond to Hyde Park where the green shoots of spring were beginning to emerge. She noticed the famous plane tree in the hotel gardens was also sparking back to life with its new spring growth. She sighed and turned away from the window.

Just for a moment she had been transported back nearly fourteen years. It had been a month after victory in Europe had been declared and she and Richard had consummated their relationship in this very hotel. She remembered having imitated her mother's voice in the telephone call to book the hotel room.

A few months later, with her pregnancy hardly showing, she had married him without her parents' knowledge and borne their son in Australia the following February. Now she was negotiating their divorce.

Yet a part of her still yearned for the love they had once had. She had been angry at his casual infidelity but she could see in her rational moments her despondency with living at Prior Park might have driven him to it. If he had agreed to live in England, she would have put it behind her but for him that was always an impossible choice. She never got the chance to say, 'but I lived in Australia for more than a decade' to point to his unfairness. Now her marriage was almost over and it felt like her life had come full circle.

She glanced across at the crumpled bed. Edward had returned to his own room in the early morning hours. Was he practised at such subterfuge, she wondered? She knew he had travelled to many exotic places with his Foreign Office work. She was not naïve enough to imagine he had been alone every night.

And yet with her, he had been restrained. Until their trip to the Caribbean. The warmth of the sun, a moonlight stroll along the beach and the soft lapping of the waves on the sand had proved to be the perfect romantic backdrop he had hoped it would be.

He had begun to make love to her on their first evening together and she had not resisted. He had shared her bed each night after that, luxuriating in his conquest of the woman he had long coveted but thought out of reach.

As they sat at dinner on their last night, he had produced a small box which he urged her to open. Nestled inside was a beautiful solitaire diamond ring. She slipped it on her finger, admiring it but removing it quickly. He lent across and kissed her, oblivious to the other diners.

'I hope you will be able to wear that publicly very soon,' he had said.

On their return home, they had resumed their separate lives thinking that no one would detect any change in their relationship.

He had not yet given up his work with the Foreign Office so she saw little of him except for the occasional weekend. In public they kept up the pretence of friendship through kinship. They were both keen to avoid public scandal even as he made light of the necessity of keeping their relationship secret.

She poured herself a second cup of tea and scraped marmalade onto a piece of toast. She looked at her watch. There was still plenty of time before she needed to dress.

Edward had arranged for a car to call for them mid-morning to take them to the National Gallery where she would officially hand over the two J M W Turner paintings from her father's estate as part payment of death duties.

She was sad to relinquish the paintings but it had solved a problem for her. She had been grateful for Edward's intervention. His network of contacts seemed to extend into all corners of London life.

Suddenly, a wave of nausea forced her to sit down abruptly. She sat very still and tried to quell the overwhelming urge to throw up. She tried to regulate her breathing. After a few minutes sitting quietly, the worst of it passed.

But she knew immediately what the nausea meant. She remembered the symptoms so vividly. As careful as they had been, they had not been careful enough. History was about to repeat itself except now she was in a panic.

Her first thought was to wonder how she could hasten her divorce, knowing that she must now marry Edward as quickly as possible. She could not pass off this child as Richard's, could she? She shook her head, although there was no one with her to see. He would never agree.

She got up and went into the bathroom to bathe her face. How would she break the news to Edward? And how would he react? With pleasure or with consternation? She realised she did not yet know him well enough to predict his reaction.

She covered her pale face with makeup and added the brightest lipstick she had brought with her. Then slowly she began to dress, desperately trying to ignore each new wave of nausea as it threatened to engulf her.

Edward slipped into the back seat of the car alongside her and directed the driver to return to the Dorchester. They both turned to wave goodbye to the Gallery director who had escorted them to the door.

'That went well,' he said, 'although I noticed how pale you looked. Are you unwell?'

She turned towards him, worried by the concern in his voice. What could she say? Their conversation could hardly be private.

'I'm fine,' she said but she could see he was not convinced.

'Are you sure?' he said.

She nodded her head and then held her finger to her lips in a gesture he immediately understood so he changed the subject.

'I was reading in this morning's paper that the executors of the second Duke of Westminster's estate have listed for sale most of the remaining part of the Melton Constable estate to meet further death duties,' he said, 'so don't feel so bad about having to give up two paintings and some minor assets. It could be worse.'

She smiled. It was true that the death duties which at first had seemed like a major impost proved to be more easily satisfied than she had at first thought.

'I thought you might have been interested in the snippet about the lunch given for the Foreign Minister of France at Carlton Gardens,' she countered. 'Isn't the MP Selwyn Lloyd who hosted it your ultimate boss? I'm surprised you weren't there.'

It was his turn to smile.

'I don't quite rate highly enough in diplomatic circles to warrant an invitation to an event like that,' he said. 'Besides I told them this week that my Foreign Office career was coming to an end. I'd like to think they were disappointed but they accepted it with polite expressions of regret.'

It was her turn to be surprised.

'You hadn't talked about the possibility of giving it up for a while,' she said quietly. 'I thought perhaps you had changed your mind or it had simply been your mother's idea.'

He did not answer immediately but instead pointed to the hectic pace of the city around them.

'You're right, it was initially my mother's idea,' he said, as the car came to a halt in front of the hotel, 'but I've grown tired of city life, knowing that I have another option.'

He helped her out of the car and together they walked up the few steps into the hotel foyer.

'Shall we have a coffee?' he asked, as he guided her towards the café.

He chose a secluded booth on the far wall, somewhere away from prying eyes where they could talk in private.

'So what is it that you couldn't say in the car?' he asked, as he slid into the seat opposite her.

She was silent for a few moments and then looked up at him. She would have preferred to say what she had to say in private but she had been taken unawares by his solicitude.

'I think I'm pregnant,' she said uncertainly. 'In fact, I know I'm pregnant.'

She waited for his reaction. He was smiling broadly.

'That's wonderful news,' he said. 'A little sooner than I had hoped, but it's wonderful news.'

She laughed quietly then.

'You seem to forget,' she said, 'there's the small matter of me being married to another man.'

But he hadn't forgotten.

'When do you think the baby will be due?'

She had already done her calculations.

'Mid November I would think,' she replied.

'Then we must get your divorce finalised by July at the latest,' he said.

He could have added, 'I don't want our baby born while you are still married to Richard' but he didn't and she was grateful for that. A baby born just a few months after they were married would be gossiped about for a month or so and then forgotten but a child born before they married would be a Belleville.

'I take it your local man is dealing with the divorce?' he asked, referring to Maurice Langton whom he had met a couple of times.

'Yes,' she said. 'I thought he could handle it.'

He shook his head.

'Perhaps not now with so much urgency.'

'What do you suggest?'

But he would not be drawn immediately into an answer.

'Let me ask around,' he said. 'That boss of mine you were referring to divorced his wife, or should I say she divorced him, a couple of years ago without much fuss. I'll find out who handled it.'

Catherine was shocked.

'You can't just call him up and ask, 'who handled your divorce', can you?'

He laughed. He could see she was quite unversed in the ways of the diplomatic world.

'No, of course I can't,' he said, smiling across the table at her, 'but I can invite his private secretary to my club for a drink. I'm sure he'll have a recommendation for me as to which firm to use and be discreet about it.'

'I hope so,' she said, now that he had raised doubts about her own solicitor's ability to progress the matter urgently.

'It will be fine,' he said, with a confidence she did not feel.

John Bertram stopped briefly to admire the garden that surrounded Richard's home and greet the gardener who was hard at work clipping the already immaculate hedges.

'Looks like you take a lot of pride in your work,' he said, nodding towards the wide expanse of freshly mown lawn and the neatly kept flower beds.

The man beamed. Compliments were rare but welcome nonetheless.

But it was Richard who answered having appeared at the top of the stairs that led up to the wide front verandah.

'I didn't think you were a gardening man, John,' he said, shaking his hand vigorously. 'I didn't expect you today. I thought you were coming tomorrow.'

'Yes, that was the original plan,' he said, returning his friend's warm greeting, 'but it turned out there was a seat on the plane today after all, so I grabbed it.'

'You should have called me from the aerodrome,' Richard said. 'I could have come and picked you up.'

'No need,' he said, as Richard ushered him inside, 'the crew were staying over in town, so I got them to divert past your place.'

Richard pointed him to a spare bedroom, one of several in the large house.

'My housekeeper has made up this room for you,' he said. 'It's on the coolest side of the house or at least away from the western sun.'

John dropped his small bag in the room and the two men headed towards the kitchen. He sat down at the kitchen table while Richard went about the unfamiliar ritual of making tea.

'Your housekeeper not here today?' John asked, surprised at Richard's willingness to perform such a domestic task.

'No,' he said, laughing at his friend's presumption that he was useless in the kitchen. 'I share my housekeeper Mrs Freestone with my sister Julia. She's at Julia's today.'

'But not your gardener?' John asked.

'Bert goes to my sister's place once a week or so but we let him make his own mind up about when he feels he needs to go there.'

John smiled. He thought Richard Belleville was probably the most easy going of men to work for.

'I hope you're here for a few days, John?' Richard asked.

His friend nodded in reply.

'Yes, I have the rest of the week off, then it's back on the Sydney-London route.'

'Do you ever get tired of flying?'

His friend had been working as a pilot since qualifying after the war.

'No,' John answered emphatically. 'I never get tired of flying or the excitement of new aircraft coming into service.'

He sipped the hot tea appreciatively. Flying from Sydney to Springfield meant a change in Brisbane which made the journey feel much longer.

'God, I envy you, John,' Richard said suddenly. 'It's too late now for me to take up flying again. I wish I'd never let it go after the war.'

Richard had been an excellent pilot. Yet he had told no one of his Distinguished Flying Cross, awarded for an outstanding act of valour in returning his stricken Lancaster bomber to the airfield and saving all his crew. But John knew, of course, because John had been his navigator.

His friend looked up suddenly.

To John, Richard had everything, well almost everything. He was wealthy, he had married Catherine, the woman John had loved from afar and he was the father to two healthy sons. By comparison, I live like an itinerant, John thought.

No wife, a lonely flat in Sydney, a series of anonymous hotel rooms on the various flight stages from Sydney to London and return. But he loved it all the same. He was proud that the airline he worked for had been the first airline outside the United States to enter the jet age with the introduction of the Boeing 707.

'Feeling sorry for yourself then?' John asked, with just a hint of concern. 'It must be a sign of advancing years.'

Richard grimaced. It was an unnecessary reminder they must both soon face the prospect of turning forty.

'You said you had something for me,' Richard said, changing the subject.

'I do,' John said. 'I saw Catherine last week in London. She asked me to give you this.'

'How is she?' Richard asked as he inspected the large envelope and noticed an unfamiliar firm of solicitors as the sender.

'She's well,' John lied. 'But anxious to have this divorce wrapped up if you'll help her out.'

He was uncomfortable acting as a messenger between the two people he cared about most but Catherine had pleaded with him that she desperately needed to finalise the divorce. He hadn't asked why but he had guessed. What makes a divorce desperately needed when it had, a month or so ago, been something that could take its course, he asked himself. There had been only one answer and her pale face and nervousness had confirmed it.

The two of them sat in silence for a while as Richard read through the documents. She was asking him to admit to adultery? He couldn't deny the facts as they were presented to him but he hated the necessity of exposing his private life in such a manner. The fact that it was all happening in a court on the other side of the world was the only reason he agreed.

'I think I need to witness that, old boy,' John said, pleased that he had escaped a deeper interrogation.

Richard pushed the documents across to him. John pulled his fountain pen out of his pocket and he began signing each page. There was a long silence between the two men as they each contemplated the end of a marriage in which they had both played a part.

John was remembering how he had stood beside Richard in the small village church when the two had married at the end of the war, Catherine already pregnant with Paul. Later, he had listened to Catherine's lament over her disappointment of life in Australia and then finally listened patiently to both as the final break loomed and divorce became inevitable. No one had ever guessed what it had cost him to listen to the intimate details of Richard's and Catherine's lives.

He was jolted out of his reverie as Richard began to return the documents to the envelope.

'We've only talked about me, John,' Richard said, in an attempt to lighten the mood. 'Maybe there's a Mrs Bertram in the wind I don't know about?'

'Ah, the life of an aviation tragic is not good for relationships,' he said laughingly.

They both turned at the sound of footsteps coming along the central hallway that led to the kitchen.

Thirteen-year-old Paul Belleville, his tie askew and his shirt parting company with his shorts, dumped his school bag near the kitchen table and headed directly for the refrigerator.

His father immediately interrupted this afternoon ritual.

'Don't you think you should say hello to our visitor first?' Richard asked, quietly frustrated by his son's lack of manners.

'Sorry, Dad,' he said, his voice contrite.

'Hello Uncle John,' he said, using the familiar form of address he had adopted in childhood.

'Hello Paul,' John said. He would have recognised the boy anywhere as Richard's son. 'How was school today?'

Now that he had turned to face them, both he and Richard could not help but notice the slight bruising on the boy's face. Before they could ask what happened, he volunteered the answer.

'Got into a fight,' he said, with unusual frankness.

His father was immediately concerned, although it was hardly an uncommon occurrence for boys to resort to fighting to settle their differences.

'What was the fight about?' Richard asked his son. 'It's better to walk away sometimes you know.'

But the young boy shook his head.

'I couldn't walk away from this one,' he said, his voice suddenly mature and decisive.

They waited for him to explain.

'Some boys were taunting my cousin John over his sister and saying awful things about Aunt Julia,' he explained. 'I heard it as I was coming out of the school gates and a group of boys were following John. I got a couple of mates together and we sorted them out.'

For a moment Richard didn't know whether to admonish his son for fighting or applaud him for coming to the aid of his younger cousin. But John Bertram chimed in.

'Well done, lad,' he said, nodding approval. 'It's good to stand up to bullies.'

'Apparently it's been going on for a while,' he said, 'John's been copping it and not saying anything. He's younger than me so I don't see that much of him at school. It was just today that class got out a bit later.'

'Should we tell Aunt Julia?' his father asked. He was reluctant to bring it up with the boy's father. He was uncertain what sort of reception he would get.

But Paul shook his head.

'I'll keep an eye on him and I'll let Marianne know to look out for him.'

Richard was concerned about involving Marianne. Would the boys be more respectful around a girl? He wasn't sure.

'Are you sure you want to involve Marianne?' his father said. 'We don't want the boys bullying her.'

Paul looked at his father in surprise.

'You don't know Marianne very well, do you?' he said with a sigh that implied adults know nothing.

'With a few words and one of her looks, she'd reduce that lot to a bunch of blithering idiots,' Paul said, with a candour that took Richard completely by surprise.

This time they couldn't help it. Both Richard and John burst out laughing, leaving Paul looking puzzled and slightly affronted.

CHAPTER 15

December 1959

Anthony Belleville, now tall enough to inspect the infant sleeping in his mother's arms, was experiencing mixed feelings about the changes in his life. It had been nearly a year since he had seen his father and his older brother.

His family now, his mother had said, was her and Uncle Edward, who had come to live with them, and his grandmother Lady Marina. And, of course, the new baby. His new baby brother.

But he missed being the centre of his mother's world. He understood why she was busy with the new baby and her new life and had less time for him, but it meant he missed his father all the more only he could not tell her that.

He pretended he had not overheard the whispered conversations that it was nearly time for him to go away to school. He immediately thought if he had to go away to school perhaps they would let him go back to his father in Australia.

His memory of life in Australia was fading but he remembered the warmth of the sun and the landscape. And the big house. Not as big as Haldon Hall, which his mother had inherited, but grand all the same.

He had mourned its loss in his childish way for it was not just a loss but a complete loss. His mother had explained the terrible fire to him but not how the fire had started. Yet he wanted desperately to return. He did not want to lose the memories of his early childhood, yet he was afraid he would.

But none of this could he tell his mother, especially on this special day, as she cradled the new baby in her arms. He stood to one side as adults jostled to admire his new brother, who had woken just at the moment the drops of cold water from the baptismal font had trickled down his forehead.

'George Edward Nicholas Cavendish, I baptise thee in the name of the Father, the Son and the Holy ....'

It was then that baby George voiced his disapproval at all the strange fuss engulfing him and let out an almighty wail to the consternation of the small congregation but to the delight of his older brother, who started to giggle until he was silenced by a stern look from his grandmother.

Lady Marina Cavendish was uncharacteristically indulgent of her young grandson but not on this occasion.

Anthony Belleville did not yet know it but he was about to be usurped in the affections of his grandmother who saw, not a red-faced squalling infant in the arms of her daughter, but the future Sir George Cavendish, the fifth baronet.

Lady Marina had never said as much but in her demeanour were the signs, for those who cared to look, of quiet satisfaction at seeing her daughter appropriately married – to the man who had inherited her father's title. Catherine's thirteen years in the wilderness, as Lady Marina might have described her life in Australia, were best forgotten, or if not forgotten, then not spoken of, except for the children, Paul and Anthony.

Lady Marina noticed letters arriving regularly for her daughter from the thirteen-year-old Paul Belleville. She noticed too that his father Richard no longer wrote to his ex-wife except on very rare occasions, and then probably only when he felt compelled to comment on their older son's progress.

As the small party moved out of the protection of the church and headed the short distance back towards Haldon Hall, a bitter wind sprang up, causing Catherine to hold the baby closer to her body for protection.

Edward, now possessed of all he desired, smiled solicitously at his wife and child. He had hardly dared hope that this day would come. When he had first met Catherine years earlier, she had been Mrs Richard Belleville and seemed likely to remain so.

Yet he had fallen completely and hopelessly in love with her.

It was the unexpected outcome of her father's death – Catherine being his major beneficiary – that had seen Catherine return to England permanently. But he knew there had been more to the breakdown of her marriage than her need to be in England more frequently. He had not expected to be able to compete with the war hero that Richard Belleville had been but, in the end, life in Australia had not suited Catherine and her growing disenchantment had seen her husband look elsewhere. That much he had gleaned in the scant details Catherine had revealed.

Suddenly, he noticed his mother Louise at the edge of the group. Reassured that Catherine was coping with the baby, he put a protective arm around his mother. She looked up at him and smiled.

'It's a wonderful day, isn't it?' she whispered to him.

'It is a wonderful day, Mother,' he said, nodding in agreement.

'And you have an heir,' she said, as if she had still not recovered from the surprise of Catherine being able to bear a child in her late thirties.

'And I have an heir,' he said, again repeating his mother's words.

He could see she was happy.

'You broke a lot of hearts you know when you announced your intention to marry Catherine.'

He smiled and shook his head, unwilling to endorse his mother's opinion on his marriageability.

'I don't think so, Mother. I didn't see too many weeping damsels at the parties I attended.'

But his mother was not to be dissuaded.

'It wasn't the girls who were weeping,' she said. 'It was their mothers. Eligible men are few and far between these days. And you were seen as quite a catch having inherited the baronetcy.'

But he remained unconvinced.

'I have a beautiful wife and now a beautiful son,' he said. There was more than a hint of satisfaction in his tone.

Just then the heavy door of Haldon Hall opened. The household staff, of which there were fewer than in the pre-war years, lined the impressive hallway to welcome the family and their guests.

Evans, who had recently replaced the family's long-serving butler, was keen to make a good impression. His eagle eye could spot even a minor indiscretion by a member of the household staff, so all the staff stood stiffly to attention and followed his lead.

'Was it a good service, Lady Cavendish?' he enquired, although he did not expect a response.

'Very good, thank you, Evans,' Catherine said in response, 'although Master George did make himself known to the entire church.'

She smiled at the memory. She marvelled at the thought she had now borne three sons. She privately hoped there would be no more. She knew she had defied her mother's expectation that she was too old to bear Edward an heir. But against the odds she had done so and now her mother was satisfied.

Her mother, exercising unaccustomed tact, had never referred to the short time between her daughter's wedding in early August and the baby's birth in mid-November. She was simply satisfied the baronetcy would not die with Edward.

Just then a small figure moved close to her. She put her arm around him in a motherly gesture.

'I must not neglect Anthony,' she reminded herself quietly.

She was well aware of the fuss being made about George. Fleetingly she wondered how, in later years, she would explain it all to Anthony.

How would she explain in future years when they were both grown up that the bulk of her wealth would be claimed by her youngest son? After all, George was a Cavendish and he naturally must inherit Haldon Hall not to mention Grantham Manor. But that was a problem for another day.

It was a little over a week later that Richard Belleville sat silently opposite John Bertram and heard sketchy details of the christening party for the baby George.

'I wonder if she will have time for Anthony now?' Richard said, voicing aloud the very same thoughts that had occurred to his friend.

But John was ever loyal. He spoke quickly in Catherine's defence.

'I'm sure she will have time for him,' he said, in a soothing tone. 'She's devoted to the boy.'

But Richard was not so easily placated. He worried about his younger son constantly.

'They will probably want to send him away to some stuffy English boarding school now there's a new baby to look after,' Richard said, as he downed his second glass of cold beer.

It was a hot December day in Sydney. From their vantage point, the two men could see the glistening harbour and the flotilla of small boats drifting languidly in the light breeze. Beyond the harbour, the city shops were busy with the Saturday morning crowd, swelled by the approaching festive season. Christmas decorations festooned every public facade.

John turned back from admiring the view across the hotel's garden terrace. The harbour was a beautiful thing but how much better it looked from the air, he thought.

He knew he must respond to Richard with an honest reply.

'Yes, it's possible they'll send him off to boarding school,' John admitted, knowing full well the pattern of life in upper class English families.

His voice brightened.

'Maybe you could suggest he comes back home to you and goes to school with Paul?'

Richard sat back in his chair, arms clasped behind his head.

'I thought about that,' he said. 'Paul's certainly doing well since he came back to live with me. It would be good for the boys to be together.'

It seemed a logical move to John, but he wondered how Catherine would react.

'Did Catherine object when you took Paul out of school in Sydney?'

He could not recall his friend mentioning her reaction.

'She was a bit put out but I got Paul to write to her explaining that he preferred it,' Richard said, remembering the tense exchange. 'I think that settled it and then of course she had other things on her mind.'

John nodded, well aware that Catherine's preoccupation during the year had been securing a divorce so she could marry Edward before the arrival of her baby. Everything else in her life had been rendered less important.

'And what's Paul going to do after he finishes school?'

Richard shrugged.

'He's only thirteen, John,' Richard said, 'I guess we will figure that out later on.'

'University in England?'

'Not if I have any say in it,' Richard said, shaking his head determinedly. 'I have one son being brought up 12,000 miles away. I'm not going to agree to Paul going across to England to university. There are plenty of good universities here at home.'

'Talking of 12,000 miles away, it must be time you and Paul went across to see Anthony?' John said. 'I am sure Paul is missing his mother too.'

He had been surprised that nearly a year had elapsed since Richard had seen his younger son. Richard nodded, his face clouded with anxiety, the pain of separation obvious.

'It is time we went,' he admitted. 'I was keeping clear while the divorce was being finalised. Then the new marriage happened. And I found I had no stomach for seeing my former wife pregnant to another man.'

'I guess you came to understand the reason for the sudden rush for the divorce to be finalised,' John said, regretting the words almost as soon as he had said them.

Richard looked at him searchingly.

'I did indeed,' he said. 'When you brought those papers over for me, did you know her condition then?'

John shook his head, relieved he didn't have to lie. No one had told him outright of Catherine's condition, although he had guessed.

'No, I didn't know about the baby,' he said, 'but I thought it was strange that she was suddenly so anxious about the divorce, but she didn't tell me why.'

Richard smiled, accepting his friend's explanation but doubting his denial all the same.

'Well, it doesn't matter now,' Richard said as he stood and pushed back his chair. 'Let's go into the restaurant and have some lunch. I'm starving.'

A quarter of an hour later, Richard looked on with approval as a satisfyingly large T bone steak was put in front of him. He began to attack it with relish.

In another part of Sydney, Julia and Philippe were enjoying an altogether different lunch, this time without Pippa.

They too had a great view of the harbour the blue waters of which were just a matter of yards from their outdoor table. A small strip of beach was all that separated them from the water. A neat line of upturned wooden dinghies lay drying in the sun.

Philippe waited while the waitress took their orders before he spoke.

'Do you realise it's more than two years since we met again?'

She smiled and nodded. The anniversary had not escaped her notice either, yet so much had happened since that day.

'Sometimes you know it seems like a lifetime ago that I saw you in the hotel dining room,' she said, recalling the scene with terrible clarity.

She shook her head then, in disbelief at the improbability of the encounter.

'Imagine if either of us had made different arrangements on that day?' she said. 'We would never have met again.'

Such an idea was unthinkable to her now but how easy might it have been, she thought, to have been in the same hotel and not meet one another.

He turned to look out over the harbour. He had been in Sydney well over a year now and he had come to know – and love – the city, especially on days when the sun was high in the sky and the magnificent harbour seemed to stretch out for miles in every direction.

But he did not tell her how he had come to know of the restaurant in the charming little bay on the southern side of the harbour. Inwardly he smiled at the memory.

Had Karen been serious about her desire to marry him or was it just a whim that struck her at the time? As they had sailed past on a friend's boat, she had pointed to an old stone church sitting high above the harbour and above the restaurant.

'That's where I plan to get married,' she had said jokingly but when he had turned towards her, he had seen the serious look in her eyes. 'That is, when you finally ask me,' she had added, with the hint of a smile teasing her lips.

He remembered how he had been caught entirely off guard by her words. How could he answer her, he had wondered, without hurting her feelings? Had he encouraged her too much with his attentive friendship and in doing so convinced her he was in love with her? Or had she convinced herself she was in love with him?

As they had stood side by side leaning on the railing and watching the scene glide by, he had tried to find the right words to let her down gently and then one of her friends had intervened and the moment was lost. But the question remained unanswered between them.

He turned back towards Julia and reached across the table to take her hand. In the period since they had met again, he had begun to realise their focus had been almost completely on Pippa and their involvement in her life.

He had begun to feel as if his life was in limbo. He wanted desperately to know if she felt the same way? Did she still feel the same way about him that she had all those years ago?

'Will we still be doing this in another two years' time?' he ventured.

She looked at him with a slightly puzzled expression.

'Doing what?' she asked.

She wanted to be sure she understood what he meant.

'Meeting occasionally like this when you come to Sydney, seeing our daughter together but not making any commitment to each other,' he replied.

'Meeting only as friends,' he added.

There, he had said it. Deep down, he wondered if he was growing tired of life as a single man. Yet he hesitated. When he had married in New York, he had found it impossible to put his first love out of his mind. And so, his marriage had failed just as he thought it would. Did he now have a second chance at happiness with Julia? Or was it all too late? Had he been holding on to an impossible dream?

For a few moments, Julia felt like a young girl again, being swept off her feet by the charming American doctor who had come to her aid all those years ago. But at thirty-five she no longer felt quite so carefree. She looked away from him towards the harbour. She hesitated, suddenly unsure of what to say.

'I understand what you mean,' she said as turned back to face him. 'There are times when I feel as if I don't know where my life is going or where I belong.'

What else could she say? As a mother she did not want to fail either of her children but it would be impossible to be with both of them. As a woman she wanted a life, a proper life, a fulfilling life.

Philippe smiled, understanding her uncertainty and the dilemma she faced.

'When your divorce is finalised, will you marry me?'

There, he had said it. There was no going back now.

Why am I hesitating, she wondered? Isn't this what I've been dreaming of all along? She smiled and then relaxed.

'Of course, I'll marry you, Philippe,' she said.

The words echoed in her mind. If only she could have said them sixteen years ago, how much simpler life would have been. He smiled and reached across the table to kiss her.

'I was worried there for a moment that you were going to turn me down,' he said teasingly, as if there had never been in any doubt in his mind he was going to ask her to marry him.

But she laughed and shook her head.

'No, of course I wasn't going to turn you down,' she said, as if there had never been any doubt in her mind about her answer.

'It's only that we have lives at different ends of the country that made me hesitate.'

Philippe nodded, aware that it was a hurdle to be overcome.

'I'm happy for your son to live with us,' Philippe said.

He had never met the boy but it seemed logical to make the offer. She shook her head.

'I can't imagine his father agreeing to that,' she said. 'Besides he needs to be brought up on Mayfield Downs which he'll inherit one day. I can go up and stay with Alice and William anytime and see him.'

He nodded. It seemed like a sensible solution. He had sensed that the boy was closer to his father than his mother.

'And Pippa?' he asked. 'When shall we tell Pippa?'

Julia considered the question for a few moments.

'I don't think we should tell her until school breaks up for the year,' she said.

They both knew how delighted she would be and how desperate she would be to tell her friends.

'Good idea,' he replied. 'I would rather tell Robert Clarke myself than have him hear the news from his gossiping daughter.'

But it solved another problem for Philippe.

It would give him the chance to tell Karen himself. He did not want her to find out the news via the expanding web of gossip that would spread once it became known he was to marry. No, he decided, the news must come from him.

'I think we should drink to our future and a winter wedding,' he said.

He signalled to the waitress and ordered champagne to celebrate the moment.

CHAPTER 16

December 1959

A week after he had proposed to Julia and a matter of days after she had returned home to Springfield, Philippe was intent on keeping his promise to escort Karen to her friend Bianca's Christmas party. He was running late as he pulled up outside her home so he quickly opened the door of his car and was about to get out only to be met by her father whose booming voice greeted him.

'Duval, it's you again,' he said. 'I thought I'd made it clear you should stay away from my daughter, but you seem to be hanging around a lot lately. You're not getting the message, are you?'

Philippe cursed the fact he hadn't noticed that Karen's father had just pulled into his own driveway opposite. But David Clarke had noticed his car.

'Good evening, Mr Clarke,' Philippe said politely, although it appeared as if the man was in no mood for an exchange of pleasantries.

'As a matter of fact, I promised weeks ago to escort Karen to Bianca's Christmas party,' he said, struggling to keep the anger out of his voice. 'As I've said previously, we're just friends. When she doesn't have a suitable escort, I step in to help her out.'

It was clear though that David Clarke was a hard man to convince.

'Which probably means any other eligible bloke who's there is going to be put off by you being at her side,' he said pointedly.

Philippe shrugged. He'd heard of one or two other young men who had partnered Karen recently, but he was not about to use this as a defence.

David Clarke turned and was about to walk off but he paused mid-stride, as if remembering something important. He turned back towards Philippe.

'You seem very sure my daughter sees you only as a friend,' he said.

'I believe so,' Philippe replied, despite his own doubts.

'According to my wife, Karen has been seen in the bridal shop at Double Bay recently,' he said, with genuine concern. 'She had it from a friend of hers who was thinking a happy announcement was imminent.'

Philippe shook his head. It seemed a flimsy piece of evidence to back up his assertion that his daughter was in love.

'Perhaps a girlfriend is getting married and she was helping out?'

He offered this by way of explanation. He did not think it signified anything important.

It was David Clarke's turn to shrug his shoulders.

'Perhaps, but I thought my wife would know if that was the case.'

It seemed a fair point but Philippe thought that Karen was now at an age when she might not share everything with her mother. He tried a different tack to distract her father.

'You know she told me last time I saw her that she's found her time with you this year learning about your business very interesting,' he said, hoping that this would end the discussion of marriage.

'I think she has,' her father said, not displeased with the observation. 'She has good instincts although she wouldn't be suited to the nine to five grind more the boardroom, I think.'

Philippe smiled at this description. He thought there would be some daytime social events she would be reluctant to miss. Her working week would need to be very flexible, he thought.

'I'd better go and see if she is ready,' Philippe said, hoping that was the end of the matter.

It was clear to him that David Clarke had calmed down and the two men walked across the road and began to climb the stairs leading to the front door.

'You really have no need to worry,' Philippe said finally, deciding then to share his big news.

'I should tell you that Julia Belleville has accepted my proposal and we will marry next year as soon as her divorce is through. I wanted to tell Karen, though, before it became widely known.'

David Clarke's attitude towards him changed in an instant. He shook Philippe vigorously by the hand and slapped his back awkwardly.

'That's good news, Duval,' he said, smiling broadly. 'I wish you all the best. I really do. That's the right thing to do, marry the mother of your child, even if it's a bit late in the day.'

Philippe smiled. He could see the relief spread across the older man's face. It was as if he had just achieved a personal triumph in seeing off an unsuitable suitor for his daughter.

'But break it gently to my daughter,' he said, as an afterthought. 'She might be a little bit upset. You never know.'

He sighed happily. He had no need to worry now. He would cast his net widely for a son-in-law among the sons of his friends and acquaintances. Perhaps even Bianca Ferrari's brother, who had just returned from a year in America? I must check him out, he thought, as Karen came down the front steps to greet Philippe. She gave her father a quick hug as she passed him on the stairs.

'You two seem to be getting along better,' she said as she slipped her arm through Philippe's and they headed towards his car. 'My father was positively beaming.'

Philippe took a deep breath as they walked across the road. Would there ever be a better time to tell her?

'Let's walk down towards the harbour,' he said softly. 'It's such a lovely night and I have something important to tell you.'

She fell into step alongside him. They walked in silence until they reached the water's edge.

'What is it you have to tell me?' she asked anxiously.

They stood together looking out over the darkening water. Here and there the lights of a moored boat brightened the fading light.

'I wanted to tell you,' he said quietly, 'that I'm going to marry Julia Belleville next year when her divorce is finalised. I have asked her and she has accepted me.'

In the twilight he could not see her face clearly. She stepped away from him as if to create some distance between them and turned away from him. The only sound was the gentle lapping of the water against the rocks that edged the harbour.

'Is that why my father appeared so happy just now?' she asked, turning to face him.

It was suddenly clear to her why her father had appeared to be so happy. Philippe had told him the news of his impending marriage. For Karen, it was all falling into place. She knew her father had never considered Philippe a suitable candidate to be her husband. Philippe could do nothing but confirm her suspicions.

'Your father was always warning me to stay away from you,' he said, 'but I always insisted we were just friends. When I told him this evening I was getting married, I could see the news came as a great relief to him.'

He smiled hoping she would share his amusement at her father's sudden change of mood. He could just make out her face in the light from the street lamps but he was not sure how she was taking the news.

And then she spoke.

'I suppose it never occurred to him that it was my decision, not his, as to who I thought would be the right husband for me,' she lamented. 'He thoroughly approved of my previous fiancé until I discovered what a hopeless drunkard he was. He was rich, that's all my father cared about.'

Philippe felt he had to say something.

'I'm sure he cares a great deal about your happiness,' he said. He could see how much David Clarke doted on his daughter.

'In his own way, I suppose he does,' she said, 'but he is more concerned with me having children, grandsons anyway, who he can draw into his world. He says if he doesn't have another generation to work for, it will have all been for nothing.'

'And so he wants you to have a young husband,' Philippe said, 'not an old man like me. Is there anything wrong with that?'

She laughed then.

'I don't think of you as old, Philippe,' she said. 'But you are right, he wants me to marry someone my own age. Except I'm not in love with anyone my own age.'

He thought he caught the sound of her sobbing but he could not be sure. It was not going well. Have I misread her all this time, he wondered?

'I'm sorry if the news of my marriage is a shock to you,' he said, trying to choose his words carefully.

He could have said 'if it wasn't for Julia, things might be different' but what woman wants to be told she's second best, he thought.

'It is a shock in one way, but in another, it isn't, Philippe,' she said finally. 'I always knew she had a claim on you that was very strong.'

She reached up and kissed him on the cheek.

'You've always been so honourable,' she said, trying hard but failing to hide her disappointment.

'I tried not to fall in love with you. I tried very hard, but I failed. And now I have lost.'

He didn't know what to say at that moment. He was torn between not wanting to hurt her and not wanting to be disloyal to Julia. He found himself admiring her all the more for her honesty.

She was standing very close to him now, so close he could smell her perfume. Despite the summer evening, she shivered, her thin cocktail dress offering no protection from the cool breeze that drifted up from the water. A sudden gust of wind caught her long auburn hair and she put her hand up to smooth it back into place.

Suddenly, she stumbled. Philippe caught her just in time to stop her from falling, his arm encircling her waist to steady her.

'Thank you,' she muttered.

But he did not let her go. For a few moments they stood together, his arm around her. Now he did not want to let her go. She slid her arms around his neck.

'This is wrong,' a voice in his head was saying repeatedly. 'This is wrong.'

But he took no notice.

He pulled her closer to him and began to kiss her.

In Springfield, it was the last day of term and last day of school for the year. Richard had somewhat reluctantly accepted an invitation to drinks from the headmaster of Paul's school. The handwritten note had been sent home with Paul and he felt he could hardly refuse. The drinks would almost certainly end in an appeal for money, he thought cynically.

Despite the warm humid afternoon, he reached for the obligatory tie. And then slipped the suit coat from the hanger. He wore these clothes rarely in his home town, preferring instead the standard moleskins and boots he'd grown up with. But he knew the headmaster was a stickler for formality.

'I'm off to your school for end-of-year drinks with the headmaster,' he called out to his son who had not long arrived home.

Paul's head appeared around the doorway of his father's room.

'If they say I play up in class, it's all lies,' he said cheekily.

Richard laughed. The fact that Paul was a good student in most subjects pleased him. His report card for behaviour had been positively glowing.

'School will start to get a bit harder next year,' he warned his son.

They were words that fell on deaf ears as Paul headed out of the house in search of his mates. Nothing mattered now to him except the prospect of seven weeks of freedom.

Richard watched as his son rode away on his bike. There were times when he envied the freedom of childhood.

Ten minutes later he was walking through the school gate and up the gravel drive to the main building. He was not the first parent to arrive. Ahead of him James Fitzroy was striding out purposefully. Richard did not increase his pace to catch up with him. Time enough, he thought. It will be a small gathering and I won't be able to avoid him, but better to see him in company. It will be awkward if Julia has been invited too, he thought.

Richard was momentarily startled by the booming voice of the headmaster who welcomed him. Fitzroy Jardine's large, powerful build matched his crushing handshake. Richard knew him only by reputation.

'It's good to meet a fellow pilot,' he said as he ushered Richard through the building to the common room that was already crowded with people.

Richard acknowledged the unexpected greeting with a dismissive shrug of his shoulders.

'It's a long time since I've flown a plane,' Richard said. 'I should have kept it up but I didn't.'

'Ah, but you didn't just fly a plane, did you? You did much more than that,' the older man said.

Fitzroy Jardine had been away when Richard had enrolled Paul at the school so he was surprised the headmaster was so well informed on his wartime exploits. He had clearly taken the trouble to discover something of Richard's past.

'Oh, the war you mean,' Richard said, ready to reject any suggestion of heroism on his part. 'I try not to think about that these days. It's best left in the past.'

He remembered then having heard something of the headmaster's own exploits in the Great War.

'Royal Naval Air Service and then the RAF, wasn't it?' Richard asked, his memory sketchy on the details except that he knew the headmaster had distinguished himself in the final years of the war.

The big man nodded his head but he too looked as if he did not relish the memories.

'Like you, I try not to remember that part of my life,' he said. 'But I've done some flying since. You should take the time to refresh your skills before it's too late.'

Richard nodded, pleased that the conversation had turned away from his wartime deeds.

'Yes,' he replied. 'I might just do that, now that my life has settled down a bit.'

Fitzroy Jardine looked slightly chastened.

'Yes, of course,' he said, 'I was forgetting just how much you've been through in the past couple of years. It can't have been easy.'

Richard was grateful he chose not to catalogue the misfortunes that had befallen not only him but the Belleville family.

'No, it hasn't been easy,' Richard said, the tone of his voice discouraging further discussion of the topic.

The headmaster changed tack.

'Your boy Paul, who came to us this year, is a good student, a promising lad,' he said unexpectedly. 'You should be proud of him.'

This was safe ground and Richard smiled.

'I am proud of him,' he said. 'And in the not too distant future I hope to have his younger brother join him at the school.'

The headmaster nodded thoughtfully.

'There's quite an age gap between the boys, isn't there?' he asked. 'I assume your younger boy is with his mother in England?'

Richard was surprised but he should not have been. Fitzroy Jardine made it his business to know about the families whose children attended his school.

'That's right, he lives in England,' Richard explained 'but my ex-wife has married again and has another son.'

Why was he telling the headmaster so much about his private life? Was it that he was particularly clever at eliciting information from reluctant parents or was he just an old gossip, Richard wondered?

Again, with another knowing nod of his head, the headmaster was quick with the next question.

'So you think she might neglect the boy in favour of the new child?' he asked.

Richard was taken aback by the blunt question. Obviously, Fitzroy Jardine had seen many families at close quarters and not all of them were people to be admired. But Richard was inclined to defend Catherine.

'I don't think she would do that deliberately,' he said, 'but with a new husband and a new son, some might think it's a predictable outcome.'

He was choosing his words carefully.

'Well, we have a new mistress starting next year to look after some of the younger boys,' he said. 'Your younger boy would be about seven I imagine?'

Richard nodded, again surprised at the headmaster's knowledge of his family.

'He was seven in September,' Richard said, hoping that was the end of what had become almost an interrogation.

Fitzroy Jardine, never one to miss an opportunity, began to guide Richard through the crowded room to the far side.

'Well, let me introduce you to our new female member of staff,' he said. 'She's very good with younger children, I'm told. This could well help you make up your mind.'

He quickly spotted his quarry and barged through the crowded room. Richard followed behind him, out of politeness rather than interest.

'Miss Saville,' he said, a little too loudly. 'I'd like you to meet Richard Belleville. He's thinking of sending his younger son to us next year so the boy could be in your care.'

Jane Saville had been standing with her back to the two men and did not see them approaching. At the sound of the headmaster's voice, she turned, as if in slow motion. She saw the shock of recognition register on Richard's face. She could see immediately he had not really heard her name. Only when he saw her did he realise who the headmaster was about to introduce to him.

His first thought was that he could do nothing but go through with the charade of an introduction. To make matters worse, he noticed, out of the corner of his eye, James Fitzroy who was clearly highly amused at the prospect of the awkward scene about to be played out in front of him.

At the last moment, Richard spoke.

'I know Miss Saville,' he said, without elaboration.

'That's good,' the headmaster replied distractedly.

'I'll leave you two to get reacquainted,' he called back over his shoulder as new arrivals demanded his attention

Jane held out her hand with a formality Richard hadn't expected. He took it and held it longer than politeness dictated.

'Can I have my hand back?' she said quietly.

He laughed and released her hand.

'Sorry, I just didn't expect you ....'

'To be here?'

She finished the sentence for him. He nodded.

'Yes, as you say, I didn't expect you to be here.'

He didn't know what to say. He had known for most of the year that she had separated from her husband but something had stopped him from seeking her out. And yet the year before, when he had come close to dying, he was aware she had visited him in hospital as he lay semi-conscious in his hospital bed. And the year before that, they had, for a brief time, been lovers.

All this flashed through his mind in a few moments.

'I've been busy making a new life for myself,' she said guardedly.

Outwardly she appeared calm but she had the advantage over him. She at least had been prepared for a possible encounter because she had known his name was on the guest list. She could see he had been caught totally unawares by her presence.

'My sister did say something about your circumstances a few months back,' he said, noncommittally.

She nodded, aware that news of her marriage breakdown must have reached him, if not immediately, then shortly afterwards. Gossip, after all, was the lifeblood of a town.

'My marriage is over,' she said simply. 'I couldn't pretend anymore.'

Richard touched her lightly on the arm. The room was becoming overheated. The noise of the conversation around them had risen markedly.

'Let's go outside onto the verandah,' he said, pointing the way through the French doors. 'We can talk there.'

He pushed his way through the crowd and she followed him. He tried to avoid eye contact with James Fitzroy who had stopped talking to the people around him in order to watch his former brother-in-law's reaction to the unexpected meeting. Others around him followed the direction of his gaze but with no idea of what was going on.

'A bit awkward when a chap comes across his mistress at a school function, isn't it?' James said, indicating the departing figures.

His words were loud enough for those standing near him to hear. He laughed with malicious delight as shock registered on the faces of those nearest him. He had made sure though that Richard was well out of earshot.

Outside on the verandah, a light breeze had sprung up. Richard was grateful for the cool air. Beside him, Jane waited for him to speak. Even though she had been prepared for the meeting, she had no idea what to say to him.

He turned towards her. Strange, he thought. Meeting her again it feels like my life has come full circle.

'I guess you know I'm divorced from Catherine now,' he said without prompting.

He was surprised it no longer hurt him to say it out loud.

'She married again and has had another baby, a son,' he added. 'She married the man who inherited her father's title. All very neat. She's now Lady Cavendish and in possession of the fine country estate in Derbyshire her father left her, somewhere I never belonged.'

She listened intently. The gossips had been mostly right, she thought.

'And, of course, you know about Prior Park burning down and my mother's death. And then the attempt on my life.'

She nodded, relieved that he was telling her the plain facts of his life.

'You've had a terrible time of it,' she said sympathetically. 'I wanted to see you and tell you how sorry I was, but it just didn't seem possible. I didn't know how you'd react. I wasn't sure you would want to see me.'

He turned away from her slightly. He was well aware of how badly he had treated her. He struggled to find the right words.

'I understand why you would feel that way,' he said finally. 'I feel very ashamed of how I treated you.'

It was an admission he had long wanted to make to her. He knew he should have apologised long ago. He wanted to explain his actions, not to excuse his behaviour but to make her understand how he felt.

She said nothing, waiting for him to continue. He turned back towards her.

'I think I wanted you to feel the way I felt when you dumped me when I was away at the war,' he said, 'but it was very ill done and I apologise.'

It had taken her a long time to come to the conclusion that he had used her in that way. He had charmed her and seduced her all over again and left her with the guilt of having betrayed her husband. He had offered her nothing but a clandestine affair to salve his wounded pride.

She looked at him intently. He still had the boyish good looks of his youth. His tall athletic figure had not yet yielded to middle age. But she could see in his face traces of sorrow and regret. She noticed a new scar on the side of his face.

She nodded, acknowledging his apology. She knew him well enough to know it was genuine.

'And so here we are,' she said. 'Two people much older and wiser.'

She was remembering the day more than seventeen years earlier when he had announced he was going off to join the RAF. He had promised to marry her but she had doubted his sincerity. What had she to offer him? He was younger than her, wealthy, good looking, with the world at his feet. Why would he settle for her? She had no money, no family connections, nothing to bring to the match except her love. But she never believed in his love. Yet he had a hold over her that nothing would ever quite sever.

He looked at her closely and felt the familiar stirrings. She was still the same elegant woman of his youth but her face too bore the sorrows and regrets of the years. Was it too late to revive the hopes and dreams of their young love?

'I'm pleased we had this talk,' he said finally.

But he drew back from asking to meet her again. He did not want to go back to the past. He did not want to risk disappointing her again as he had once before.

He turned then and walked away.

CHAPTER 17

December 1959

'I can't believe another year has passed,' Alice said, as she brought the ham to the table which was already groaning with festive fare.

The housekeeper Mrs Duffy, following closely behind, struggled under the weight of a large platter of roasted meats. Marianne had been given the task of bringing in the gravy boat. She was concentrating hard to make sure she didn't spill any of it. Even Julia had been pressed into service, carrying a serving plate heaped with roasted vegetables.

William, who took his job of carving the meats very seriously, was working furiously on the knife blade to produce a satisfactory edge.

Richard lounged against the wall of the dining room, in deep conversation with Charles Brockman who had earlier volunteered his services only to be evicted from the kitchen.

Richard's contribution had been to open a bottle of claret, several boxes of which had accompanied him home from his trip to England the previous Christmas.

William, on being offered a glass, eyed it suspiciously and opted for beer. Julia accepted but sipped the wine cautiously while Alice refused it, declaring she couldn't stand the smell of it. Charles, like William, preferred beer but graciously accepted a glass. Mrs Duffy could not be lured away from her glass of sherry.

It was a more relaxed and settled family party that sat down to Christmas dinner at William and Alice's table compared with the previous year.

William, taking his place at the head of the table, felt a surge of satisfaction, looking at the family around him.

To his left his sister and her son John; to his right his brother and his son Paul. At the other end of the table, his wife Alice and daughter Marianne. Their trusted friend and manager Charles Brockman sat opposite Mrs Duffy, whose Christmas feasts were legendary.

He felt like the patriarch of the family even though his brother Richard was older. It was as if Richard had abdicated the position in his favour.

They were all seated, except Alice, who was busy passing plates around and making sure everyone was being served and William who stood to do the carving.

'It's a pity young Anthony isn't with us,' he said, as he carefully transferred a slice of pork to Richard's plate.

Richard nodded. He missed his young son and resented his own role as father being usurped by Edward Cavendish, who had made it his mission to charm the young boy from the very beginning of his relationship with Catherine.

'I'll make sure he's here next year for Christmas,' Richard said, as if it was a promise he was making, not just to the wider family, but to himself.

William turned towards his sister.

'And you didn't have Pippa come up to us this Christmas?'

She shook her head.

'She wanted to have Christmas with her father and then she is going to Nancy Lester's family for a week or so.'

Richard looked up from his plate at the mention of the Lester family.

'I'm taking Paul down to stay with the Lester family next week,' he said. 'He's been staying in touch with Tim Lester, even though they're no longer at school together. Perhaps we will see her there.'

Marianne had been listening to all this with a growing sense of disappointment. She had hoped to see her older cousin again this Christmas. Instead she had to make do with the boys and in her opinion, they were no substitute at all.

'Aunt Julia,' she said, 'will you make sure Pippa comes for Christmas next year?'

Julia heard the disappointment in Marianne's voice and smiled. She too knew what it was like to be surrounded by boys growing up and she sympathised with her niece.

'I will, I promise,' she said to Marianne, who looked only slightly mollified by the promise.

There was a hush over the table as everyone began to eat their Christmas dinner. With the general lull in conversation, Julia seized her opportunity.

'I have some news for everyone,' she announced.

She paused as all eyes turned towards her expectantly. She took a deep breath.

'A few weeks ago, when I was in Sydney, Philippe asked me to marry him and I have accepted his proposal,' she said.

She did not feel it necessary to add 'when I am divorced'.

She waited, wondering what the reaction would be. It was Alice who broke the silence.

'Oh, that's wonderful news, Julia,' she said. 'I'm so happy for you.'

She got up and moved around to embrace her.

To Alice it was all impossibly romantic. Even though it had meant the breakup of Julia's marriage to her brother, she knew Philippe had been Julia's first love and, without the intervention of Julia's mother, she would have married him long ago.

William was less enthusiastic at the news, although he tried hard not to show it. All he could see were the difficulties she would face in balancing her life in Springfield, where her son was, and Sydney, where her future life would be with Philippe and her daughter.

Richard, who had the advantage over the others of having met Philippe in Sydney, smiled broadly. It was happy news as far as he was concerned. He raised his glass and urged those around him to toast his sister and her future happiness.

'When is the happy day likely to be?' he asked, as he replaced his wine glass on the table.

The announcement had come as a surprise to all of them, even Richard, who might have been the only one who could have predicted it.

'Hopefully, I will be free to wed by the winter,' she said. 'June at the latest, I hope.'

She had not forgotten her young son in all the hubbub that followed her announcement. He frowned, not knowing what to say or what it would mean for him, although he had not harboured any false hopes his parents would reunite.

She bent down towards him.

'It will mean I will live most of the time in Sydney,' she said to him quietly, 'but I will come up to see you often. Your father wants you to be with him at Mayfield Downs and to continue going to school just as you have this year.'

He nodded, saying he understood. He did not want to cry, not in front of everyone. He desperately wanted life to go back to the way it had been but he knew that would never happen now.

Across the table, Paul noticed his young cousin's unhappiness but could do nothing to help him. Like me, he'll come to realise it's the adults who mess everything up, he thought, but I can hardly say that out loud.

At least he'll know I understand because I've already been through it all. He thought about the photo his mother had sent him of her smiling happily alongside Edward Cavendish with his brother Anthony in front of them on their wedding day. He'd been very tempted to tear it up. He had shown his father, who had handed it back to him without comment. I bet John gets a photo like that, he thought. Adults know nothing, he decided.

Marianne's reaction was as far from that of her cousin Paul as it was possible to be. She ignored the warning glance from her father as she bounced up and down in her chair.

'Aunt Julia,' she said breathlessly. 'Can I be your bridesmaid? Can I please?'

Julia sat back in her chair, not quite laughing, but a little overwhelmed by Marianne's eagerness.

'My darling girl,' she said. 'It won't be a big wedding like you have when you first get married. I won't have any attendants. It will be a very small quiet affair.'

It seemed as if Marianne was to be disappointed for a second time. It was Alice who saved the day.

'We will get you a wonderful new dress and it will feel like you are a bridesmaid,' she said to her daughter.

Marianne turned towards her mother. This concession opened up new possibilities.

'Can I have a taffeta dress?' she asked. 'With lace over the top and a floating panel from the back, with a V neck, just like the one I showed you in the magazine the other day.'

At this point William decided to intervene.

'That's far too grown up for you, young miss,' he said, in an effort to bring her back to earth.

But she would have none of it.

'I'll be nearly fourteen then,' she retorted. 'I'm not wearing a child's dress.'

William shook his head. He was about to respond but Alice intervened.

'We'll take a look at it and see if my dressmaker can make it for you, perhaps with some minor changes,' she said to her daughter while sending a warning glance towards William at the other end of the table.

He sank back in his chair. He knew that look. He had been seeing it more and more of late as Marianne began to voice her own very definite opinions.

But he was comforted by the thought that Alice was a woman of infinite good sense and he knew he could rely on her to make sure his daughter was appropriately dressed for her aunt's wedding.

He grew impatient with the women's chatter about dresses and weddings so he turned towards Richard and Charles and began to bemoan the low prices for their cattle in the latest round of sales.

Several days later, Richard and Paul stepped off the plane in Sydney to be met by John Bertram who had offered to lend Richard his car to drive to the Lester property near Bowral.

'Are you coming back to Sydney straight away?' John asked, as they stowed their luggage in the boot. He had assumed Richard would leave Paul with the family for a few days.

But Richard shook his head.

'Even though I don't know them, Mrs Lester has invited me to stay for the duration of Paul's visit. I could hardly say no.'

'So when will you be back?' John asked.

'Friday probably,' Richard answered. 'Will you be back in the air by then or lolling about on the ground?'

John laughed.

'Oh, how I wish I could be lolling about on the ground,' he replied, 'but I'm off tomorrow.'

'How's the new plane going?' Richard asked, aware that John was now flying the Boeing 707 which had been introduced mid-year.

'Beautiful,' John replied.

He might well have been speaking about a woman he admired, such was his enthusiasm.

Richard smiled. Same old John. An aviation tragic who would never grow up.

Paul had been listening to the friendly banter between the two old friends, not quite understanding it all but pleased to see his father so relaxed.

John turned to Paul.

'Want to see over the new plane?'

The boy's eyes lit up.

'Yes please,' he said, looking towards his father for confirmation he was allowed to accept the invitation.

With the luggage safely stowed, the three of them walked around the terminal and on to the tarmac. John flashed his credentials to the ground staff and within minutes they were climbing up the stairs into the plane.

Paul looked at the complicated cockpit and tried to understand what he was being told. Richard looked at it and shook his head.

'A lot more complicated than the old crate I flew back in the war,' he said.

But John shook his head.

'It only looks that way, mate,' he said. 'It's really quite simple when you get the hang of it.'

Then he looked at Paul who was wide eyed and completely captivated by what he saw. Richard noticed it too.

'I think it's time we went,' he said, 'before you end up with an extra passenger on your flight to London.'

Paul left the cockpit reluctantly. There was still so much to see, so much to understand.

'Dad,' he said, as they descended the stairs, 'I want to be a pilot like Uncle John.'

Since this was about his third or fourth declaration of what he would do in the future, neither of them took any notice at all.

'Do we need to give you a lift back to your place?' Richard asked.

John shook his head.

'No, mate,' he said. 'I'll get a lift with Jock who runs the ground crew,' he said. 'He lives in the next street to me so it's no trouble for him to drop me off.'

Richard slid in behind the steering wheel. He was grateful that John had chosen a Holden rather than one of the British models that Richard thought were totally unsuitable for Australian roads.

With Paul settled beside him, he turned the key and the engine came to life immediately. Before long, they were heading through the suburban streets towards Canterbury Road and the Hume Highway that would take them out of the sprawling city.

A couple of hours later, Richard turned into the driveway of Berrima Park, relying solely on Paul who had visited the house previously to recognise the driveway. The entrance, flanked by two impressive sandstone pillars, gave way to a narrow road lined by magnificent oaks and elms that had obviously been planted the previous century.

Already Richard was impressed but he was quite unprepared for the majestic three storey sandstone house surrounded by manicured lawns and clipped hedges that greeted them.

'Wow,' he said to Paul as they followed the driveway around to the back of the house. 'I thought Prior Park was grand but this, this is something else again.'

Paul shrugged.

'It's nice,' he said, 'but it's no match for what we had.'

Richard smiled. The boy's loyalty would never be in doubt.

As he brought the car to a standstill, he noticed a lone figure emerge from the back of the house.

'That's Mrs Lester,' Paul said, helpfully. 'The others must be out fishing or something.'

Kate Lester extended her hand to Richard as he climbed out of the driver's seat.

'Welcome to Berrima Park, Mr Belleville,' she said, smiling warmly.

'How do you do, Mrs Lester,' Richard replied. 'Thank you for inviting me and Paul. It's very kind of you.'

She turned to Paul, who was smiling but wary of being kissed and embraced. He knew from experience that Mrs Lester was that kind of woman. But he understood he must submit gracefully to her greeting because she had been so good to him when Prior Park had burnt down and he had no home to go to for the Christmas holidays.

'Tim has missed you at school this year, Paul,' she said as she ushered them inside. 'But they should all be back very soon and then you can catch up with him.

'Your cousin Pippa is staying too,' she said, almost as an afterthought.

'You must be very patient to have so many children staying during the holidays,' Richard said, although he had already sensed she was a very capable woman.

She smiled. Richard noticed how her face lit up. She has a very natural beauty, he thought, to go with her bright generous personality. There was nothing contrived or artificial in the way she looked. He found himself unexpectedly drawn to her.

'Well, Nancy and Tim spend a good part of the year away at school,' she said, as if she needed to justify herself. 'It's just too far for them to go to local schools and so I think it's only fair they have a chance to have some young friends to share the holidays with.'

Richard listened politely. He felt it was the perfect opportunity to thank her again for having taken Paul in at the time of the fire.

'I was so grateful for you taking Paul in when we had the fire at our home at Prior Park,' he said.

But she cut him short.

'Oh, there's no need to thank me at all,' she said. 'Your son is a joy to have around. We were worried that Tim wasn't making friends but then he and Paul became friendly. I think it helped that Paul was from a country background too.'

Paul was standing silently listening to this exchange. He wasn't sure that it was all true. He knew Tim had made other friends at school but he was happy to be singled out as special.

'Mrs Norman, our housekeeper, will show you to your rooms,' she said. 'You'll be on the first floor, Mr Belleville. I'm sure Paul can find his way to the next floor where all the children's rooms are, can't you Paul?'

The boy nodded and grabbed his bag. He assumed he would be sharing Tim's room as he had on his previous visit. She turned to Richard.

'Come down when you're settled,' she said, 'and I will show you the house and make you a drink before dinner. My husband Gerald should be back soon and I can introduce you. We'll have dinner at seven.'

Richard looked at his watch. It was already four o'clock.

Grace Norman, a woman who looked as though she bore a permanent grudge against the world, gestured to Richard who followed her through the hallway and up the main staircase.

He hardly had time to admire the red cedar staircase and the fine chandelier that hung in the front entrance to the house. It's an easy house to admire, he thought. But would such a house be practical in the tropical north, he wondered?

For the first time he felt a profound sense of disappointment that he and William had decided not to rebuild their own grand home after the fire. William's new home may be comfortable, he thought, but it was certainly not the showpiece their old home had been. It had made a statement to all who saw it that the Bellevilles were a rich and powerful family.

Now, there was almost nothing to distinguish them from their neighbours. Practical it might be but Richard felt a wave of desolation engulf him at the memory of what had been and now was no more. It was as if it had taken this magnificent house to remind him of what they had lost.

Half an hour later he descended the stairs in search of Kate Lester. He found her in the dining room, checking the settings for dinner. She welcomed him with a warm smile.

'I hope you found the room to your liking,' she said. 'It has a very nice view of the garden.'

'Thank you,' he said, 'it's very nice and very comfortable.'

She continued putting the finishing touches to the table. He wondered if there were other indoors staff. It would be a big house to run with just a housekeeper.

'I think your son has headed down to the river,' she said. 'He is a very keen little fisherman. I told him that's where the other children are.'

Richard smiled. He remembered Paul having extolled the virtues of the river fishing after he had stayed with the Lesters two years ago.

'He's always pestering me to take him fishing,' Richard said, pulling a face, 'but it's not a pastime I care for very much.'

She laughed. It was a tinkling happy sound.

'Gerald is pleased that Tim has a friend who likes fishing because he doesn't like it much either.'

'And the girls?' Richard asked. 'I don't know many girls who like it.'

Kate Lester shook her head.

'No, they don't like it much either, but they enjoy messing around in the swimming hole in the river,' she said. 'Scaring the fish, according to Tim.'

Richard was curious. It sounded as if there were quite a few girls staying with the Lesters.

'You said my niece is here?' he asked.

'Yes, Pippa is here along with Anita Clarke,' she said. 'Normally Lucy Dixon would come too but her family has gone to visit relatives in New Zealand so it's just the two girls staying with Nancy and your son to keep Tim company.'

Richard was remembering then what Julia had told him. It had been Nancy Lester who had stood by Pippa when the story of her illegitimate birth had become known. And, of course, it had been his own son who had inadvertently laid bare the information about Pippa's father. It was all coming back to him. It had been, as it turned out, a big fuss about nothing. He made a mental note to see Philippe on his return to Sydney.

'I remember now,' Richard said. 'It was your daughter, wasn't it, who saved my niece from being ostracised by the other kids at school?'

Kate Lester looked up at Richard who was now standing alongside her. She nodded.

'Yes, Nancy really liked Pippa and I think she felt sorry for her too,' she said. 'It's been a difficult time for Pippa. I'm not sure people really understand how difficult. First of all, she thinks she has lost her adoptive parents. Then she finds her real parents but people tell her she can't talk about them because her mother is married to a man who doesn't know about her and her father will be embarrassed in his job if it comes out that he has an illegitimate daughter.'

She paused, wondering if she had said too much. She could see that Richard was listening carefully to what she was saying.

'I'm proud of my daughter for standing up for Pippa and not allowing the other kids to bully her,' she said. 'After all none of what happened was Pippa's fault.'

Richard saw in her eyes just a hint of rebuke. He knew he would have to explain how it was that his sister's child had been given up for adoption. How her family had not stood by her. He let out a deep sigh. He was ashamed of how his sister had been treated.

'It's a sad story that could only really be described as tragic.'

He began to explain.

'My mother intervened and stopped any of Philippe's letters reaching my sister. She thought she'd been abandoned. When she found out she was pregnant, my mother arranged everything, insisting she give up the baby for adoption. My only defence is that I was away in England in the RAF. I knew nothing of it until it all came out very recently when she met Philippe quite unexpectedly in Sydney.'

Kate Lester reached out to touch his arm briefly in a gesture of reassurance.

'I'm sorry,' she said. 'I didn't mean to offend you. I didn't know the story, or at least not all of it but thank you for telling me. On a happier note, according to Pippa, her parents are going to marry next year, when your sister's divorce is finalised.'

'Yes,' he said. 'She told us on Christmas Day that Philippe had proposed and she has accepted.'

'You must be relieved at that news?'

'Relieved? I guess so,' Richard said although he was surprised she thought it would be a relief. 'But I think my sister will find her life split between Sydney and up north where we live a bit of a challenge. It won't be easy for her. She has a ten-year-old son from her first marriage.'

'She will work it out,' Kate Lester said confidently.

'I hope so,' he said. 'I hope so for her sake. And for Pippa's sake.'

Richard had been unprepared for such an awkward conversation. Kate Lester, ever the perfect hostess, felt she too had gone too far in speaking so frankly about Pippa's situation so she retreated to the usual civilities.

'Let's get some fresh air,' she said, 'before we lose the light. Let me take you around the garden and then I'll fix you a drink.'

She led the way to the French doors and flung them open. It was still light enough to see the magnificent garden that lay beyond the verandah. Richard wondered how many staff it would take to keep a garden in such immaculate condition.

'It's Gerald's pride and joy,' she said. 'That and his stud cattle.'

As he followed her on to the verandah and down the few steps to the garden, he thought perhaps Gerald had his priorities all wrong. If I was Gerald, he thought, my pride and joy would be my wife.

CHAPTER 18

December 1959

It was Richard's last evening at Berrima Park and he was surprised to find himself sad at the prospect of leaving the following morning.

Dinner had finished and he had declined the offer of port, so he wandered out onto the front verandah in search of a breeze. It had been a hot day and despite its high ceilings the atmosphere in the house had become oppressive.

He leaned against the railing and breathed in the sweet cool air of the evening. He noticed the decorative iron lacework that surrounded the verandah on three sides had been repainted here and there where rust had begun to break through. It would be an endless and thankless task, he thought, to keep it looking so good.

He heard a movement behind him and was pleased to see it was his hostess and not her husband who had followed him out in search of cool air.

Had he imagined it or had he detected disappointment in Kate Lester's response when he had said they would leave the next day?

'It's lovely out here in the evening,' she said. 'The house is usually quite cool but it does get rather stuffy on hot nights.'

He smiled at her.

'I don't think you could blame the house,' he said. 'The past few days have been quite hot, especially for this area I imagine.'

He was being polite, she thought.

'You don't think it was the conversation at dinner that made you desperate to seek cool air outside?' she asked.

He could see she was teasing him and he laughed.

'Some men get very earnest about their politics, don't they,' he said, pulling a face.

She nodded in agreement.

'My husband certainly does,' she said, with just a hint of exasperation. 'He and his friends want to order the world just to suit them.'

Dinner that evening had been a much larger affair than the family dinners of the previous evenings. It was, after all, New Year's Eve.

But two couples had left early. Richard suspected the women had reached their limit of listening to Gerald Lester opine with absolute authority on every subject under discussion, leaving only two of his single male friends to share the after dinner port with him. Richard, having declined the invitation to participate, had thus escaped the endless blustering and ranting that was likely to go on for hours yet.

Kate Lester stood beside him in silence for a few minutes, as they both revelled in the cool night air.

Would it overstep the bounds of propriety to tell her how much I admire her, Richard wondered? In the end, he decided not to, choosing instead the far safer ground of complimenting her on her house.

'You have a wonderful house and property,' he said. 'You must be very proud of it.'

He wanted to ask, but could not, how they came to own it. Above all, he wanted to know how she came to marry a man ten years or more her senior, a man who hardly paid her any attention at all, a man who seemed so totally at odds with her own character.

She guessed what was on his mind as the two of them stood companionably together. Like Richard, she chose the safe conversational route.

'It's a really wonderful house,' she said.

He noted she did not use the word 'home'.

'Gerald inherited everything from his father just as we were about to get married,' she added. 'We moved in when we returned from our honeymoon. I was only nineteen years old and suddenly in charge of this big house.'

He sensed there was more to the story. He waited for her to continue.

'My father lost just about everything in the Depression so there was pressure on me, as the eldest, to make a good marriage,' she explained. 'Gerald gave my father a job managing one of his properties near Gundagai. It restored my family to some level of respectability.'

Richard was silent for some moments. He didn't know quite what to say. But he caught the despondency in her voice. She had done her duty and married Gerald Lester to save her family.

What else was there to say, she wondered? Should she tell him that, apart from her two children, there was nothing left in the marriage? Nothing for her anyway. But she did not. How could she give voice to those thoughts to a man who, until a few days ago, had been a perfect stranger to her?

'The Depression was very tough for a lot of families,' he replied diplomatically. 'My own father did not manage our family investments well. It was down to my brother and I to restore them.'

She did not know much at all about the Belleville family. She was suddenly curious to know more. Pleased too that he had not pressed her with more questions.

'And have you, restored them I mean?' she asked, stumbling over the words.

It had been a clumsy question to ask.

'I think so,' Richard said. 'We did quite well out of the woollen mills in Goulburn for a while but I sold out of those, perhaps a little early but I think the future is in synthetic fabrics.'

She was surprised at what he was telling her and said so. She had thought the Belleville family were simply a wealthy country family.

'My husband sees no investment prospects beyond sheep and cattle,' she said, with a sense of regret. 'He won't listen to my suggestions at all.'

Again, he replied diplomatically.

'It doesn't suit all men to move outside what they know,' he said.

She laughed at him in her kind amusing way.

'You are so diplomatic,' she said. 'You know, I could see straight away that Gerald is not your type of man.'

Should he continue to be diplomatic, he wondered, or should he agree with her?

'Well, let's just say there are lots of issues on which he and I would not see eye to eye,' he said.

He wondered if she would accuse him again of being less than honest, which is what she had really meant, he thought. They could hear the high-pitched laughter of the three girls who had congregated in the sitting room. He wondered if the boys were there too. If they were, they were being drowned out by the girls.

'Your niece seems very fond of you,' she said.

This time it was her who was being diplomatic by changing the subject.

'I'm fond of her too,' he said. 'She reminds me so much of my sister at that age. Julia is just over four years younger than me, but I remember her so clearly growing up. She had her eighteenth birthday just after I went away to train with the RAF.'

Kate nodded, aware that her own daughter resembled her very closely, so it was no surprise to learn that Pippa looked very much like her mother.

'The girls will all turn sixteen next year,' she said. 'Gerald thinks I should start looking around for a good match for Nancy, but I want my daughter to have her own life and make her own choices.'

He could see Kate Lester understood the battles ahead of her to ensure her daughter had a say over her own future.

'I agree with you,' he said. 'I don't think girls today want their parents arranging marriages for them. It sounds like a very nineteenth century idea.'

But he was thankful all the same to have two boys and not be faced with the dilemma of a daughter bringing home an unsuitable partner.

'Gerald is very old fashioned about girls,' she said. 'That's what I keep telling him. But you won't need to worry. You have another son as I recall?'

'Yes, Anthony will be eight next year,' he replied. 'He lives in England with his mother, but I would like to have him live with me and Paul. His mother has had another baby to her new husband. I think he might get a bit overlooked. Besides I want him to grow up in Australia, not in England.'

He had revealed much more than he had intended. They were sharing confidences as if they were friends of long standing, not two people who had only just met. For her part, she worried she had over-stepped the mark.

'Oh, I'm so sorry if it sounded as if I was prying,' she said. 'I didn't know your ex-wife had remarried. Young boys are not very good at conveying family news.'

'No, they aren't, are they?' he said. 'Paul told me almost nothing of your beautiful house and estate. All he could talk about was that he could go fishing.'

She laughed.

'That's so typical of a boy but the girls gossip like mad,' she said.

Richard had overheard snippets of the girls' conversation in the few days he had been at Berrima Park and he could do nothing else but agree with her.

'You're right,' he said. 'The girls seem to talk about their friends endlessly. Imagine what they're going to be like when they have boyfriends to gossip about.'

Again, Kate laughed.

'Oh, what a thought,' she said, her voice suddenly serious for a moment.

'Thank goodness Nancy hasn't shown any interest in boys yet but I think Anita might have a crush on your future brother-in-law, the handsome surgeon. She's always asking Pippa about him.'

Richard didn't quite know what to say. He was sure Julia had told him Philippe was about to turn forty-five.

'I'm sure you must be wrong there, Kate,' he said, incredulous at the prospect of a young girl even noticing him. 'He's older than me.'

She thought for a moment.

'Yes, I would have thought so but it's not only Anita who has a crush on him I believe,' she said. 'I understand Anita's cousin Karen Clarke has a crush on him too. Anita's father, of course, is a surgeon and works alongside Dr Duval.'

She was sorry then the conversation had taken this turn. She berated herself for bringing Karen's name into it. There were things Anita had said about Philippe Duval that she could not repeat to

Julia's brother. She hoped he would let the conversation lapse, but he did not.

'I take it that Karen Clarke is much older than her cousin?'

'Oh, yes, I think she would be late twenties, if not thirty,' she said candidly. 'I met her once when I went to pick up Anita from the Clarke's home. She is a very striking girl, not to mention a very rich girl. Her brother died tragically while having an operation, so she is now an only child.'

Somewhere in the back of his mind, a memory stirred.

'Of course, I remember. My sister told me about her,' he said. 'Julia was in Sydney and Duval cried off from seeing her one evening, citing hospital business as the reason but it turned out he was escorting Karen Clarke to a hospital fundraising ball. That didn't go down too well.'

Kate Lester hesitated. Nothing good came of meddling in other people's affairs. And nothing good would come of telling Julia's brother that Anita had boldly declared she had seen Pippa's father kissing her cousin Karen when they thought no one was around to see.

She had quickly silenced the girl and told her not to repeat the story. She was grateful Pippa had not been in the room at the time. Kate knew it would have led to a terrible row and floods of tears. If there was one thing Pippa believed in, it was that her mother and father were still very much in love with each other, despite the years of separation. Kate could see if that belief was proven to be false, her whole world would collapse. She had spoken sternly to Anita who had not repeated the story, at least not within her hearing. Pippa appeared happy so she assumed the girl had heeded her warning.

She let the moment pass. She chose not to comment on Philippe Duval's apparent duplicity. Instead she mused aloud on the unlikely set of coincidences that now connected them all.

'If you think about it,' she said, 'it's quite extraordinary that your son was at school with my son and your niece, whom you've only recently met, is at school with my daughter.'

'And then there's the link with Dr Duval through Anita's father,' she added.

He too had realised what a strange set of coincidences linked them in a way he was only just beginning to understand. He mistrusted coincidences. But he didn't mistrust his instincts.

As he stood beside her, he wondered idly if he should cut their conversation short and bid her 'goodnight'. He was beginning to feel unsettled by her proximity. He sensed that she too was feeling the same way. 'Don't be a fool, walk away now before it's too late.' He heard the voice of reason in his head but he ignored it. What had started out as admiration had given way to an urge much more powerful, the urge to possess her.

He turned to look at her. She met his gaze briefly then looked away. They were standing very close together now. It was at that moment he found he could not resist her. He reached out and began to stroke her hair, just the lightest of touches.

'I know I shouldn't say this,' he said quietly, 'but you look very lovely tonight. You are a very beautiful woman.'

She stepped back to put a little distance between them but not as quickly as she should have.

'You're right,' she said, shaking her head, 'you shouldn't say that to me. I'm a married woman. It's not appropriate for you to say such things.'

But she did not walk away. She could not walk away. He lifted her fingers to his lips.

'I can go away from here tomorrow and we need never meet again,' he said. 'I didn't mean to offend you. I apologise if I have.'

But did she really want me to apologise, he wondered? Was she really offended or just felt she should say it?

She looked up at him. What if I never saw him again? What if, tomorrow, he goes out of my life forever? She couldn't bear to think about the possibility. He knows I find him attractive, she thought. I should send him on his way now, I should walk inside and forget he ever spoke to me in such a fashion. I should do what is right ... but her resolve weakened.

'You haven't offended me,' she said, 'not at all. Please don't think I'm offended. Far from it.'

In her softly spoken words he found encouragement.

'I'm very pleased to hear that,' he said, as he stepped closer to her, close enough to put his hand on her waist. 'That's the very last thing I would want to do.'

He lent forward to kiss her but she turned her head slightly. In the dim light, he could see her eyes had filled with tears.

'Until a few days ago, I was happy,' she said. 'I would never have dreamed of looking at another man ...and then you came.'

Her words trailed off. In him she had glimpsed the romance that was long gone from her marriage, if it had ever existed at all. She could not remember. She had married not for love, but for money and security for her family. And she had not regretted it. Until now.

He began to caress her gently. This time she did not step away. He pulled her closer to him. His lips brushed hers. When he sought her lips, this time she did not turn away from him. He kissed her passionately. She could not then mistake his intentions.

Can I give myself to this man, she wondered? Am I really capable of betraying my marriage vows so easily? Even thinking about it is a betrayal.

She looked around nervously. What if someone chose that moment to walk out onto the verandah?

'There is a more private place,' she found herself saying.

At the end of the garden, away from prying eyes, they sought the privacy of the garden folly.

She ignored the warning voice in her head as he began to make love to her.

He caressed her body gently, as if she was some fragile thing that might break easily. He is so practised at this, she thought. Does he seduce every woman who takes his eye?

Then he kissed her again and began to undo her dress which slipped easily off her shoulders. She felt his hand close over her breast. She tried to banish her doubts.

'I can't ... not here,' she said, the words catching in her throat.

'But you want me,' he said soothingly, 'and I want you. It's too late, there's no going back now.'

To Richard, she felt warm and inviting in his arms. Her body is betraying her, he thought. Then she slid her arms around his neck.

She had never before felt the deep physical ache for a man as she was feeling now.

'I do want you,' she whispered. 'But it doesn't seem right …..'

She hesitated. She had never felt this way before. Before tonight, sex had been some perfunctory activity she had endured rather than enjoyed. But this was different. And in the end she could not deny him. And she could not deny herself.

Afterwards she lay in his arms, her dress lying in a crumpled heap on the floor.

'You are so beautiful,' he said, stroking her hair. 'I tried very hard to deny I was attracted to you. I don't make a habit of this.'

'I'm glad of that,' she said. 'I thought perhaps you seduced the wives of all your friends up and down the country.'

He laughed. He had never considered himself to be serial seducer of women.

'I don't make a habit of it,' he repeated.

It was a little lie. A very small lie, he told himself. There had been one other married woman. He was not about to admit that to her.

She reached up to kiss him. With her finger, she traced the line of the most recent scar on his face. She could just make it out in the dim light.

'Not a jealous husband, I hope?' she teased.

'No,' he said. 'A madman who caught me by surprise. I'll tell you the story one day.'

She sighed. She had given herself to him and there was no going back now. Regrets were useless. Would she ever lie in his arms again, she wondered? Or would this be a memory she would hold close to her heart for the rest of her life? He would only have to touch me, she thought, and I would be in his arms and in his bed. Willingly. Wantonly. Lying naked beside him.

The sound of voices from the house startled her. She got up suddenly and began to dress.

'I must get back to the house,' she whispered urgently, aware that they had been missing for almost an hour. 'Can you help me?'

She hoped no one would notice her tousled hair. She could do very little to smooth it down.

He smiled. He wanted to say, no, I won't help you, I prefer you the way you are, but instead he sat up and refastened her dress which she could not manage by herself. He began to kiss her again, but she pulled away from him.

'I must go in, otherwise I'll be missed,' she said.

But he held her for a brief moment. He was too strong for her to break free.

'We must make sure this is not the last time,' he said, 'only the first time' as he released her and watched as she walked quickly back across the manicured lawn.

He began to dress. He hoped he could slip into the house and up to his bedroom without being seen. He was not practised at such deception.

Would she now have to accept her husband's caresses, he wondered? He would be if not drunk then hardly sober, he thought. That might save her from his amorous attentions tonight.

He shivered. The thought of her husband in her bed, enjoying her body as he had done, suddenly became intolerable.

He began to walk slowly back to the house. Would he ever have another chance to be with her, he wondered? If only she wasn't another man's wife ....

Chapter 19

January 1960

Richard had already placed his bag into the boot of the car and was waiting patiently for his son, who was playing an impromptu game of cricket with his friend Tim.

At the last minute Richard had agreed to return his niece Pippa and her friend Anita to their respective homes in Sydney to save the girls the tedium of the train journey the following day. He looked at his watch. He expected them to appear at the back door at any moment.

This late change of plans had delayed his departure but he did not mind. He had not yet caught sight of Kate so he was in no hurry to leave. He would not leave without seeing her.

Gerald Lester, who was off early to look at a new calf that had been born at his Hereford stud twenty miles away, had earlier bid him farewell and invited him to come back any time.

Richard had taken the chance to look closely at him. He was certainly closer to fifty than forty, Richard thought. He was a heavy set man who seemed to have modelled his appearance on his outdated idea of a country gentleman. His naturally ruddy complexion had not been improved by regular evenings of heavy drinking. He would not be a man to cross, Richard thought. It troubled him to think that Kate might feel the backlash of his temper if some small thing upset him.

'God, I hope he never finds out about last night,' Richard thought, 'especially if I am not around to protect her.'

In being farewelled by Gerald Lester, he felt as if guilt was etched in his face but the older man showed no sign of being aware of anything untoward.

Richard had passed a sleepless night, mostly reliving the pleasure of being with Kate, but also thinking of how his desire to see her now complicated his life, not to mention her life.

He was jolted out of his reverie by a misdirected cricket ball. He reacted quickly enough to catch it just before it reached the windscreen of his car. There was a sheepish silence from the two budding cricketers but he wasn't angry with them. He and William had laid waste to a couple of windscreens and several ground floor windows in their time so he could hardly reprimand his own son.

He walked across to the patch of ground they were using as a wicket, but he did not return the ball. Instead he bowled his version of leg spin to Tim, who gave all the appearance of wanting to follow in the footsteps of the great Don Bradman. The boy gave the ball a hearty whack and it looped back towards the house, falling harmlessly at the back steps.

'Nice one, Tim,' Richard said.

'Nice one?' a voice behind him said. 'He might have knocked me out with that shot.'

Richard turned. Kate was walking towards him. She was dressed very much as she had been when he first met her. A simple cotton dress, her tanned legs bare. He wanted to reach out and stroke her long glossy hair which had drifted across her face with the breeze.

She smiled at him. He walked across to her.

'You look as beautiful as you did last night,' he whispered.

She was pleased there was no one close by to see the rising tide of colour that engulfed her face at the intimacy his compliment implied.

Standing close to her and struggling against the urge to put his arm around her, he noticed a slight red mark on her cheek which she had tried unsuccessfully to cover with makeup. Surely, he had not done that. Surely, he had been gentle with her.

He pointed to his own cheek to ask the question silently.

She shook her head.

'Not you,' was all she said.

If not him, then there was only one other explanation, he realised. 'Sometimes, not often, his temper gets the better of him.'

It was a simple horrifying statement. She turned away from him, knowing that he would want to ask more questions. He wanted to grab her hand. How could she say that and turn away from him?

'Last night?'

She nodded.

'Don't ask more,' she said quietly. 'You won't want to know.'

He shook his head slightly. What could he do? The knowledge that he was powerless to protect her from her brute of a husband made him angry. He loathed men who treated their wives in that way. Gerald Lester should put his wife on a pedestal, he thought.

It took him a few moments to realise the full import of what she had said. 'You won't want to know.' Had Gerald Lester gone so far as to force himself on his wife, Richard wondered? Had she resisted his clumsy, boozy attempts at lovemaking. Enraged by her rejection, had he slapped her and then forced her to submit to him? Richard was sick to his stomach at the thought.

He walked back towards the two boys and called to his son.

'Time to go.'

And then he caught up with her.

'I can't leave like this,' he said quietly. 'I must know I'm going to see you again.'

He could do nothing to help her domestic situation but he could at least indulge her if she would only agree to meet him.

'Do you travel to Sydney often on business?' she asked.

To anyone who overheard, it would sound like such an innocuous question. His response was equally discreet.

'As often as I need to,' he said.

She smiled. Their eyes met briefly.

'I have to take Tim and Nancy back to school at the end of this month,' she said in a whisper. 'Perhaps I could meet you then ...'

Her voice trailed off.

'Just say the word,' he said, 'and I will be there.'

She nodded.

'I'll let you know,' she said.

She walked back to the house and began organising the two girls who were finally ready to leave. He followed and helped her stow their luggage in the boot.

Paul, fearing competition for the front passenger seat, was already in the car. The two girls, having said their good-byes, slid into the back seat.

Kate stood, with her two children beside her, ready to farewell them all.

At the last moment, she held her hand out to him and he took it. He understood that to kiss her good-bye, even on the cheek, was over-stepping the bounds of propriety. Would she meet him in Sydney? He desperately hoped so.

With his passengers all settled, he fired up the engine and let out the clutch. He drove the first few yards carefully so he did not leave a cloud of dust in his wake. He took one final glance in the rear vision mirror but she had already gone back inside the house.

In the span of a few short days, he felt his life had changed. Did she feel the same, he wondered? She was everything, and more, that he admired in a woman. She had reawakened something in him, something more than desire.

He pushed thoughts of her to one side and turned to the children.

'Did you all enjoy your stay?' he asked, as he stopped to negotiate the turn back on to the main road.

There was a chorus of agreement.

'I hope we can go back soon,' Paul said. 'Tim said his father is going to get a plane and next time I will be able to go up in it.'

Richard nodded. John Bertram's to blame for this, he thought.

'Sounds exciting,' he replied, noncommittally.

'It is,' Paul said, as if that fact was beyond doubt. 'And Tim is going to have flying lessons soon. So, Dad, I want flying lessons too.'

He was in no mood to deny his son, so he agreed.

'OK,' he said. 'You can have flying lessons, but I think we need to wait another year until you are taller.'

He doubted the boy was big enough to manage the controls, even of a small aircraft.

'Wait for this, wait for that, that's all I hear,' Paul said, with mock outrage.

Richard laughed. Sometimes it seemed like that, he thought, when you're a child.

But I have to wait too for some things. I'll have to wait for Kate, for when she can get away. Already he was impatient for their reunion.

The trip back to Sydney was slower than Richard had anticipated but eventually he pulled up in front of Edith Henderson's house in Strathfield.

He was gratified to see how warmly she welcomed Pippa home. She's going to miss the girl, Richard thought, when Julia and Philippe marry, assuming that they become a family then.

'Thank you for bringing her home,' she said, as she greeted him at the front door. 'It's a complicated journey by train. I really think the girls are a bit too young yet to travel that distance alone.'

He doubted that Anita's parents, or Kate Lester for that matter, would allow the girls to travel on the train if they didn't think it was safe for them, but he didn't express an opinion.

He had met Edith Henderson briefly on a previous trip to Sydney. He was aware how fortunate Pippa had been to have been placed in her guardianship.

'Would you like to come in and have some tea,' she asked. 'You look a little tired.'

Both Paul and Anita had got out of the car.

'I see you have your son Paul with you,' she said. 'Are you planning to stay on in Sydney for a few days?'

Richard nodded.

'Yes,' he said. 'I have some business to do. It's an awkward time of year but I want to take advantage of being here.'

'Of course,' she said. 'Why don't you let young Paul stay here with me and Pippa. It would give him a chance to get to know his cousin better and I could take them to a matinee. And to Luna Park perhaps?'

Paul looked a little doubtful but Pippa added her voice to her great aunt's invitation.

'Please do,' she said. 'Please stay. It would be so much fun.'

Richard looked towards his son.

'It would be more fun than being with me couped up in a hotel room for the next couple of days,' he said. 'I have to attend a board meeting of a freight company on Monday morning.'

'OK, Dad,' he said. He liked Pippa and the lure of an afternoon matinee was very powerful. He headed back to the car to get his bag.

Richard reached into his pocket and pulled out his wallet.

'It will be an expensive weekend, I think, Mrs Henderson,' he said, as he drew a wad of notes from his wallet and handed them to her.

'There's no need ....,' she started to say.

But he waved away her protests. He gave Paul a quick hug.

'I'll be back Monday afternoon, probably around three, to pick you up.'

With that, he headed back to his car, having declined the offer of tea. All that remained was to drop Anita back to her home.

'You'll have to show me where you live, Anita,' he said. 'I don't know Sydney all that well.'

'That's no problem, Mr Belleville,' she said politely. 'I travel to this area all the time. That's our school up the road.'

He could see the deserted school building along the street.

'So, where do you live?' he asked. He couldn't remember her telling him.

'In Woollahra,' she replied.

'That's a long way to come to school every day, isn't it?'

He was puzzled because he was sure there were very prestigious girls' schools much closer to her home.

'My mother went to school at Meriden, that's why I'm there,' she said. 'Sometimes I get the train. It depends whether my dad has time to drive me in the morning before his surgery starts or whether he just drops me at Central Station.'

Under her expert navigation, it seemed no time at all and Richard was pulling up in front of the Clarke home. It was a generously proportioned two storey home which looked as if it had undergone very recent renovation.

'Looks like someone's home,' Richard said, as he got out of the car and went around to the boot to retrieve Anita's bag. He had noticed that all the windows and the front door were open.

'Dad likes to let the fresh air into the house,' she explained. 'I think it's because he's cooped up in the hospital all day.'

She pushed open the front gate and Richard walked in behind her.

Anita's mother Patricia had been expecting them for some time. She came half way down the pathway to meet them, having been alerted to their arrival by the creaking of the gate.

'Mr Belleville, I presume,' she said, extending her hand. 'Thank you for bringing my daughter home. It's very good of you. Won't you come in for a moment.'

He was about to refuse but he realised she was not a woman to whom one said 'no', so he followed mother and daughter into the house.

'This is my husband, Robert,' she said as they entered the house.

The two men shook hands.

'Your son isn't with you?' she asked. 'He was visiting Tim Lester, wasn't he? Has he stayed on?'

Richard smiled. Patricia Clarke was no doubt someone who knew all the arrangements, especially arrangements that involved her daughter, down to the finest detail.

'No, as a matter of fact, Mrs Henderson, Pippa's aunt, invited him to stay with her for a few days so the two children could get to know each other a bit better,' he said, although he wished he hadn't been so forthcoming.

'I have some business to attend to so it would have been boring for him, being with me,' he added.

She made no comment but he thought afterwards he had detected just a slight change in attitude at the mention of Pippa's name.

She motioned for him to follow her through the house. It was her husband though who broke the silence.

'Would you like a beer, Richard?' he asked. 'I'm just about to get myself another one.'

Robert Clarke had in any case pre-empted his acceptance. He was already pouring the ice cold liquid into a glass. Richard accepted it gratefully. It seemed a bit early but then it was New Year's Day.

They had walked through the kitchen and out onto the back terrace. Richard had become aware that the Clarke family were not alone.

Patricia Clarke performs her hostess duties flawlessly, Richard thought.

'Of course, you know Dr Duval?'

Of course, Richard thought, Robert Clarke and Philippe work together. How natural would it be that he is invited to their home on New Year's Day?

Philippe extended his hand and Richard greeted him warmly.

'Julia told me you were going to Bowral although she didn't exactly say when,' he said, genuinely pleased to see Richard. 'I see you were co-opted to bring the children back with you.'

'I didn't mind,' he said. 'They were no trouble at all. The girls talked nonstop but at least they were in the back seat. I've only just come from dropping Pippa off.'

'That's very good of you,' Philippe said. 'I had volunteered to go down and pick them up but Kate Lester said there was no need, they could come back by train.'

The unexpected mention of her name caught him by surprise, so he sipped his beer to cover his momentary confusion.

'We must have lunch together,' Richard said. 'Are you free tomorrow?'

Philippe nodded. It was a Saturday and unless there was an emergency, he would be free.

'I'd enjoy that,' he said. 'Are you staying at your usual hotel?'

Richard nodded.

'Meet me in the foyer at 12.00 and we'll head out to a pub I know with a great view of the harbour,' he said, remembering the long lunches he'd enjoyed there with John Bertram.

Before Philippe could reply, they were interrupted by the sound of stiletto heels on the hard-tiled floor.

Karen Clarke had not heard Richard's name when he had first arrived so there was no hint of caution in the way she approached Philippe. She stood alongside him, sliding her arm through his, positioning her body provocatively close to him. Richard noticed how Philippe tried subtly, but without success, to put some distance between them.

'A stranger in our midst?' she said brightly. 'Isn't someone going to introduce me.'

Philippe took a deep breath. He could see exactly what Richard was thinking by the look on his face. This will require some explanation, he thought. But will he believe me, he wondered?

'Karen, this is Julia Belleville's brother Richard,' he said, his polished, educated voice disguising his discomfort. 'He's been staying down with the Lesters. He brought Anita home just now.'

Richard extended his hand towards her. She took it politely. Was that a look of triumph in her eyes, Richard wondered? He remembered Kate Lester having described her as 'striking'. Kate was seeing her through a woman's eyes, he thought, definitely not through a man's eyes. A mass of auburn hair framed her perfectly-shaped face. 'Striking' is the wrong word. I would have said she was ravishing, he thought.

In those few seconds, when he met her for the first time, he understood immediately the danger she represented, especially to Philippe. Would she be deterred by Philippe's commitment to another woman or would she see that as the ultimate challenge? Richard was suddenly aware that he too was the subject of appraisal.

'Miss Clarke, how do you do?' he said.

'It's Karen, please call me Karen,' she replied.

He smiled and acknowledged the offer.

'Karen,' he said. 'Kate Lester mentioned you. You're Anita's cousin,' she said.

She smiled.

'Yes, that's right, she's my cousin,' she said. 'My father David is Uncle Robert's elder brother. My parents decided to go skiing in Aspen, but I have no taste for cold weather so I remained at home.'

That explains her presence here, Richard thought.

'Me either,' he said, conversationally. 'I endured enough bad weather in England during the war. I prefer the sun.'

He did not say he had also endured many visits to Haldon Hall, some of them in the depths of winter.

Robert Clarke had been listening intently to the exchange. He too wondered what Julia's brother would make of his niece's very public attachment to Philippe. He thought perhaps his own brother had been premature in celebrating Duval's impending marriage to Julia

Belleville. There had been no date set because she was still waiting on her divorce, so they said.

'So what were you doing in England in the war?' he asked as he joined them.

He was genuinely interested. He knew Philippe had practised as a doctor in the US Army. But what had taken a young Australian to the other side of the world?

Richard turned towards him. He was unsettled by the spectacle of his future brother-in-law with another woman on his arm, so he welcomed the diversion.

He almost never spoke about the war but he didn't want to be rude, so he replied with as little embellishment as he could.

'I was a pilot,' he said, as if it was an everyday job. 'I flew Lancaster bombers over Germany. I was one of the lucky ones. I lived through it.'

Robert Clarke let out a low whistle. He had a particular interest in military history. If pressed, he could probably recite the attrition rate of crews in RAF Bomber Command. The numbers were appalling. Richard Belleville was one lucky man to be alive and intact. They both knew it.

'Close calls?' he asked.

His curiosity had got the better of him despite Richard's obvious reluctance to speak about the topic.

'One in particular,' Richard said. 'The old crate copped too much anti-aircraft fire. I managed to bring it home, with all the crew intact.'

He did not want to sound like a hero. It was another life, a life he'd buried deep in his past.

'I remember,' Robert Clarke said, unexpectedly. 'DFC if I'm not mistaken, Squadron Leader.'

Richard nodded in acknowledgement. How could the man possibly know that? He must have a prodigious memory and have pored over the lists of casualties and commendations.

'Yes, that's right,' he said quietly. 'But there were no heroes, only those who survived and those who didn't. We all just tried to do the job we were asked to do.'

Robert Clarke shook his head. Both he and Philippe had played their part, in different forces, helping to repair the badly injured men that ended up on their operating tables. But it took a special kind of courage to fly a heavily laden Lancaster across the Channel into enemy territory, knowing that every flight could be your last.

'I think you're being far too modest,' he said. 'Far too modest. I'd like to hear more about it, but my wife will accuse me of monopolising the conversation. Why don't you come back and have dinner with us tomorrow night?'

His wife, who had come back to stand alongside her husband, reiterated the invitation.

'We would love to have you, Mr Belleville,' she said.

His presence would solve a problem for her too. She was short a man at her table. He would round it off nicely. If you set aside his sister's disgrace, she thought, he has much to recommend him. He's tall and good looking, socially at ease and a war hero. Is he rich, she wondered? Certainly, his sister seemed to travel at will and stay at the best hotel. There must be money in the family, she concluded.

Richard, for his part, felt he'd been outmanoeuvred. He could do nothing but accept the invitation.

'I'd like that,' he said politely. 'Thank you.'

'Is there a Mrs Belleville,' Robert asked, as an afterthought. 'She would be most welcome too.'

He shook his head.

'No, I'm divorced,' he said simply. 'My wife returned to England and has since remarried.'

Patricia Clarke repeated the invitation. She remembered now someone telling her that he had married into the British aristocracy but the marriage had failed.

'We look forward to seeing you again,' she said. 'It's just a few friends. Some interesting people but mostly medical. Come at seven for cocktails. We usually dine at eight.'

He smiled his thanks.

'I'll see you out,' Philippe said, eager to have a private word with him.

The two men walked out of the house together but neither of them spoke until they were sure they were out of earshot. It was Philippe who spoke first.

'Don't read too much into how Karen is with me,' he said. 'She's a very warm and friendly girl. I act as her regular escort when there is no one else around.'

Richard smiled at his explanation. He's clearly embarrassed at being caught out, he thought, but her behaviour with Philippe was not that of just a friend. Far from it. He might deny it, Richard thought, but his relationship with Karen was much more than simple friendship.

'You're playing with fire, Philippe, but you already know that, don't you?' he said. 'Just don't break my sister's heart.'

Philippe shook his head and looked down. He could not, just at that point, meet Richard's eyes.

'I'm aware of how it looks,' he said quietly.

'I'll say nothing to Julia,' Richard said, 'but you should not encourage that girl.'

It was meant as a friendly warning but he was alarmed when Philippe laughed in response to it.

'I've never encouraged her, that's the trouble,' he said. 'Her family is very unhappy about her attachment to me. I try to keep her at arm's length, but it's not always easy. Or possible. But one day she will tire of me.'

What did he mean by that, Richard wondered? But his attitude softened a little. How could he judge someone else's behaviour? How could he criticise Philippe for doing exactly what he himself had done? We're not monks, he thought. I've seduced the mother of my son's best friend, right under the nose of her husband. Except it felt different for him.

After all, Philippe had offered marriage to his sister and, in Richard's eyes, that was a commitment he should honour. Could I resist Karen Clarke if she set her sights on me, he wondered? I don't think I'm her type but a week ago I might have been vulnerable, he mused. But Philippe? Julia had always been so sure of him but I've said all I can say, Richard thought. The rest is up to him.

'Let's hope that she tires of you very, very soon, for all our sakes,' Richard said finally.

Philippe smiled and nodded, in full agreement. Richard's appearance at the Clarke's home had been so totally unexpected he felt he'd been caught out like a naughty schoolboy.

The two men parted and he turned back towards the house. Karen had walked along the pathway to meet him. Glancing towards the house to make sure they were not observed, she put her arms around his neck.

'I think I've got you into deep, deep trouble, haven't I, my dear Dr Duval?'

He laughed. What else could he do?

'You didn't know who he was, did you?'

She shook her head.

'No, I didn't,' she admitted. 'Not until I heard his name and then the penny dropped.'

'The penny dropped alright,' he said.

She laughed and kissed him lightly on the lips. Against his better judgement he put his arms around her. She was so affectionate towards him he found her hard to resist, as if rebuffing her was like rebuffing the innocent affection of a child, except she was not a child. And the affection was far from innocent. She knew it. And he knew it too.

'I told him I have tried to keep you at arm's length,' he said.

'And so you have,' she agreed. 'And so you have. But you didn't tell him that you'd failed, did you?'

Again, she laughed softly at him. He shook his head.

'No, I didn't tell him that I had failed,' he admitted.

He put his hand under her chin and tilted her face upwards.

'You are just plain trouble, Miss Clarke,' he said.

He was trying to be serious with her for a moment but everything about her rendered that ambition hopeless.

'I know,' she said teasingly.

'Terrible, aren't I?' she said, as she yielded to his embrace.

He did not respond except with a sigh that signalled his crumbling resistance.

CHAPTER 20

January 1960

Richard slept late to be woken by the sound of the telephone. He rolled across the bed and lifted the receiver. Through the haze of sleep, he recognised the voice on the other end of the line.

'John,' he said, 'what are you doing ringing at this hour? I thought you'd still be on your way back from London.'

John Bertram, on the other end of the phone, was surprised that his friend was still in bed and said so, rather crudely.

'So what's her name?' he asked.

'What do you mean?' Richard replied.

'If you're sleeping this late, you've probably had a tiring evening.'

Richard laughed then but stopped short of swearing at him. Only John could get away with such ribaldry.

'I'm alone, John,' he said. 'Quite alone. Paul is staying with his cousin Pippa.'

John had been about to ask that question.

'You still haven't told me why you are here in Sydney and not flying your precious 707 back from London,' Richard said.

'I got sick on the Sydney – Singapore leg going over and my superiors decided to replace me and send me home for some R&R,' John replied. 'Nothing serious, probably just a stomach bug. I'm alright now. I thought I'd call to see if you were back in town. How was Bowral?'

What could he say? He did not have many secrets from John

Bertram but he was hardly going to give him the full story of Bowral over the phone at eight o'clock on a Saturday morning.

'I enjoyed my short stay with the Lester family,' he said, giving no hint at all of what had happened.

'What are you up to today?' John asked. 'I thought we could catch up for lunch at our usual pub.'

'Sure,' Richard replied, 'but there'll be three of us. I made a date to meet with Philippe Duval, Julia's intended, for lunch. He's meeting me here at 12.00.'

'Ah, the vile seducer?' John said jokingly, having remembered Richard's description of him. 'I get to meet him at last.'

Given what Richard had discovered about Philippe the previous day, he thought it might well be an apt description of the man.

'Come at 11.00, John,' Richard said. 'We can have coffee before Philippe arrives.'

He heard John chuckle on the other end of the line.

'Coffee huh? Sounds serious. Got something on your mind, old man?' he asked.

He knew the signs.

'Just be here, John,' Richard said, and hung up.

He lay across the bed for a few moments before heading for the bathroom.

He's right. I do have something on my mind. My desperate desire to see Kate Lester again, he thought. Not to mention the shock of discovering Philippe is what? Betraying Julia? Or simply having an innocent flirtation with a woman who oozes sex appeal from every fibre of her being. The thought of that possibility made Richard laugh out loud. If Karen Clarke was offering herself, he thought, no red-blooded man would be able to refuse her.

What a terrible web we all weave, Richard thought. Life should be simpler than this.

Richard was already on his second cup of coffee when John Bertram walked in. He spotted Richard immediately in the hotel café and sat down opposite him.

'Well, you don't look like a man whose been partying until the small hours,' John said by way of greeting. 'Or was that the previous evening catching up with you this morning?'

Richard sipped his coffee. Trust John to get straight to the point, he thought. No small talk. No 'how are you, how've you been?'.

'You're right, John' Richard said. 'I was a bit tired from the previous evening which is why I slept late this morning.'

It was not what Richard said but the way he said it that alerted John to there being something more significant about the events of the past few days than Richard was letting on.

'Ok, let me guess? You drank too much? Or there's a woman involved?'

When Richard did not respond immediately, John opted for the obvious solution.

'OK, so my money's on a woman,' he said flippantly.

Richard looked across at his friend. Am I that transparent, he wondered? Richard, for his part, felt he had to share what had happened with someone. Who better than John Bertram? In weighing his options, he decided William would be much more disapproving than John was ever likely to be.

'I've met a woman I really admire,' Richard said finally, having tried to find the right words. He knew there was a risk it would all sound sleazy and sordid.

'That's good, isn't it?' John said, as he stirred copious amounts of sugar into the cup that had just been placed in front of him.

'Well, it's good and it's bad,' Richard said obliquely.

Why good and bad, John wondered, and then it struck him. Richard had been visiting the family of his son's best friend. Perhaps the boy had a much older sister, but that seemed unlikely. An aunt perhaps. John ran through the possibilities in his mind.

'So it was someone you met down at Bowral during your visit?'

Richard nodded. How do I tell him who it is? But John was ahead of him. There's only one reason, he thought, why Richard's being so deliberately vague.

'She's married, am I right?' he asked straight out.

Richard nodded slightly, surprised yet relieved that John had uttered the words.

'But there's more isn't there?'

Richard nodded again.

'Yes, there's more,' he said, again without going into any detail.

'OK, you didn't keep your admiration to yourself, I suppose,' John said, filling in the blanks in the conversation.

He looked at Richard as he said it and he saw the slight shake of his friend's head.

'Bloody hell, you've seduced her, haven't you?'

John really didn't expect him to confirm it so he was surprised when Richard nodded his head.

John, as only John could, shook his head from side to side and let out a curious sound that Richard knew only too well. It's was John's way of scolding him, of disagreeing with him or of questioning his behaviour.

'Does her husband know?' John asked, looking carefully at his friend's face. 'You don't look as though anyone's taken a swing at you in a jealous rage lately.'

After such an admission he felt entitled to know the basic details. Richard laughed but then he became serious.

'No, he didn't take a swing at me,' he said. 'I'm sure he has no idea. But he took a swing at Kate.'

John put his cup down. It clattered in the saucer but he took no notice of it.

'You mean he hit his wife? How do you know?'

'I saw her the next morning with a faint but visible red mark on her face,' he said. What he had to say next he found extremely painful. Painful because of his impotence in not being able to defend her.

'It seems she tried to resist his drunken advances but he had other ideas,' he said. 'When I pressed her for details, all she said was, 'you won't want to know'. I think you can draw your own conclusions.'

The two men sat in silence for some time. John could see how much it had cost Richard to walk away and not do something to protect her.

'Let me get this right,' John said. 'You were staying in Bowral with the family of one of Paul's friends from school. A family by the name of Lester, as I recall. And you've seduced the mother of your son's best friend, am I right? And discovered that her husband is handy with his fists?'

Again, Richard nodded, confirming John's understanding of what he had just told him.

'And are you planning to see her again?' he asked.

'Yes, I am,' he replied.

John noticed there was no uncertainty at all in his response.

'Hopefully at the end of this month here in Sydney,' Richard said. 'Her son Tim goes to Shore and her daughter Nancy goes to the same school as my niece Pippa. She's coming up to bring them back to school.'

John sat back in his chair. On the one hand he was pleased his friend had met someone new. For a long time, he worried Richard had been so bitter about the breakup of his marriage to Catherine that he looked as if he would never get on with his life. Now this. A woman married to another man. A woman likely to remain married to that other man.

'You don't believe in the simple life, do you?' John said, shaking his head in disbelief. 'Where do you think this will lead?'

It was a pertinent question but Richard could only shrug his shoulders by way of response.

'Who can tell where it will lead,' he said, 'but I know I can't walk away and never see her again.'

It was clear to John that this was much more than a one-night stand. Richard had never used his charm and his looks to sleep with women indiscriminately, not in his experience anyway, so his answer came as no surprise.

'I assume she's around your age?' John asked, curious now for a little more detail. She has to be special, he thought. She has to be special to help him forget Catherine.

'Possibly a couple of years younger,' Richard said. 'She married at nineteen but her husband must be eleven to twelve years her senior or possibly more. She married him because her family had fallen on hard times and he offered to give her father a job.'

'Which means she didn't marry for love,' John said.

That's a classic scenario, he thought. The woman who marries for reasons of security, and then finds it hard to go on living with that decision, year after year.

'No,' Richard replied. 'She didn't marry for love.'

John shook his head. He done quite a bit of that in hearing this story over the past half hour. He didn't know quite what to say. He didn't condemn his good friend for his behaviour. He knew Richard was a decent man who would not casually seduce a married woman, or any woman for that matter. In John's experience, he had never been heartless nor deliberately cruel.

'I hope it works out,' was all John could think to say.

What more could he say? To him, it seemed like a hopeless situation that was only going to lead to more heartache for his good friend. But he didn't want to say that. He'll find that out soon enough, he thought. He doesn't need me to tell him.

'Thanks, mate,' Richard replied.

John signalled for another cup of coffee and then he turned back to Richard, who sat back in his chair, his arms behind his head.

'And your sister?' John asked, deciding it was time to change the topic of conversation. 'Her divorce must be through soon so she can marry again. Any news on that front?'

Richard lent forward and lowered his voice. He was aware that Philippe could walk in at any moment.

'Well, as it turns out, I ran into my future brother-in-law yesterday afternoon,' he said. 'I brought the other children who were staying with the Lesters back to Sydney. One of them was Anita Clarke. Anita Clarke's father is Philippe's colleague at the hospital. There was a small family lunch at the Clarke's home and I arrived just at the end of it. Who should I find there but Philippe, with the ravishing Karen Clarke, who happens to be Dr Clarke's niece, being very familiar with him? He had the good grace to be embarrassed at being caught out.'

John heard all this in silence. Then he laughed quietly.

'So, he was being a naughty boy too,' John replied. 'I take it he wasn't expecting you to turn up?'

'No, he wasn't,' Richard said. 'And she didn't know who I was so in effect she dropped him right in it.'

John pulled a face.

'Bloody hell, what am I doing wrong?' he declared. 'You have women throwing themselves at you. Your future brother-in-law does too. And no woman ever takes a second look at me.'

Richard laughed out loud at this. Apart from John's enduring hopeless love for his cousin Catherine, he had rarely seen his friend with a woman on his arm, which he'd always assumed was John's lack of interest rather than anything else.

'I don't think it's quite like that, John,' he said, but he did not get a chance to say anything further to his good friend.

He had not seen Philippe until he came up to their table.

'May I share the joke?' he asked, as he extended his hand to Richard, who in turn, introduced him to John Bertram.

John got up and greeted him. Inwardly he groaned. He understood then why women might fall for Philippe Duval. He was perfectly groomed, urbane and sophisticated. His dark hair had just begun to show a hint of grey which only made him look more distinguished. His foreign accent only added to his slight air of mystery.

If I was Richard's sister, he thought, I wouldn't let him out of my sight.

'Shall we head out?' Richard said.

As they walked towards the entrance of the hotel, the concierge handed Philippe's car keys back to him.

'Your keys, sir.'

'Thank you,' he said, as he handed the young man a tip.

'I couldn't get a park so I parked right out front. Perhaps I should drive us?'

Both John and Richard nodded in agreement and followed him through the front door of the hotel. Richard was surprised to see a brand new Mercedes in the driveway. It looked like it had just come off the showroom floor.

'Nice car,' he said. 'Is it new?'

Philippe nodded.

'Karen organised it for me,' he said, without thinking. 'Her father owns several dealerships.'

So, thought John. Not only do the women throw themselves at this handsome American surgeon, they organise new cars for him too, no doubt at a discounted price. What the hell am I doing wrong, he thought, as he and Richard took their seats in the luxury saloon.

Half an hour later, with their meals and drinks ordered, the three men chose a table with a good view of the harbour. It was a hot day but umbrellas shading the outdoor tables made it possible to sit outside in the fresh air, rather than the smoke fogged bar and restaurant.

Philippe did not know the history of Richard's friendship with John Bertram. As they sat down, he put the question to the two of them.

'So how do you two know each other?' he asked.

He assumed the friendship might go back a long way, school perhaps? Richard answered him.

'John was my navigator on the Lancaster crew back in England,' he said, 'and he is also my ex-wife's cousin. He was the one who introduced me to Catherine so we go back a long way.'

The waiter brought their drinks and Richard was grateful for the interruption. He left John to take up the story.

'We've stayed in touch since then,' John said, glossing over his role as an intermediary in the marriage breakdown. 'I upgraded my skills after the war and now I fly the Sydney-London route for Qantas. But Richard was the best pilot I ever knew.'

Philippe nodded. He sipped his glass of wine. He did not share their taste for beer.

'I heard something of that story yesterday when he was telling Robert Clarke about it,' he said. 'So you were his navigator? Robert would be so interested in that. He's very keen on his military history and particularly military aviation.'

'We don't talk about it much,' John said warily. Neither he nor Richard were very keen on reliving that part of their shared history.

'Richard is coming to dinner tonight to the Clarke's place,' Philippe said. 'You should come too.'

Richard interrupted this time.

'Not, I think, before you clear it with Patricia Clarke,' he said with a smile. 'I think she organises her dinners with military precision. An unannounced guest would throw everything into turmoil.'

Philippe reached into his pocket and drew out his wallet, from which he extracted a business card. It turned out to be Robert Clarke's and it included his home telephone number.

'Would you like an invitation?' he asked John. 'It would make a change from all those boring medical people that turn up at their dinners. I could call Robert now.'

John shrugged. He had nothing better to do with his evening and he was curious to see the luscious Karen Clarke, who would probably be there.

'If you feel it is appropriate,' he replied.

Philippe got up and went in to the bar to use the telephone. Within a few minutes he had returned.

'Patricia and Robert would be delighted for you to attend,' he said.

He took a small notebook from his pocket and scribbled the address for John. He then looked towards Richard.

'What did Patricia say?' he said. 'Come at seven for cocktails. We dine at eight.'

Richard laughed.

'It did have the feeling of military precision about it, I must say,' he said.

'Oh, and I should warn you,' Philippe said, looking towards Richard. 'There's every chance they'll seat you next to my friend Karen this evening.'

Richard smiled at him.

'How can you be so sure?' he asked.

'Because they want to distance her from me,' he said candidly, 'but they don't realise the more they go on about how unsuitable I am, the more interested she is in me.'

John could not help himself at this point. Perhaps it was because he was on his third beer.

'Richard was telling me about the lady before you came to meet us,' he said. 'Good looking, he says, ravishing in fact, and very keen on you.'

Richard wished he could have silenced John at that point but Philippe only laughed.

'Yes, I was rather caught out, like a naughty school boy,' he said smoothly, 'but Karen sometimes makes a big display of her interest in me just to annoy her family, including her uncle, who would be under strict instructions to report every misdemeanour back to his older brother.'

Well, he's had all night to think up that excuse, Richard thought, but I'm not going to challenge that statement just yet.

The three of them ate in silence for a few moments. Once again, it was Philippe who spoke first.

'By the way, Robert said Patricia was quite relieved to have another man added to the party at the last minute.'

'Oh, why was that,' John asked, although it had just sunk in that Patricia Clarke was a hostess who liked a balanced dinner party of equal numbers of men and women.

'Apparently Lucy Dixon's parents are coming to dinner too,' he said. 'Lucy is the other girl in the group at school with Pippa. I haven't met them yet. I think he's something in the law.'

'But they're a couple,' Richard said. 'That wouldn't make her dinner table unbalanced.'

'No, you're right,' he said, 'but apparently Kate Lester, Nancy's mother, has made a quick visit to Sydney for some reason and Patricia felt she couldn't invite the Dixons without inviting her as she's staying with them, hence the need for another man at the table. Her husband isn't with her, apparently, which Patricia thought was unusual.'

John could hardly dare look at Richard who had suddenly become very interested in the remnants of his meal. But Philippe noticed the sudden tension.

'Something amiss?' he asked.

As a doctor he was attuned to unexplained changes in his patients, especially changes in their emotional state. Looking at Richard he was starting to go through all the possibilities of what might have caused his reaction to the news of Kate Lester's presence at the dinner.

'Of course, you've just spent several days with the Lesters,' Philippe said, using his professional skills to probe for the reason for the sudden change in Richard's mood.

'I'm told she is a quite lovely woman who has thrown herself away on a less than appreciative husband,' he said. 'According to Karen anyway.'

Richard could not trust himself to reply. Once again, John came to his rescue.

'Why is it that fellows who have perfectly lovely wives don't always appreciate them,' he said.

Philippe knew there was no answer to this rhetorical question. He himself had been guilty of not appreciating his wife in his short marriage. He knew something of Richard's protracted divorce from his wife. But he hazarded a guess that John was single.

'What about you, John?' he asked. 'Is there a Mrs Bertram?'

John shook his head.

'No, afraid not,' he said. 'The life of a pilot isn't conducive to a stable family life.'

'A bit like the life of a surgeon,' Philippe said. 'People need critical operations at the most inconvenient times.'

He drained his glass.

'Don't worry, I'm not on call today,' he said, having caught John's querying look. 'You need a very steady hand to do neurosurgery.'

'And to fly a plane,' John said.

Both professions demand abstention from alcohol at times, he mused. Philippe suddenly looked at his watch.

'I really need to go,' he said. 'I got a call from Edith Henderson this morning to pick up your son and my daughter from their matinee at three o'clock.'

Richard laughed. Philippe was probably the most highly paid taxi driver in the city this afternoon and certainly the only one driving a brand new Mercedes Benz.

'I take it she doesn't think they can get home by train by themselves?' Richard asked.

He would have been disappointed to think Paul was incapable of looking after his cousin. In a month's time, the boy would turn fourteen. But he didn't attempt to interfere in the arrangements.

'No, she is a little over protective of Pippa,' he said, 'but I don't mind that. I help out when I can.'

'I should come with you,' Richard said.

'No, it's fine,' Philippe said. 'Stay here and enjoy a beer with John. You look as though you need it. I'll see you tonight. No doubt you can get a taxi back to your hotel?'

Richard nodded and looked at his watch.

'We'll be fine,' he said. 'You go otherwise those kids might get up to some mischief.'

With that, Philippe was gone and he and John were left to contemplate the evening ahead of them. As soon as Philippe had left, John let out a low whistle.

'I bet you weren't expecting that news?' he said. 'I could see the shock on your face. So could Philippe. You'll have to be very careful this evening, otherwise Kate Lester's reputation will be in tatters.'

He knew that. He didn't need John to remind him. The big question was: why had she come to Sydney at such short notice? There had been no mention of it just over twenty-four hours ago.

Well, this is going to be an interesting dinner, John thought. Very interesting indeed.

Chapter 21

January 1960

A weak southerly change had cooled the city by the time Richard and John walked up the garden path of the Clarke's home in Woollahra just before the appointed time. Richard shrugged on his suit coat as he walked. He hoped dinner jackets were not expected as he had not packed for such an occasion.

Their hostess greeted them at the door and Richard performed the necessary introduction.

Patricia Clarke has spent the entire afternoon in the beauty parlour, Richard thought. She was immaculately groomed extending a well-manicured hand to each of them in turn. She looks as if she was born to the role of hostess, Richard thought, but obviously her love of entertaining did not mean slaving away in the kitchen for hours.

Robert Clarke was standing just behind her. He was clearly delighted to meet John Bertram. Robert had brightened at the prospect of having two World War Two heroes at his dinner table and had insisted that his wife seat them either side of him at one end. By the end of most dinners he was usually bored by the medical talk or the small talk of the women. Or disturbed by the sight of his niece flirting outrageously with Philippe Duval, who did not discourage her quite as vigorously as Robert would have liked.

But Richard Belleville's arrival in their midst had changed all that. He hoped some good food and good wine would encourage him and his friend John Bertram to regale him with stories of their wartime exploits. It was so rare to meet bomber crew that he could not pass up the opportunity. He had forsaken his medical journals that afternoon in favour of his expanding library of military history to refresh his memory of the war in Europe and particularly the air war. His wife, in exasperation, had finally evicted him from his study to get changed with only half an hour to spare.

He was already monopolising both Richard and John as they walked through to the drawing room. Richard glanced around quickly. He could not see Kate Lester although he and John were by no means the first to arrive.

The two of them greeted Philippe, who in turn introduced them to the woman with whom he had been in deep conversation. Richard was surprised it wasn't Karen by his side. But he conceded the woman would represent no threat to Karen.

'Barbara is the best theatre nurse I've worked with,' Philippe said generously.

'I'll second that,' Robert Clarke said enthusiastically.

Richard noticed how she reddened at the unexpected compliment from the two doctors who clearly valued her professional skills.

He acknowledged the introduction. He was amused to see her eyes flick back quickly to Philippe. Another conquest, Richard thought. That woman would walk through a brick wall for him.

Richard turned as a waiter offered him a drink. He was grateful Robert Clarke's hospitality extended to single malt. As he took the drink from the tray, he caught the flash of a swirling skirt out of the corner of his eye. Karen Clarke was suddenly by his side.

'Hello again,' she said exuberantly as she raised a glass of champagne to her lips.

'Good evening, Karen,' he said. 'May I introduce my good friend, John Bertram.'

He had managed to extricate John from Robert Clarke's clutches as the host's attention was temporarily distracted.

'John,' she said, her smile dazzling. 'How wonderful to meet you. My uncle has been talking non-stop about the two war heroes who are coming to dinner tonight.'

John blushed. He wished he had Richard's easy charm.

'Not a hero, Miss Clarke,' he said at last. 'Just did a job, that's all it was.'

'And what do you do now, John?' she asked. 'Something exciting and interesting?'

Richard almost laughed out loud at the charm offensive she had directed at his good friend.

'I'm a pilot for Qantas,' he said, as if it was just an everyday job. 'I fly the Sydney-London route so next time you go to Europe for a holiday, you might find I'm at the controls.'

'Oh, that's wonderful,' she said, her eyes lighting up. 'My friend Bianca and I are planning a trip in the late northern spring. It would be such fun to know the captain of our flight over.'

John was captivated by everything about her. Her deep blue green eyes, her stunning good looks, the sensuous movement of her body, he couldn't recall having met a woman quite like her. Richard watched all this with great amusement. He wondered if John would ever fully recover from the encounter.

She moved on to Philippe who smiled too warmly at her for Richard's liking. But it was not even the way she glided up to him and claimed him that troubled Richard the most. It was the way she looked at him, just for a brief moment. The girl's not simply being flirtatious, Richard thought. She is in love with him. Completely and utterly in love with him. And Philippe? It was hard for him to judge. Was he simply flattered by the attention? What man wouldn't be? Or was he in danger of succumbing to her undoubted charms? John Bertram followed his gaze and saw what he saw.

'Looks like your sister might have some competition,' he said quietly. 'Or is it that our doctor friend just enjoys the attention? From what I can see he would only have to say the word and she would be in his bed in a flash. Lucky bastard.'

For once, Richard was annoyed by his friend's outspoken assessment of what they were seeing but he could see with his own eyes what John was saying was probably true. He sipped his whisky as he contemplated the implications. He noticed that more people had arrived and with them the noise in the room had risen markedly. He turned as the voice of his hostess cut through the noise.

'You know Kate Lester, of course,' she said to Richard, catching him completely off guard.

Kate had been following behind Patricia, whose objective was to introduce her to her dinner companions.

'Kate, this is Richard's friend, John Bertram,' she said.

'John,' Patricia said. 'I've put you near Robert so he can chat to you about goodness knows what but Kate will be on your other side, opposite Karen, who's next to Richard on the other side of the table.'

Philippe's prediction had come to pass, Richard thought. She's doing her best to find another target for her irrepressible niece. In the crush and distraction of introductions, Richard held Kate's hand and raised it to his lips.

'We meet again,' he said quietly. 'It's unexpected.'

She smiled, uncertain of what to say in a crowded room where anything at all could be overhead. Or perhaps the noise rendered it safe? She glanced quickly to both sides, worried that either her friend Angela Dixon or her husband Ian might have seen the greeting. She relaxed when she was sure they had not. They were busy being introduced elsewhere.

But Philippe had noticed the intimate greeting and instantly understood its meaning, having remembered Richard's sudden change of mood when her name had been mentioned that afternoon.

So, he thought, my future brother-in-law wants to take me to task for my behaviour, yet he seems impervious to the impropriety of romancing another man's wife? He smiled to himself. Karen's gaze too had followed his. She had not missed the significance of the greeting either. There was obviously more to the war hero than meets the eye, she thought. And what a challenge he would be, she thought, as she looked him up and down. How jealous could she make Philippe, she wondered?

It was John Bertram who forced Richard to relinquish Kate's hand by extending his own hand in greeting.

'How do you do,' he said courteously. 'I've heard so much about you and Bowral.'

She heard John's words and the colour drained from her face. She looked imploringly at Richard. But, as ever, he was quick to cover his friend's poor choice of words.

'John means I told him what a wonderful house you have down at Bowral and how much I enjoyed my stay,' he said reassuringly.

She relaxed then and smiled at him. It was a warm, generous smile and John was entranced by it.

'It was really nice to have Richard and the children visit,' she said to John. 'It's a pity it was so short. My son is still talking about his slow bowling.'

They all laughed. That's a new pick up line, thought John. Impress with your bowling ability.

'And what brings you to Sydney?' John asked, knowing that this was the very question his friend wanted to ask but couldn't.

She smiled.

'My daughter decided at the last minute she wanted to go to see the ballet matinee this afternoon, so I called Angela Dixon to find out if she and her daughter Lucy were going,' she explained. 'We were lucky to get tickets, but Angela is very well connected in the theatre world. We were lucky that the Dixons got back from New Zealand yesterday.'

Richard heard the explanation with some relief. He had, in his worst moments, imagined that Gerald Lester had become even more intolerable which had caused her to leave her home suddenly.

As Kate finished speaking, Karen came to stand alongside Richard and put her arm through his. She was so close he could feel the warmth and softness of her body. Does she do this to men all the time, he wondered? Or does she pick her targets? If she does this to John Bertram, there's a good chance he'll faint.

'My aunt sent me to gather you all to go into dinner,' she said brightly. 'John, give your arm to Kate. She's sitting next to you.'

John Bertram obeyed her immediately.

'Looks like we've been given our marching orders,' he said, as he offered his arm to her.

She took it gratefully. How much harder would it have been if she had been seated next to Richard. But she felt just a tinge of jealousy that Karen Clarke was free to flirt shamelessly with him and she was not.

'Are you and Richard good friends?' she asked John.

There was so much she did not know about Richard. It seemed a safe question to ask.

'The best of friends,' John said. 'We met in England during the war. I was the navigator in his crew. And he married my cousin.'

'But that marriage has ended,' he added hastily.

'Yes, I know that much about him,' she said.

John then said in a quiet voice.

'Don't be perturbed but I know what happened between you and Richard.'

He felt her hand tremble, so he put his hand over hers. She clung more tightly to his arm. She appreciated his gesture of reassurance.

'You have no need to worry,' he said quietly. 'Your secret is safe with me.'

She nodded and smiled. He could see the relief in her face. She was free to talk to him about Richard and not worry about the consequences. In front of them, Karen was guiding Richard to the dining room.

'I see you've made a good friend of Kate Lester very quickly,' she said, with just the hint of a secret smile on her lips.

Richard looked at her. You little minx, he wanted to say, you don't miss anything, do you? Behind him, he could hear Philippe being introduced to Kate. He half turned but Karen stopped him.

'Worried Philippe might turn her head?' she whispered.

He looked back at Karen who was smiling conspiratorially at him.

'And what makes you say that?' he asked, as he deliberately tried to make her feel uncomfortable by drawing her closer to him.

But she was a match for him, enjoying nestling closer to him. She noticed the scar on the side of his face which added a touch of danger to his looks.

'Your body language gives you away,' she said. 'I saw the way you greeted her tonight.'

He laughed it off.

'That's absurd,' he said, but then lowered his voice. 'And what do you think your body language tells me about you?'

Two can play at this game, he thought, as his eyes travelled provocatively over her body. He continued to hold her close to him.

It was not an unpleasant sensation. Far from it and she did not protest. But she wouldn't be drawn further into the tease.

As they reached the table, he drew her chair out for her and sat down beside her. Diagonally across from him, John had done the same for Kate Lester. Then Philippe sat down next to her. He immediately claimed Kate's attention so that she had to look away from Richard, who was immediately accosted by Robert Clarke, eager to continue their conversation about Richard and John's wartime exploits.

Out of the corner of his eye, he watched as Philippe lavished attention on Kate.

Was that deliberate, Richard wondered? Is he trying to tell me something? He felt his irritation rising. She's mine, he wanted to say. Stay away from her. But that's crazy, he thought. I have no claim on her.

During the course of the evening, food came and went, Richard found his wine glass refilled at regular intervals without asking and he answered Robert Clarke's eager questions without irritation. Fortunately, he could call on John Bertram to fill in the gaps in his memory.

Beside him, Karen Clarke shared her attentions between Richard and Jules Hamilton, her uncle's regular anaesthetist, on her other side. Across the table, Philippe, who had mastered the art of dinner table conversation, charmed the women on either side of him.

More shop talk with Barbara Thomas, Richard guessed, but with Kate? He doubted Philippe was the type to talk endlessly about the children. He'd detected a reticence in Philippe to talk openly about Pippa. He no longer denied she was his child but Richard guessed there was an awkwardness in knowing that almost everyone he met knew the salacious details of how he had fathered a child out of wedlock.

At that moment, Kate turned her head and smiled at him, before turning to John Bertram, who bent his head to hear her question. This dinner is endless, thought Richard. How will I get Kate alone for a few moments? Just then, Patricia Clarke stood up and said it was such a fine night, she would have coffee served on the terrace.

There was a general scraping of chairs as guests began to leave the table. Before Richard could leave, his path was blocked by Kate's friend

Angela, who held her hand out towards him.

'Mr Belleville,' she said, 'we didn't meet before dinner but Kate has told me all about you. My name's Angela Dixon.'

He was momentarily speechless. Did she really mean 'all' about me, he wondered? Was Angela Dixon as close to Kate as John is to me? He thought it would be a dangerous admission on Kate's part to tell anyone what had occurred between them.

He replied politely.

'It's very good to meet you,' he said. 'My son is a friend of Kate's son Tim.'

He thought he should say something. Her husband came forward then to be introduced. Ian Dixon extended his hand towards Richard and he shook it. He was a distinguished looking man of around fifty, his grey hair framing a lightly tanned face.

'I was trying to listen in to some of what you and your friend were telling Robert,' he said. 'It was so interesting. I said to Patricia just now it would be better to sit all the men together, but she was having none of that idea. I have a feeling she won't invite me back any time soon.'

Richard laughed.

'What, put all the men together?' Richard said. 'And spoil her niece's fun, flirting with the men next to her.'

Not to mention, Richard thought, that I'd then have to listen to men pontificate on politics and argue pointlessly about the state of Australian cricket.

Ian Dixon smiled.

'She's a very pretty girl, I grant you that,' he said, 'but it's you young blokes who attract her eye.'

Ian Dixon was clearly a master of understatement, Richard thought.

'You must have been quite young when you went off training in Canada?' he said.

'I was,' Richard said. 'Very young and very green.'

He had set off on what he thought was the adventure of a lifetime until the grim reality of war caught up with him. But he didn't want to say that. He didn't want to continue the conversation in that vein.

'I take it you would have been overseas when your niece Pippa was born?' he asked, clearly trying to get all the tangled web of relationships right in his mind.

'Yes,' he said. 'That's right. I was.'

But he did not say anything more. He did not want to retell the complicated story of Pippa's illegitimate birth and her being given up for adoption. He thought it possible Julia's fall from grace might be dinner party gossip forever. They must all know the story, or a version of it, he thought.

Except it occurred to him then that Philippe didn't appear to be paying any price socially or professionally for his role in leaving Julia pregnant and unmarried at nineteen. It seemed the fuss that had surrounded his son's disclosure of Philippe being Pippa's father had evaporated, much as he had expected it would.

'Your niece is a nice kid,' Ian Dixon said, unprompted. 'My daughter Lucy has a good set of friends, with her and Nancy Lester and Anita Clarke.'

Richard was surprised there had been no sign of Anita all night. Too young for an adult dinner party, he thought. Probably shipped out to a friend's place for the evening.

'I think the other girls missed your daughter at the Lesters' place last week,' Richard said, with a smile.

'Well, you'd think three girls under one roof would be enough, wouldn't you, without wanting to add to them,' he replied, with just a hint of humour.

Richard laughed. He was inclined to agree. He found Ian Dixon refreshingly straight forward.

'What work do you do, if I may ask?' Richard said.

'Nothing useful like Robert and Philippe, I'm afraid,' he said. 'I'm a lawyer. My uncle is Chief Justice of the High Court. Sort of runs in the family. Angela finds her theatre pals much more interesting than my legal friends. I have to say she is right.'

Richard's experience of lawyers had been limited to dealing with Belleville family business and his divorce. He could not imagine socialising with them.

'And you, Richard?' he asked. 'You're not local, I understand.'

Richard shook his head.

'No, I come from up north, Springfield,' he said. 'My brother and I have a big cattle property Prior Park and other business interests. My brother tends to look after our rural interests.'

The two men walked out of the dining room together.

'You took your son down to stay with the Lesters, I understand?'

Richard nodded.

'Yes, my elder son Paul lives with me,' he explained. 'He was at Shore for a couple of years. That's how he met Tim Lester and the boys have stayed in touch. My younger son Anthony lives in England with his mother.'

'That must be difficult for you?'

'It is,' Richard admitted. 'I'm hoping to bring Anthony back to live with me when he is a little older. My ex-wife has had another child to her new husband. I think my son might get overlooked.'

'Surely not,' Ian Dixon said.

'Not deliberately, you understand,' Richard said, 'but the new child is going to inherit the baronetcy which means my boy will be less important, if I can put it that way, in the household, and I don't like that idea.'

The older man nodded his head. He could see the problem now. He had dealt with so many family issues, nothing surprised him. He reached into the inside pocket of his jacket. He handed Richard his card.

'If you ever need help with a legal matter, especially where your child is concerned, I think I can help,' he said.

Richard looked down at the card. It read simply, Ian Dixon, LL.M., Q.C.

'Thank you,' he said. 'I may need your help one day.'

Ian Dixon was about to walk away but he turned back.

'We're having a few friends for a bar-b-que lunch tomorrow,' he said. 'Why don't you and your friend John Bertram come along. Say 12.00 o'clock. My home address is on the back of the card.'

Richard nodded.

'I'd like that,' he said. 'I'm sure John would too.'

'Very casual,' Ian Dixon said, gesturing to the tie around his neck he was desperate to remove.

Richard laughed and sympathised. He too preferred casual dress.

John Bertram came up beside him and held out a cup of coffee to his friend.

'Thought you might need this,' he said. 'God knows they plied us with enough alcohol in that dining room. I'm pleased I'm not flying tomorrow.'

Richard nodded in agreement. The hospitality had been very generous.

'I think you'll find our host has a very good cellar underneath this house,' he said.

From the back terrace, the lights of the harbour sparkled below them. The two men leaned against the railing. Richard lit a cigarette. He rarely smoked these days but just occasionally the urge struck him.

'You seemed to get on well with Kate,' Richard said.

It was half a question, half a statement

'I did,' he said. 'I can see why you're attracted to her. She's very natural and unaffected. The complete opposite to a woman like Karen Clarke. She's lovely, in fact.'

Richard listened closely to what John was saying. His friend's opinion of her was suddenly very important.

'But I don't think she's practised at this type of deception,' John added quietly. 'It troubles her, if I'm not mistaken.'

'And you think I'm completely untroubled by it?' Richard replied.

As he spoke, he noticed her standing alone near the tray of coffee cups that had been brought on to the terrace. He moved quickly to stand beside her. She glanced up at him and half turned to face him.

'I noticed you got the full treatment from the striking Miss Clarke,' she said teasingly. 'You must be very tempted. Or was she simply trying to make the good doctor jealous?'

He laughed and moved a little closer to her.

'She's quite a package, isn't she?' he said, smiling. 'But I'm not tempted. Not at all.'

Kate shook her head disbelievingly.

'She may be disappointed after all that effort,' she said. 'For an hour or so, you were the envy of every man at the table, apart from her uncle.'

He desperately wanted to touch Kate but he dare not. Even though it was quite dark on the terrace, he could not risk it. John Bertram's words echoed in his mind, 'her reputation will be in tatters'.

'You look beautiful tonight,' he whispered. 'I'm struggling to keep my hands to myself.'

She blushed, grateful there was no one close enough to notice. She sipped her coffee.

'I'm not going to suggest we get lost in the garden here,' she said, 'if that's what you were hoping I'd say.'

He laughed. The Clarke's home was way too public for assignations of that kind, he thought.

'And I suppose I can't even say I will drive you home,' he said. 'The Dixons might suspect something was going on.'

She shook her head.

'If it was just Angela, it would be OK,' she said. 'I've covered for her before, but not with Ian in tow.'

He looked slightly taken aback.

'Don't look so shocked,' she said. 'Ian's a nice man, just a little boring.'

Richard laughed then. So women had their secrets too, he thought.

'And how many times has she covered for you, may I ask?'

In the darkness he had slipped his arm loosely around her waist. She shook her head.

'Never for me, but in future, who knows?' she said provocatively.

He was serious then, remembering how her husband had hit her. How could he ask her if such a thing had happened again?

'I was worried the day I left,' he said. 'I wanted to protect you but I know I have no right …'

She put a single finger up to her lips.

'Don't talk about that,' she whispered. 'I don't ever want to talk about that part of my life. Not when I'm with you.'

He nodded. He understood then there were some things that were off limits.

As they talked, they had walked to the darkest corner of the terrace. He pulled her into his arms quickly and kissed her, and then released her reluctantly. For that brief moment, he felt the softness and willingness of her body.

'Are you sure you would be missed? he whispered. 'We could go back to my hotel right now.'

But she shook her head. As much as she wanted to be with him, she couldn't take the risk. There was too much at stake. Even being seen with him like this could start the gossips talking, she thought.

'You'll have to be patient,' she said. 'Perhaps Karen might be a consolation prize after all?'

He laughed at her impudence.

'Not a good idea,' he said. 'Besides, I think Philippe might have something to say about that. What do you think?'

He had asked the question to test her reaction to Karen's flirtation with Philippe. Was he reading too much into it? Was it just harmless fun?

'I think he might too,' she said, suddenly thoughtful. 'He's a very charming man. I think he's almost blasé about female adulation, it's happened so often. He's meant to be marrying your sister when her divorce is through, isn't he?'

Richard nodded.

'He is indeed. I was hoping his interest in Karen was just a harmless flirtation.'

Kate looked doubtful.

'Does she really look harmless to you, Richard? she asked. 'I can tell you her behaviour raises a few eyebrows, among the women of course. But it's probably envy.'

Again, he laughed, remembering just how provocative Karen has been when he first met her.

'I'm sure it's envy,' he said, 'but you have nothing to be envious of.'

He started to caress her slowly, sensuously, deliberately. He was remembering the pleasure of making love to her. She caught his hand and shook her head.

'You must stop,' she said. 'You must stop.'

He dropped his hand.

'I did not expect to see you again so soon,' he said.

'Me either,' she said, as she turned to walk away to rejoin her friends. 'I must go. I hope it's not too long ….'

Her words trailed off. Standing next to him had become too risky.

She knew she would be the one to suffer if gossip started, not him. There was too much at stake for her and she knew it only too well. But for all her caution, they had not been unobserved.

Philippe had noticed their intimacy and knew immediately the two were already lovers. He admired Richard but in him he could see just that hint of arrogance that money and privilege had bred. Richard was a man used to getting what he wanted, he thought. If Kate continued to see him when he chose to come to Sydney, it would be her, not him, who would suffer any fallout from their affair becoming public knowledge. He hoped Richard would do whatever he could to protect her. I've survived a scandal, he thought, but for a married woman, the stakes were much, much higher. Without doubt, her Sydney friends would be forced to abandon her.

Angela Dixon had noticed Richard's interest in her friend too and smiled to herself. I hope he's kinder to her than her husband is, she thought to herself. She remembered times when Kate had tried to cover up multiple bruises. She deserves better than that, she thought. Much better than that. She deserves to be loved.

She looked around for her own husband, who was deep in conversation with Robert Clarke. Does Ian ever look at another woman, she wondered? Or is he simply the loyal, faithful husband he appears to be? She might have added 'dull' to the description, but she thought that was unkind. Unromantic perhaps? He looked up and caught her eye and smiled. He motioned to her to join them.

'Sorry, darling,' he said. 'We've been talking about war stuff.'

She groaned inwardly. There's Richard Belleville romancing her friend in full view of just about everyone and these men want to talk about war. What's wrong with them, she thought. Is it any wonder we women look around occasionally for a distraction?

The two men hardly drew breath as they resumed their earnest discussion about Hitler's military tactics that had failed spectacularly in the Ardennes.

'He's very handsome,' she said in an undertone to Kate, who had just rejoined the group. 'Divorced, isn't he?'

Kate nodded.

'Yes, his wife went back to England. She inherited the family pile when her father died,' Kate said. 'She never came back to Australia and now she's married again and had another baby.'

'Have you, you know….?' Angela asked obliquely.

Kate simply blushed. Angela needed no other answer.

'Be careful, my dear,' she said. 'You don't want to end up with unexpected consequences.'

It's too late for that, Kate thought. I will just have to trust to luck.

'By the way, Ian's invited Richard and his friend John for lunch tomorrow,' she said. 'Do you want to stay on?'

Kate had already said she would leave for home in the morning.

'No, I won't,' she said, with a mixture of sadness and regret. 'It's too dangerous. Nancy is old enough now to be aware of anything unusual. I couldn't risk it.'

She paused.

'I would be so desperate to be with him,' she added, 'I might do something I regret in front of my daughter.'

Angela smiled and nodded. She put her arm around her friend in a reassuring gesture.

'When you bring the children back for school, that's going to be a good opportunity if he is around,' she said, already planning Kate's next assignation with Richard.

'You should stay a few extra days. Husbands believe any pretext. Medical appointment, shopping, catching up with an old school chum.'

Angela rattled off the list of plausible excuses. Kate laughed.

'You sound very expert at this,' she said.

'No, not expert,' she said. 'Far from it. But just occasionally. And you're just lucky you met Richard Belleville before me.'

Kate laughed again. She was sure Angela's taste ran to slightly younger men than Richard. Like her, Angela had married a much older man. At least your husband is a much kinder man than Gerald, Kate wanted to say, but didn't.

'I fell for Richard the moment I met him,' she whispered.

Angela nodded.

'Some men have that effect, I must say,' she said. 'In the present company the only other one is Pippa's father and he, I have to say, has his hands full already.'

Just a few yards away, Philippe was sitting alongside Karen, his arm draped along the back of the patio seat. Two of his medical colleagues, who had been at the dinner table, sat opposite them, drinking coffee and chatting.

'That's Dr Jules Hamilton on the left,' Angela said, 'and Dr Mark McDermott on the right.'

Kate followed her gaze. She could see both men were trying hard to concentrate on what Philippe was saying, while being distracted by Karen, who had just kicked off her shoes and had tucked her legs up under her body, forcing Philippe to put his arm around her to support her.

'They've got no hope with her,' Kate said. 'Absolutely none. I think she's in love with Philippe. The question is, how does he feel about her?'

'Do you think they are lovers, Kate?' Angela asked, cocking her head on one side, as if she was trying to decide.

How delicious it is to gossip about other people, Kate thought. As long as she keeps her hands off Richard. She was not entirely convinced by Richard's denial that he was not tempted by her. She had seen how he had played up to her, probably to annoy Philippe, she guessed, but it had been a very convincing performance.

'Perhaps, perhaps not,' Kate answered uncertainly. 'Philippe seems to enjoy his flirtation with her but just how far it has gone is anyone's guess.'

And then she noticed Richard walk across to bid Philippe good night. As he approached, Karen stood up and put her arms around Richard's neck in an unnecessarily extravagant farewell. She kissed him lightly on the cheek.

'She's very friendly with Richard,' Angela said.

They both thought Richard had held her just a moment too long and too intimately.

'Did you notice his hands?' Kate said. 'All over her. I think he's trying to make Philippe jealous, or annoyed.'

'Do you think he's succeeding?' her friend asked.

'Perhaps,' Kate said. Or is he just succeeding in making me jealous and uncertain of him, she wondered.

They watched as the two men shook hands. Even at a distance, they could see an unmistakable frisson of tension in their handshake. They were not the only ones to notice it.

John Bertram, who stood alongside him, said a cheery good-bye to everyone and quickly guided his friend through the house and out the front door. He knew Richard well enough to know he was getting very annoyed with Philippe. It was clear that watching Philippe with Karen had almost been the last straw for him.

'So, what was that back there?' John asked. 'Trying to make him jealous? Or just push him to see how far you could go before he told you to back off and leave Karen alone? What were you trying to prove?'

'What was I trying to prove? Nothing,' he retorted.

He took a deep breath.

'But you're right, I was trying to push him so far that he would reveal his true feelings about Karen.'

'Through his reaction, you mean?'

'Yes,' Richard said, 'but he is a very smooth operator. He just seemed to smile slightly.'

John was sure Philippe had known what Richard was trying to do.

'If he lets my sister down again,' Richard said testily, 'there will be consequences.'

John thought it was probably not the time to remind Richard that it had really been her family who had let her down, not Philippe. He had tried to keep in touch with her but her mother had intercepted every letter he had ever written her.

'You know, I'm tempted,' he said, as they walked towards John's car. 'If I bedded her, he'd lose interest. It might just save my sister a whole lot of heartache.'

For a moment, John was shocked into silence.

'You seem very sure of yourself,' he said. 'She might tell you to bugger off. Had you thought of that?'

Then again, not many women have ever told Richard to bugger off, he thought. Richard shook his head.

'I don't think so,' he said. 'I don't think she'd turn me down.'

'And what sort of strife would you be in then?' John asked. 'Kate would certainly find out and that would be the end of that.'

Richard laughed, as if he was suddenly coming to his senses.

'That's the only thing that's stopping me,' he said.

'Well, I'm pleased something's stopping that ridiculous idea,' John said.

John was preparing to drive off. He reached up to adjust the rear vision mirror before he pulled out from the kerb.

In the dim street lighting, he could just make out Philippe helping Karen into her car, except she was heading for the passenger's seat. He watched as Philippe held the door for her. He probably thought she'd had too much to drink to drive herself, he surmised. Then he watched as Philippe slid into the driver's seat and the Mercedes sports roared into life.

John paused in the act of starting his own car, curious to see which direction he headed. By the swiftly executed U turn, he assumed he was heading east.

'As a matter of interest,' John said, 'where does Karen live? Near her uncle and aunt here in Woollahra?'

Richard thought for a moment.

'No, I think she lives with her parents in Vaucluse but they're away skiing in Aspen,' he replied, 'so she's probably staying with her aunt and uncle tonight rather than go home late at night to an empty house.'

John smiled to himself.

I don't think she's going home to any empty house, mate, he wanted to say, but his good sense prevailed.

CHAPTER 22

January 1960

In less than twenty minutes, Philippe was pulling into the driveway of Karen's home, manoeuvring her car into her allotted parking space in the garage.

'Thank you for driving me home,' she said. 'I think I could have managed but perhaps I did drink one glass of champagne too many.'

He got out and walked around to the passenger door to help her out.

'I thought it better to be sure by driving you myself,' he said, as she held his hand to get out of the low car.

When he had noticed her imbibing so freely, he had deliberately refused repeated offers to refill his glass at the dinner table.

'Was I really outrageous tonight?' she asked, with just a hint of concern in her voice.

He smiled at the question. He had a feeling she had asked that question on other occasions.

'I think you know the answer to that,' he said, not unkindly.

He did not think it was his place to pass judgement on her behaviour but he could not help teasing her just a little.

'You certainly flirted outrageously with my future brother-in-law,' he said.

She laughed and leaned against him as he opened the front door for her.

'He's quite a charmer, isn't he?' she said, walking ahead of him and switching on lights as she went.

It was his turn to laugh.

'I think he expected me to get very annoyed with him,' he said, as he followed her into the house.

'And were you, annoyed with him I mean?' she asked, as she draped her wrap over a chair and kicked off her stilettos. She did not ask if he was annoyed with her.

'A little,' he said. 'I'm sure he was trying to get me to react by being over friendly with you. But then he was only responding to you, wasn't he?'

He was challenging her to admit she had deliberately flirted with Richard. She smiled at him. It was a sly smile, meant to provoke him.

'Mmm..' she said, her head cocked to one side as if trying to compare the two men. 'He would be a challenge. Should I try my luck?'

He pretended to be disinterested.

'If you like,' he said, to her disappointment.

Oh, you are so annoying, Philippe, she wanted to say. You are so polite and detached. But she did not.

'Sadly, I think he might already be spoken for,' she said, with a tinge of regret in her voice. 'I couldn't help but notice his keen interest in a certain lady ...'

Philippe silenced her there. He knew she could be indiscreet, not through malice but because of her open friendly nature.

'For that lady's sake,' he said quietly, 'don't go repeating that bit of gossip and especially her name. Richard is divorced so it doesn't matter for his sake, but her reputation would be in tatters, and her marriage with it, if it came out.'

But Karen shook her head in obvious disagreement with his warning.

'I won't mention her name,' she said, suddenly becoming serious, 'but perhaps it might be a good thing for her if it did come out.'

They had walked through to the living room and he sat down beside her on the sofa.

'Why do you say, 'a good thing'?' he asked, curious about her response. 'I don't know the family except for her daughter being a schoolfriend of Pippa's.'

She sat up on the edge of the seat and turned so she could look directly at him.

'Of course, you don't know that sometimes, when the mood takes him, Gerald Lester is very free with his fists?'

Philippe was shocked. He did not know.

'Are you sure?' he said. 'Are you absolutely sure?'

It was such a serious allegation that he felt she was wrong to repeat it unless she was certain of her facts. She nodded her head, quite vigorously, as if to make the point.

'Of course, I'm sure,' she said. 'Angela Dixon is Kate Lester's particular friend and I heard Angela telling my aunt one day how Kate had been visiting and tried to hide the most recent bruises she'd suffered at his hands.'

Philippe was silent for a few moments. The thought of a lovely woman like Kate Lester having to put up with a husband like that sickened him. He noticed then that Karen had started to tremble. He put his arm around her and she nestled close to him. She's upset by the story, he thought. He began to stroke her hair in a soothing gesture. But there was something about her reaction to the story that troubled Philippe. There's more to her reaction than mere sympathy for another woman, he thought.

'Tell me if I'm on the wrong track but did something like that happen to you?' he asked gently.

He was sure she was on the verge of tears. And then she nodded.

'The official reason why I broke off my engagement with Alec Fairholm was because he was a drunk,' she began.

'The truth was much worse,' she said. 'He was a drunk and a bully. I lived in an apartment in Rose Bay at the time. He stayed over with me sometimes, but one evening, after we had been out, something annoyed him. I never really understood what it was, but that night he was drunk. And violent. I ended up with a cracked rib where he punched me and bruises where he'd held me down.'

She took a deep breath but Philippe said nothing. He knew there was more she wanted to say.

'I managed to get away from him and grab my keys,' she said. 'I drove to Uncle Robert's house. His house was the closest. I was a mess but he was so kind. I didn't want a fuss but Uncle Robert knew his father, so he called him, told him what had happened and if his son ever came near me again, the police would be called and he would be charged. Being a respected surgeon and the fact that he had examined me and recorded details of my injuries meant he could give evidence against Alec, so he disappeared from my life.'

It was a heart wrenching story she had never told him before.

'Oh, my poor girl,' he said, appalled at what she had told him. 'I had no idea. No idea at all.'

He held her closely. He wanted to make her feel safe.

How does a man do that to a woman, he wondered? How is it even possible to contemplate doing such a thing. But it explained some of her behaviour, he thought. She so mistrusts men now, the fact I've never tried to take advantage of her has made her feel safe with me. And kept other men at bay perhaps? And her outrageous flirting? It's always somewhere where she feels safe, he thought, where it's ultimately harmless. He realised then why she was so close to her uncle and his family.

'I'm fine now,' she said, knowing he would want to be reassured, 'but it did take a while for the sore rib to heal.'

'Your parents, do they know?' he asked.

She shook her head.

'No,' she said. 'I didn't tell them about it. Only that he drank too much. I didn't want a fuss. Just to be rid of him.'

He wondered then if her behaviour might have provoked the violence. It did not excuse it, Philippe thought, but it might explain it. A jealous violent man would be the worst possible husband for her, he thought. Every time she even looked at another man, such a man would feel threatened and want to demonstrate his control over her in the only way he knew how.

'Thank you for trusting me enough to tell me,' he said softly.

'Thank you for listening to me,' she said. 'And for understanding.'

He moved to get up from the sofa.

'Perhaps it's time for me to go,' he said.

But she shook her head and turned towards him.

'I don't want you to go,' she said. 'I don't want you to go. Not yet.'

He looked at her and saw the vulnerability of a young woman who, deep down, yearned for affection. She leaned towards him and kissed him. He could not push her away. He could not reject her. Instead he kissed her lovingly. Tenderly.

She looked at him. It was not the first time he had kissed her but there had never been a danger it would go further. Until tonight. He could feel his self-control deserting him. Did she understand what she was doing, he wondered? Did she understand where this might end up? Does she know how much I desire her?

'Tell me you were jealous tonight,' she said. 'Just a little?'

Her teasing tone had returned. He laughed. It was no use denying it.

'Yes, I was,' he admitted. 'I didn't like watching Richard put his hands all over you. Not at all.'

She laughed softly and nodded her head. He had finally admitted it.

'I hoped you would be. Jealous, that is.'

He pulled her into his arms.

'I've told you this before,' he said. 'You are just trouble. Big trouble.'

'I know,' she said, as his hands began to explore her body.

'If you want me to leave, say so and I will go,' he said, kissing her gently.

He did not want to be accused of forcing himself on her, but she shook her head.

'Don't go,' she said. 'Stay with me tonight. Please.'

He began to caress her body more intimately with the lightest of touches. She got up then and held her hand out towards him and led the way to her bedroom, as he began to unzip her dress.

He knew then it was too late for regrets. He had tried hard to distance himself from her but it had proved impossible. He could no longer deny himself the pleasure of being in her bed, of making love to her, of possessing her.

In the darkness, she allowed herself a small smile of triumph as she responded to his caresses and the pleasure of his lovemaking.

For the second time in a matter of days, Richard Belleville was woken from his sleep by the insistent ringing of the telephone in his hotel room. It had taken some minutes for it to wake him. Eventually he lifted the receiver.

At the same time, he switched on the bedside light and checked his watch for the time. It was two o'clock in the morning. A phone call at this hour always meant trouble, he thought. He recognised the voice on the other end of the phone immediately. It was Edith Henderson. She was calm despite the urgency of her call.

'Richard,' she said. 'I'm sorry to ring you at this hour. It's your son, Paul. He's been injured. I think he's needs medical attention.'

Richard was immediately wide awake and alert.

'What's happened?' he demanded.

A hundred scenarios flitted through his mind.

'He was playing with some boys down the road late this afternoon and he fell out of a tree,' she explained. 'I didn't think anything of it really. Boys fall out of trees all the time. He seemed OK when he came home. He had his tea and went to bed. But when I got up just now to go to the kitchen for a glass of water, I heard him groaning and his breathing was laboured. I can't wake him properly. What will I do?'

Richard thought quickly.

'I'll call Philippe and ring you back.'

He hung up and dialled Philippe's number but there was no answer. Two o'clock in the morning and he's not answering his phone? Perhaps he's a heavy sleeper, he thought.

He reached into his wallet. Robert Clarke had also given him a card. He dialled the Clarke's home number. The telephone was answered immediately.

'Dr Robert Clarke,' the voice on the other end said.

This is a man used to being woken in the middle of the night, Richard thought. He explained the situation as quickly as he could then Robert Clarke took immediate control.

'Tell her to ring an ambulance, take him straight to St Vincent's Hospital. I'll be there by the time he arrives. You meet me there.'

And he hung up, leaving Richard to ring Edith Henderson with instructions.

Robert eased out of bed, trying not to disturb his wife. She was used to his frequent late night call outs. He scribbled a note for her as he dressed hurriedly. It did occur to him to wonder why Richard had not called Philippe but he spent no time thinking about it. His mind was now focused on a young boy with unknown injuries, perhaps internal injuries, that might require his intervention.

He walked down the length of his driveway to open the gate and then went back to the garage to get his car. He reversed quickly down the driveway. He did not bother to stop to close the gate but he did notice as he drove away that Philippe's car remained parked in the street outside his house. I hope that doesn't mean what I think it means, he thought. Karen's car is gone but Philippe's remains. He shook his head. Had Richard tried to call Philippe at home and got no answer? But he pushed that thought to the back of his mind and focused on the short drive to the hospital.

Within fifteen minutes, he was pulling into his dedicated parking space and heading towards the emergency department at a quick walking pace.

It was eerily quiet in the hospital in the early hours of the morning. He was greeted with deference by Dr Steve Hancock, the registrar on duty. It had been a quiet night, he said. And then they heard the wail of the ambulance siren and a screech of tyres in the hospital's forecourt. The emergency team, whom he had just briefed, swung into action and he watched as Richard's young son was lifted out of the ambulance and onto a stretcher to be wheeled into the hospital.

He could do nothing now until the emergency medical team had made an assessment of his condition. He knew they would not welcome his presence so he went in search of Richard, whom he found alone in the waiting room. Richard looked up as he walked in.

'Thanks for helping out, Robert,' he said. 'Is he here? Can I see him? I just heard the ambulance arrive.'

'Yes, he's here,' Robert said calmly, 'but, no, you can't see him at the moment. The team need to assess him. You'll only get in the way.'

Richard nodded. He understood but it did not make it any easier for him.

'I should have been there to take care of him,' he said, clearly blaming himself for his son's accident.

But Robert Clarke shook his head.

'You can't be with them every minute of the day,' he said. 'I bet you and your brother got into some scrapes, just like this. It goes with the territory. Boys being boys.'

Richard agreed reluctantly. He and William had certainly caused their mother some anxious moments but they had escaped the rough and tumble of childhood with little more than the occasional sprain and gashed knee.

'I was surprised to get your call although pleased that you did contact me,' Robert said, as he sat down alongside Richard. 'I would have thought you would have called Philippe.'

His curiosity had got the better of him. He could not resist the opportunity to ask the question.

'I tried calling him,' Richard said, 'but he didn't answer. Perhaps I didn't give him enough time to get to the telephone. That's when I decided to call you and you answered straight away. Thank goodness.'

Robert nodded. He made no comment about Philippe not answering his phone. What excuse could he make that sounded plausible? They were all so attuned to irregular callouts that even when they were not on call, telephones were usually answered within seconds of them starting to ring. Richard doesn't want to hear my speculation about where Philippe is spending the night, he thought. After all, it is just idle speculation on my part. I may be wide of the mark, he thought.

Just then, they heard the bang of the swing doors that separated the reception from the emergency ward. Robert went forward to greet Dr Hancock. Robert was a few paces ahead of Richard. He wanted to know if there was bad news before Richard was told.

'The boy's going to be OK, but he is concussed, and I think he's got a compound fracture of the left arm,' the doctor told Robert quickly. 'I've sent him off for an X-ray just now.'

Robert was relieved.

'Is this the boy's father?' he asked Robert, motioning towards Richard.

'Yes, Richard Belleville,' Robert said, as he introduced the registrar to Richard. 'The child is Paul Belleville, he's thirteen, I believe.'

'Mr Belleville,' Dr Hancock said. 'Your son is going to be fine but we think he has sustained a pretty nasty fracture of his left arm. He'll need an operation and we'll need your permission.'

Richard felt he could breathe again.

'Can I see him? Is he aware of what's going on?' Richard asked, thankful that the news sounded positive.

'Yes, of course you can, as soon as he gets back from X-ray,' the registrar said.

The doctor then turned to Robert.

'I suppose you want Mark McDermott to operate?' he asked. 'He's not on call this weekend but he's the best.'

Robert smiled. His reputation in the hospital counted for something. No one would suggest a young intern be called in to operate on the son of one of his friends. As head of orthopaedics, Mark McDermott would always be the obvious choice.

'I had the whole surgical team at my dinner table last night,' he joked, 'so you might as well call up Dr Jules Hamilton for the anaesthesia and Barbara Thomas too. We might as well ruin all their plans for Sunday.'

Besides, he thought, if they weren't all called for the emergency operation on Richard's son, their professional egos would be bruised. They would complain about having to be 'dragged into the hospital on a Sunday' but they'd be secretly pleased because in being asked to do the operation, it meant they'd been anointed as the best in their fields by someone whose opinion mattered a great deal.

Richard spent the next half hour immersed in paperwork. He scrawled his signature where they asked him to sign. He then went to sit beside his son's bed. Paul had been given painkillers but he was clearly still in pain. Richard was careful to avoid the injured arm. He put his hand on his son's right shoulder.

'How are you feeling?' he asked.

He could see the boy was drowsy.

'It hurts, Dad,' he said. 'It hurts a lot.'

He reassured him as best he could.

'They are going to have to operate to fix your arm,' he said. 'They have to call people into the hospital to do it, so it won't be for a few hours yet, but I'll stay here with you until you go into the operating theatre, except I will have to go out and telephone Mrs Henderson.'

Paul nodded. He closed his eyes and drifted into an uneasy sleep.

By eight o'clock in the morning, the surgical team was assembling. First to arrive was Mark McDermott who greeted Richard with a wry smile.

'Your lad's got himself in a spot of bother, I understand,' he said, as the two men shook hands. 'Don't worry we'll soon have him right again.'

'Always on bloody Sunday,' he muttered to Robert. 'Jules coming in?'

Robert nodded.

'And Barbara.'

'Thank God for that,' he said. 'You can get all sorts of greenhorns doing weekend surgery. Takes twice as long.'

Then he looked at Robert.

'Are you going to scrub up and watch a master at work?'

It was meant as a joke but Robert knew there was a serious reason for the invitation. If there was something in Paul's condition that was undiagnosed or the initial examination had missed, an extra surgeon might prove life-saving.

'Might as well,' he said, as they both headed towards the prep room.

As Paul was wheeled away, Richard went back to the waiting area, this time to telephone John Bertram, who had only just woken from a long and dreamless sleep.

John listened while he told him what had happened.

'I'll be there as soon as I can,' his friend said.

'Before you come to the hospital, can you call Ian Dixon and tell him we'll have to skip lunch,' he said, 'and perhaps you should call Catherine. Can you do that for me?'

'OK, I'll do that,' he said but he did not relish being the one to tell Catherine her son was about to undergo an emergency operation.

But he would do it because Richard had asked him to do it.

Well before dawn began to lighten the night sky, Philippe had slipped quietly out of Karen's bed, dressed and headed down to the garage. She had hardly stirred as he left so he had picked up her car keys from the hall table. He had one objective: to make sure Robert Clarke didn't wake to the sight of his car still parked outside his house.

He drove into the street and parked Karen's car several hundred yards away and then walked towards his own car. He glanced up at the house. It was in darkness but he noticed the garage door and driveway gate stood open.

He groaned inwardly. Everything about the open garage door and the gate that had been left open pointed to a quick departure. He didn't need to guess. It would be a patient of Robert's who had taken an unexpected turn for the worse and he had been called into the hospital in a hurry.

I hope he didn't notice my car still parked in the street, Philippe thought. If he did, he'll only draw one conclusion and unfortunately it will be the right one. Philippe slipped into the driver's seat of his car. Within minutes, he was pulling up in the driveway of his own house just a few minutes away.

He berated himself for his weakness. He had spent months keeping her at arm's length or if not at arm's length, at least resisting the temptation she put in his way. But watching her flirt with Richard and watching him overstep the bounds of propriety at her invitation had been the last straw. She was right. He had been jealous. And his jealousy had been his undoing.

Now all he felt was guilt that he had betrayed Julia. But in the midst of his guilt and his anger with himself, he recalled the pleasure of being with Karen. It's not her fault, he thought, it's mine. I was the one who succumbed. I had the chance to walk away and I couldn't.

As he unlocked the door of his home, he stripped off and headed for the shower.

For a long time, he stood under the hot shower, letting the water cascade over his body, trying hard not to think about what lay ahead and the implications of what had happened. But he failed spectacularly.

CHAPTER 23

January 1960

John Bertram sat alongside Richard in the hospital waiting room. He had strict instructions from Catherine to call her as soon as the operation was finished, no matter that the time in England would be well after midnight.

'This is taking too long, John,' Richard said, looking at his watch. 'This is taking way too long.'

Just then they heard the familiar thud of the swing doors leading to the waiting room. Richard looked up in time to see Robert Clarke walking towards them, still gowned but pulling off his mask as he walked. He was smiling and Richard took that as a good sign.

'He's fine, Richard,' he said, understanding they were the first words a parent wants to hear. 'The op took a bit longer than we thought. A slightly more complicated break than Mark had anticipated and there was a broken rib we didn't know about, but it's all fine now.'

Richard breathed an audible sigh of relief.

'He'll be here for a few days,' Robert said. 'Mark doesn't want the full plaster to go on until he's sure the swelling has gone down. He'll probably be in plaster for six weeks or so.'

'And then?' asked Richard. 'Can I take him to the local hospital in Springfield?'

Robert Clarke nodded, although he hoped there was some type of specialist physician where they lived. Even Brisbane would be an option, he thought.

'Mark will provide some instructions for your local hospital,' Robert said, 'but should you have any concern about anything, you should take him to Brisbane to a specialist, if there is none locally.'

Richard nodded, understanding that a surgeon plying his trade in Sydney might have a low opinion of medical care elsewhere.

'He will take a little while to come around from the anaesthetic,' Robert said. 'Then you can see him, but no other visitors.'

The two men shook hands.

How fortunate, Richard thought, that he had met Robert Clarke. The calm authority he exuded had given Richard confidence. But he would never know how much he owed Robert Clarke. It had been Robert Clarke who had saved Paul's life on the operating table. He had been the one to spot the internal bleeding in the chest cavity.

As the team had left the operating theatre, they had all looked towards Robert. With a simple nod of the head, each of them had acknowledged his vital role.

'Thanks, mate,' Mark McDermott had said. 'Didn't spot it.'

Robert had nodded.

'Easy to miss sometimes when you think an op is simple,' he said.

'Broken rib,' Mark said. 'That will explain the chest bandage to the father.'

Again, Robert nodded. The boy would be fine now. No need to alarm his father unnecessarily.

'He comes from the country in Queensland,' Robert said. 'You'll need to write some instructions for post-operative care.'

Mark grimaced. He would have preferred the post-operative care to take place where he could oversee it.

'I'll do that before he's discharged,' he said. 'I hope they can follow some simple instructions.'

'I'll tell him to take the boy to Brisbane if there are any concerns,' Robert said.

'Good idea,' his colleague replied. 'One or two decent blokes there but we'll keep him here for a few days longer than strictly necessary to make sure everything's OK.'

Robert had agreed and headed out to tell Richard only the good news.

'I need a shower and a change of shirt,' Richard said, as he and John headed out of the hospital.

They had made the necessary phone calls, first to Catherine, then to Edith Henderson, who was more relieved than she could say, and then to William, who had been shocked and relieved in equal measure.

Richard had seen Paul briefly but had been hustled out of the ward by the ward sister who had declared her patient needed to rest. He had thought about calling Philippe but decided against it.

'I'll call him later,' he said to John, as he slipped into the passenger seat of John's car.

'Strange he didn't answer when you called him in the early hours,' John said, and then wished he hadn't.

Richard said nothing but John thought there was every chance he had figured out exactly where Philippe had been and with whom.

'Me and my big mouth,' thought John as he navigated the light Sunday traffic through the city to Richard's hotel.

'Let's have some lunch,' Richard said, pointing to the dining room.

'I'll wait in the bar,' John said. 'I could murder a beer.'

'On my tab, remember,' he said to his friend, as he headed to the lift.

John needed no second invitation to charge his beer to his friend's room. Where would he be without me, he wondered?

As soon as Edith Henderson had put down the phone and told Pippa that Paul would be fine, she had insisted on calling her father. It was eleven o'clock and he answered promptly, half expecting to hear Karen's voice. Instead, he listened intently as Pippa began telling him a garbled story about her cousin Paul. In the end, he asked her to put her aunt on the line.

'I'm pleased we called you,' Edith said. 'Richard tried to call you in the early hours of this morning after I called him about Paul's accident, but he couldn't raise you.'

She had said it in all innocence. In her experience, people often claimed they could sleep through a ringing telephone but obviously Philippe could. She attached no significance to it whatsoever.

Inwardly, Philippe groaned. He knew Richard would know immediately why he hadn't answered his phone. He did not really need to ask who Richard's next call was, but he did anyway.

'Who did he contact, Edith?' he asked.

'He phoned your colleague Dr Clarke,' she volunteered. 'Dr Clarke organised the medical team to operate on Paul earlier this morning.'

Philippe was silent for a few moments. He could have named the team without even asking. Jules Hamilton. Mark McDermott. Barbara Thomas. He was the only one missing, yet he was the one who had the most reason to be there. He was soon to become an uncle to the boy. I should have been there, he thought.

'And the operation went well?' he asked, with just a touch of anxiety in his voice.

'Yes, Paul's got a compound fracture of the left arm and a broken rib,' she said. 'He'll be in hospital for a few days.'

Philippe heard this prognosis with relief but interest. Several days seemed a long time to keep a healthy child in hospital, even one with a broken arm and a broken rib.

Before he could speak, he heard Pippa's voice on the line again.

'We were going to go to Luna Park today but with Paul in hospital Aunt Edith says we can't go now,' she lamented. 'Can you take us to lunch at that hotel in the city instead? You know, my favourite?'

There was no way out, he thought. I can hardly say your Uncle Richard stays there and for reasons I can't explain, I don't really want to run into him today. Instead, he agreed.

'If your aunt is happy to go along with the plans, then yes, I will,' he said.

Edith Henderson took the phone that Pippa held out to her.

'Yes, we can meet you there at half past twelve,' she said, and hung up.

Philippe sat for a few minutes collecting his thoughts. He sipped his coffee as he contemplated the potential fallout from the events of the past few hours.

I need to ring Robert, he thought, but he will grill me, once he's given me a rundown of what happened. But he knew he couldn't avoid the phone call. He picked up the phone and dialled the Clarke household. Patricia Clarke answered and handed the phone to her husband as soon as she heard his voice.

'Philippe,' he said, 'the missing man.'

Philippe ignored the jibe. If I lie, he thought, and he's noticed my car outside his house when he left for the hospital, he'll never trust me again.

'Sorry I wasn't contactable, Robert,' he said, in his best professional voice. 'What happened with Paul Belleville? Any problems?'

Philippe listened intently for several minutes as Robert Clarke described the incident, Richard's early morning phone call and the subsequent operation.

'We almost missed the internal bleeding in the chest cavity,' he said, knowing Philippe would understand the urgency of dealing with such a problem.

When he had finished, Philippe already knew the answer but he asked the question anyway.

'You spotted the problem, I take it,' he said. 'Thank God for that. It's easily missed.'

Would he have seen it if he had been assisting? Goodness knows, he thought. Such speculation was useless, but he agreed with Robert there was no point in telling Richard. The boy was making a good recovery now. Richard had been told he had a broken rib which explained the bandaging on his torso.

'I notice my niece's car is now parked some way up my street,' he said, 'yet I noticed your car was still outside my house when I left for the hospital at about two thirty. There was no sign of her car then.'

He hardly paused for breath.

'I hope you know what you're doing, Philippe,' he said. 'I know my niece is a very attractive young woman. She may fancy she's in love with you, but you have promised to marry another woman, so don't forget that.'

Philippe could do nothing but listen politely, knowing that the lecture had been a long time in the making.

'I hear you, Robert,' he said, out of respect for his colleague.

Had it been anyone else, he would have told them to mind their own business. He was certainly not used to being lectured on how he lived his life.

'I hope you do, Philippe,' he said, 'for all our sakes.'

Robert, for his part, couldn't bring himself to interfere any more than he had already done in his niece's life. He knew her father had pushed her into the relationship with Alec Fairholm and look how that turned out, he thought. Philippe at least treated her with respect and tenderness. If only my niece had fallen for someone else, he thought, life would be much simpler.

Philippe thanked Robert for what he had done for Richard's son.

'The Belleville family are going to be in your debt for a very long time,' Philippe said, 'except they won't ever know just how much in your debt they are.'

'That's why we're doctors, Philippe,' he said finally. 'We can give back to a father a son he might otherwise have lost.'

'Most of the time,' he added, remembering the loss his own brother had suffered.

Karen sat on the edge of her bed with a towel wrapped around her slim body. She had slept late but she had been aware that Philippe had slipped out of her bed in the early hours of the morning. She guessed her car would be gone from the garage although she hadn't checked.

The ringing of the telephone on her bedside table sounded unusually loud in the quiet of the otherwise empty house. She picked it up and heard the familiar voice, the voice she'd been expecting.

'So you cut and ran?' she said, teasingly. 'And took my car into the bargain.'

Despite his simmering anger with himself and to a lesser extent with her, he couldn't help but laugh. Then he was serious for a moment.

'There's a slight problem with that,' he said.

She was only half listening. Had he crashed her car, she wondered?

'I had to take your car,' he said apologetically. 'For obvious reasons I couldn't leave my car parked outside your uncle's house all night but unfortunately events conspired against us.'

'How?' she asked. 'What do you mean?'

Philippe sighed.

'At half past two this morning your uncle responded to an emergency call from Richard Belleville about his son Paul and he left for

253

the hospital in a hurry. Despite his rush to leave, he noticed my car was still parked outside his house and the fact that your car wasn't there. He put two and two together, I'm afraid, so you and I are in the bad books. At least I am.'

He then told her about Paul Belleville and what had happened.

'Is his son OK?' she asked, with genuine concern.

Talk of emergency operations revived painful memories of losing her brother.

'He's fine as I understand it,' Philippe said, 'thanks to your uncle and his team, but I should have been there too. He tried to call me but of course I wasn't at home.'

'Oh, that's bad,' she replied. 'Richard will not be happy with you at all if he figures it out.'

'No, he won't be happy with me,' he said. 'He won't be happy at all. But I'm hoping what's happened with his son may distract him.'

'That's possible,' she said, 'but I wouldn't get my hopes up.'

He laughed at this. She's incorrigible, he thought. And she enjoys teasing me but she can hardly claim to be a disinterested bystander.

'I've promised to take Pippa to lunch,' he said. 'Unfortunately, it's at the same hotel where Richard stays. I probably won't be able to avoid seeing him.'

'Enjoy your lunch,' she said, wondering what he would say to Richard that would explain away his not being contactable at home in the early hours of the morning. That will be a tense conversation, she thought. Very tense indeed.

'We need to talk about last night,' he said. He was going to say, 'it must never happen again' but that sounded lame, as if she was to blame for everything. He paused.

'I'll call you later,' he said and hung up.

She lay back on the bed. Was it really only a month ago he told me he would marry Julia Belleville as soon as her divorce was finalised, she thought? So where does that leave us now? Where does it leave me? Was I just a one-night stand he couldn't resist?

She began to dress. The telephone in her bedroom rang again. She was relieved to hear her friend Bianca's voice on the other end of the line.

'Doing anything?' Bianca asked. 'My brother has a friend in town from Melbourne. He wants us to make a four for lunch.'

Karen agreed readily. She did not want to stay at home alone waiting for Philippe's call.

'But you'll have to pick me up,' she said. 'I don't have my car.'

Bianca expressed surprise. Karen and her distinctive sports car were hardly ever parted. And she knew her friend had been banned from driving either of her parents' cars after one or two mishaps.

'It's a long story,' Karen said, 'and I'm not sure I should tell you.'

But Bianca knew there was very little likelihood her friend would keep her in the dark.

'I'll pick you up in half an hour,' she said, 'and then you can tell me all about it.'

So, the gorgeous doctor has finally succumbed, she thought. She shook her head then.

'She's playing with fire,' she said to herself. 'She'll be the one who'll be hurt. He'll have his fun and move on to his long lost love.'

Karen was already waiting at the bottom of the stairs when Bianca pulled up in front of her house in her little Fiat.

'Where are we going?' Karen asked.

She had dressed casually in a summer frock and sandals, assuming that a Sunday lunch would be very relaxed.

'There is a restaurant just the other side of the bridge,' she said. 'We're meeting them there.'

'Would you mind a detour via the Australia Hotel?' Karen asked. 'I can pick up my car keys and then you can drop me back to my car on the way home.'

Bianca looked sideways at her friend, seeking an explanation.

'Sure, I can do that,' she said, as she mentally adjusted the route she would travel. 'So let me get this right, your car keys are at the hotel and your car is, where?'

Karen smiled. And then explained why she needed to pick up her keys and how they came to be at the hotel.

'Which means my car is sitting in the street outside my uncle's house in Woollahra while he sits inside tut tutting at my behaviour.'

Bianca laughed.

'Well, if I was your uncle, that might be my reaction too,' she said.

She wanted to say 'do you think it's a good idea to front Philippe in front of his daughter' but she understood Karen too well. She has a mischievous streak, she thought, which could well get her into even more trouble.

The first person Philippe spotted when he walked into the hotel restaurant was the one person he had hoped to avoid. Richard looked up, saw him and beckoned to him. He could do nothing else but walk across to where he and John Bertram were sitting. Richard had already replaced his menu on the table. John continued to study it carefully, even more so when he saw Philippe approaching.

'God, I hope Richard doesn't thump him,' he thought. 'Surely he won't do that.'

Richard got up and politely extended his hand. John followed his lead, somewhat more tentatively.

'I spoke with Robert Clarke this morning,' Philippe said. 'I hear your son had an accident. But everything has gone well with the operation, according to Robert. But I'll look in and check out the situation on my way home to make sure he's comfortable and doing well.'

How clever, thought Richard. How bloody clever he is. He knows I tried to call him at two o'clock this morning and he didn't answer. But he's deliberately side tracking me. What else can I say other than that I'd be reassured if he checked Paul out? He was about to respond when he heard Pippa's voice.

'Uncle Richard,' she said, as she came up to him to claim a hug, 'Daddy didn't tell me you would be here.'

Edith Henderson was a few paces behind her. She greeted them all and then turned to Richard.

'What can I say,' she said. 'I was so sorry that I didn't look after your son well enough. I never thought for a moment he'd get into such a scrape. Can you forgive me?'

Richard held up his hand to silence her.

'It's not your fault, Mrs Henderson,' repeating what he had previously said to her. 'I'm afraid boys will get into strife. But he's in good hands and doing well.'

He looked around for a waiter.

'I think we'll need a bigger table.'

John Bertram breathed a small sigh of relief. He thought he noticed Philippe too look a little more relaxed. With Pippa and her aunt lunching with them, the two men would need to postpone any terse exchange.

They had just settled around a larger table when John looked up and saw Karen searching the room before spotting the group.

'Here comes trouble,' he thought.

Karen, smiling brightly, greeted everyone at the table. She had met Pippa once through her cousin Anita and she acknowledged the girl. Philippe performed the introduction to Edith Henderson.

She then held her hand out to Philippe.

'My car keys,' she said. 'I think you may have them. I'm lunching with Bianca and her brother and a friend of his. I want to pick up my car on the way home.'

There was a twinkle in her eye. Philippe said nothing but fished them out of the pocket of his trousers.

'Philippe was kind enough to drive me home last night from my uncle's dinner party,' she explained to the interested onlookers. 'He thought I'd drunk too much to manage it myself.'

Edith was about to compliment him on his thoughtfulness, but she thought better of it. That isn't a look of wide-eyed innocence, she thought. But what disturbed her more was the mixture of guilt and pleasure on Philippe's face at the sight of the young woman.

John Bertram had the good sense to divert Pippa's attention by beginning to tell her one of his wild flying stories, how he'd almost aqua-planed off the runway at Singapore airport during a heavy rainstorm.

Karen reserved a special smile for Richard, who could only admire her audacity.

'I hope your son is OK?' she asked, her mood suddenly serious. 'If there's anything I can do to help, please let me know.'

Richard thanked her and then she turned and walked out of the restaurant. Philippe watched her walk away and then sat down again. Richard did the same. Neither man spoke.

'A very pretty girl,' Edith Henderson said. 'Very pretty indeed.'

Someone needed to say something about her, Edith thought. If Julia was here, he'd be behaving himself. Men are like that, she thought, even the best of them. So predictable. I hope he doesn't break Julia's heart over a pair of seductive eyes. Her brother doesn't look happy with him.

'Have you decided what you are going to have to eat, Pippa?' she asked, in the hope of easing the tension at the table.

She turned to John Bertram.

'They do a very good Sunday roast here,' she said.

Philippe was grateful for the diversion. Karen's appearance had caught him totally off guard and he knew the look on his face had betrayed him. Richard knows, he thought. Richard now knows, with absolute certainty, where I spent last night.

Richard half turned towards John and said in an almost audible undertone.

'I told you I should have bedded her,' he said, 'but it's too late now.'

All John could do was shake his head. This is going to get very, very messy he thought. Very messy indeed. He drained his glass of beer, signalled the waiter for another one and followed Edith Henderson's lead and ordered the roast of the day.

CHAPTER 24

January 1960

Richard checked his watch as he stepped out of the lift. It was Monday morning and he was dressed for business. He carried an attaché case bulging with papers. As he approached hotel reception, the reception-ist looked up and recognised him.

'Can I help you, sir?' she asked politely.

Richard checked the address on the meeting notice.

'Hunter Street?' he asked. 'Can you give me directions please.'

The receptionist pointed to the street outside.

'If you walk two blocks towards Circular Quay, you'll come to Hunter Street, sir. Then you need to turn either left or right depending on the number of the building you're after.'

He thanked her and was about to walk away.

'Mr Belleville,' she said, holding up an envelope. 'I'm sorry this should have been delivered to your room yesterday afternoon.'

He took it and glanced at the perfumed notepaper. He had at least twenty minutes before he was due at the board meeting of Curtis Transport. At most, the walk would take ten minutes, so he paused to open the envelope.

It was a short note.

Dear Richard,

I heard about Paul's accident from Ian Dixon. I'm on my way home this morning but I just wanted to say if there is anything I can do, please let me know.

*I hope Paul makes a quick recovery. He's welcome to come
to us at Berrima Park if he needs to recuperate down here.
You only have to call me to let me know.*

*Seeing you again so soon was so unexpected. I can't wait
to see you again …..*

K xx

He smiled to himself and tucked the letter back into the envelope.
He slipped it into his case and headed out the door.

His mind now went to the business at hand. He had made an investment recently in Curtis Transport. It amounted to a ten percent stake
in the company which entitled him to a seat on the board. This
extraordinary meeting to discuss the possible takeover of a smaller
Victorian company would be his first opportunity to sit as a director.

'Ten percent won't give me much say,' he had said to William, 'but
I'll go to the meeting as it fits in with my plans anyway.'

William had agreed. Transport was something they both understood. It was essential for the rural sector and both of them could see
the potential in an industry where demand would only grow.

Within fifteen minutes, Richard was being shown into the boardroom on the third floor of the company's Sydney headquarters. He
was greeted immediately by the chairman, Sidney Curtis, who introduced him to the other directors.

The name Jack Fairholm meant nothing to him when the two
shook hands, except that Richard realised he and Fairholm were by
far the youngest members of the board.

Sidney Curtis's secretary handed Richard a cup of coffee and indicated the position at the board table where he was to sit. She's probably been with Sidney Curtis for at least thirty years, Richard guessed.
I wonder how many board meetings she's organised. Hundreds probably.

'We're waiting for one other person,' she said, 'then Mr Curtis can
begin the meeting.'

Richard put his papers down on the table and turned to chat with
Jack Fairholm. Just as he did so, the door opened and a familiar figure
walked in.

'Miss Clarke is deputising for her father today,' the chairman announced. 'I hope you will all make her very welcome.'

Karen had not looked in his direction. Instead she focused her attention on Sidney Curtis, who insisted on pulling out her chair and fetching coffee for her. Richard was watching all this with great amusement. His companion, however, was clearly annoyed.

'The old man's fussing over her,' Jack Fairholm said, contemptuously. 'I wonder if he knows she's just a slut really.'

Richard was shocked. Did I really hear him call Karen a slut, he thought? Surely not.

'I see you're shocked,' Jack Fairholm said to Richard quietly, 'but she's got form. My brother had her first up but he got rid of her when he got tired of her. Said he'd passed her on to some of his mates. They enjoyed themselves with her, he said.'

'And you think it's amusing to talk about her in that foul, disgusting way, do you?' Richard retorted. 'As it happens, I don't.'

He pushed his chair back and in one swift, decisive movement he hauled Jack Fairholm out of his chair and forced him back against the wall of the boardroom. Richard had never needed his wartime unarmed combat training until now. The pressure points, how to immobilise an opponent. It all came back to him. In seconds, Fairholm was gasping for breath.

'What the bloody hell do you think you're doing,' he sputtered.

Richard's angry face was inches from his.

'If you ever speak like that again about Karen Clarke, make no mistake, I will finish what I started,' Richard said, as he released him and let him fall.

Sidney Curtis was the first to react. He walked around the table to where Richard was standing and put his arm on Richard's shoulder.

'What's going on here?' he demanded. 'We don't fight in the boardroom. This is not some sleazy bar.'

Richard turned to him.

'It isn't, Mr Curtis,' he said. 'You're right, but that's why it's no place for sleazy bar talk either. I've just reminded Mr Fairholm of that.'

Karen was immediately behind Sid Curtis. She smiled at Richard and reached up and kissed him on the cheek. He held her briefly.

'Very impressive reflexes, Richard,' she said admiringly. 'Jack Fairholm passed some rude comments about me, I expect.'

He smiled at her. He had never previously encountered a woman who could cause so much trouble and yet look so innocent. And he said so.

'Are you always this much trouble?' he whispered quietly to her.

'Apparently,' she said, with a broad smile and a twinkle in her eye.

She watched with interest as Jack Fairholm was helped up from the floor. He was straightening his jacket and tie. Although not yet forty, his face was beginning to show the early signs of too much high living.

'Come and sit next to me, Richard,' she insisted, 'and give me some advice. My father owns twenty percent of this outfit and he wanted me to sit in for him at this meeting. I have his proxy to vote on the takeover proposal.'

She's very calm and collected about Jack Fairholm's comments, he thought. I wonder if it's happened before?

For his part, Jack Fairholm glared at Richard, annoyed that he had got the better of him in a fight. And who was this Richard Belleville anyway? Some country yokel with an inflated opinion of himself, he said to the man next to him.

'I don't think that's quite fair,' his fellow director replied evenly.

He had not heard the remark Jack Fairholm had made but he had taken the trouble to read Richard's biography which had been circulated to all the directors prior to the meeting.

'He's a war hero, Distinguished Flying Cross, flew Lancaster bombers during the war,' he said. 'I wouldn't take him on, if I were you. He knows how to handle himself. And Miss Clarke obviously knows him.'

Jack Fairholm turned to face his companion.

'Is that in the biblical sense, do you think?' he asked, the leering grin having returned to his face. 'She looks very pleased with herself. And he can't take his eyes off her.'

It was not a discussion his fellow director was prepared to continue so Jack Fairholm was left to ponder how it was she had failed to succumb to his charms when he had caught her by herself at a party. And how it was that she ended up running out on his brother who had, after all, just got a bit too vigorous in his amorous attentions. And yet some country oaf had clearly won favour with her. He shook his head in disbelief.

The meeting was then called to order and Richard listened carefully. He suspected not all the board members were in favour of the takeover. He whispered to Karen.

'What's your voting percentage?' he asked.

He was unfamiliar with just how much each director controlled.

'My father has twenty percent,' she said, without having to refer to the papers. 'Sid Curtis has twenty-five percent. The Fairholms have twenty percent.'

He did the sums quickly. After his ten percent, that left twenty-five percent held by the remaining directors.

'Did your father think the takeover of the Victorian company was a good idea?' he asked quietly.

'Yes, he did,' she said, 'but he said I should make up my own mind. He said I could vote whichever way I wanted to.'

After an hour or more of sometimes heated discussion, the chairman asked for a show of hands on the proposal. Karen voted with Sidney Curtis in favour but no other hands went up.

I can't let her lose her first vote as a director in place of her father, Richard thought, so his hand went up too.

Jack Fairholm scowled. Richard's ten percent had swung the day for Sidney Curtis. He wouldn't forget that. He had hoped to defeat the proposal so his father could buy the operation outright as a way into the transport industry.

He got up and left the meeting without another word.

Richard and Karen said their farewells and left the meeting together. It was now twelve o'clock and the city was buzzing with the lunchtime crowd, although being early January, it was a smaller crowd than usual.

'Let's walk down to the harbour,' Karen said. 'There's a little Italian café that Bianca and I have been to many times. We could have lunch, unless you're committed elsewhere.'

He fell into step alongside her.

'Lead on,' he said. 'I'm going to the hospital this afternoon to see Paul but not until the afternoon visiting hours.'

'Is Paul recovering well?' she asked, looking up at him and holding her hand to her eyes to shield her face from the sun.

'He is, yes, thank you,' he replied. 'Philippe called in to see him late yesterday and he telephoned me to say he's recovering well.'

Did he see just a tiny reaction at the mention of Philippe's name, he wondered, or was he just imagining it?

They walked on in silence for a short way. He could see she was thinking about something, debating perhaps whether to confide in him.

'Thank you for what you did in the boardroom with Jack Fairholm,' she said. 'He's a horrible man, worse even than his brother Alec.'

'I certainly didn't warm to him,' Richard said. 'And I'm certainly not going to repeat what he said.'

He had never heard a man utter such an ugly slur against a woman. Karen laughed but it wasn't a happy sound.

'You don't have to tell me what he said, I can guess,' she said. 'I had to knee him in the groin once at a party to get away from him. And I was engaged to his brother, who took to me with his fists one night. I managed to get away from him too, fortunately.'

She went on to tell him the story she had told Philippe. When she had finished, Richard's instinct had been the same as Philippe's. He wanted to protect her. He drew her arm through his.

'I'm so sorry,' he said. 'I have no idea how a man can treat a woman like that. They're cowards really. Jack Fairholm would run a mile if he saw me coming towards him and he was alone, yet he and his type think nothing of using their superior physical strength on a woman.'

'I'm sorry I went so easy on him,' he added. 'He deserved a good thumping.'

She shrugged as if to say, 'it's in the past, let's forget about it'. But the thought of her being subjected to such behaviour disturbed him.

'None of this is your fault,' he said gently. 'You must never think that. You deserve to be loved and cherished, not abused.'

She smiled at him. It's like being with Philippe, she thought. I feel safe with Richard. I feel protected.

They had arrived at the entrance to the café where she was greeted warmly by Mario, the owner. He fussed over her and found her the best table which had mysteriously just become available.

He looked Richard up and down and then raised his eyebrows in her direction, as if to say, 'is this your new man?'

But she shook her head slightly and he smiled. Then Mario whispered to her.

'He's a good man, I think,' he said. 'You work on him. You'll get him.'

She laughed then. How sweet Mario is, she thought. So gentle. So warm.

'I see you're well known here,' Richard said.

He'd been surprised by the restauranteur's warm, familiar greeting. He had always thought cities were cold and impersonal places.

'Yes, I am well known here,' she said, with a wry smile. 'Mario's always trying to get Bianca and I married off but we keep disappointing him. But he says he'll keep trying.'

Richard laughed.

'Your father probably agrees with him,' he said, guessing that an unmarried daughter nearing thirty was not in David Clarke's plans.

'He does,' she said. 'He does indeed. Except he was the one who pushed me into the relationship with Alec Fairholm. I couldn't bring myself to tell him the full details of what had happened, only that he was a drunk.'

He wanted to say, 'and how does he feel about Philippe?' but he did not. In the end, he did not need to ask the question. It was as if she had read his mind.

'He doesn't like Philippe,' she said, without prompting. 'He doesn't like the scandal of him having an illegitimate child. And he investigated his background and doesn't like that either. His mother wasn't married, never married in fact.'

It was Richard's turn to be shocked. It seemed incredible that her father would go to such lengths and he said so.

'Outrageous, isn't it?' she said. 'But my father likes to know everything. I was very angry with him when I found out.'

He wondered then if David Clarke had inadvertently pushed his daughter towards Philippe, such was her outrage at his investigation of Philippe's family background.

He was reminded of how his own son had been responsible for identifying Philippe as Pippa's father.

'But Philippe seems to have survived the revelation of being outed as Pippa's father,' Richard said. 'I remember when my son inadvertently let it out, there was a great to do. Julia was sure he'd lose his job.'

Karen smiled, a slightly knowing smile.

'It might well have had those consequences except that my father is a significant donor to the hospital foundation,' she said. 'I said it wouldn't please me to have Philippe sacked so he told Uncle Robert to tell the board he'd withdraw his support if Philippe's employment was terminated.'

It had never occurred to Richard there might have been more to Philippe's apparent ease in riding out the scandal.

'I had no idea you'd intervened on his behalf,' Richard said, shaking his head. 'No idea at all.'

'I think my father has since regretted it at times,' she said, with a laugh. 'But it's now well known Philippe has a daughter and who she is. It's hard to believe the coincidence of her going to the same school as Anita. And being Anita's friend.'

'Thinking back, I did need to use a little more persuasion,' she said enigmatically.

She sipped the white wine that Mario had placed in front of her before she continued.

'My friend Bianca is a fashion buyer for one of the big department stores,' she said. 'One of the wives of the men who sit on the hospital foundation board has been known to help herself to merchandise and not pay for it. He was threatening to be difficult about what he called Philippe's unsavoury private life. I got to hear about it so I cornered him one day as he was coming out of a meeting at the hospital. I told him I had a friend who knew about his wife's little problem. Did he want to discuss it further? He got the message.'

By this time, it was all Richard could do not to laugh but he was smiling broadly.

'Remind me never to pick a fight with you, my dear girl,' he said. 'You would be far too clever for me.'

He began to tackle the vast plate of pasta that had been put in front of him. She followed suit and then paused.

'But you haven't asked me the one question you are desperate to ask me, have you?' she said, looking directly at him.

'I've no right to ask you that question,' he said, surprised at the turn of the conversation which had been mostly light hearted.

'No right at all,' he repeated.

He was caught between his disappointment at Philippe's behaviour and his growing affection for a young woman he found impossible to dislike.

She smiled at him. He could see she was teasing him, provoking him even.

'You can't deny it,' she said playfully. 'You want to know about my relationship with Philippe. I've seen how angry you are with him at times. With me, too.'

He was startled. He thought she was incapable of surprising him further, but he was wrong. He shook his head. She was wrong there. He wasn't angry with her.

'Not angry,' he corrected her. 'Disappointed. In him, not you.'

'Because of how friendly he is with me?' she asked.

He nodded. Friendly hardly covers it though, he thought.

'To be quite frank, it's not a good look to have another woman on his arm if he really plans to marry someone else,' he said, choosing his words carefully. 'And as that someone else happens to be my sister, I think I have a right to have an opinion on his behaviour.'

He had seen them together. He knew it was much more than a simple flirtation. And it was not one sided, he had seen that too.

'You do realise he could not live with his guilt if he did not marry her?'

'Has he said that?' Richard asked.

'No, not in so many words,' she said. 'But I know him. He's not a man to go back on his word.'

The conversation had taken a totally unexpected turn. For just a brief moment he saw the desolation in Karen's face.

'And if he does that, as you say he will, where does that leave you?'

He had focused solely on how his sister might feel at Philippe's inappropriate behaviour with another woman. He had not given much thought until now about how Karen would feel. He wanted to reach out and comfort her but he hesitated. A public restaurant seemed the wrong place for such a gesture.

For the first time, he was seeing it from her point of view. Philippe had not discouraged her but, in the end, she believed he would keep his promise to Julia.

There was so much more he wanted to ask her. He had thought it was so simple. Philippe should just distance himself from her. But Richard guessed that slowly, against his better judgement, he'd been drawn to her. He had enjoyed her attention. What man wouldn't, thought Richard? But he'd always thought he was in control. That he could stop seeing her at any time.

For the first time Richard understood the power she exerted over men. A century ago, he thought, men would have fought duels over her. She almost has me under her spell too.

He had been waiting for her to answer his question but it never came. Instead she jumped out of her chair to hug the man who had just walked up to their table.

'I thought you were back tomorrow,' she said.

He shook his head.

'Your mother and I decided to come home early,' he explained. 'She got sick of the cold weather. We must have just missed each other this morning. We got home around nine.'

'And who's this?' David Clarke almost growled the question at his daughter.

Richard stood up and was introduced.

Well, at least it's not Duval, he thought.

'Richard helped us get the takeover proposal through the board meeting this morning,' she said.

It explained our lunching together, she thought. He won't pepper me with questions if he thinks it's just business.

'I noticed there was a new shareholder on the register,' David Clarke said. 'Ten percent if I'm not mistaken?'

Richard nodded.

'Yes, it was my first board meeting,' he said. 'I voted with Karen and Sid Curtis. That got the vote to fifty-five percent so it was passed.'

David Clarke gave a hearty chuckle. He pulled out the empty chair alongside his daughter and sat down uninvited. Mario produced a glass of wine for him, seemingly from nowhere.

'Thanks,' he said to Richard. 'I'm very pleased. I knew old man Fairholm was trying to scupper the deal so he could buy the Victorian company outright. Good to put a spoke in his wheel.'

'You should have told me Jack Fairholm would be there,' Karen said. 'At least I would have been forewarned.'

Her father looked perplexed.

'They usually send a proxy or Roger Fairholm attends himself,' he replied. 'They must have sent Jack as he's the bully boy. I'm sorry you had to face him.'

Then she laughed, remembering the look on Jack Fairholm's face as Richard tackled him.

'Richard looked after me,' she said, casting a smile in his direction. 'Jack Fairholm made the mistake of making some unsavoury remarks about me. Richard had him up against the wall in a chokehold before he knew what was happening to him.'

David Clarke raised his glass towards Richard in a gesture of thanks.

'Well done,' he said. 'Thanks for looking after my daughter. He's a nasty piece of work is Jack. Worse than his brother Alec.'

'Ah, Mr Clarke, here is your favourite dish, just for you,' Mario said, as he put a large bowl of spaghetti on the table.

'Thank you, Mario,' he said.

Mario grinned broadly. A good man, Mr Clarke. Such a shame about his son. His daughter should be giving him grandsons. Perhaps this new man will be the one, he thought.

Karen and her father walked out of the restaurant together having farewelled Richard earlier.

They were walking slowly along Circular Quay, past the ferry terminals and the tourist shops. Every now and again, the rumble of a train overhead interrupted their conversation.

'So, who's this Richard Belleville?' he asked. 'Where have I heard that name before?'

She had realised her father had not made the connection when he had joined them at lunch but she had not bothered to explain who he was. Now she could not avoid it.

'He is Julia Belleville's older brother,' Karen said simply.

'Now I know,' he said, nodding, as the name resonated in his memory. 'Julia Belleville is the girl who is going to marry Philippe.'

She nodded. There was nothing she could add. Or wanted to add.

'Richard is married, I assume,' her father said. 'He said he had to visit his son in hospital.'

He worried then his daughter might be getting mixed up with a married man. He guessed Richard would be in his late thirties.

'He's divorced,' Karen said. 'He has two sons, the younger one lives in England with his ex-wife, who has married again and had another son.'

Her father looked at her quizzically.

'You know a lot about him,' he said, with just a hint of suspicion in his voice.

'I sat next to him at dinner at Uncle Robert's on Saturday night,' she said. 'He'd been staying down with the Lesters in Bowral and brought Anita back when he came back to Sydney. Uncle Robert found out he had flown bombers in the war and wanted to talk to him about his experiences.'

To David Clarke, it all seemed straightforward and unremarkable.

'I expect Robert wanted a change from the usual medical talk at his table,' he said. 'I suppose Philippe was there too?'

She nodded.

'Of course,' she said. 'There were quite a few people from the hospital at the dinner. You'd expect him to be there.'

'And tell me, did he see you home?'

'Why do you ask?'

She was suddenly wary. It was an unlikely question. She wanted to be sure of the reason behind it.

He reached into his pocket and then opened the palm of his hand to reveal a single silver cuff link with a very fine etching of the American flag.

'Maria was cleaning your room this morning and found this under the bed,' he said. 'Fortunately, she gave it to me thinking somehow it was mine and that it had got caught up with something you'd taken into your room. Your mother doesn't know about it.'

She took it from him. They had stopped walking. They were standing side by side looking out over the harbour.

'Thank you,' she said. 'I'll return it to its owner.'

'He spent the night with you, didn't he?' he asked.

'Do you want me to lie to make you feel better?' she replied.

He shook his head and they resumed walking slowly back along the quay. As they reached his car, he stopped and looked at her.

'Does this mean he's going to go back on his word and won't marry Julia Belleville?'

'I don't know,' she said. 'That's up to him. I don't think so.'

'So where does that leave you, Karen?' he asked.

He wanted to say why don't you make better choices but he could see the disappointment in her eyes. She shrugged her shoulders.

'I don't know where it leaves me,' she said. 'Moving on, I guess, trying to find someone else. Trying to pretend I'm no longer in love with him.'

He swore under his breath. Americans, never liked them. They were trouble here during the war and they're still causing trouble. He put his arm around his daughter and she rested her head on his shoulder. I should be angry with her, he thought, but I can't. It's not her fault.

Does he really understand, she wondered? Does he really understand I have no idea how I'm going to live without Philippe in my life?

She watched as her father drove away and then she headed back towards the city to retrieve her car.

CHAPTER 25

January 1960

Pippa sat perched on the edge of Paul's bed, flipping through the comics he had discarded, looking for the latest issue of Phantom, which was her favourite. Edith Henderson was tidying his things, arranging fresh flowers in the vase beside his bed and urging him, possibly for the twentieth time, not to get up to any mischief.

He was very relieved to see his father. All these females fussing around him was more than a boy could stomach, he wanted to say, but thought better of it.

'How are you?' Richard asked, although he could see his son was in good spirits despite being confined to bed.

'Getting bored,' he said. 'When will they let me out?'

'I'm not sure,' his father replied, 'but complaining won't get you out any sooner. I have to call your mother later tonight to give her a report. I know she'll wonder if she should make the trip out to see you, but she has a young baby. It would be difficult for her.'

Paul shook his head. He missed her terribly and especially at a time like this, but he knew it was impossible for her travel so far with his new baby brother.

'I understand, Dad,' he said, 'but can we go and see Mum soon? Maybe I can take an extra week off school in the May holidays? That would give us enough time.'

Richard nodded. He knew Paul needed something to look forward to. Living together, just the two of them, had worked well, but he knew

Paul was missing his mother and his brother.

'It was better when we all lived together at Prior Park,' he had told his father on previous occasions.

With just me for company, the boy is lonely Richard had thought at the time. Is Pippa another lonely child, he wondered? Richard motioned to Edith Henderson and she followed him outside to speak in private.

'He seems to be recovering well,' she said.

She was still very conscious of Paul having been injured under her care.

'I'm sure he'll be fine,' Richard said. 'But I was thinking he needs company. What if I arrange for Pippa to come back with us for a couple of weeks? I plan to send Paul out to Prior Park to my sister-in-law Alice who will do a much better job of looking after him than I can. He'll be much better off there with Marianne and Pippa for company. I know Marianne is very keen for Pippa to visit again.'

Edith smiled and nodded.

'I think she'd be delighted,' she said. 'None of her close friends from school live nearby and I only have people my own age visiting me. But that means you'll have to come back to Sydney to bring her back. Or Julia will.'

'That won't be a problem,' he said. 'And she will be with us to celebrate my fortieth birthday at the end of next week.'

He added a cautionary note.

'Don't mention it to her until you get home,' he said, 'otherwise she'll disturb the other patients.'

Edith laughed.

'She is inclined to get over exuberant,' she said, 'but she is a delightful child.'

He thought Edith Henderson would very soon have to stop describing Pippa as a child. Richard had noticed the early signs of womanhood in his niece. By the time she's seventeen, he thought, she'll be a very pretty young woman. He wondered if by that time she would be under the guidance of her actual parents. It occurred to him, not for the first time, how difficult it must be to enter a child's life late in the day. Can the bond ever be as strong, he wondered?

273

As he walked out of the hospital, Richard sensed there was someone behind him. He stopped and turned. Philippe was a few paces behind him.

'Richard,' he said, 'have you time for a coffee?'

He nodded and followed Philippe to a small coffee shop alongside the main hospital building.

'I assume you've just come from seeing Paul?' Philippe said.

'Yes, he seems to be recovering well, thank goodness.'

Philippe was relieved. It could have easily turned out so much worse, except Richard didn't know it.

'I think they will put a bigger cast on tomorrow, I believe,' Philippe said. 'You just need to make sure he doesn't start playing and fall over. Boys are notoriously difficult patients to keep quiet.'

Philippe sipped his coffee and checked his watch.

'Are you pushed for time?' Richard asked.

'I have a few minutes,' he said, 'but I do have to check on a patient I operated on this morning.'

'By the way,' Richard said. 'I've suggested Pippa come back with me and Paul. I plan to send them both out to Prior Park to Alice and William to look after.'

It occurred to him then he should have asked Philippe's permission before suggesting the trip to Edith Henderson. Who has parental authority over the girl, he wondered?

'That's a good idea,' Philippe said, 'but you'll have to bring her back in time for school.'

Then he remembered. For Richard, it provided the perfect excuse to be back in Sydney as the private schools were going back for the new school year. Kate Lester would be in Sydney settling her children back in school.

'By the way, I ran into Karen today unexpectedly,' he said, watching Philippe's face closely for any reaction. 'I ended up having lunch with her.'

But Philippe was already aware of their meeting.

'She called me earlier,' he said simply. 'It's good to see her father putting his confidence in her. I keep telling her she needs to do some-thing meaningful with her life.'

'You mean something more than the life of the Sydney socialite she was raised to become?' Richard asked.

Philippe smiled and nodded.

'Yes, if you put it that way,' he said. 'She's very bright and engaging. But how fulfilling can a life be of endless lunches, dinners, fashion shows and gala balls? There has to be more, doesn't there?'

'You and I probably think so,' Richard said. 'Surely it's up to her?'

'Of course,' he said. 'Her father has started to bring her into his business, although she doesn't like it much. She finds the all-male culture difficult.'

'That doesn't surprise me at all given what happened this morning,' Richard said, remembering the incident in the boardroom earlier in the day.

'Yes,' Philippe said. 'She told me briefly about what happened with Jack Fairholm. She was very impressed by your chivalry.'

Richard laughed. It seemed such an old-fashioned word.

'I couldn't stand idly by and let that foul-mouthed boor trash her reputation,' Richard said. 'I couldn't repeat what he said, it was so appalling.'

'Neither could I have stood idly by,' Philippe said, 'but your response was probably more direct than mine would have been.'

'More physical, you mean,' Richard said, with a laugh. 'Some of my combat training came back to me just at the right time.'

Philippe nodded but said nothing.

'By the way I met Karen's father,' Richard said. 'He came up to us while we were having lunch. Sat down uninvited, as I recall.'

'She told me that too,' Philippe said. 'He would have sized you up as a potential son-in-law.'

Richard laughed at this suggestion.

'You cannot be serious,' he retorted. 'I'm too old for her for a start.'

He drained the last dregs of his coffee and looked at Philippe.

'He can hardly approve of you seeing her?'

'He disapproves very strongly,' Philippe said. 'But then, you don't approve of my friendship with her either, but for different reasons.'

Richard inclined his head slightly. He could not deny it.

'You know my feelings,' he said. 'I just hope when the time comes for you to fulfil your promise to my sister, your relationship with Karen is over.'

Philippe did not answer him directly.

I think he's got himself in much deeper than he cares to admit or planned to, Richard thought. And he feels terribly guilty about it, although he wouldn't admit that either.

'I must go,' he said. 'Duty calls. Perhaps I'll see you tomorrow when you visit Paul again.'

Richard watched him walk back towards the main building. He began to wonder how well his sister would fit into Philippe's life in Sydney. He wondered if they had even discussed it.

For the first time, he began to think Karen might have been a more suitable wife for Philippe after all.

Richard arrived back at his hotel to two messages. He glanced at them quickly. One was from John Bertram. The other was from Karen, asking him to call her.

Karen can wait, he thought, as can John. He found Ian Dixon's card and rang his office number. As he expected, he did not get through to the man himself but to his clerk.

'What is the possibility of seeing Mr Dixon in the next few days?' he asked.

There was silence for a few moments while the clerk checked the lists.

'You're in the luck, sir,' the clerk said. 'The judge he was to appear before tomorrow is off sick this week, so the matter has been stood over. Shall we say 10.00 o'clock tomorrow?'

Richard thanked him.

'And may I ask, sir, who your instructing solicitor is for the matter you wish to discuss with Mr Dixon?'

'I don't have one,' Richard replied. 'Who do you recommend?'

There was just the smallest of sighs from the clerk, who was unused to dealing with people unfamiliar with the niceties of the legal world.

'I'll check with Mr Dixon. I'm sure he'll recommend someone, probably from Allen Allen & Hemsley,' he said.

'That's fine, thank you,' Richard said, already impatient with the rigmarole of setting up a simple meeting.

He then lifted the receiver to call Karen. He was surprised when she answered. He had half expected to hear her father's voice. Or perhaps her mother's.

'My father asked me to call you,' she said, as if she did not want the message to be misinterpreted. 'He's having a few people out on his boat tomorrow afternoon, sailing at around five and then having dinner on board. He'd like you to come. The harbour looks wonderful at this time of year, you shouldn't miss it.'

'I'd like you to come,' she added, as if the invitation had sounded too impersonal.

It was a totally unexpected invitation. He wondered what lay behind it. Was it just a 'thank you' for having helped get the takeover proposal through the board at Curtis Transport? He hoped the motivation was as straightforward as that.

'Yes, of course, Karen,' he said. 'I'd love to come. It's very thoughtful of your father to think of me. Where do I go? How do I find the boat?'

'I'll pick you up at your hotel at 4.30,' she said and then rang off.

He put the phone down, not displeased with the idea of a dinner cruise on the harbour but nonetheless curious at the reason for the unexpected invitation. He checked his watch. It was too early to book a call for England. He dialled John Bertram's number.

'Have you been staying out of trouble, mate?' his friend asked.

'More or less,' he said. 'I had coffee with Philippe this afternoon. It was very civilised, you'll be pleased to know.'

'That's good,' John said. 'What about catching up for dinner tomorrow night? I'm busy from Wednesday onwards with work.'

'Dinner's out, I'm afraid,' Richard replied. 'I've been invited on a harbour cruise by Karen's father, on his own boat no less.'

'You better watch out,' John said, 'he might be checking you out as a potential replacement for Philippe.'

Richard laughed.

'I don't think so,' Richard said. 'He wants a young man without baggage who's going to make sure Karen gives him grandchildren.'

'I wonder what she thinks of that plan,' John mused aloud.

'I don't think she's wildly in favour of it, from what I can see,'

Richard replied. 'I had lunch with her today. Her father turned up unexpectedly. I think he expects the world to dance to his tune.'

'Interesting,' John said, without explaining what was so interesting about it. 'Perhaps we can do lunch tomorrow.'

'Good plan,' Richard said. 'I have a lawyer meeting tomorrow at ten. Maybe see you around twelve?'

'Done,' his friend said.

John Bertram hung up the phone. So how did Richard end up having lunch with the delightful Karen, he wondered? There's a story there, he thought.

Richard's next call was to his sister who thanked him for his thoughtfulness in arranging to bring Pippa back home with him.

After he had hung up the phone, he felt a vague sense of unease at the answers he had given to her questions about Philippe. What purpose would it serve, he argued with himself, to tell her Philippe had certainly spent the night in another woman's bed? But in knowing that and deciding not to tell his sister the truth, he felt somehow complicit in the deception. And he knew he would have to go on being complicit. For her sake.

He headed down to the hotel bar for a much-need drink. Outside, the streets almost vibrated from the bustle of weary workers heading home to the vast spread of suburbs beyond the city. It was a life he could not imagine. A life he could never live. A life he would never have to live.

He downed the remains of his beer in one gulp and called for another.

Philippe closed his eyes and sat back in his chair. It had been a difficult day, not made any easier by his terse exchange with Richard. I should have avoided him, he thought. How have I let my life become so complicated, he wondered?

He was listening intently to his latest jazz record from New York. It was something he missed about New York, the jazz clubs. Music had always been part of the background to his life. He had not realised how much he missed it.

Occasionally he sipped his glass of wine. Will I get this chance to simply listen to music, he wondered, when Julia is with me? How will that work? Will it work?

Then his thoughts went to Karen. Once again, he felt a surge of guilt overwhelm him. He berated himself. How could I have let that happen, he thought? I should have walked away. But I didn't. In fact I couldn't, he finally admitted to himself.

He had left the front door of his house open in the hope of catching the breeze. It had been a warm day. He thought of New York. Central Park would by now be blanketed by a thick carpet of snow. The city streets would be wet and slushy. So different from the hot steamy month of January in Australia. What a shock it must have been to the first European settlers, he mused, to discover the seasons were completely reversed.

He had been so immersed in the music he did not hear Karen calling him. She had opened the screen door and walked along the hallway calling his name. He got up and walked across to the record player to turn down the volume.

'I didn't hear you come in,' he said as he greeted her. 'Was I expecting you?'

Surely, I'd have remembered her saying she was going to call to see me, he thought. She shook her head.

'No, it was a spur of the moment decision,' she said. 'I was out with Bianca. She wanted me to meet a young local designer to look over some sketches for the spring range. She values my opinion. I realised it was only a couple of streets away from your house.'

'Let me get you a glass of wine,' he offered.

While he was gone, she began to browse his bookshelf. It differed markedly from her own. It was dominated by medical texts. Then she glanced further along the shelves. Biographies, American history, American thriller writers. A book about Sydney was the only one she recognised.

There's so much about him I don't know, she thought. She had never before had the opportunity to see his life at close quarters. She had only ever previously been to his house once before and then only briefly.

'You're welcome to borrow anything you want,' he said, seeing her glance along his bookshelf, 'but you might find the medical texts heavy going.'

She laughed.

'It's just like Uncle Robert's study,' she said, as she picked up a framed photo and turned towards him.

'This is your mother?' she asked, as she held it out in front of her.

'Yes,' he said, taking it from her. 'It was taken not long before she died.'

'She must have been proud of what you achieved,' Karen said, aware that she was trespassing into the most private part of his life.

'I think she was,' he said, and put the photo back on the bookshelf.

He could not look at a photo of his mother, even after all the years since her death, without seeing an unselfish lifetime of struggle ultimately tainted by her single wilful act of failing to pass on Julia's letter to him.

Karen took the glass of wine he held out to her.

'Is there a reason why you came by tonight?' he asked.

He was determined to keep his distance from her. Forget how enchanting she looks, he reminded himself.

She took a sip of wine then opened the palm of her hand, just as her father had done, to reveal a single silver cufflink. He took it from her.

'Where did you find this?' he asked, only because it seemed the logical question to ask, not because he didn't already know the answer.

'I didn't find it,' she said, with a faint smile. 'Our cleaning lady found it, where you might expect, and she gave it to my father, who returned it to me today.'

'Oh, that's bad luck,' he said, shaking his head. 'Was he very angry with me? With you?'

He knew her father would guess who the cufflink belonged to. Who else would wear a cufflink finely etched with the famous stars and stripes?

'Not as angry as I thought he would be,' she admitted.

She walked across to the sofa and sat down. She placed her glass of wine carefully on the coffee table in front of her.

He wanted to avoid sitting next to her but to sit away from her seemed almost disrespectful of their friendship, as if he no longer wanted to touch her. As if what had happened between them had rendered her contemptible.

'About Saturday night,' he said, groping for the right words. 'I should not have ..'

'Made love to me?' she said, filling in the words he could not bring himself to say.

'The blame is mine for what happened,' he said quietly. 'I should not have taken advantage of you as I did. It was wrong.'

She was silent, considering what he had just said. Then she spoke.

'You did not take advantage of me,' she said. 'There is no need to apologise.'

Now that she was sitting beside him, he could see for himself how the mask of bravado has slipped. Beneath it, he glimpsed her vulnerability. He saw the hurt in her eyes. He understood, by apologising, he had reduced the act of making love to her to a simple act of sex she thought he did not want to remember.

She had looked away from him to hide the tears in her eyes.

'Look at me,' he said tenderly, as he moved a little closer to her. 'I think you are misunderstanding me. I am sorry because I feel guilty. Because I'm pledged to marry someone else. But I enjoy being with you. You know that, don't you?'

He reached across to her face and wiped a single tear from her cheek. She's too desirable, he thought. She's too dangerous. I shouldn't be doing this. I should get up and send her home. She nodded her head. She could not trust herself to speak.

'You know I find you very hard to resist,' he said, as he began to stroke the hair that had fallen across her face.

He put his arm around her and bent forward to kiss her. How can I feel this way about a woman who is not the woman I've promised to marry, he wondered?

'Is this something you're going to regret tomorrow?' she asked, her old feistiness returning as she responded to him.

'Probably,' he said, as he began to caress her. 'I cannot claim to be a saint. I've tried to convince myself I don't want to make love to you again. But the truth is, I do. Desperately.'

She laughed softly, as his lips caressed the tops of her shoulder and his hands began to explore her body lovingly.

I want him so much, she thought. Tomorrow, or the next day, I'll worry about the future. Not now, not tonight.

'Stay with me tonight,' he said, as he held out his hand and led her to his bedroom.

CHAPTER 26

January 1960

John Bertram sat sipping his beer and listening intently as Richard related the events of the previous day, carefully omitting some of his discussion with Karen which seemed too private to share even with his best friend.

'So, you were a knight in shining armour, riding to the rescue of the fair Karen,' his friend joked. 'You should have given him a good slap, just to make sure he understood.'

Richard laughed.

'I had a feeling brawling in the boardroom would be frowned upon,' he said. 'Besides there were two ladies present.'

'Two?'

'Yes,' Richard explained. 'Karen and Curtis's secretary. She was organising the papers and taking minutes.'

'Of course,' John agreed. 'It might have been a bit unseemly. But he would have deserved it.'

Where Richard had declined to repeat the slur to Philippe, he had repeated every word to John, who was as horrified as Richard. He despised men who demeaned women in such a way.

'You said you had a meeting with a lawyer this morning,' John said, changing the subject. 'Anything you want to tell me?'

'I wanted to find out what I should do in relation to Anthony,' he replied. 'I was happy to leave him with Catherine while he was young but now she's had another baby, I want him to come back and live with me. I've promised to take Paul over in May, so I want to do some investigation before I go.'

'Let me get this right,' he joked. 'You thought you'd go straight to the top of the lawyer tree and secure the services of a Queen's Counsel. You must be anticipating trouble.'

Richard smiled. He hadn't quite seen it like that.

'Actually, I'm not anticipating anything yet,' he said, 'but I thought the local firm we use for our business matters would be out of their depth quite frankly. Meeting Ian Dixon the other night was an opportunity I couldn't pass up.'

'And what does he say?'

'Well, he wants to get the divorce papers from England,' Richard said. 'He wants to see if there were any provisions in our agreement. I said there weren't but you know what lawyers are like, they have to see it for themselves.'

John grimaced at this news.

'You know that's going to expose your private life,' he said. 'As I remember you agreed to the adultery admission so Catherine could get her divorce quickly.'

He laughed mirthlessly.

'Yes,' he said, 'I did. If you remember I did that as a courtesy to my former wife. I did not know it was to make sure she did not end up having a baby fathered by another man while she was still married to me.'

John again protested his innocence.

'She never told me she was pregnant, mate,' he said, which was true.

He did not say I guessed she was pregnant.

'I never thought those divorce papers would ever surface again,' Richard admitted, 'but I'm prepared to do it for Anthony's sake.'

He took a sip of his beer which had almost gone flat. He pushed it away and called for a fresh one. He sat back in his chair, his arms behind his head. It was a habit of his when he wanted to think.

'If Anthony grows up in England but inherits a share of Prior Park and the Belleville business interests, it will be meaningless to him,' Richard said, having thought about it for some minutes.

'If he grows up in England, I believe he will eventually be made to feel like the poor relation because he'll be excluded from any inheritance in England now that Catherine has a son who'll inherit the title. If she makes provision for our children, it will be a minor provision. She'll want to keep her wealth intact for the new baronet.'

John listened to this sympathetically. He could not deny Richard was right. He had seen at close quarters the snobbishness of the English upper classes. Anthony would be mercilessly teased as a colonial at any public school he attended. As he began to mix in polite circles, he would probably be whispered about as the offspring of Lady Cavendish's unfortunate first marriage.

'You should discuss this with Catherine when you go over there,' John said.

'I will try and have a civil discussion with her,' Richard said, as he thanked the waiter for the fresh glass of beer. 'That's why I want to find out where I stand in law and which jurisdiction might apply.'

I'll probably regret this, John thought.

'If you need my help, let me know,' he said.

'Thanks, mate,' Richard said. 'Hopefully I can keep you out of it this time. I don't want you to have to take sides.'

John smiled to himself.

'I've walked a tightrope between the two of them for years,' he thought. 'And that's not likely to change any time soon.'

Their meals arrived. John began to tackle the large rump steak that hung over each side of the plate. Richard, on this occasion, had opted for grilled fish.

Richard was thankful it looked as if it would be a calm evening on the harbour. David Clarke greeted him enthusiastically as he came aboard the Lady D, which proved to be a sizeable boat, capable of holding quite a number of guests.

'Richard, welcome,' he said, extending his hand. 'We meet again.'

Richard returned the powerful handshake and thanked his host, who waved aside his gratitude.

'I wanted to introduce you to a few people,' he said. 'It occurred to me after your help with the Curtis Transport matter we might be able to do more business together or at least I might be able to introduce you to some people who might be useful to you.'

Richard was unsure what David Clarke expected him to say so he remained silent. He looked around the crowd already gathered on the back deck. Apart from Karen and one other young woman, it was an all male gathering.

No wonder Karen finds it all very difficult, he thought.

'This is Norman Cowper,' David Clarke said, 'partner at Allen Allen and Hemsley.'

Richard shook the older man's hand.

'I met one of your colleagues today,' Richard said, by way of conversation. 'He sat in with me while I was having a chat with Ian Dixon about a legal matter.'

'That's good, Dixon's a good man,' he replied, before his attention was diverted by the offer of a drink.

In quick succession, Richard was introduced to four or five other men, none of whose names he could remember, so he was relieved when Karen came alongside him.

'Shall I rescue you?' she whispered as she slipped her hand through his arm.

He noticed some looks of envy from the men around him who secretly wished David Clarke's daughter would do the same to them.

'Please,' he said quietly, as he followed her to the foredeck.

'You look prettier every time I see you,' he said. 'By the way I thought your driving was really outstanding. You handle your car so well.'

She laughed. It had been short drive along familiar roads from his hotel in the city to Rose Bay. She thought it hardly merited such an extravagant compliment.

'You were going to say, for a woman,' she said teasingly.

He shook his head.

'Did I say that?'

He could not let it go unchallenged although it might have been what he meant subconsciously. She shook her head.

'No, but it's what you meant.'

The gentle throb of the engines signalled the boat was getting under way. It was still light enough to see the vast expanse of water that stretched ahead of them. It is possibly the most beautiful harbour in the world, Richard thought. He lent against the side rail watching the southern shore of the harbour drift by. Karen stood beside him, remembering that she had stood in a similar position with Philippe by her side months before.

'I will introduce you to my friend Bianca when I get a chance,' she said. 'I take it my father has introduced you to a number of people already.'

'Yes, he has,' Richard said. 'If I remember their names and faces tomorrow it will be a miracle.'

'Me too,' she said, 'although I've met most of them before. They're all aware that if my father drops dead, I'll be the person they'll have to deal with.'

'Obviously, that day is a long way off,' Richard said. 'Your father looks to be very fit and active.'

'Perhaps,' she said, suddenly thoughtful, 'but he is sixty-five this year. A dangerous age for a man.'

'Like twenty-nine,' he said with a wry smile, 'which is clearly a dangerous age for a woman.'

She couldn't help but smile at his flirtatiousness.

'You are a practised flirt, my dear Richard,' she said, dismissing his protests he was no such thing.

'I've seen you in action, remember,' she said. 'Except you seem to prefer to lavish your attention on other men's wives.'

He laughed at the sheer audacity of what she had said.

'Now that,' Richard said, slipping his arm around her waist to make his point, 'is a piece of pure fiction.'

Before she could reply, a voice cut across their conversation and they both turned to see who the voice belonged to.

'Karen, my darling, how delightful to see you.'

Richard watched as Michael Ferrari lifted her fingers to his lips in a theatrical gesture and then put his arms around her. He noticed how she tried to step back from his embrace. She's uncomfortable with him, he thought.

'Michael, this is my friend Richard Belleville,' she said, using the introduction as an excuse to evade his clutches.

Richard shook hands with him. He guessed he was around Karen's age. He was classically good looking and well groomed.

'Belleville,' he said. 'The name is familiar. French in origin, I think?'

Richard nodded. Probably a couple of centuries ago, he thought, but he didn't say so.

'Related to Julia Belleville perhaps?'

'Yes, she's my sister,' Richard said.

He was cautious. He didn't know where the conversation was heading.

'Ah, the lady who shares a scandalous past with the good Doctor Duval,' Michael Ferrari said sarcastically. 'When they finally marry, then I can marry Karen.'

'What a ridiculous thing to say, Michael,' a voice broke in.

Bianca Ferrari held her hand out towards Richard.

'Please excuse my brother's appalling manners and that dreadful comment,' she said, disarming Richard so completely the tension immediately dissipated.

'I can only think he's already had too much to drink. Throw him overboard if you think it's warranted. You have my permission.'

Richard was relieved at Bianca's intervention. In truth he had been very tempted to throw Michael Ferrari overboard for the outrageous and totally unnecessary remark he had made.

'It was just a joke, sis,' Michael Ferrari said petulantly. 'No one can take a joke anymore.'

'No one appreciates your failed attempt at humour, Michael,' she said sternly. 'Go and find some coffee and sober up before you embarrass our family even further.'

He turned and sidled off. He was clearly chastened by the dressing down his sister had delivered.

'Karen has told me all about you,' she said, as she turned back towards Richard.

Richard wanted to say 'well done, Bianca' but he thought better of it.

'Some of it might have been embellished,' he said laughingly.

'But not your reaction to Jack Fairholm, surely?' she said.

'It's what anyone would have done in that situation,' he said, determined to play down his growing reputation for gallantry.

'Not many these days,' she said, as she surveyed the groups of men scattered around the vessel. 'I keep Karen company at these events so she doesn't feel quite so outnumbered.'

'Her mother doesn't attend?' Richard asked, surprised that David Clarke's wife was not on board to act as hostess.

Bianca shook her head.

'Deborah Clarke despises these all-male events,' she said. 'If you invite their wives, then I will come, but not otherwise, I've heard her say to David Clarke.'

As they had been speaking, Karen had responded to a signal from her father to join him. They both watched as Karen began to negotiate the narrow space down the side of the boat to reach him on the back deck. What Richard observed as she moved through the groups of guests shocked him.

Several men, surreptitiously, grabbed her by the waist or patted her backside as she tried to make her way to where her father was standing with a group of men.

He turned to Bianca.

'Did you see what I saw?' he asked, unable to keep the sense of shock out of his voice. He thought, but did not say, they are treating Karen like a trollop.

'That's why I come with her,' Bianca said. 'To keep the worst of them at bay. To rescue her from them.'

Richard was perplexed.

'Doesn't her father see it happening?' he said.

'Not all of it,' Bianca said, 'and then he's inclined to dismiss it by saying they don't mean anything by it. He's more concerned not to offend certain of his business friends than defend his daughter.'

'That's dreadful,' he said, shaking his head slightly. He couldn't imagine William standing by and watching Marianne being groped in public. Nor would he for that matter, as her uncle.

'Why do you think she finds you so charming, Richard?' she said. 'And Philippe too. You both treat her with respect.'

'Don't forget too,' Bianca went on, 'many of them have heard what Jack Fairholm and his brother have to say about her. They believe it.'

'Then they're idiots,' Richard said, shaking his head in disbelief.

They watched as her father put his arm around her.

'If David Clarke wants to draw you into his business web,' Bianca said, 'I would turn and run in the opposite direction.'

'Are you telling me that from personal experience?'

'My father does some deals with him,' Bianca said, 'but he doesn't like him much. He told me he's seen other men flattered by David Clarke's attention only to find their own interests are suddenly expected to come a distant second to David Clarke's interests.'

Richard smiled.

'I was beginning to get that feeling myself,' he said. 'Thanks for the warning. I don't readily dance to another man's tune. I have no need to.'

'Then you are a lucky man,' she said.

They watched as Karen extricated herself from her father's group and headed back towards them. Before she could reach them, her path was blocked by a very inebriated guest who pulled her into his arms and began trying to kiss and fondle her as she struggled to break free.

Richard looked at Bianca. She nodded.

'I think she needs help.'

In seconds, Richard was by her side.

'I think you should leave the lady alone,' he said, with icy politeness.

'Wait your turn, mate,' the fellow slurred.

Richard hit him hard and he let her go suddenly. He crumpled to the deck but Richard was totally unconcerned. He put his arm around Karen to prevent her from falling. She smiled up at him.

'What am I going to do without my knight in shining armour when you go home?' she asked, as she smoothed her hair back into place.

'I was appalled at how those men were treating you,' he said gently. 'You shouldn't have to put up with that.'

'They are appalling,' Bianca said, as they watched the offender being helped to his feet.

He turned and glared at Richard before reaching for the glass of whisky being offered by the steward.

'I'm sure he's a friend of Jack Fairholm,' Karen said. 'A gullible friend, should I say.'

The other partygoers had barely noticed the altercation, thought

Richard. What's wrong with them?

The fine afternoon had given way to quite a chilly evening and he took off his jacket and placed it around Karen's shoulders.

'Thank you,' she said, as she pulled it closer around her.

Bianca smiled at him.

'You are the only gentleman on board,' she said, raising her glass in a mock toast.

If he doesn't watch out, Bianca thought, Karen will fall in love with him. But he is not the right man for her. He is a country man at heart. He would hate city life.

She did not know he had already disappointed his first wife with his distaste for the superficiality of life on the society merry-go-round.

CHAPTER 27

January 1960

The Viscount turboprop lifted effortlessly off the tarmac. The post-card view of Sydney Harbour Bridge was quickly replaced by fluffy white clouds and blue sky as the aircraft climbed steadily towards its cruising altitude on its journey north.

Richard eased his tall frame back into the airline seat, closed his eyes and breathed a sigh of relief. He was pleased to be leaving the city behind him. Such living would quickly turn a man soft, he thought.

He longed to get back to Prior Park to do a day's hard physical work. It was not demanded of him. He and William employed enough men to do what was needed but just occasionally he would ride out with them at daybreak to muster cattle for sale or get calves in for branding. He looked forward to it.

He began to think over the events of the past ten days. He remembered Kate Lester with a mixture of pleasure and concern. She had captivated him. Against his better judgement, he knew he would seek her out again. Her husband does not deserve her fidelity, he thought. And Karen. Philippe will have to make a decision and he knows it. He will have to be the one to end the relationship. I wonder if he realises Karen will not go willingly.

He turned towards his son, who sat next to him. Paul was uncom-fortable with his plaster cast but pleased to be heading home too. He had begun to mark off the days on his cast. He still had a long way to go before he would be free of it.

Across the aisle, Pippa sat quietly reading the latest *Girls' Annual* which had been among her Christmas presents.

Does she really belong to us, Richard wondered? There will always be a missing part, he thought. The part we never knew. The baby. The young child growing up amongst us. She's not part of our shared memories. It's not her fault but it feels like that all the same. There will always be a small part of her that is a stranger to us.

It's the very reason I must move heaven and earth to get Anthony back, he thought. He belongs with us, not to a household where his younger brother is much more important than he is. He drifted into a fitful sleep and woke with a start as the aircraft hit the Brisbane runway hard.

'Wind shear,' Richard explained to Paul who looked towards him for reassurance. 'An unexpected wind gust just at the moment of landing.'

He'd experienced similar problems himself despite the bulk of the Lancaster.

'One more leg and we'll be home,' he said, as they disembarked into a steamy Brisbane afternoon.

William greeted his sister Julia as he walked into the terminal at Springfield.

'Any sign of the plane?'

She shook her head.

'Not yet,' she said, looking at her watch. 'It's due in another five minutes or so.'

'I expect you are looking forward to seeing Pippa?'

She nodded.

'It's good of Richard to think of bringing her back with him,' she said.

'Marianne's very excited,' William said. 'When will you bring her out to us?'

'Probably tomorrow,' Julia said.

'Richard is coming out too,' he said. 'He thinks Paul will be better recuperating with us with Alice to watch over him and having the girls for company.'

'You didn't really need to come to pick them up today,' Julia said. 'I could have managed.'

William shrugged his shoulders.

'I was in town anyway,' he said. 'I said I would stay over at his place tonight, so I called by to let his housekeeper know. I picked up his mail too.'

He held up a perfumed envelope for Julia to see.

'I think our brother might have met someone while he was away,' he said, with an emphasis Julia could not mistake.

She took it from him and looked at the return address. K Lester, c/- Angela Dixon with a Sydney address. She looked quizzically at William.

'I may be getting this entirely wrong,' he said, 'but Richard took Paul to visit Tim Lester at Bowral. The parents, if my memory serves me, are Gerald and Kate Lester. There may be an innocent explanation as to why she is writing to Richard, but then again ….'

Her brother left the sentence unfinished. Julia laughed. William has become so pompous, she thought.

'Well, let's see how he reacts when you show him the letter,' she said as she handed it back to him. 'If he snatches it out of your hand, you know he's guilty.'

Even William raised a smile at this. His brother had shocked him once before with an admission he had been romancing another woman while he was married to Catherine.

Now he's divorced, William expected him to marry again but why couldn't he find a suitable single woman, he wondered? Why complicate his life by going after another man's wife?

They both looked skywards as the sound of an approaching aircraft signalled the imminent arrival of his flight.

It was only a matter of days after his return home that Richard fulfilled his desperate need to put in a hard day's physical work. The sun had only just broken above the horizon. It would be another hot, dry day.

Charles Brockman waited while Richard mounted his horse, which proved more difficult than he had anticipated. The gelding was proving to be fractious.

'He hasn't been ridden for a couple of months,' Charles said. 'He'll be frisky. Hold him tight otherwise he'll get away from you.'

Richard cast a quick glance in Charles's direction.

'I do know how to ride, thank you, Charles,' he said, as he settled himself into the saddle.

'So how was the trip, apart from young Paul's mishap?' Charles asked, as they rode side by side in the direction of the farthest paddock at Prior Park.

The stockmen had already gone on ahead. All hands were needed to brand at least a hundred calves with the Prior Park mark of L4.

'Interesting,' Richard said.

How much detail could he go into, he thought? Where to start?

'And the Lester place at Bowral?' he asked. 'I bet that gets a lot more rain than we do.'

Richard smiled, remembering not the property but the owner. Or more precisely the owner's wife. He had snatched her letter out of William's hand when they met at the airport. He was still puzzled by the knowing smile that passed between William and Julia.

'It's a wonderful place,' he said. 'A grand home even bigger than ours, beautifully manicured gardens and some terrific grazing country.'

Charles knew he was referring to their grand old house at Prior Park that now lay in ruins.

'It must be quite something to be bigger than your old home,' Charles said. 'And the cattle? Fat as mud I suppose?'

'I saw some good young steers but I missed seeing the Hereford stud which was about twenty miles away on a separate property,' he said. 'But it made me think it's time for us to get serious about expanding our cattle business.'

He had in the past left this to William but seeing part of Gerald Lester's operation had renewed his enthusiasm for cattle.

'It's going to be hard to do that here,' Charles said but Richard already knew that.

To the west they were hemmed in by Tom Warner's place. To the north and east, James Fitzroy now owned all the viable land.

'Maybe we should look south,' Richard said.

'South of here?' Charles asked, surprised.

In his opinion, the country wasn't much good for grazing immediately to the south of Prior Park

'No,' Richard said. 'I mean in New South Wales perhaps. A separate
operation. Somewhere where the rainfall is more reliable.'

There's more to this idea than meets the eye, Charles thought. He's
never mentioned it before as a possibility.

'Well, don't include me in your plans,' Charles said, 'I'm not moving at my age.'

Richard laughed.

'Nor am I suggesting you move,' he said. 'Just a thought to get us
into more reliable country.'

Well, we'll see if anything comes of that, Charles thought. It wouldn't
be a cheap move.

'And Julia's intended? Did you see him?' he asked.

'I did,' Richard said. 'Several times as a matter of fact.'

'How's he going? Any sign of Julia's divorce becoming final so they
can tie the knot?'

Richard looked at Charles. Should I tell him? I need to tell someone. If I tell William, he'll fret and possibly let something slip to Julia.

'I hope Julia's divorce happens very soon, Charles,' he said, as he
eased his horse to a complete stop. 'For her sake. There is a very delicious piece of womanhood called Karen who has taken a liking to the
good doctor. And I think he's taken a liking to her too.'

Charles let out a low whistle and shook his head.

'Not good by the sound of it,' he said, as he reined in his own horse
so they could speak without difficulty.

That, thought Richard, was an understatement.

'You're right. It's not good at all,' Richard agreed. 'Duval says they
are just good friends but I've seen her with him and I don't believe it.
He says he will fulfil his commitment to marry Julia. I'm holding him
to that.'

Charles was silent for a few moments. He had never considered
Julia might face a rival for Duval's affections. She had spoken so confidently of their relationship. This is what comes of being apart, he
thought.

'And you told your sister exactly what about this situation?' Charles asked, hoping Richard had the good sense to keep it to himself.

'Nothing at all, Charles,' he said. 'I told her precisely nothing. Julia knows the girl so I didn't even mention that I'd met her. It seemed safer somehow.'

'Good plan,' Charles said. 'Anyway, from what I've been told, Mr Fitzroy will be wanting a divorce sooner rather than later so he may push it along. I heard there's one angry father in town claiming he's made his daughter pregnant.'

'Any truth in it, do you think?' Richard asked.

'I don't know,' Charles said, 'but I'll keep my ear to the ground.'

'Thanks,' Richard said. 'I'd like to let Julia know if we can confirm the gossip. She needs to have something she can hold over him.'

Richard could feel his horse getting restless, so he dug his heels into its flanks and the horse responded immediately.

Beside him, Charles followed his lead, but he restrained his horse to a slightly slower pace. He would turn seventy very soon and for the first time, he was beginning to feel his age.

A week later, the entire family was once again gathered around William and Alice's dining table only this time it was to mark a milestone for Richard which he had hoped had been forgotten.

It was left to Marianne to present the family's special gift to mark his fortieth birthday. He carefully opened the gift she and Pippa had spent practically all afternoon wrapping and rewrapping.

He opened the box carefully to reveal a pair of gold cufflinks embossed with the Belleville family crest and his initials. He realised they matched the signet ring he had inherited from his father.

'Just don't lose them,' William said, in his usual practical way. 'Or worse, lose one. They should be passed on to Paul eventually.'

'I promise I won't, William,' he said, laughing.

There was something about William, he thought. He always manages to reduce everything to the most practical, mundane level. There are times I feel sorry for Alice, he thought. He can't be the most romantic of husbands. But she looks happy so maybe that suits her.

Just as he had done on Christmas Day, William once again took the business of sharpening his carving knife very seriously.

It's almost a repeat of the Christmas Day lunch, Richard thought, except Pippa is with us. Once again, Anthony is missing. He was sorry he would grow up with no memory of these events. Shared history is so important, he thought. Richard noticed Julia hand Pippa a package. It was clearly something she'd been expecting.

'Uncle Richard,' she said, as she undid the package of photographs. 'Remember I took some photos at Berrima Park with the camera Daddy gave me for Christmas.'

He'd forgotten completely. He noticed with interest William set aside his carving knife to inspect one particular photo.

'Who's this Pippa,' he asked, as he prepared to pass it along.

'That's Mrs Lester with her daughter Nancy, Anita Clarke, Tim Lester and Paul. Anita Clarke is Dr Clarke's daughter,' she explained. 'He works with Daddy at the hospital.'

William took particular notice of Kate Lester. But he noticed his brother was absent from it.

'Uncle Richard isn't in the photo?'

'No,' she said, shaking her head. 'He was off somewhere with the men.'

'You're very clever to be able to load the film all by yourself,' Julia said.

She assumed Philippe had given her some instructions.

'I didn't load it,' she replied. 'Daddy did and he said he took a photo just to be sure it was working properly before he gave it to me.'

She rummaged through the photos and held up the one he had taken. Richard had joined Alice to look at the photographs over William's shoulder. He immediately recognised the subject of the photograph.

Why didn't he take a flower or a tree or a shot of the harbour bridge, he thought? Why did he have to take a photo of Karen, who smiled happily back at the camera. But, of course, she wasn't smiling at the camera, Richard thought, she was smiling at the photographer.

'Who's that?' William asked, innocently.

'That's Karen Clarke,' Pippa answered, without any hesitation. 'She's Dr Clarke's niece. Uncle Richard will remember her. She came into the hotel on Sunday while we were all having lunch together to get her car keys ….'

It was at that point Richard pretended to overbalance, knocking William's glass of beer across the table. In the general pandemonium that followed, Charles Brockman looked at him and mouthed the words, 'Well done, mate.'

Pippa had quickly gathered up the photographs William had discarded on the table so they wouldn't be spoiled by the beer that was beginning to spread in all directions.

Alice, Julia and Mrs Duffy began to mop up the mess and remove everything from the table so it could be reset.

'I'm sorry, Alice,' he said. 'I made a terrible mess of your nice table.' But she waved away his apologies.

'These things happen, Richard,' she said. 'Don't worry about it. We'll have it cleaned up in a jiffy and a new tablecloth put on.'

While he had been speaking, he had edged around to where Pippa was standing.

'Bring the photos over here where there is better light,' he said quietly to her, 'I didn't see them properly.'

As he flipped through them, he asked if he might keep one.

She nodded, happy to oblige him. She did not notice him slip two photos into his pocket. If Julia remembered to look for the photo of Karen, she must not find it, he had decided on the spur of the moment.

'A word of warning,' he said to Pippa. 'Your mother might get the wrong idea if she thinks your father is driving another young woman home. He only did it because he thought she had drunk too much. But it would be better not to mention it.'

She nodded.

'Promise me?' he said, wanting to be sure she understood.

'I promise,' she said. 'I think Daddy really likes Karen.'

'I think he does too,' Richard said, 'but just as a friend. Your mother might get the wrong idea if you told that story and you don't want to make her unhappy, do you?'

She shook her head. Of all the things she wanted in the world it was for her mother and father to marry. To be happy together. To be a family. The family they should have been from the moment she was born. If Uncle Richard thought she shouldn't mention Karen Clarke, then she wouldn't. She went back to the table to sit alongside Marianne.

Richard wandered out to the verandah and Charles followed him. They knew it would be a few minutes before order was restored at the dinner table.

'I take it you've removed the incriminating photograph,' Charles said.

Richard pulled it from his pocket, careful to show him only the photo of Karen Clarke. Charles studied it thoughtfully for a few moments before pronouncing his verdict.

'That lady is trouble with a capital 'T',' he said finally. 'How did he leave that evidence around so casually?'

'He probably forgot and, in any case, he wouldn't have considered the possibility of Pippa showing the photos to us here,' he said.

'He probably thought she would give him the film to arrange for processing but I bet she took it to the local Kodak agent near where she lives,' Richard added. 'I imagine Mrs Henderson picked them up and sent them on to her without looking at them.'

Both men were leaning on the verandah rail, contemplating the problem. They did not hear William come up behind them.

'What's so interesting about that photo you're holding?' he asked.

Before Richard could react, William took the photo from his hand and surveyed it critically.

'Karen Clarke isn't it? Isn't that what Pippa said?'

And then they could see the realisation dawn on him.

'What's Duval doing taking a photograph like this of a pretty young woman?' he demanded.

He had hardly glanced at the photograph when Pippa had first shown him. Now he was inspecting it closely.

Richard was silent. How could he answer William without telling him of his suspicions?

'That was no accident back there, was it, Richard?'

Richard shook his head.

'I couldn't let Pippa finish what she was going to say about Karen Clarke,' he said. 'And I've had a word to her just now to make sure she doesn't repeat the story to Julia.'

'Which was?' William asked.

'Philippe drove Karen Clarke home from a dinner John Bertram and I attended at her uncle's place,' he began. 'I met her uncle when I brought the children back from Bowral, one of whom was his daughter Anita. He invited John and I to a dinner the following evening. Robert Clarke is mad keen on war history so he wanted me to tell him about my experiences. I let John do most of the talking.'

Neither man interrupted.

'After the dinner, John dropped me back to my hotel. He didn't tell me but I know he spotted Philippe helping Karen into her car, but into the passenger side, as we were leaving. When Edith Henderson called me to tell me about Paul's accident, around two o'clock the following morning, my first thought was to call Philippe. I'll leave you to draw your own conclusions when I couldn't raise him at home. I called Dr Clarke instead and that's how Paul got to be operated on so quickly.'

He had hoped to avoid telling William but he had been put on the spot.

'So, you've met this girl?' William asked.

'Several times,' Richard said. 'I didn't want to mention her name in front of Julia because she has met her. Some time ago I understand. That's why I've deliberately said nothing about her.'

'Do you think Duval's serious about her?' William asked.

'I don't honestly know,' Richard said, 'but he has given me his word he will marry Julia.'

'What good is that if he starts two-timing her as soon as they get back from the honeymoon,' William said. 'Let's not forget he seduced our sister. He has form.'

Richard laughed. Visions of Karen came to his mind.

'In this case, I couldn't vouch for who would be doing the seducing,' he said, which shocked William and caused Charles to have a quiet chuckle to himself.

'So, let me get this straight,' William said. 'She came to the hotel on the Sunday after the dinner. You were having lunch with Philippe and Pippa and she walked right up to Philippe and asked for her car keys. Am I right? In full public view? With everything that request implied?'

'That's pretty much the way it was,' Richard said, remembering the incident. 'Mrs Henderson was there too, of course, and John Bertram.'

He had thought at the time it was curious how Philippe had reacted. If he was annoyed or angry with her, he had hidden it well.

'And afterwards?' William asked, curious as to how the lunch proceeded after the interruption.

'You could have cut the atmosphere with a knife,' Richard conceded.

Richard quickly put the photograph back in his pocket as he spotted Julia emerging from the French doors onto the verandah.

'Well, after that fine exhibition of clumsiness from my brother,' Julia said, 'we can now get back to enjoying our dinner.'

The three men followed her back to the dining room without another word.

CHAPTER 28

Late January 1960

Ian Dixon hardly noticed the distant hum of traffic or the far-off rattle of trains on the bridge of which he had an excellent view from the rear terrace of his home on the north side of the famous harbour. He was instead concentrating hard on reading the divorce papers sent from England at his request.

He made a note in his careful spidery handwriting of key dates. He did not miss the fact that Richard and Catherine had married in England in October 1945 with their first son being born in February the next year in Australia, a mere four months later. That one fact told the whole story of the marriage, he thought. It was probably always doomed to failure.

He assumed Richard had insisted his wife accompany him back home to Australia. She, a blue blood, distantly related to the Duke of Devonshire, left behind the comfort and privilege of the country estate she has now inherited. What sort of a life could she possibly have built in an unsophisticated country backwater half a world away, he wondered?

He wondered idly how much time she had spent on a ship going backwards and forwards to England. Too much time by the look of it.

He turned over the pages and read through Richard's statement, admitting adultery, which had been the reason the divorce had proceeded to its final decree in time for Catherine to marry again before the birth of her third child.

Out of curiosity, he checked the dates. Was it something he had done just to give his former wife the evidence she needed? But the dates did not correspond.

He noted she had returned to England in August 1957 when her father became ill and then subsequently died. She had never returned to Australia.

His admission of adultery occurring in June of that year confirmed what Ian Dixon had already suspected. Richard had sought solace in the arms of another woman, a married woman it appeared, as his wife's dissatisfaction with her life in Australia increased. Was that his excuse? He had felt abandoned and ignored?

Ian Dixon set the file of papers down on the small table beside him. Richard had been right. There was nothing in the divorce papers except the salacious details that had formed the basis for the divorce action to succeed. Their children's future arrangements had been dealt with in one line. 'Private agreement between the parties.'

How receptive was a young mother going to be to allowing the younger boy to return to Australia to the father's care, he wondered? Yet he knew Richard was determined it would happen.

If he goes into the discussions with his former wife with a legal team, that might backfire but on the other hand he needs to be ready with a legal team to press his claim for custody, Ian pondered, debated the case for and against in his mind.

He sat back thinking through the likely legal scenarios. These matters are never amicable, he thought, no matter what goodwill exists. He closed his eyes briefly to consider the best strategy. Was there another way to approach it all, he wondered?

A sudden gust of wind began to scatter the papers everywhere. He jumped up and scrambled to stop the remaining pages from joining those already scattered across the small back garden.

'Let me help,' Kate Lester said, as she walked onto the back terrace. 'You'll never get all these papers back together in the right order without some help.'

Kate had arrived the previous evening with her son and daughter to stay for a few days while she settled her children into school for the new year.

'Thank you, Kate,' he said. 'I should have been more careful with them.'

He began to gather the ones closest to him while she knelt down to pick up the pages lying flattened against the back fence. But she stopped suddenly. She was holding the statement Richard had made admitting adultery.

'Please don't read that, Kate,' he said, suddenly alarmed at the breach of trust it represented. 'It's confidential. It's a private matter.'

He walked over to her and prised the statement from her grasp.

'It's about Richard Belleville's divorce, isn't it, all this,' she said, pointing to all the pages still to be collected.

He nodded. He wondered how much of the statement of Richard's confessed adultery she had read.

'It is,' he said. 'I had the papers sent out from England. I needed to see them.'

'Why?' she asked, perplexed.

Should he break a client's confidence by telling her? Then he remembered the attention Richard had paid her at the Clarke's dinner earlier in the month. Would that explain her interest? Surely not, he thought? Kate is a sensible woman, married, with two nice children. Admittedly her husband is an overbearing charmless man but surely she wouldn't look seriously outside her marriage, would she?

And then he looked at her carefully and for the first time saw a quite different woman. A woman on edge. Nervous even. Taking slightly more care with her appearance. Her dress emphasising her womanly appeal in a way he hadn't noticed before. Lucky Richard Belleville, he thought, if it's all for his benefit.

'If you must know,' he replied cautiously, 'he came to me for legal advice about custody of his children. That's all.'

She nodded. She had guessed he would not leave his younger son to be brought up in England indefinitely. But the adultery? She had not read all of it before Ian had snatched it from her but what she had read disturbed her. Was she just one of a long line of his conquests? She had accused him of that in a teasing way but he had denied it. Yet here he was, in black and white, admitting adultery.

Ian struggled for something to say, something that would lessen the impact of the salacious detail in Richard's statement.

'He made that statement to help his former wife,' he said finally. 'She was pregnant and desperate to marry again before the baby arrived. It must have felt like history repeating itself for her.'

'What do you mean, history repeating itself?' she asked.

'Catherine Cavendish was already pregnant when Richard married her after the war,' Ian admitted.

What harm could there be in her knowing?

'He did the right thing,' he said. 'Their son Paul was born four months after they married. After they had arrived back to Australia.'

'And the marriage lasted how long?'

He calculated quickly.

'A little under twelve years,' he said. 'She went back to England when her father got sick. He subsequently died and she inherited the estate, which gave her the perfect excuse not to return.'

She nodded her head slowly. Richard had already told her that much.

'I shouldn't be discussing this,' he said, 'although most of the facts would be generally known in his circle.'

'So, he admitted adultery to save her the embarrassment of having a baby out of wedlock?' she asked.

Ian answered carefully. If she assumed he admitted adultery to assist his ex-wife, it would not look quite so bad, he reasoned. It would seem as if he had concocted the story for that purpose.

'Yes,' he said. 'Because of his admission, the divorce happened more quickly than it might otherwise have done but technically, the child would not have been born out of wedlock in any case. She would still have been married to Richard if they had not divorced, so the baby, as far as the law is concerned, would have been his.'

'Even though she had conceived it with another man?'

'Even though she had conceived it with another man,' he said. 'The husband would always be regarded, in law, as the father. So technically it would not be out of wedlock.'

'But the baby wouldn't have been able to inherit the father's title, I assume, if they had not been married before he was born?'

'That's correct,' Ian said, as he attempted to gather the remainder of the loose pages.

As Kate was considering what Ian had said, Angela Dixon appeared at the door leading to the terrace. She was surprised to see her friend and her husband in earnest conversation.

'You sound as if you're getting legal advice, Kate?' she said laughingly.

She shook her head but did not reply.

Should I tell Angela what we've been discussing, Ian wondered? In the end he decided against it. He had already broken client confidentiality. He did not want Richard's affairs to be the subject of discussion among the three of them.

'Ian,' Angela said loudly, to make sure he was paying attention. 'Don't forget you are looking after the children tonight. The dinner is ready to be heated up in the oven. Kate and I are going out for a girls' night out.'

He smiled and nodded. He had not forgotten the arrangements. Earlier, he might have taken the arrangements at face value, but not now.

He couldn't help but notice the slight colouring of Kate's cheeks and the careful emphasis his wife had placed on it being a girls' night out.

He had no doubt Kate would be meeting Richard Belleville. He already knew Richard was in Sydney because the solicitor from Allens had contacted him for a further meeting. But he said nothing. He would go along with the charade.

But what would his wife be doing, he wondered? Going off somewhere with some of her theatre friends perhaps? Was she casting an eye elsewhere, he wondered? There were times he suspected it but he chose to ignore the small signs. Better not to know, he thought.

And Kate Lester? He wouldn't fancy being in her shoes if her husband ever found out. He's the type of man who would leave her penniless, he thought. And deny her access to her children.

He was about to reply but Kate and Angela had already disappeared back into the house together.

He tied the legal file securely with tape and went inside. He dumped the file in his study and headed straight for the cocktail bar. He poured a generous measure of his favourite single malt whisky and sank thankfully into his favourite armchair.

Kate reached across to the bedside table to check the time by Richard's watch in the dim light cast by the outside street lights.

'I must go,' she said, as his arms closed around her to pull her back towards him.

He began to kiss her passionately and caress her with an intimacy she had never before experienced. He's so good at this, she thought, as she succumbed once more to his lovemaking.

'So you still want to leave?' he asked as he stroked her body.

This time, though, she was determined.

'I have to go,' she said. 'You know that. I have to get back to Angela's place at a reasonable hour.'

She kissed him for a final time and swung her legs out of the bed. She began to dress.

'Will I see you again?' he asked, as he watched her dress.

'Do you want to see me again?' she asked, with just a hint of uncertainty in her voice. She couldn't quell the niggling doubt that he was a man who had made a habit of illicit meetings like this.

'I think you know the answer to that, my darling,' he said.

For the first time since Catherine had left him, he began to imagine a new life for himself. With a new wife. What would it take, he wondered, for Kate Lester to divorce her husband and become his wife? She was everything he admired in a woman. But it was too soon to make such an offer.

Now fully clothed, she reached across the bed to risk another kiss.

'It will be difficult to see you again this trip,' she said. 'I'm taking the children to their respective schools tomorrow and then Gerald expects me back home.'

He wanted to ask if her husband had been treating her kindly but she had forbidden him from asking such questions. He did not enjoy the fact he shared her with another man.

'Then next time will be when?' he said, hopefully.

'I will be in Sydney just before Easter,' she said, 'to bring the children back home.'

'That's not until April,' he protested. 'I can't wait that long to see you again.'

But she shook her head. As much as she wanted to see him, unusually frequent trips to Sydney might alert Gerald.

'I would suggest you bring Paul and come and stay with us at Berrima Park for Easter,' she added, 'but that might be just a little too risky.'

He nodded. It was far too risky, for her in particular. It would only take a word out of place, a gesture, a hint of familiarity and the fact they were lovers would be exposed. And she would be the one to suffer. Not him.

He lay back in bed as he heard the door of his hotel suite close softly. If only she wasn't married, he thought, life would be so much less complicated.

At forty, he had expected his life to be settled. As it had turned out, it was anything but settled, he thought. And now the one woman he really wanted was unattainable, except for the occasional illicit encounter.

He sighed and fell into a fitful sleep.

John Bertram looked out to the west where ominous dark clouds were building on the far horizon. It had been a very warm humid day, the type of day that was always a precursor to thunderstorms in Sydney.

'I hope these storms don't come up tomorrow,' he said to Richard. 'It makes for a rocky ascent out of Sydney for the passengers. Not good for nervous flyers.'

Richard sipped his beer and followed his friend's gaze to the far horizon.

'It looks like it's going to be a serious storm,' he said.

His immediate thought was for Kate driving home in such weather. Looking at the direction, she would be driving right into it.

'You look a bit wrung out today, if I may say so,' John said, with just a hint of concern in his voice.

Richard smiled, remembering the reason for it.

'It's nothing serious,' he said. 'Just a bit tired.'

John nodded his head. He'd seen that look before.

'Your friend from Bowral, I assume?' he said, enigmatically.

Richard laughed and nodded. Am I really so transparent, he thought?

'I really like her, John,' he said finally.

'But she's married, mate,' he said, as if he needed reminding.

'I know,' he said, 'and her husband would make life extremely difficult for her if she asked for a divorce. He has the money and the power. He'd probably attempt to cut her off from her kids and she wouldn't want that.'

John considered this for a few moments.

'So she's locked into a marriage she doesn't want,' John said. 'Am I right?'

'Pretty much,' Richard said.

'But you'll go on seeing her when you can?'

Richard nodded.

'Yes, I will,' he said. 'She's not someone I can walk away from and never see again.'

'You don't believe in any easy life, do you, mate?' his friend said with a deep throated chuckle as he drained his glass and called for another beer.

The following morning, Richard walked the short distance to Phillip Street for his meeting with Ian Dixon who greeted him with a smile and a firm handshake.

Should I tell him about the incident with his divorce papers? He thought about it for a few moments and then decided against it. Mentioning it would, in a roundabout way, be an acknowledgement of Richard's interest in Kate. It's better if that goes unacknowledged, he thought. Far better.

'Did you look through the papers?' Richard asked.

Ian Dixon reached for his glasses as if he was about to read something and then changed his mind and put them on the desk.

'You were right,' he said. 'There is no formal agreement on custody arrangements.'

'That's exactly as I remember the arrangements,' Richard said. 'So what do you advise?'

Ian Dixon considered his response carefully.

'The easiest way is to approach your ex-wife with a sound argument for returning the boy to your care in Australia,' he said. 'Failing that, you can take it to court but probably in England, given that the marriage was in England and the subsequent divorce was granted by an English court. And the boy is in England.'

Richard heard all this in silence.

'You'll know that courts favour mothers getting custody, but there are always exceptions, of course.'

He paused and then went on.

'The fact too that you haven't married again and established a new household might go against you,' he said. 'A court might think a young lad needs at least a step-mother to look after him.'

Richard smiled at this.

'I can't just whistle up a new wife like that,' he said. 'My brother's wife Alice was very close to Anthony. I'm sure she would be happy to help.'

'That might count in your favour,' Ian Dixon said. 'The other thing to propose might be a temporary arrangement. For a year, for example. Far be it from me to suggest it, but once the boy is here and he is settled, it would be much easier for you to resist his return.'

Richard considered this for a few moments.

'Is that legal advice?' Richard asked. 'Or is that practical advice?'

'Well, let me put it this way,' he said. 'You won't ever find that advice in any written opinion I would give you on how to go about securing custody of your son. But you might want to consider it. You might want to try it and if it fails, then take the matter to court.'

Richard nodded and got up to leave.

'Thank you, Ian,' he said. 'You have given me an idea that might just work.'

'Good luck with it,' he replied.

What a shame, he thought. A woman like Kate Lester would have made him an excellent wife. She would have been a good step-mother to his children too. I can see now why Angela says she's wasted on that blustering fool of a husband. One day, he thought, it will be easier for women like her to leave an unhappy marriage but right now, the cards are all stacked in the husband's favour. And that is wrong. So wrong.

He set aside the now tidy file containing Richard's divorce papers and picked up his next matter, a straightforward case of insurance fraud.

Chapter 29

Late January 1960

It was nearing lunchtime as Richard stepped out onto the street following his meeting with Ian Dixon. He looked up to check the weather, although he could see little of the sky between the tall buildings surrounding him.

For no particular reason, he began to walk in the direction of Circular Quay, an easy walk of just a few blocks.

As he walked under a new elevated roadway taking city traffic to the harbour bridge, he wondered how someone could conceive of such an ugly blight on the harbourside streetscape. This will be complained about for decades, he thought, if someone doesn't tear it down.

Far to his right, he could just make out the beginnings of the construction work for the new opera house on Bennelong Point. There'll be a scramble for invitations to that official opening, he thought.

Again, for no particular reason, he wandered into the small café where he had lunched with Karen Clarke on his previous visit. The restauranteur recognised him immediately.

'Miss Clarke is not with you?' he asked, as he showed Richard to a table. 'You make a fine couple.'

Richard laughed. What a matchmaker, he thought. Karen at least had the advantage of being single. He could imagine bedding her, but not marrying her.

'I haven't seen Miss Clarke for a few weeks,' Richard said, hoping to deflate Mario's enthusiasm.

'Neither have I,' Mario said, a little forlornly. 'She must be busy or lunching elsewhere.'

She's clearly a favourite customer, Richard thought.

He began to study the menu. He had been guided by Karen in his choice previously so, after a few minutes, he gave up and was about to suggest Mario surprise him. As he looked up, he saw a familiar face smiling broadly. He stood up and she came forward to kiss him on the cheek.

'You naughty boy,' she said, with an impish smile. 'You didn't tell me you were in town.'

Behind her, her friend Bianca smiled and extended hand.

'It's lovely to see you again,' she said.

A beaming Mario was quickly behind them, pulling out chairs for the ladies and generally making a great fuss of them. Glasses of wine appeared as if from nowhere.

'And what brings you back to Sydney so soon?' Karen asked. 'But, of course, you had to bring Pippa back for school, how silly of me.'

She refrained from saying, 'and so did Kate Lester.'

She glanced at the menu before reassuring Mario they would have whatever he suggested. He bustled away, smiling broadly.

'And other business,' he said. 'Other boring business.'

'Not Curtis Transport,' she said. 'There's no meeting scheduled until next month.'

'No, something personal in fact,' he said. 'I was getting legal advice from Ian Dixon.'

She wanted to ask about what but she did not. There might be many reasons why he would want legal advice.

'Have you seen Philippe?' she asked, offhandedly.

Richard smiled to himself. I bet she knows very well I haven't seen him yet.

'No,' he said, shaking his head. 'There hasn't been an opportunity. I caught up with John Bertram yesterday. You'll remember John, I'm sure. I think Philippe was busy seeing Pippa.'

But she would know that too, Richard thought.

'I may try and catch him for a drink when he's finished work,' Richard said. 'Have you seen much of him lately?'

He couldn't resist the question. She looked directly at him and lied unconvincingly.

'Once or twice,' she said as she fidgeted with her wine glass.

He was surprised to see Bianca. Why isn't she at work, he wondered? It was Karen who volunteered the answer.

'Bianca and I have been reviewing some designs for next season,' she explained.

Richard guessed it must be something she regularly did with Bianca.

'Fashion is something I know absolutely nothing about,' Richard said, holding his hands up in mock surrender to avoid a more detailed discussion.

'And why would you?' Bianca said. 'Most men are perplexed by it or simply grumble at the cost of their wife's wardrobe.'

At least I can never be accused of that, he thought.

'My ex-wife Catherine was very fashion conscious,' he said. 'Now she's back in England, no doubt her wardrobe has doubled in size.'

Bianca smiled at the prospect of shopping in London and Paris. Milan perhaps. And having the money to do it. She sighed.

'How lucky she is to have the major European fashion houses close by,' she said, wistfully.

'But you will soon have your own fashion house here, Bianca,' Karen said.

She understood there were times Bianca pined for a life in Europe.

'Are you planning on it? Your own fashion house?' Richard asked.

Bianca shrugged her elegant shoulders but Karen nodded, smiling broadly.

'My father set up a trust fund for me which I will control either when I marry or when I turn thirty,' she said. 'Which means by September this year, I will be able to provide the financial backing for Bianca's fashion house.'

Richard smiled at Karen's absolute confidence in her friend. He couldn't help wondering, though, what David Clarke would make of it. And clearly, she didn't plan on marrying in advance of her thirtieth birthday.

'We shall see,' she said to her friend. 'It is a big step for you to put your money up for my dream.'

But Karen was insistent.

'We will be partners,' she said. 'I cannot abide the businesses my father runs. When I inherit it all, I plan to sell his dealerships and dismantle his car racing team. All those horrible men.'

Richard sympathised with her plans. He had seen just how badly the businessmen had treated her. Despite her initial reluctance, Bianca began to enter enthusiastically into Karen's dream.

'We could set up a bridal boutique too,' she said. 'And shoes. We can import Italian shoes. They are the best.'

Richard laughed.

'Good luck with all that,' he said, as the two women chatted happily about the future.

Women's fashion was not necessarily his idea of a good investment but who could know, he thought. It may all turn out very well.

Large bowls of spaghetti had been placed in front of them and they were all quiet for a few minutes while they tackled the difficult task of eating the long slippery tendrils.

He sensed a new maturity in Karen that had previously been missing. Was that a good sign, he wondered? Or was it a bad sign? Could it be there are new things in her life to engage her interest apart from Philippe?

There's something about her, he thought. A sense of quiet triumph perhaps? A new-found confidence in herself? He noticed a slight smile. She has a secret, he thought. Something she won't share, even with Bianca.

Karen could feel his eyes on her, as if he was trying to read her thoughts. Shall I shock him by telling him Philippe left my bed at midnight last night? But she knew Philippe would be angry with her if she did.

She wanted to say, 'don't worry, he will marry Julia as he promised. I won't stop him doing that but until he does, he's mine. And there's a part of him that will always be mine. I'm the guilty secret he will carry with him for a lifetime.'

But she did not say any of it.

Being with Philippe had forced her to rethink her life. Her girlish dreams of a fairy tale wedding had faded. With the tantalising prospect of financial independence within her grasp, her world had suddenly opened up.

And as that world opened up before her, she began to question whether she would want to swap her newfound sense of freedom for marriage. She had seen any number of husbands at close quarters and how the wives were forced to mould their own lives and their own ambitions to suit the men they married.

With Philippe, it might have been possible, she thought. But there would be no one else. This would be her golden summer with him. When it was over, she would have to move on. To a new lover, perhaps. To a new life.

As they left the restaurant, Richard put his arm around her.

'I look forward to seeing you next time,' he said, and he meant it.

She had lifted his spirits. He did not blame her for Philippe's misbehaviour. He could have walked away, he thought. He should have walked away. He was the one who had made the commitment to marry someone else. Not her. He should have resisted the temptation. But it was clear, very clear, he had not.

'Make sure you do let me know,' she said, with an engaging smile, as they parted.

He watched as she and Bianca walked off in the opposite direction.

It was late afternoon and the bar at the Australia Hotel was unexpectedly crowded. Richard pushed his way through the throng and signalled to the barman who recognised him and handed him a glass of his favourite beer. He turned and retreated to a vacant table in the far corner of the lounge.

A few minutes later he spotted Philippe who negotiated the crowd to sit down opposite him. He was holding a glass that looked to be mostly ice.

'Not a beer drinker, are you?' Richard remarked.

Philippe shook his head.

'I never acquired the taste for it,' he replied. 'Bourbon is my drink of choice. Or wine.'

Richard had tried bourbon once but he found it too sweet and less refined in taste than the single malt whiskies he favoured. But beer was always his preferred thirst quencher.

'How is Paul getting on?' Philippe asked, his professional concern showing.

'Everything is as it should be with his recovery, I believe,' Richard said. 'He finds the plaster cast very hot and annoying but I remind him that complaining about it won't help.'

Philippe smiled.

'I did say boys were the most difficult patients to keep amused when their movement is restricted.'

'How true,' he said. 'My sister-in-law Alice is keeping a strict eye on him which is good.'

Richard had already downed his first glass of beer and caught the barman's eye to bring him another.

'Thanks for bringing Pippa back,' Philippe said. 'She was full of stories of what she got up to with her mother and with Marianne. It was very good for her to see everyone.'

'I know she enjoyed it,' Richard said. 'It's good to have her as part of the family. By the way I saw Karen today, quite by chance, which reminds me to suggest that you don't leave photos of your girlfriend on your daughter's camera.'

Richard sat back watching his reaction carefully. Philippe took a sip of his drink and grimaced.

'I forgot about taking that photo, to be honest,' he admitted. 'And I thought in any case Pippa would give me the roll of film to have processed when it was finished.'

'But she didn't, did she? Instead she had the photos processed and sent to her at her mother's place.'

'And don't tell me,' he said, 'she passed them around for everyone to see?'

'She did,' Richard replied, 'at my birthday dinner at Prior Park.'

Philippe thought for a moment, trying to remember when he had taken it. He had ignored the jibe about 'girlfriend'.

'Was the photo so suggestive as to raise comment?' Philippe asked. 'Surely not.'

He hadn't thought so but you never quite know how a photograph is going to turn out. Richard frowned, remembering the incident.

'It wasn't the photo so much,' he said finally, 'it was the story that went with it.'

Philippe was still bemused. What story, he wondered?

'Your daughter started recounting the day Karen walked into the dining room here and came right up to you at lunch and demanded her car keys,' Richard said. 'Pippa started to say how you had driven Karen home the night before from a dinner and ......'

For the first time, Philippe's face betrayed him. He interrupted Richard.

'And you let her go on telling this story in front of Julia?' he demanded.

'As it happens, I didn't,' Richard said, noticing the immediate look of relief on Philippe's face. 'I knocked over my brother's glass of beer as a diversion. Then I got Pippa to show me the photos away from the table and I pocketed the one of Karen, so if Julia remembered what Pippa said and looked for it later, it wouldn't be there.'

Richard pulled out his wallet and handed the photo to Philippe, who looked at it with a mixture of relief and guilt.

'May I suggest you don't keep that photo anywhere where it will be found again,' he said. 'The camera loves that woman. Or was it the photographer she was smiling for?'

Philippe ignored the question. He refused to be drawn into a discussion about Karen. He continued to look at the photo. In it, she was smiling suggestively at him.

'She's got you wrapped around her little finger, hasn't she?' Richard said, as he continued to observe Philippe's reaction.

'I'd really rather not talk about it if you don't mind,' Philippe said, his tone of voice challenging Richard to drop the subject.

'Very well,' he said. 'I'll say nothing further. I'm protecting my sister for her sake, not for yours, though. You should be clear on that point.'

Philippe nodded. Richard has every right to be angry, he thought.

If he was asked to explain how he felt about Karen, he would struggle for the right words, he thought. Less than two months ago he had told her he was going to marry Julia. Until that moment, he had been able to keep her at arm's length. But something had fundamentally changed. He didn't quite know what. Or how. Or why.

'Everything will turn out fine,' Philippe said finally, more to convince himself than Richard.

'I hope so,' Richard said, as he drained his second glass of beer. 'I certainly hope so.'

'A final word of advice,' he said. 'I know you're sleeping with her so don't treat me like a fool and deny it. If I were you, I'd get her out of your system now, before you marry Julia. I can turn a blind eye to it because Julia's not here, but I'll be very angry if my sister finds you're cheating on her after you get married.'

Philippe was shocked but not surprised by Richard's stark warning. 'I hear you,' he said.

He finished his drink and extended his hand to Richard, who stood up and shook hands with him, as if a deal had been struck between them.

I hope he takes my advice. I sympathise with him in a way, he thought. Karen would be a delightful armful in any man's bed. He understood only too well how hard it would be to reject her advances. Would I say 'no' to her, he wondered. Probably not. But Philippe should, he thought.

'I hope to hear good news when I get home of the date Julia's divorce will become final,' Richard said. 'Perhaps next time we meet you'll be standing at the altar.'

'I hope so,' Philippe said. 'I sincerely hope so.'

He walked away quickly, anxious to avoid any further interrogation from his future brother-in-law. He sat in his car for some time, making no move to start the engine, as he thought over what Richard had said.

'Get her out of my system,' he had said.

He remembered the first time he had made love to her. He had promised himself it would be the only time. It would never happen again.

Yet each time he had seen her his resolve had weakened. He had been unable to deny himself the pleasure of being with her, of making love to her. And she had given herself willingly and completely to him. Yet in doing so she had eroded his belief in himself as a decent man, incapable of deceit.

But he was caught now. Caught between his desire for her and his desire to fulfil his promise to Julia. He finally understood how Karen had completely disarmed him with her light-hearted, flirtatious nature.

At first, he had been indifferent to it. And then, bit by bit, he had begun to enjoy the attention she lavished on him. And then she had pushed him to jealousy which had been his undoing. He could no longer pretend he was indifferent and she had known that. In that moment, he had capitulated and she had triumphed.

There is going to be nothing easy about saying 'no' to Karen, he thought. Nothing easy at all.

CHAPTER 30

February 1960

Hardly anything stirred in the countryside beyond William and Alice's house. In the heat of the early afternoon, everything had fallen eerily silent, except for the tireless insects.

It was Sunday and for William it was the perfect time to sink into his new squatter's chair, a present from his wife and daughter, which now took pride of place on the verandah.

He was more than two years off his fortieth birthday but there were times he looked older than Richard. His daughter teased him often saying he had adopted old man habits. Perhaps she's right, he thought, as he opened the latest edition of *Queensland Country Life*. It had become a regular Sunday habit.

There was, after all, always something for William to worry about. He fretted that the price of cattle was never good enough when it was time to sell and too high when he wanted to buy. The season had been good but he worried it would mean a drought was imminent. And the run of hot days? Well, that would sap the remaining moisture from the ground.

And he worried about his sister Julia. He set down his newspaper and twisted around in his chair to look at his brother. It was his first chance to have a quiet word with Richard since his return from Sydney.

'It's good that Julia's divorce is set to be finalised by the end of March,' he said.

It was news they had already discussed over lunch.

'She must have got notification while I was away,' Richard said. William nodded.

'I think James pushed it along in the end,' he said.

'Is he planning on marrying again?'

Richard assumed Alice would know even though he and William now had very little contact with him. He was civil towards them but their friendship had not survived the revelations about their sister.

'Alice says not,' William said. 'There had been rumours about a girl but they were just that. Rumours.'

'Probably the same gossip I heard from Charles,' Richard said. 'I assume John is going to live with his father?'

'He is,' William said. 'I think that's very fair of Julia. It wouldn't suit the lad to be taken to live in the city. But I expect we will see her often.'

'I expect we will,' Richard said, wondering just how his sister was going to adapt to life in Sydney.

No doubt she'll be caught up in the social whirl through Philippe's circle, he thought. Which means there'll be times when she comes face to face with Karen. At least I won't be there to see it, Richard thought.

There was no way to avoid the next question William asked.

'I take it you saw Philippe in Sydney?'

He knew Alice and Marianne were helping Mrs Duffy clear the table after lunch, but he was concerned they might appear at any moment. He had lowered his voice for fear of being overheard.

'Yes, I had a drink with Philippe at my hotel one afternoon,' Richard replied.

He did not volunteer any other information forcing William to ask the question.

'Is he behaving himself?'

William makes it sound as if he's a schoolboy who has earned the wrath of a headmaster rather than a man cheating on his fiancée, Richard thought. For his part, he wanted to say 'yes, everything's fine' but he couldn't lie outright to his brother.

'Let me put it this way,' Richard said, diplomatically. 'He's promised to follow a straight and narrow path when he marries Julia.'

William looked puzzled. What did that mean?

'I take it he's not following a straight and narrow path at the present time,' he said. 'Am I right? He's still seeing that girl?'

Again, Richard did not quite spell it out for William. He did not want to completely ruin Philippe's reputation.

'I've told him to get her out of his system,' he said. 'He knows what I mean.'

'And will he take your advice?'

'I think so,' Richard said. 'At least I certainly hope so.'

He could see it was beyond William to imagine how a man might struggle to say 'no' to a woman like Karen, who broke all the rules of behaviour that William was familiar with.

'Well, the wedding date has been set,' William said. 'That should focus his attention on Julia and their future life together.'

At that point Alice interrupted. She and Marianne had just walked on to the verandah. Her preferred reading after Sunday lunch was the latest edition of *The Australian Women's Weekly*.

'You two don't sound very cheered by the prospect of your sister's wedding,' she said, as she sat down and opened the magazine.

She had been reading for only a few minutes when she folded back the magazine to point to a story about Princess Anne having a fitting for a bridesmaid dress.

'Look at the name of the designer,' she said to Marianne. 'Belinda Belleville, can you believe it?'

Mother and daughter, heads together, devoured the article with greater interest. Richard got up and went in search of his son. He did not want to be drawn into a discussion on women's fashion.

'I've heard enough about women's fashion from the mischievous Miss Clarke and her ambitious friend,' he wanted to say but he did not.

No one needs to know I met Karen Clarke again in Sydney, he thought. Or Kate Lester.

He would have protested had anyone suggested he was following the time-honoured tradition of the Belleville family by keeping things to himself.

'I'm not in love with her,' Philippe repeated to himself as he stood before his bathroom mirror and attempted for the third time to coax his black tie into an acceptable bow.

For the past couple of weeks, he had failed to return Karen's calls, refused to go to places where he knew she was bound to be and did his best to avoid her.

If he wasn't on call, his home telephone went unanswered. He explained it away to Julia whose calls had also gone unanswered by saying he was getting calls from patients and he did not want to encourage the practice of them calling his private number out of hours.

But he could not avoid Karen tonight. He had promised months ago to escort her to the first night of *Giselle* and he could hardly go back on his word. Besides he had convinced himself it was the ballet he wanted to see and not Karen.

He was finally satisfied with the bow and he shrugged on his jacket. He tugged at the sleeves of his white shirt and adjusted his cuff links. He smiled to himself at the memory of how she had brought back the missing cufflink. He had been very careful since then not to repeat that mistake.

How many times had he succumbed to her charms? He couldn't bring himself to make a tally but he was sure it had been the reason she had moved back to her own Rose Bay apartment. Away from her parents' watchful eyes.

Allowing her to cook dinner for him one night had been a huge mistake, he reflected. Had she been trying to demonstrate her domestic skills, he wondered? The excellence of the dinner had surprised him, as had the charm of her art deco apartment, which had been a legacy to her mother from an aunt who had never married.

He remembered it had been a Sunday evening because he had seen Pippa during the day. Wasn't it the next day she ran into Richard at that little Italian café she likes? He shook his head. She wouldn't have said anything, surely? Yet Richard's anger with me had grown to a new level after that, Philippe thought. Had he simply guessed the extent of my relationship with her? Whichever it was he had been angry.

He sighed. Since then, I've tried hard to stay away from her. He did a final check in the mirror. Tonight. I have to end it with Karen, finally, tonight, he told himself.

He switched off the lights in the living room and the hallway, leaving the porch light ablaze, and headed out to his car.

'Am I Giselle?' Karen asked, as she sipped champagne amidst the crush of opening night revellers.

Around them the hum of conversation was growing as waiters battled to refill empty champagne glasses.

'You are hardly a peasant girl.' he replied with a smile and a small shake of his head. 'Peasant girls do not wear real diamonds at their throat.'

She pretended to pout at his put down.

'But my lover is betrothed to another,' she countered, seeking parallels to her own story in the ultimately tragic story of the peasant girl.

'That's true,' Philippe conceded. 'But you've always known that. You've always known I would marry Julia.'

She shook her head, her glossy auburn hair threatening to escape the diamond clip in her hair. How much more beautiful can she look, Philippe wondered?

'That isn't true,' she said, defending herself. 'When I met you, you were unattached. I did not know about your past. No one knew about your past.'

He inclined his head slightly. She was right. He had deliberately hidden the details of his private life. Then bit by bit they had been exposed. He was very aware he owed her a great debt. Without her intervention, he believed he would have been forced to resign.

She held her glass up for the waiter to refill.

'You've been avoiding me lately,' she said, repeating what she had already said to him earlier in the evening.

'I've been busy,' he said.

'Preparing for your wedding?'

'Partly,' he said.

'Seventh of May, Uncle Robert says?'

He nodded. She's well informed, he thought. He had only told Robert Clarke two days ago.

'So now it's time to give me up,' she said with a resigned sigh, as if she was going to make it easy for him.

Again, he nodded, not quite trusting himself to speak. He was trying hard to keep a physical distance between them.

'Tell me,' she said, 'do you love her?'

It seemed a very intimate conversation to be having in the middle of a crowded reception. He looked around but no one was paying any attention to them, so he answered her.

'Yes,' he said simply. 'I do love her.'

Karen smiled, a sad wistful smile. How do I tell him he only thinks he's in love with Julia because he expects to be in love with her? Because it's the right thing to do. Because he wasn't there for her when Pippa was born. He feels guilty. Guilty that she had to give birth alone. Guilty that Pippa was given away.

But there was no way to tell him, she realised. No way he'll give up the dream of Julia. There's no way to tell him no man makes love to a woman the way he's made love to me without being in love with her. And there's no way a woman responds to that lovemaking without being in love.

She placed her empty glass on the nearest table and slipped her arm through his. He could hardly push her away.

'Shall we go?' she said. 'I've suddenly lost interest in ballet. The stories are too sad.'

They made their way to the front entrance of the theatre, carefully avoiding the people they both knew. It was a short walk along the street to his car. He held the door for her and then he walked around to the driver's side. But he did not start the engine immediately.

He reached across and put his arm around her. She was surprised and turned her head towards him.

'I never meant to hurt you,' he said softly. 'And I cannot say to you I love you. That would be wrong. You will always be special to me. Always.'

He started the engine and headed off in the direction of her apartment. She was silent until he brought his car to a halt outside her building.

'I promise I won't ruin your marriage, Philippe,' she said quietly. 'I plan to go away very soon so you won't see me again. Not for a very long time.'

This wasn't meant to be as difficult as this, he thought. He got out of the car and went around to open her door. He offered her his hand to help her out of the car.

'Must you go away?' he asked, concerned that he was forcing her to flee the city. Where would she go? Would she go by herself?

'It's for the best,' she said. 'I don't want to be here and see you with Julia as her husband. I don't want to be the other woman. And I don't want people to feel sorry for me.'

What could he say? He had nothing to offer her. To offer friendship sounded banal. Could they be just friends? He doubted it. Could he trust himself around her? There was too much at stake for him to take the risk.

He followed her up the stairs to her apartment. At the front door, she fumbled for her keys. After several attempts, she slotted the key into the lock and turned it. She turned to face him. He lent forward and took her face in his hands. He began to kiss her tenderly.

'You will always be special to me,' he said softly.

'But not special enough,' she sobbed, as tears cascaded down her cheeks.

There's nothing I can say, he thought, nothing I can do that will make this any easier. With supreme effort, he turned and walked away from her. As he headed down the stairs, he heard the door of her apartment close.

I should feel relieved, he thought, but I don't. I feel desolate. I feel absolutely bereft.

A week later, Julia sat with her older brother on the front verandah of his home in Springfield. There was only one possible topic of discussion between them. She sipped the tea he had made for her and began to run down the list of things she still had to do.

'Is the guest list finalised?' he asked.

He assumed it would be dominated by Philippe's friends in Sydney. She held it out for him to inspect and he ran his eye down the page. He recognised many of the names. Dr and Mrs Robert Clarke and Anita, Dr and Mrs Steve Hancock, Dr Mark McDermott, Dr Jules Hamilton, Barbara Thomas, Mr and Mrs Ian Dixon, Lucy Dixon, Mr and Mrs Gerald Lester, Nancy and Tim. He hadn't really expected their names to be on the list.

Julia couldn't help but notice his surprise.

'Pippa insisted her special friends be invited so that means inviting the parents too,' she said. 'But, of course, I forgot. You will know some of them, which is good.'

He nodded.

'I've met quite a few of them,' he said. 'Robert Clarke and some of the medical people I know. Mark McDermott operated on Paul. Ian Dixon has been giving me legal advice regarding custody of Anthony.'

He avoided mentioning the Lester family.

'It's not like they're small children,' Julia said, thinking he was surprised children were being invited. 'All the girls will be sixteen or nearly so, except Marianne. The boys are fourteen.'

'And your son?' Richard asked.

'James has refused permission for him to travel down with Alice and William,' she said. 'I'm sorry for that but there is nothing I can do about it.'

Richard agreed. There is nothing she can do about it. Far better not to create a fuss for the boy. He seems settled, he thought, and Julia can see him anytime. He's well looked after between his father and his grandmother.

He scanned the guest list again to make sure the one name he hoped wouldn't be there hadn't somehow made it on to the list. But Karen's name wasn't there. Richard was relieved Philippe had obviously had the good sense not to include her. His own name was on the list, together with William and Alice. Paul and Marianne too. Charles Brockman had already said he would feel like a fish out of water in a big city and asked to be excused. The same sentiments had come from Mrs Duffy, the Prior Park housekeeper.

'Not too many people from up here?' Richard said.

It looked like Julia was making a complete break from her old life. She shook her head, with just a hint of sadness.

'Too many of them are James's friends,' she said. 'And somehow it's easier for me too knowing that I have a sixteen-year-old daughter fathered by the man I am marrying among the guests. The wedding is seventeen years late.'

Richard looked at her closely. Was she a woman in love or a woman determined to fulfil the dream she had as a teenager?

He lent back against the verandah railing. He noticed his gardener was working quite close by, pruning the shrubs bordering the fence. The regular click of his secateurs signalled his ongoing battle with the unruly vegetation in the garden.

'Are you marrying him for the right reasons?' he asked, in a quiet voice.

Julia looked up at him. It seemed an odd question to ask now. She remembered he had voiced similar concerns before.

'Why do you ask that now?' she demanded, as if there might be another reason why she should reconsider.

He suddenly realised he was on dangerous ground, so he resorted to his earlier arguments against the marriage.

'I've said before that Pippa is very nearly a young woman now,' he said. 'If you are marrying just for her sake it would be the wrong reason.'

Julia smiled. To her that was an easy question to answer.

'I'm marrying Philippe because I love him,' she said.

'And your new life in Sydney?' he asked. 'What do you imagine that will be like?'

She shrugged her shoulders.

'An adventure? I don't know,' she said, 'but it's where Philippe must practice medicine so that is where my future is. But I will come back here often.'

He smiled then, making an effort to reassure her. Privately he wondered how it would all turn out. But it wasn't his decision to make. As a family, we interfered once before, he thought, with tragic consequences. Now we must do everything to ensure she is happy.

'You are welcome to stay with me here when you come up,' he said, 'rather than keep your house on.'

She considered the offer for a few moments.

'Thank you for the offer,' she said finally. 'I haven't decided yet what to do. It may be important for John to feel I have a home here. That I haven't abandoned him.'

That too made sense to Richard.

'And when are you off to Sydney to finalise arrangements?' he asked.

'Next week,' she said. 'Philippe has suggested I stay with him. I hope you aren't shocked.'

Richard shook his head. It seemed a very odd thing to think but the sooner she welcomed Philippe into her bed the better, he thought. But where was Karen in all this? To ask Julia to stay with him, he must have ended it with Karen. He must be certain she's not going to turn up on his doorstep unannounced.

'By the way, I had a letter from Pippa yesterday,' she said, holding it up as if she needed to provide proof.

'She's always full of gossip,' she said laughing. 'Apparently Karen Clarke, Anita Clarke's cousin - the girl who flirted outrageously with Philippe when he took me to dinner at Robert Clarke's house – has jetted off overseas for an indefinite period, to study the fashion business, apparently.'

Julia put the letter down.

'It reminds me of the time when Mother and I made a sudden unexpected pilgrimage to Melbourne under cover of her mystery illness,' she said. 'I wonder if she's been tempting too many men and has found herself in trouble.'

Despite the heat of the day, the news sent a sudden chill down Richard's spine. He turned to look at the work his gardener was doing to cover his sense of shock at sister's interpretation of the unexpected news.

Surely not, he thought. It can't be happening a second time. I hope there is some innocent explanation. There must be. She had talked about the fashion business, he remembered. Perhaps we're reading too much into it.

He emptied the remainder of the tea in his cup into the garden and turned back towards his sister to continue discussing the interminable details of her forthcoming wedding.

CHAPTER 31

May 1960

Sixteen-year-old Pippa Jensen looked at the piece of paper and held it out in front of her to read and reread the words. The paper said she wasn't Pippa Jensen any more. The piece of paper declared she was Pippa Anne Duval. It was a single sheet of paper precious beyond measure. She folded it carefully, replaced it in the envelope and dropped it back into the drawer of her dressing table. She had looked at it daily since she had received it a week earlier.

Just then the door to her bedroom opened after a tentative knock. 'Are you ready?'

Aunt Edith's head appeared around the door.

'Yes, I'm ready,' Pippa said.

For the first time she was being allowed to wear lipstick. And stockings.

Aunt Edith inspected her from every angle and declared herself satisfied. She checked her watch. Philippe had ordered the car to pick them up at three o'clock.

'Such a pity,' she thought. 'They should be getting married in the cathedral. Not in the registry office.'

She put her arm around the girl and gave her a hug.

'This is a very special day, my dear,' she said. 'A very special day.'

Pippa nodded and smiled broadly. Finally, her parents were doing what they should have been doing before she was born.

'It's a beautiful May day,' her aunt said, as she locked the door behind her and waved to the driver who was moving slowly along the street looking for her house.

Philippe lent in close to Julia, as they sat side by side at the main table.

'You look beautiful today,' he said as he lifted her fingers to his lips. She smiled at him.

'You know we should have done this seventeen years ago,' she whispered to him.

He smiled back at her.

'Our lost years,' he said gently, 'but we will make up for it. Beginning with today.'

She looked at her left hand, the wedding ring all shiny and new, the engagement ring sparkling when it caught the light, her old rings packed away along with most of her old life.

She looked around her. She hardly knew anyone at the reception, apart from their daughter Pippa and Edith Henderson, and her own brothers and their children. She had met only Robert and Patricia Clarke previously that she could recall.

It was hard to tell how they all reacted, she thought, when Philippe had risen to his feet to respond to Richard's toast.

Was that a collective intake of breath she had heard as Philippe acknowledged Pippa? Or was she imagining it? Did they expect he was going to ignore her in his wedding speech? After all, she's the reason we're here, she thought. Without her, there would have been nothing that would have brought us back together again. He would have slipped out of my life and out of my thoughts eventually. Except for the fact he had fathered my child.

Now she had a new role in a new group of people, as Pippa's mother. How would Patricia Clarke, Angela Dixon and Kate Lester receive her? And for the time being anyway, Pippa would continue to live with Aunt Edith so that Pippa's schooling would not be interrupted.

'Good old Edith,' Julia thought. 'She wants us to have the chance to establish our marriage first before we become a threesome.'

She let out an almost audible sigh. Richard, sitting to her left, touched her arm to gain her attention.

'You look a little serious for your wedding day,' he said, hoping to lighten her mood.

She shook her head and smiled back at him.

'I was just reflecting on how I came to be here,' she said. 'Life's strange, isn't it? If I had never had Pippa, Philippe would have probably receded from my memory. But the thought of my baby kept our romance alive.'

Richard wanted to say that's a strange thing to say on your wedding day. But he refrained. It was the very reason he had been anxious about her commitment to Philippe. Was it a memory of love she felt? Or was it the genuine enduring kind of love that would be the basis for a strong marriage?

Next to him, Alice leaned across to her sister-in-law. Alice, too, understood her doubts and anxieties.

'You look really beautiful today,' she said, admiringly.

Julia had dressed simply in a short dress of ivory satin with a lace bodice that had taken Alice a full fifteen minutes to button up the back. She had dispensed with a veil and instead had worn a fascinator of net and flowers.

A woman should only wear a long white frock and veil once, Alice had explained to Marianne, who had expected something far grander. Still, Marianne was pleased with the day. She had worn her first truly grown up frock, despite being only thirteen. Her mother noticed she had borrowed some lipstick from one of the other girls. She hoped William wouldn't notice.

Alice glanced across to where Pippa was sitting between Nancy Lester and Marianne.

'I wonder how she feels today?' Alice thought. 'How does it feel to be a child who's grown up with one mother only to find you actually have a different mother, a real mother?'

She looked again at Marianne and could not have imagined giving her up as a baby. Unthinkable.

She hadn't voiced these thoughts to William. She understood now how William had helped Julia's mother in the whole terrible episode. She learnt never to broach the subject with him. Instead, she had confided all her thoughts to her own mother, who had agreed it must be difficult. Privately Amelia Fitzroy had simply given thanks it had never happened to Alice who had been safely married for two years or more before Marianne made her appearance into the world.

Alice noticed movement along the table. It was Julia and Philippe heading to the dance floor as the band began to play the traditional waltz. She nudged William alongside her.

'You go and get our daughter up,' she said, crossing her fingers the dancing lessons she'd been paying for at the Girls' Grammar School would finally pay dividends.

Richard, taking the hint, guided Alice to the floor. Very quickly, the floor was crowded with dancers.

'It's a bittersweet day for you, isn't it, Alice?' Richard said.

She nodded. Life had been so settled with Julia married to James and living just up the road from her.

'It is,' she said.

'Do you think James ever regretted being so hasty in ending the marriage?'

She shook her head slowly.

'James would have always thrown it back at her,' she said, 'if they had a row or he was in a bad mood, or something wasn't going his way.'

'You know your brother too well,' Richard said, admiring her honest answer.

'He was always so indulged when we were children,' she said, 'much like you, I expect.'

But she said it with a smile.

'Do you think he'll marry again?' Richard asked, ignoring her little jibe.

'I hope so,' she said. 'I believe he is seeing a girl who stands to inherit a property out in the central highlands. He met her when he was buying cattle out that way. My mother and I hope something comes of it.'

'Sounds like a good match,' Richard said.

'And what about you?' she asked. 'You should be looking to marry again. It would be good for the boys.'

He laughed good-naturedly.

'I knew that was going to be your next question.'

'Well?' she said, expectantly.

'I'll let you know when I find a new wife, I promise,' he replied with a smile as he spun her around the dance floor.

The music came to an end and he escorted Alice back to the table. He wasn't inclined to sit down again so he headed across to the bar, which was doing a brisk trade.

'I think William will be shocked at this bill,' he thought as he watched the spirits being drunk at a rapid rate. It had been William who had said they should pay for Julia's wedding reception and he had agreed, saying jokingly that he wouldn't pay for a third.

He turned back towards the dance floor as the music started up again.

'Could I risk asking Kate to dance?' he wondered.

But he already knew the answer to that. He could not. Not in front of her husband. The risk was too great. He had limited his contact with them to a simple greeting, shaking Gerald Lester's hand and moving on quickly, but not before Kate had given him the faintest of smiles.

Besides, he could not see her anywhere. It was in fact Mark McDermott who spotted him and came across the room to greet him.

'Your boy seems to have fully recovered from his injuries,' he said.

'Thanks to you, yes he has,' Richard replied. 'I've tried to keep him from any further mishaps.'

'It's probably quite hard to do,' he said, nodding towards Tim Lester and Paul. 'Those two boys are getting restless with this whole thing.'

Richard followed his gaze.

'Another few years and they'll be a bit more interested in the girls around them,' he said. 'That should have a civilising influence on them.'

Robert Clarke, nursing a refilled glass of whisky, came to join the two men.

'I don't know whether it's better to have boys or girls,' he said, catching the drift of the conversation, 'but I do know girls are expensive. Every other day my wife says, Anita must have this, or Anita must have that. Never ending.'

They all laughed but there was no sympathy for his predicament.

'I imagine your brother probably felt that about his daughter Karen,' Richard said, hoping by introducing her name into the conversation he might find out something more about her sudden decision to travel overseas.

Robert Clarke shook his head, as if to say, 'I'm lucky I'm not her father'.

'He never complained,' he said, 'plenty of money of course, not like us poor surgeons.'

Richard doubted that surgeons of Robert Clarke's standing were actually poor. But he hadn't offered up the information Richard wanted.

'I didn't expect to see her here,' Richard said, turning more towards Robert Clarke.

'She went overseas at the end of February. Or was it early March?' he replied. 'Very suddenly. I believe she's in London but we haven't heard from her. Her father said she's gone to study the fashion business.'

'Do her parents expect her back soon?' he asked, casually.

'I don't think so,' Robert said. 'Actually, I don't know to be honest. David was very cagey about it. But I think Philippe must have been quite relieved.'

Richard simply nodded. It did not seem to be quite the right conversation to be having on the day his sister married Philippe.

'I'm going to England very soon,' Richard said. 'Perhaps I should look her up if you can get her address for me. She was very charming company at your dinner table.'

Robert Clarke nodded.

'Patricia probably has it or can get it from Deborah,' he said, as if the goings on of the women in his family were a complete mystery to him or something from which he was excluded.

He excused himself and wandered off to find his wife. Richard was about to head back to his table when he felt a subtle pressure on his arm. He smelled her perfume first before he realised Kate had come up alongside him.

'I wanted to ask you to dance,' he said quietly, 'but I thought perhaps it would not be a good idea.'

She gave the slightest shake of her head.

'Not a good idea,' she said. 'Not a good idea at all.'

He had not seen her since late January. Their Easter plans had not eventuated. But she had written to him quite regularly and he had responded.

He had known she would be at Julia's wedding but he had accepted there would be no opportunity to be alone with her. He was desperate for her, but in a loving way. He wanted to be with her. He was sure now he wanted her to leave her husband and be with him. But would she break up her family for him?

'Let's move along to the corner,' she said, indicating a less well-lit area of the reception room.

He followed her, hoping no one would notice them.

'I have something to tell you,' she said quietly.

He wondered if she was going to tell him her husband had discovered their affair. He was however totally unprepared for what she had to say.

'I'm pregnant,' she whispered, her voice hardly loud enough for him to hear her.

She watched his face as he absorbed the news. At first, she saw disbelief. Then she saw shock. He took a deep breath.

'Is it …?'

'Yours? Yes, it's your baby,' she said, with a confidence he knew not to challenge.

'When?' he asked.

'Late January.'

'But I thought ..?'

'It doesn't always work,' she said, with a faint smile, 'as I've discovered.'

'And your husband?'

'Thinks I'm further along with it than I am.'

It was too public a place to be having this conversation, he thought. He couldn't ask the questions he wanted to ask. He couldn't make any gesture of support nor offer any comfort at all beyond mere words. He calculated quickly. By now she would be slightly more than three months pregnant.

'You didn't say anything in your letters to me?' he said, looking puzzled.

Again, she shook her head.

'I didn't want to commit this news to paper,' she said, 'and I knew I would see you here. I've been summoning up the courage to tell you.'

He fought the urge to reach out and hold her in his arms.

'And your husband knows what?'

'That I'm pregnant but he thinks I conceived at New Year,' she said. 'He hasn't been welcome in my bed since then. He knew he'd over-stepped the mark that night.'

'And when the baby doesn't come when he expects it?'

'I'll deal with that then,' she said, with a confidence she did not feel. 'The other two came early so perhaps he will think this one is simply late.'

'And you are going to bring up my baby as his child?' Richard asked, beginning to understand the full implications of what she was saying.

'I don't have a choice, do I?' she said.

He could see the disappointment in her eyes.

'You do have a choice,' he said. 'Leave him and come and live with me. Or with Alice and William until the baby is born and the divorce is through and I can marry you. I want you to be my wife.'

'Are you just saying that because you're a gentleman and you feel you should say it?'

He shook his head. The news had left him stunned, almost speech-less, but not senseless. He did not relish the prospect of another man bringing up his child.

But more than that. He wanted Kate to be his wife. He wanted them to bring up the child together. He had seen how she was with Paul. She would be an excellent step-mother to his children. Like Alice, she was kind and warm and loving.

'I can't leave him,' she said. 'There's too much at stake. He would cut me off from my children. He would turn my parents out.'

Before he could say anything further, William appeared beside him, as if from nowhere.

'You're being noticed,' he muttered under his breath.,

'Thanks, mate,' he said as he introduced him to Kate, who was quick to take William's hand and greet him warmly.

'I've heard so much about you,' she said, 'from Paul, of course. And your brother.'

Alice too had decided to join them, which necessitated a further introduction.

'Richard told us about your wonderful home at Berrima Park,' Alice said, in her usual chatty way. 'And I know young Paul really enjoys his visits to you. It was so kind of you to take him in when we had the disaster at Prior Park at the end of '57.'

Kate smiled at Alice, grateful for her presence and for having returned the conversation to the commonplace.

'You and William must come and visit us at Berrima Park next time you are down this way,' she said. 'And Marianne too. She's a lovely young girl. Just a bit younger than Nancy I understand.'

William and Alice's timely intervention had settled Gerald Lester's temper. He liked Richard Belleville but there was something about him that made him edgy where Kate was concerned. Probably just my imagination, he thought.

He joined the group, just to be sure. He shook hands with both William and Alice.

'You must come and visit us at Berrima Park,' he said, reiterating the invitation his wife had already extended.

'But after the baby is born in the spring,' he added. 'I don't want my wife to have extra stress just at the moment.'

Alice, unknowing, kissed Kate on the cheek and offered her congratulations.

'Boy or girl?' she asked. 'What do you think it will be?'

Kate smiled at the innocence of Alice's question.

'It's early days,' she said, 'but it feels like a girl.'

'Another wedding to pay for,' Gerald Lester grumbled, but this time with a smile.

He'd given up hope of more children, thinking he was no longer capable of fathering a child. At least that's what the doctors had told him, but what would they know. He was quietly pleased his virility had been proven.

William had the good sense not to look directly at his brother at that moment. Even he could sense the tension among them. His first and only thought was to extricate Richard from the group.

'I've got to drag my brother away,' he said apologetically. 'I need his signature on a cheque to pay for this shindig.'

It was all he could think to say as the three of them excused themselves and headed back to the bridal table.

As they sat down, William swapped chairs with Alice. He turned to his brother.

'Is that what I think it is?' he asked. 'I've seen the letters from her remember, including the one you accidently left in the Curtis Transport papers.'

Why did William have to ask that question right now, he wondered, as he was trying to process the news himself and think about the implications of it all? But he couldn't deny it. He couldn't lie to his brother.

'Yes,' he said, quietly so that Alice would not hear him. 'Kate and I have been lovers. The baby is mine.'

'Are you sure?' William asked. 'Are you absolutely sure?'

'I'm sure,' he said. 'She was with me at the end of January. It tallies.'

William thought for a moment. I can hardly ask whether she still sleeps with her husband, he thought. Obviously, Richard doesn't believe she does.

'So, let me get this straight,' William said. 'You believe Gerald Lester is going to be bringing up a child whose name should be Belleville?'

Richard nodded.

'Is divorce an option?' William asked.

'She's concerned about her two kids,' he replied. 'Gerald Lester would almost certainly get nasty.'

William sat back, trying to decide what he should make of it all. Their earnest discussion had alerted Alice but he had rebuffed her questions.

'Well, this is a fine mess, brother,' William said. 'I take it she means more than a one night stand to you?'

He ignored the insult in his brother's question. William, after all, had never been known for his tact.

'Much more, William,' he said, with a deep sigh. 'I want her to be my wife.'

Angela Dixon had been observing all of this from the other side of the room. She leaned in to her husband who was sitting beside her.

'I think the charming Richard has just found out he's to be a father again,' she said, in a very low voice.

Ian Dixon looked at his wife, opened his mouth to speak, and then closed it again.

'Didn't you tell Kate a few months back the law would always regard the husband as the father when you were discussing Richard's former wife's predicament?'

He nodded. He remembered the conversation well. He couldn't believe Kate herself faced the same predicament.

'Are you sure it's his and not Gerald's?'

He hoped she was wrong. But she never is, he thought.

'Absolutely sure,' she replied. 'I saw her briefly at Easter when she came to pick up the children at school. We had coffee together. I knew something was wrong. She had to tell someone.'

'Should she have told Richard though?' Ian asked. 'Perhaps she would have been better saying nothing and ending the affair.'

Angela shook her head.

'Richard would have found out and guessed anyway,' she said. 'Kate says he's desperate to go on seeing her but it's easy for him. He's divorced but for her everything is at stake.'

'And how does she feel about him?'

'If it wasn't for the children, she would leave Gerald Lester tomorrow,' she said.

'Does Richard feel the same way about her, do you think?'

'She says he does and I believe her,' she replied. 'Despite everything, I think he is a decent man.'

Perhaps that assessment is open to question, Ian Dixon mused. He wanted to say getting another man's wife pregnant hardly rates as decent behaviour, but he did not.

'What do you think will happen now?' he asked.

'Gerald Lester will bring up a child he thinks is his and she will be trapped in a loveless marriage with a man she can't bear to touch her.'

Ian Dixon looked up then and noticed a fleeting look of devastation cross Kate Lester's face.

'What a disaster for her,' he said, with genuine pity in his voice.

Then he looked across at Richard, in deep conversation with William.

'He won't like the idea of Gerald Lester bringing up his child one little bit,' he said, shaking his head.

How complicated can one man's life become, he wondered?

He put his arm around his wife's shoulder. She nestled closer to him, pleased at the small display of affection.

'I'm pleased our life is uncomplicated,' he said. 'Very pleased.'

She smiled and nestled closer to him.

CHAPTER 32

May 1960

Two days after arriving at Haldon Hall, Richard sat opposite his former wife in her study. He sipped his coffee and waited for her to speak.

'It's lovely to see the boys back together again,' she said. 'I can't tell you how much I've missed Paul. It was so difficult being so far away when he had his accident in January.'

'I can tell you he missed you very much then but I explained, with such a young baby, it wasn't possible for you to travel,' Richard said.

They both realised they were experiencing all the difficulties they had envisaged of sharing custody of the boys.

'He's grown so much, he's almost a young man now,' she said. 'I hardly recognised him.'

At fourteen, Paul was at the awkward stage of leaving childhood behind but not yet fully grown. Richard had been amused to see it had taken the two boys less than twenty-four hours to start fighting with each other. Anthony was not yet eight, so he invariably came off second best, causing Richard to intervene frequently.

He deliberately changed the subject. He did not want to remind her constantly of the pain of the separation from her eldest son.

'Your baby seems a very happy little fellow,' Richard said. 'You must have found it strange to have had a baby after so many years.'

Catherine smiled.

'It did seem a little strange at first,' she said, 'but I coped.'

She did not know he was thinking of Kate Lester who would find herself in a similar situation at the end of the year. He had written to Kate before he left Sydney repeating his offer of marriage but knowing, deep down, she would never leave her husband.

'Thank you for making the divorce possible,' she said. 'It was a great favour to me. And to Edward.'

He nodded slightly. He could see she was sincere in thanking him, but he preferred not to speak of it.

'And your new marriage?' he asked politely. 'Is it going well?'

'Very well, thank you,' she said. 'Being a father seems to suit Edward. Did you know he's given up the Foreign Office?'

Richard nodded.

'We were talking about it last night at dinner,' he said. 'He says he doesn't miss it but there are probably times he feels out of things.'

He was doing his best to be civil. He had not warmed to her new husband but he did his best to hide it. There was almost no subject of common interest between the two of them.

'He'll hear all the gossip when we attend Royal Ascot next month,' she said.

'In the Royal Enclosure, I assume?'

Richard was curious as to just how good Edward's connections really were.

She smiled and nodded but said nothing more about the often hectic social calendar around which their lives now revolved.

'You said there was something you wanted to talk to me about,' she said. 'I'm assuming it's about Paul and Anthony?'

He drew a deep breath. This was the critical moment in their conversation. How would she respond?

'I'd like Anthony to come and live with me and Paul in Australia,' he said. 'For a short period.'

She was immediately defensive, as he knew she would be.

'I think that would interrupt his schooling too much,' she said, searching for ways of saying 'no' that didn't make her sound unreasonable.

Richard, for his part, refused to be put off by her concerns.

'The English school year runs from September to July,' he pointed out. 'I could hire a tutor to teach him for the remaining two terms from Christmas.'

She could see immediately he had put quite a lot of thought into it.

'It would be possible to do it while he's still young,' Richard said, pressing his argument. 'When he gets older, it would be harder.'

Perhaps I'm being unreasonable, she thought.

'And when would you bring him back?' she asked.

'In time for the following school year to start in September.'

He had thought it all through very carefully. He recalled John Bertram's warning that Catherine and Edward would be thinking about sending Anthony to boarding school before long. When he had left Anthony with her, there had been no suggestion of her remarriage but her second marriage had made him more determined to secure custody of Anthony.

'Once he outgrows the local school, did you have a plan of where to send him?' Richard asked.

They had never discussed it but it was suddenly an important question.

'Edward would like him to go to Eton,' she said, realising her mistake as soon as the words were out of her mouth.

'I don't mean to sound ungrateful for his interest,' he said tersely, 'but the fact is where Anthony goes to school is none of his business.'

It was as close as he had come to being angry with her. To calm down, he got up and walked across to the window. Beyond the immediate garden, he could see lush green meadows with, here and there, drifts of pretty wildflowers that added colour to the landscape.

'Don't get angry,' he reminded himself. 'Admit you're annoyed seeing your own son getting along so well with his step-father. It's not the boy's fault.'

She smiled and apologised.

'Of course, it isn't,' she said, although she was inclined to disagree with him, 'but he does want Anthony to have all the advantages that George will have growing up. He can get them into Eton. It's not always easy you know.'

Will Eton be an advantage when he's back in Australia running the Belleville interests with his brother and Marianne, Richard wondered? Probably not.

'You don't see it, do you?' he wanted to say. 'Anthony is Australian, not English. His future lies with me because you have another baby and that baby will be the next baronet and inherit most of what you have. And where would that leave Anthony? As the poor relation on the fringes of society, belonging, but not belonging, just as I didn't belong.'

But he said none of it. He sensed she was on the verge of agreeing to Anthony spending at least six months with him. Once he was settled, unless the boy was bitterly unhappy without his mother, he would find a reason to keep him in Australia.

'What do you suggest?' she asked.

'You could bring him out to us in December,' he said, 'if you feel you can leave baby George for a week or ten days. Otherwise I'll make the trip over to collect him.'

She sat quietly for a few minutes, as if mulling over his suggestion.

'It should be possible,' she said finally. 'George will be over twelve months old by then. I think I can leave him with Edward and his nanny.'

'But I would want to be back here for Christmas,' she added.

He inclined his head slightly in agreement.

'That sounds good,' he said. 'You will have a chance to see Paul too. Come and stay with Alice and William for a few days. They would love to see you.'

'I'd enjoy seeing Alice and William again,' she said. 'And Paul too of course.'

'Are we agreed on it then?' he asked, anxious to get her to say 'yes' before she talked herself out of it.

She nodded.

'Yes, I'll do that for you,' she said. 'It seems only fair since you helped me out.'

She could see how relieved he was that it hadn't descended into an argument. But she had her own reasons too. It would give her and Edward a chance to be together with their own child, without the constant reminder Anthony represented of her first failed marriage. She walked across to stand beside Richard at the window. The weather was fine for once and the day promised sunshine and warmth.

She found it impossible not to look at Richard without a pang of regret. There was a robust masculinity about him she missed. He had been her first real love. He had always, or almost always, had the ability to charm her and smooth over their troubles. If only he hadn't insisted on living in the wilds of Australia, she was sure their marriage would have endured.

In Edward, she had chosen the sort of husband her mother had always planned for her. But with Richard she had strayed outside the accepted boundaries. She remembered how much in love with him she had been. She remembered too their first carefree days together as lovers against the improbable backdrop of war-ravaged London. It seemed so long ago.

She sighed. Regrets were useless. She reached up and kissed him on the cheek. He put his arm around her. He too was remembering the good times and felt a pang of regret for what they had lost.

'I'm pleased we didn't have an argument about the children,' she said. 'I don't want to argue with you anymore.'

The two different worlds they inhabited had, ultimately, forced them apart.

'Now tell me everything that's been happening,' she said, 'especially about Julia's wedding. I'm so pleased she's finally married her first love.'

He smiled and relaxed for the first time since his arrival at Haldon Hall.

Everything about the streets of Manhattan was new and exciting to Julia as she and Philippe walked hand in hand along the famous streets. They rode to the top of the Empire State Building, drank cocktails in the Oak Bar, dined in the adjoining Oak Room at the Plaza Hotel and danced at the Peppermint Lounge on West 45th Street.

They dined with his friends from St Luke's who were all curious about his position at St Vincent's and welcomed her warmly as his new wife but expressed no curiosity at all about how they had met. She was surprised none of them knew the real reason why he had moved to Australia.

It was their first disagreement.

'You never told them about Pippa, did you?' she had said after the dinner, when he had warned her his friends believed she was a divorcee with two children. He had never told them one of her children was his or that he had met her during his wartime posting in Australia.

He had simply shaken his head and shrugged his shoulders.

'It didn't seem necessary to share that part of my private life,' he had replied.

'How does a man keep such secrets?' she wondered. 'Was he so used to keeping information about his patients private that it was simply natural for him to do the same about his own life?'

As they walked along Fifth Avenue, she could see he still loved the city he had called home for more than a decade. Would he want to return one day, she wondered? His former colleagues were all unanimous in their agreement he should return without delay.

But where would that leave her if he wanted to? She knew she could never embrace a city where the roar of traffic was constant, where street upon street was so dense with buildings there was no space at all for the natural world, where the constant flashing of neon lights and the proliferation of advertising hoardings assailed her senses constantly.

And Pippa? She was an Australian girl. Would she ever adapt to life in a city like this?

On their last morning in New York they woke to a heavy sky and a fine mist of rain descending on the city.

'We've been lucky so far,' he said, as he joined her at the window to check the weather. 'May is actually the wettest month here.'

'You said you had a surprise for me today?' she said, as he put his arms around her.

'I do indeed,' he said. 'I want to show you where I grew up. At Sag Harbor out on Long Island.'

He had been deliberately vague about the final three days of their honeymoon. No amount of teasing or coaxing on her part had persuaded him to tell her what he had planned.

'I'd love that, Philippe,' she said excitedly, 'but how will we get there?'

'I've organised a rental car to be dropped off here at ten,' he said.

She realised then how well he had planned everything. She looked at her watch. It was already nearly eight o'clock and suddenly she had so much to do. But he would not let her go.

'We'll be late,' she started to say as she tried to break free from his grasp.

'Then we'll be late,' he said playfully, as they tumbled backwards onto the bed.

'I'm making up for lost time,' he said, as he began to kiss her.

In London, Richard had been walking close on an hour, trying to remember the route he had taken with Catherine on their visit to London immediately after victory in Europe had been declared.

He made his way slowly along the Mall which he noticed had still not quite returned to normal following the royal wedding of the Friday before. Small piles of litter remained here and there along with discarded photographs of the smiling couple. Every gust of wind undid much of the work of the cleaners who were trying but failing to rid the streets of the rubbish that had been left behind by the crowds of well-wishers.

It must have been like this after the victory celebrations, he thought, except we never noticed it.

He checked his watch again. He was due at the Savoy in twenty minutes to meet Karen for lunch. He had not seen her since the day in Sydney in January when he had run into her so unexpectedly.

Then suddenly she had left Sydney. Was that because Philippe had finally broken with her? Because he and Julia had set a wedding date? Or was it for some other reason altogether?

He was first to arrive at the Savoy Grill. There was no sign of Karen so he followed the maître d'hôtel to the table. The restaurant was already crowded.

A few minutes after he sat down, he spotted her and waved to attract her attention. She smiled broadly when she saw him. He stood as she approached the table. When he saw her, he breathed a sigh of relief.

'You look wonderful,' he said, as he greeted her warmly. 'London suits you.'

'And you too,' she said. 'You look very relaxed. Are you staying in London for long?'

He shook his head.

'Just a couple of days,' he said. 'Both the boys are with their mother at Haldon Hall in Derbyshire. There is only so much of her new husband I can stomach quite frankly. I needed an excuse to get away for a few days.'

She laughed at his honesty.

'I take it Sir Edward Cavendish is not quite your type?' she replied.

Again, he shook his head.

'And you?' he asked. 'You made a very quick exit from Sydney. It raised some eyebrows. Or should I say it gave rise to some speculation.'

'And gossip too,' she said teasingly. 'Don't forget the gossip.'

The waiter hovered expectantly by Richard's side, waiting for their drinks order.

'Champagne?' he asked.

She smiled.

'Champagne at lunch time? How wonderfully decadent.'

Richard turned to the waiter who ran down the list of possibilities, most of which meant little to Richard, so he settled for a bottle of Dom Pérignon.

'You look different,' Richard said.

She couldn't resist teasing him.

'Older, perhaps?' she said.

'No, definitely not older,' he said, realising how ungallant his comment had sounded. 'More beautiful, more confident perhaps. At least seeing you has eliminated one explanation for your sudden departure.'

'Oh,' she said, 'have people been saying I was pregnant? What terrible gossips people are?'

Should he tell her it was Julia who had put the idea in his head? It seemed a possible explanation at the time, but seeing her now, there was no visible evidence to support the speculation. And he was relieved.

'Well, your departure was so sudden,' he said. 'And without explanation.'

She sat back in her chair as the waiter poured a glass of champagne for her and then circled around to Richard's glass. They were both silent while this ritual was being performed. When the waiter had gone, she raised her glass to him.

'To friendship,' she said.

'To friendship,' he replied.

She set her glass down carefully on the pristine white tablecloth. Richard noticed the slightest of trembles in her hand.

'I had to leave,' she said finally. 'After I saw you at lunch on that Monday, you must have seen Philippe later that day. You knew, didn't you, how involved I was with him. And he with me. But then he dropped me. For nearly three weeks, he didn't return my calls. But he kept his promise to take me to the opening night of Giselle. That night, I knew it was finally over. He dropped me back to my apartment and turned and walked away.'

She paused. He didn't know what to say. She looked devastated.

'She's blaming me,' he thought, 'ignoring the fact that Philippe had promised to marry Julia.'

'He should not have encouraged you,' he said finally. 'He was in the wrong. He wasn't free to have a relationship with you. If he was in love with you, he should have broken it off with Julia.'

But she shook her head sadly.

'He would never do that,' she said. 'He couldn't admit to himself he was in love with me. I think he only realised it after he had proposed to Julia. By then it was too late.'

'And now they are married and honeymooning in New York,' Richard said, not meaning to be unkind.

He wanted to bring the discussion to a close. It served no purpose now. The girl had been hurt, badly hurt, but there was no happy ever after solution for her. Perhaps she'll meet someone new in London.

'It rains in New York in May, a lot,' she said, 'according to some of my friends. I hope it rains every day.'

He laughed then. He could see her old spirit returning.

'And you've found London to be interesting?' he asked, as they began to peruse their menus.

'It's wonderful,' she said. 'I actually work part-time at a boutique in Chelsea called *Bazaar.*

'Not for the money,' she added quickly, 'but for the experience of the fashion business.'

He groaned inwardly. *Now I'm going to spend the rest of lunch hearing about women's clothes.* But he relented and encouraged her to talk about it.

'So, you and Bianca are really serious about the fashion business?' he asked.

She put a hand across to pat his arm reassuringly.

'Don't worry, I don't plan to bore you with all the details of how women's fashion is changing,' she said. 'And society too for that matter. Women no longer want to be under a man's thumb.'

He resisted the temptation to say he could never imagine her in that position. But then her situation, like his sister's, was a privileged one. They had their own money, or at least she would very soon have her own money. Yet he had seen with Kate how women without independent means were compromised. In their lives, their husbands held all the power.

He tossed the menu down on the table.

'Too much bloody French in that menu,' he said impatiently, as he opted for a sirloin steak.

She laughed at him.

A typical Australian response, she thought, as she chose La Darne de Saumon d'Ecosse confident she would be having Scottish salmon. Philippe would have read it all with ease, she thought wistfully.

'Now,' she said, as she closed her menu and set it aside, 'tell me what you are going to do about Kate Lester having your baby?'

He was glad he had just put his champagne glass back on the table, otherwise he might have dropped it.

'So where did this tittle tattle come from?' he asked, trying not to sound annoyed.

'Aunt Patricia wrote to me last week,' she said, with a knowing smile. 'She said she saw Kate briefly at Easter time when they were all picking up their daughters from school. Kate was with Angela Dixon, she said, and she didn't look well at all.'

Richard remained silent. She went on.

'Afterwards, Aunt Patricia spoke to Angela and apparently Angela told her Kate is pregnant,' Karen said, recalling what her aunt had written. 'Incidentally, Aunt Patricia thinks it's quite shocking, *at her age.*'

How do I respond, Richard wondered? Deny it? She won't believe me. Get angry with her? For what purpose? It's Karen being Karen, he reminded himself. She loves to shock.

'But you've decided to embellish the story,' he said, 'over and above what your aunt has written. That's true, isn't it?'

She smiled then. And nodded

'But you didn't deny it, did you?' she said. 'I saw the look of horror on your face, but that was because you thought it was generally known she is pregnant to you and not her boor of a husband, not because it's not true.'

He was serious for a moment. Karen had put two and two together. It was important she not spread the gossip. Not for his sake, but for Kate's.

'I'm relying on you not to spread this story,' he said. 'I've asked her to marry me. Well, let me rephrase that, to leave her husband, get a divorce and then marry me, but she won't because he would cut her off from her children. She has no choice but to bring up the baby as his.'

'But I'm relying on you, Karen, as a friend, not to tell anyone,' he pleaded. 'It must never come out.'

She smiled at him reassuringly.

'Of course, I won't say anything,' she said. 'But some people will know. You must know that. Angela and Ian Dixon will know. Philippe may guess. Even my uncle may suspect.'

He could have added my own brother knows too but he did not.

'I realise that,' he said, reluctantly, 'but none of those people will openly acknowledge it I hope.'

'Perhaps not,' she replied. 'But the question remains. How do you feel about another man raising your child?'

Richard was a proud man who attached great importance to his family name. She knew it would really hurt him not to be able to give his child the Belleville name.

'I'm not happy about it,' he admitted. 'The fact is I'm in love with Kate but I can't have her. Just as you are in love with Philippe and you can't have him.'

Richard hadn't realised the wide-eyed waiter was standing beside him waiting to take their meal orders until Karen suddenly picked up her menu. When the waiter had finally gone, she laughed quietly.

'He's going to have some lovely gossip to entertain the kitchen with, isn't he?' she said.

He was able to laugh then. At least he wasn't known in London. And the people they were speaking about weren't known. There was a wonderful anonymity about it all.

'To broken hearts,' he said, as he raised his champagne glass.

'To broken hearts,' she responded.

'And when will we see you back in Australia?' he asked.

She shrugged her shoulders.

'When I'm tired of London,' she said. 'But probably by the end of the year. My parents are already pressuring me to come home.'

'And still pressuring you to get married?'

She smiled.

'Nothing changes with that,' she said. 'But I'm afraid they are doomed to disappointment. I've vowed never to marry.'

'They'll be disappointed,' he said.

'I know,' she said, 'but I can't help that. I tried to please them once and he used me as a punching bag. Then I fell in love with Philippe and he chose someone else. Why would I try again?'

Richard knew there was no answer to that. He was disinclined to look elsewhere too so he couldn't blame her.

This time they were silent as the waiter placed their meals in front of each of them with a grand flourish and generally fussed around them.

The aroma of chargrilled steak reminded Richard he was hungry. He began to tackle the perfectly cooked sirloin with relish.

CHAPTER 33

May 1960

'How's married life?' Richard asked, as he and Philippe sat together on the back deck of the home he now shared with Julia.

'I'm getting used to it,' Philippe said, with surprising honesty.

There had been times he had felt lonely and very alone, but he had come to realise with something of a shock how much change marriage to Julia had brought to his life. He had been back at work for a week since they had returned from New York. That routine at least had been unchanged.

'It would take a bit of adjustment,' Richard conceded, although he had hoped for a more cheerful response.

Philippe smiled and nodded.

'Particularly at my age,' he said. 'A man does get rather set in his ways, which I've been told a couple of times.'

Richard laughed. He had overheard women say things like that repeatedly of their husbands. Perhaps it was true. It would be true of his brother, he thought.

'By the way,' Richard said, 'I had lunch with a mutual friend in London.'

He waited, watching Philippe carefully. He thought he saw just the faintest reaction but he could not be sure.

'How is she?' Philippe asked, as if Karen had been the most casual of acquaintances.

'She's very well, as beautiful as you'll remember,' Richard replied

355

cautiously. 'She's using her time to learn the fashion business. We drank champagne at lunch which even she described as decadent.'

Philippe smiled, the pleasure of his memories of her plain to see for just a few fleeting seconds. He glanced around nervously but Julia was keeping Pippa and Paul occupied with setting the table for lunch.

'I'm pleased,' he said simply. 'I was worried when I heard she had left so suddenly.'

'She was very upset,' Richard said.

'I know,' he replied. 'My fault entirely.'

'You did the right thing,' Richard said. 'You had no option.'

'I know that too,' he said. 'But afterwards, her leaving so suddenly led to all kinds of speculation, as you can imagine.'

'I thought that might be a possibility myself,' Richard admitted. He didn't want to spell it out. He could see Philippe understood what he was trying to say.

'But it's unfounded speculation?' Philippe asked, looking towards Richard for confirmation.

His question surprised Richard. So Philippe had been worried too about the real reason for her sudden departure.

'Unfounded,' Richard said, without elaboration.

'Thank goodness,' he said.

Philippe's sense of relief was obvious. Richard realised then Philippe had no way of finding out. He could not ask for her address. He could not enquire after her from her uncle. Or from her father.

'You should be prepared for her return home eventually,' Richard said.

'When?'

'By the end of the year, I believe,' Richard replied.

'Thanks for telling me,' he said, as he turned to greet Pippa who had just appeared at the back door to tell them lunch was ready.

Richard followed him inside. His conversation with Philippe had left him with a vague sense of unease. Was it just that Philippe was a man who did not easily reveal his inner thoughts, he wondered? Or was there more to it? Or was he simply imagining something that wasn't there? He smiled at his sister, who seemed relaxed and happy in her new role as Mrs Philippe Duval.

'I hope she finds happiness in this marriage,' he thought. She deserves it.

A week later, Richard and William sat together in William's study at Prior Park. It was a smaller room but it looked much the same as their father's study in the old house. Deep leather armchairs, a solid timber desk that two men had struggled to move into place, matching bookshelves and cabinets that only Alice was allowed to dust and polish. Richard wondered if such a replica served only to remind William of what they had lost.

For an hour or more, the two of them discussed the various investments that now made up the Belleville family interests. Despite his natural tendency for pessimism, William had surprised Richard by being, for him anyway, remarkably optimistic.

'Any move on another cattle property?' Richard asked.

He knew William had been looking more seriously. He hoped he had come up with some options.

'Southern Highlands is too expensive,' he said, dashing Richard's hope of a base close to the Lester's home.

What would that serve anyway, Richard thought? It would be better if I stayed away from Kate. Better for her peace of mind. Better for mine too, he decided.

'But you have something else in mind?' Richard asked.

'I do as a matter of fact,' William replied. 'Twenty-five thousand acres of prime country out at St George. It's watered by artesian bores. There would be a lot of scope to improve it, according to the agent.'

'How has it come up?' Richard asked.

'The owner has passed away I understand,' he said. 'The property has to be sold to split the estate between two daughters. They're not interested in keeping it.'

'And how would we run it?' Richard asked.

'In the past year, a manager was appointed to run it,' William said. 'The agent says he's very competent and keen to stay on.'

'Are you planning to go out and look at it?' Richard asked.

He couldn't imagine William making such a big investment, sight unseen.

'Next week, probably,' he replied. 'Would you like to come? Charles is going to come with me for a look.'

Richard shook his head. He could rely on Charles to assess the property. And he could rely on William to do the investment numbers. He was no fan of long road trips. He guessed the drive would take at least nine hours. Perhaps even longer.

'If you buy it, I might have to go back and get my pilot's licence again,' Richard said. 'Check and see if there's an airstrip on it or a site for one.'

For once William didn't disagree with him. A Cessna might just be the thing if they were to have properties spread around the country. Not to mention that young Paul had ambitions of becoming a pilot. In a few years' time, he could prove to be very useful, William thought.

Richard watched as his brother got up and went across the room to close the door. It was a habit that signalled to the household he did not want to be disturbed.

'I bet I know what's coming,' Richard thought.

'So your little problem?' William began, hoping Richard would make it easy for him.

'My little problem?' he retorted. 'That's an ugly turn of phrase, William, even for you.'

'For God's sake, Richard,' he said, suddenly exasperated with his older brother. 'I don't go around the countryside getting other men's wives pregnant. I just want to know if you have heard from Kate Lester since the wedding.'

Richard got up and began to pace the room, much as he had often done at the old house, but this new room was too small for easy movement. He let out a deep sigh. He reminded himself that his brother had his best interests at heart.

'I wrote to Kate before I left for England,' he said, 'offering to help her get a divorce and repeating my offer of marriage. I've had no reply.'

'So that's it?' William asked. 'Your son or daughter is going to be brought up in another household with another father and you aren't prepared to do anything about it.'

'William,' he said, trying to keep his frustration in check, 'it's not that I'm not prepared to do something about it. It's that there is nothing I can do about it if Kate won't leave him. That is the simple fact.'

He paused, before continuing.

'Think about it. What woman wants to openly admit she's been cheating on her husband? Which is what she'd be doing if she left him and came to me,' he said.

William looked closely at his brother. He could see Richard was unhappy but resigned to the situation.

'I'm sorry,' William said, 'I didn't mean to pry into your private life. I can see why you were so taken with her. She's a lovely woman. She would have made you a great wife. A great step-mother too. Alice really liked her.'

'I hope you didn't tell Alice about my involvement with her?' Richard asked, alarmed at the prospect of his private life being discussed between William and his wife.

'No, of course not,' William lied, before changing the subject.

He too had been worried about Julia's marriage to Philippe, especially following Richard's revelations about another girl.

'How's married life working out for our sister?' he asked, assuming his brother had seen them on his way back from England.

'I had lunch with them last Sunday,' Richard said. 'They seem fine together.'

'And the young lady whose photograph you took from Pippa?'

'Is in London now,' Richard said. 'I had lunch with her when I went up to London for a few days.'

He could see the relief on William's face. London was a good place for her. No temptation for Philippe.

'She left Sydney suddenly a couple of months before their wedding,' Richard added.

'She's not … ?'

William couldn't bring himself to say it.

'No, rest assured, she's not pregnant,' Richard said. 'She couldn't have hidden a pregnancy in the tight-fitting dress she wore to have lunch with me.'

'Thank God for that,' William said. 'Is the move to London permanent?'

Richard shook his head.

'It isn't,' he said. 'I warned Philippe she would be back in Sydney by the end of the year.'

'How did he react?' William wanted to know.

'Not much reaction at all, if you want my honest opinion,' Richard said.

'And your son in England?' he asked. 'What's happening with him?'

'He's coming out with his mother at the end of the year,' Richard said. 'I've issued an invitation for them to stay with you and Alice here.'

'For a short visit?'

Richard shook his head.

'No, Anthony will stay on with me and Paul for at least six months.'

'And then what?'

'I'm going to use whatever means available to keep him here with me,' Richard said.

William did not miss the determination in his brother's voice.

'Will that mean a custody battle in the courts?' William asked.

'If that's what it takes,' Richard said. 'Just imagine how you would feel if Marianne was being brought up by another man and that man was usurping you as her father.'

'You're right,' he said. 'I wouldn't like it at all. I understand how you feel.'

'And besides, Anthony's future is as a Belleville. He belongs here. If he spends all his childhood and young adult life in England, he won't ever feel he belongs in Australia.'

William nodded. He agreed wholeheartedly with Richard.

'He does belong here,' William said. 'And Catherine's new husband and baby?'

'Her husband is everything you imagine an English aristocrat to be,' Richard said disparagingly. 'A pale patrician face, Savile Row suits, hands that have never done a hard day's work, immaculate manners, a charming host. A man with social ambitions with just that ever so slight disdain for us colonials.'

'Bloody hell,' William said, with a laugh. 'You don't like him much, do you?'

Richard shook his head.

'Is it that obvious?' he said, joining in William's amusement.

'And he'll be raising a son in his own image, I imagine,' William said.

'Absolutely,' Richard said. 'But not Anthony. I don't want him raising my son like that.'

Before William could reply, there was a determined knock followed by Alice's head appearing around the door.

'If I don't rouse you two now,' she said, with a smile, 'you'll be complaining your meals are cold.'

Richard looked at his watch. He hadn't realised he and William had been talking together for over two hours.

'Coming, Alice,' he said, as he and William both headed to the door.

'Never keep a wife waiting,' William said quietly. 'First rule of a happy marriage.'

Richard smiled. He was pleased William had found such contentment with Alice, who had proven time and again what an ideal wife she was.

I wonder if William realises just what a debt we owe Alice, Richard thought, as he took his seat at their dining table alongside his son.

Unusually for a Sunday, it was only family seated around Alice and William's table. Charles Brockman was off seeing his ailing sister in town and Mrs Duffy, too, had opted for a long overdue weekend away.

'We're a small group today,' William said, as he sliced into the thick piece of sirloin steak that dominated his dinner plate.

Even though it meant extra work for her, Alice was not unhappy about it. She wished though her brother would come to lunch on Sunday and bring his son. He was still so angry with the Belleville family, she doubted he would ever unbend and visit her and William at Prior Park. Yet he was always happy to see her and Marianne. It was Marianne who broke the silence that had descended on those gathered around the table.

'John got a photo of his mother's wedding,' she volunteered, 'but Uncle James won't let him keep it, not at home anyway, so he's left it with his grandmother.'

This was news to Alice, who had also received a couple of photographs from Julia.

'How does John feel about his mother getting married again?' she asked her daughter, ignoring the not unexpected response from her brother to the wedding photograph.

Marianne shrugged.

'He hasn't said much,' she said. 'I think he's pretty disappointed though. I know he misses her, but there's nothing he can do about it. But he said she's coming up to see him very soon, according to her letter.'

This was news to the adults at the table, who had thought it would be some months before Julia would make the trip north.

'Does he write to his mother?' Alice asked. She hardly expected her brother to encourage his son to keep up correspondence.

'I doubt it,' Marianne replied. 'Boys aren't really the writing type, in my experience.'

Her mother wondered what experience that was exactly but, in the end, chose not to ask.

'You had a letter from Pippa the other day,' Alice said. 'Did she have any news? How is she coping now with her mother and father having married?'

Marianne put her knife and fork down as if she needed all her concentration to consider the question.

'I don't think her life has changed as much as she thought it would,' Marianne said earnestly. 'She's still living with her Aunt Edith during the week because her house is close to the school but she spends most of the weekend with her parents. She said Aunt Julia went to the mothers' day at the school for the start of the new term. She said Nancy Lester's mother couldn't attend this year because she's expecting a baby and hasn't been well. Pippa thought she might have actually been in hospital. She said Nancy was shocked that her mother would be having another baby.'

William looked at Richard and noticed his quick intake of breath at the mention of Kate Lester's name.

'I hope he doesn't ask Marianne about Kate Lester,' he thought. 'She won't know anything more.'

'She also said her father has been talking more and more about New York since they got back from their honeymoon,' Marianne said. 'He's promised to take her for a visit when she finishes school.'

She looked towards her mother then.

'Mum, can we go to New York for a holiday when I finish school?' she asked.

Alice's face grew serious. The last thing she needed was Marianne getting such ideas in her head but she knew from past experience not to say 'no' to her outlandish requests directly.

'We'll see, my dear girl,' she said calmly. 'You're only thirteen so we'll think about it in a few years' time. And it will be up to your father then.'

Putting decision-making back on William's shoulders was something Alice did infrequently but to good effect. Marianne might well be prepared to argue with her mother but, as yet, she was inclined to defer to her father's decisions without argument. Long may that continue, Alice thought. When she stops taking notice of her father, life will be just that little bit more difficult.

Paul had listened to all this chatter with growing exasperation. The one thing he did know was that Nancy's brother Tim wasn't exactly ecstatic about having a baby in the family either.

'Tim Lester thinks it's very odd his mother is having a baby too,' he said. 'He told me his parents hardly spoke to one another for months. And he said it's months since his father moved into one of the guest bedrooms permanently.'

Richard was the first one to break the deathly silence that had descended around the table. It was his son, after all, who was spreading this gossip. He was only fourteen. What's a boy of fourteen doing even talking about these things, he wondered?

'I don't think that's an appropriate thing to say, son,' he said, in his sternest voice. 'I don't know what Tim's doing talking about his family like that. How his parents live is a very private matter.'

Paul shrugged.

'They don't think he notices things,' he said, 'but he does. He told me he noticed his mother reading private letters when she thinks no one is looking. He said she looked happy when she was reading them, not like when she's with his father.'

'What can I say,' thought Richard. 'I don't want to prolong this discussion.'

'Perhaps it's better you don't speak about what Tim tells you,' Richard said finally. 'It's very private. If he chooses to tell you, it's because he regards you as his good friend. But sometimes, you have to keep things that good friends tell you to yourself.'

The boy nodded. Besides, he would rather talk about fishing and aeroplanes than someone's mother having a baby.

'I'll go and see if the pudding is ready,' Alice said, jumping up quickly from the table.

'Marianne,' William said, 'go and give your mother some help.'

She got up reluctantly.

'Why do I always have to help?' she complained.

'Well, Paul can help too,' Richard said.

He groaned and rolled his eyes but got up to help his aunt.

When they had left the dining room, William turned to Richard, letting out a deep sigh that was more eloquent than any words he could utter.

'That was a shock, hearing Marianne talking about Kate, and Paul too,' Richard said. 'What do I do now? How do I find out if she's OK?'

William shook his head. What could he say? It all seemed so tawdry. Then Richard remembered Angela Dixon. She would certainly know. He and Kate had been using Angela as a post box.

'I'll contact Angela Dixon,' he said quietly. 'She'll be able to tell me how Kate is.'

'Good idea,' William said.

He was running out of enthusiasm to talk about his brother's complicated life. He was relieved then to see his daughter come through the door.

She placed bowls of hot steamed syrup pudding covered in creamy custard in front of her uncle and her father, who set to work devouring his favourite dessert.

CHAPTER 34

Late October 1960

It was late afternoon. The storm clouds gathering on the south western horizon promised much but, in the end, delivered nothing in the way of rain.

'Rain,' thought Richard. 'It's always about rain in this country.'

He and William had spent the day going over contracts and signing documents to buy the new property to add to the Belleville holdings. William had suggested the property be renamed Belleville Park and Richard had readily agreed.

With the purchase imminent, he had fulfilled his promise to regain his pilot's licence. It had seemed strange to be in the cockpit of an aircraft as small as the Cessna. His last memory of flying had been of the Avro Lancaster with its hundred-foot wingspan and its belly loaded with bombs.

'I'm next for lessons, Dad,' Paul had said, when his father talked to him about having to learn to fly all over again. Paul thought of nothing much else other than getting his pilot's licence.

Richard sat reading the minutes from the latest Curtis Transport meeting. It seemed the company was doing well. He made a mental note to plan to be in Sydney for the next meeting, or perhaps the one after that. He looked for the list of directors who had attended the latest meeting. Karen's father's name appeared immediately after Sid Curtis in the list of attendees. Roger Fairholm was also listed. Richard noted he was the only director who had been absent.

He reread the latest letter from Kate. He was surprised she continued to write to him at infrequent intervals. Nothing had changed, she would not leave Gerald for fear of being cut off from Nancy and Tim, she said. He folded the letter and added it to the small pile of letters he had received from her. It seemed hopeless to even go on keeping in touch with her.

Lucky William, he thought. He and Alice have just celebrated sixteen years of marriage. 'I doubt William ever looked at another girl,' he mused.

He heard the familiar creak of the garden gate opening and looked up, expecting to see Paul returning from cricket training. Instead it was an unexpected but welcome visitor. What better sight to see, he thought, than John Bertram?

'To what do I owe this pleasure, John?' he asked, as his friend took the front stairs two at a time.

'I felt like a change of scene,' his friend replied. 'I have a couple of weeks off. I could have gone to my cousins in the Hunter but they're a dull lot so I hitched a ride on the plane north instead.'

'Any chance of a cold beer, mate?' he asked, as the two men shook hands warmly.

Richard was about to head in the direction of the kitchen but his housekeeper, having heard the visitor arrive, had pre-empted the request, emerging with two glasses of beer, which were quickly claimed by the two men.

John sipped his beer with the relish of a hot thirsty man before settling into a chair alongside Richard.

'By the way,' he said, with a slight smile, 'our mutual friend was on the last flight I flew back to Sydney from London before my leave.'

No names were needed. Richard knew exactly who John was talking about.

'That's a bit earlier than she anticipated returning,' Richard said, with a frown. 'Perhaps it was getting too cold and gloomy for her over there. How was she?'

'Very bubbly, very beautiful, flirting outrageously,' he replied, smiling broadly.

'Did she say anything about why she was returning?' Richard

asked. 'She told me she wouldn't be back until December when I saw her in May.'

John shrugged his shoulders.

'I don't really know but I got the impression she was keen to get on with her business plans with her friend Bianca,' he said.

Richard nodded. He too hoped that was the reason.

'I hope she stays out of Philippe's way,' Richard said.

'I shouldn't worry,' John said reassuringly. 'He's an old married man now.'

But Richard shook his head.

'He's a newly married man with a wife who spends some of her time up here with her son,' Richard said. 'More time, actually, than any of us thought she would.'

'So, what are you saying, mate?' John asked. 'Their marriage is not quite the fairy tale ending you thought it would be? Or she thought it would be? You told me the wedding seemed to go off well.'

Richard had added John's name to the guest list, but in the end, work had kept him away, so he was relying on Richard's opinion entirely.

'I don't know to be honest,' he replied, with just a hint of uncertainty. 'She says everything is fine so I have to believe her. But when she's here, she goes out to Prior Park to ride her horse. She spends time with Alice and William and with her son. She sees some of her old friends. It's as if this is where she belongs. It's as if she's living two lives.'

John could see Julia's divided life had begun to worry Richard.

'I wouldn't worry about it, mate,' John said. 'Sydney can be an overwhelming place if you're not born to it. I imagine Philippe's busy with his work too. Maybe she's trying to find a way to fit in and there might be times when there is some embarrassment for her about Pippa's birth.'

Richard nodded.

'John's right,' he thought, 'I'm just worrying for worry's sake.'

'By the way, Karen asked after you,' John said, with an extra glint in his eye. 'She said she was so pleased to see you I was beginning to wonder just how friendly you got with her in London?'

'Not that friendly, John,' he said, holding his hands up in mock alarm. 'That girl would be more than I could handle right now. Besides, when I saw her, she still hadn't got over Philippe.'

'Well, let's hope that's all in the past now,' John said, draining his glass and hoping another beer wasn't too far away.

Just as Richard got up to go in search of more beer, the shrill ringing of the telephone began to echo down the hallway.

It was some time before Richard rejoined his friend on the verandah. He sighed and slumped down in his seat, before immediately getting up again.

'Bad news, mate?' John asked.

Richard mumbled in reply.

'Yes .. and no,' he said.

'This calls for whisky,' he added, as he led the way into his house.

He splashed generous measures of single malt into two crystal glasses and handed one to John, who wanted to say 'I'd have preferred another beer' but did not.

'Are you going to tell me what the call was about?' John asked, finally.

It appeared for a few moments as if Richard did not know what to say. Finally, he spoke.

'That call was from Kate's friend, Angela Dixon,' he began. 'She was calling to tell me Kate's husband Gerald was killed in a riding accident at one of his properties two days ago.'

'That's terrible news,' John interjected. 'How did it happen?'

Richard nodded. It was terrible news.

'Apparently, he hadn't ridden much of recent times but insisted on getting on a horse to go and inspect some cattle,' Richard explained, retelling the story Angela had just told him. 'He was very unlucky it seems. His horse shied at a bird or an animal, they don't know which, and he came off and hit his head on a rock in the grass. It could happen to anyone.'

John listened to this in silence. He understood the implications for his friend but it would be just plain wrong to point them out, he thought.

'How is Kate bearing up?' he asked.

'According to Angela, the shock of it put her into early labour,' he said. 'This afternoon, she had a baby girl. Angela was with her. Fortunately, both mother and baby are doing well.'

The relief on Richard's face was obvious. He had feared the worst when he had recognised Angela's voice on the telephone.

'And Angela called you because ..?'

John didn't need to finish his question.

'Because Kate asked her to call me,' Richard replied.

Richard drank the pale amber liquid in his glass in one quick gulp and reached for the decanter again.

'Bloody strange way to become a father again,' John said, in his reassuringly down to earth way.

He did not know he was echoing Richard's own thoughts.

'I couldn't have put it better myself,' Richard said. 'It feels very strange. Surreal if you must know. Today I was lamenting the fact that nothing would ever come of my relationship with Kate because she wouldn't leave her husband. That another man would be raising my child as his. And now, suddenly, she's a widow. And I have a daughter I can acknowledge.'

Despite the circumstances, he managed a smile.

'I had hoped she would have a girl,' Richard said.

'And what will you do?' John asked. 'You can hardly rush down there claiming your child in front of the mourners at her husband's funeral.'

Richard shook his head. Only John Bertram could state the obvious, he thought.

'Of course I'm not going to do that,' he retorted. 'Angela said I should wait for a month or two, possibly just before Christmas, before I go to see Kate, but that I should write to her.'

'Sounds like sensible advice,' John said, as he too drained his glass.

For the first time in their friendship, he was lost for words. Do I congratulate him, he wondered? Somehow, it seemed inappropriate.

John could see his friend was restless, anxious to do something, anything. He will look back in years to come and remember this one telephone call, John thought, and how it changed the course of his life.

'Let's drive out to Prior Park for dinner,' Richard said suddenly.

Despite the sad news of Gerald Lester's death, he could see Richard was in high spirits.

'Maybe call your sister-in-law first?' John suggested.

'Good idea, mate,' he said.

He headed back towards the hallway and picked up the telephone receiver. It was a quick call.

'All clear,' he said. 'Alice always has a well-stocked pantry. It's six o'clock, we'll be there by seven. Mrs Freestone will give Paul his dinner when he gets back from cricket practice.'

It was obvious to him Richard was keen to share the news with his brother and sister-in-law.

'What are you going to be telling your brother and his wife?' John asked cautiously.

'Everything,' Richard said. 'William knows about Kate and I doubt he would have kept the details from his wife, although he claimed he hadn't told her.'

For the first time in a long time he looks genuinely happy, John thought, as the two men headed towards Richard's car.

After telephoning Richard, Angela Dixon returned to sit quietly alongside Kate's hospital bed. She held her friend's hand in a gesture of reassurance and felt her stir.

'Did you call him?' Kate asked anxiously. 'Is he pleased with a girl?'

'I spoke to him,' Angela replied. 'And, yes, he's very pleased to have a daughter.'

'And did you tell him about Gerald?'

'I did,' Angela said. 'I don't think he quite knew what to say.'

Kate nodded her head slightly.

'It's a terrible tragedy,' she said. 'For some reason I don't understand Gerald was so looking forward to the birth of this baby. He had made such an effort to make it up to me. He knew he'd overstepped the mark.'

Angela tried to silence her.

'Don't talk now,' she said. 'You must sleep now. It's been a trying few days for you.'

But Kate shook her head.

'I must tell you,' she said. 'Lately he's been quite a changed man, so full of confidence. The fact he thought he'd been able to father a child made him feel young and vigorous again. He hadn't been on a horse for a couple of years but apparently he insisted he would ride as the rest of the men were planning to ride. And he had been a very good rider.'

Tears began to flood down Kate's cheeks. Angela handed her a clean handkerchief which she held to her eyes.

'I should feel more, Angela,' she said between sobs. 'My children have lost their father but it's awful. A part of me feels nothing but relief. I just didn't love him, but I didn't realise it until I met Richard.'

Angela gathered her up in her arms and let her cry until finally she pulled away.

'Did you tell Richard not to come down straight away?' she said. 'I need time to come to terms with everything.'

'I did,' Angela replied. 'He's very understanding. He said to give you his love. I told him to come and see you, probably just before Christmas.'

Through her tears, Kate nodded and managed a smile.

'That's good,' she said, relaxing just a little.

'Did you tell him I thought of Susan for the name?' she asked.

Angela smiled reassuringly.

'I did and he loved it,' she said. 'Now get some rest. You'll be swamped with visitors tomorrow.'

Kate closed her eyes then and began to drift off to sleep.

When she was sure her friend was sleeping soundly, Angela gathered her things together and crept silently out of the room. How fortunate, she thought, that Kate had been staying with her for a few days when all this happened.

On her way out of the hospital she couldn't resist one final look at the baby girl in the nursery. Her name was already on her crib: Susan Marie Lester.

'I imagine she won't have that name for long,' Angela thought to herself. 'I'm sure Richard will want it changed to Susan Marie Belleville. I wonder what awaits her in the future? Will she be accepted by Richard's boys? And by Kate's older children?'

Angela turned away from the glass that separated her from the row of new born babies.

'Who can tell what the future holds?' Angela thought, as she checked her watch as she headed out into the carpark to make the short drive back to her house.

'Just enough time to change and make the birthday dinner,' she calculated.

At the very time Angela was making her way out of the hospital, in another part of the city, Julia was putting the finishing touches to her make up. She had looked hard for signs of ageing despite Philippe reassuring her there were none.

He watched her for a few minutes and then came up behind her.

'You look beautiful,' he said, kissing her lightly on the shoulder.

She smiled, looking at his face reflected in her dressing table mirror.

'You always say that,' she said smiling, but she was secretly pleased he did.

He handed his cufflinks to her. She was pleased to see he had chosen to wear her wedding gift to him. They were gold, embossed with the Belleville crest. She had long ago given up her treasured name but at least these would be something to remind him of her family.

'It must have been difficult to do this when you lived alone,' she said, as she fixed first the right and then the left cufflink through the sleeve of his white shirt.

'It was,' he said. 'It required some dexterity.'

She stood up then to examine her reflection in front of the full length mirror. A stray strand of blonde hair was tucked carefully back in her hairdo. She smoothed the embroidered chiffon skirt of her dress and then put her head on one side, as if critically examining the frock. Was it too much?

'It's not too much is it?' she asked uncertainly, spinning around to see herself from all angles.

The heavily embroidered bodice hardly needed decoration but she had added the diamond earrings which had been Philippe's present to her on their wedding day, and the diamond bracelet she had received from her brothers.

Philippe shook his head.

'You seem to be making a lot of effort this evening,' he said, having observed the amount of time she had taken to get ready. 'It's just a fiftieth birthday party for Patricia Clarke.'

Julia smiled.

'You forget,' she said. 'They haven't seen much of me. I want to make a good impression on your friends and colleagues.'

He realised then that, apart from their wedding day more than five months earlier, she had not socialised with what he called the usual crowd. They had been away on their honeymoon for the annual fundraising ball and she had missed two dinners because she had been visiting her son. He understood then why it was so important for her to make a good impression.

For his part, he felt an extra frisson of anxiety about the dinner. Just before he had left work, Robert Clarke had mentioned to him ever so casually that his niece had returned from London several days earlier. She would almost certainly be at the dinner to celebrate her aunt's fiftieth birthday.

It was more than ten months since he had seen her. Whenever he thought of her, he felt a surge of guilt that never seemed to diminish. How would he feel seeing her again? How would she react seeing him for the first time as a married man? Privately, he berated himself. 'I mustn't think about her. Whatever she does, don't react.'

He slipped his jacket off its hanger and went in search of his car keys.

It was early evening and Patricia Clarke stood with her husband at the entrance to the private room at the cruising yacht club to greet their guests. She thanked everyone graciously for their good wishes but privately wished her husband had not made such a fuss of a milestone she would have rather forgotten. Or at least not advertised quite so widely to all their friends.

But very quickly, her birthday was usurped as the main topic of discussion.

'Really, Angela Dixon could have waited with that news,' she hissed to her startled husband after they had greeted Angela and her husband.

Robert Clarke shook his head. It simply confirmed what he had always known. Life is a fragile thing. An apparently healthy man through sheer bad luck was now lying lifeless at the undertakers awaiting burial.

And his wife? She was lying in a hospital bed, having been safely delivered of a baby girl the dead man would have celebrated as his child. A child that was most likely fathered by another man, Robert thought.

'I must tell Julia and Philippe,' Angela said in a whispered aside to her husband as they made their way into the room.

But her husband put a restraining hand on her arm.

'Don't mention Richard's role in all this,' he warned. 'It will come out soon enough.'

His wife nodded. 'As if I would blurt that out tonight,' she wanted to say. But her tone was much more conciliatory.

'Julia needs to know so she can tell Pippa,' Angela reminded him. 'Her friends will be wondering why Nancy Lester was withdrawn from school at such short notice.'

'But Lucy knows about it,' Ian pointed out.

'Yes, but Lucy has been at the conservatorium all this week and not at school,' she said. 'She only knows because Kate was staying with us.'

Then she spotted Julia and Philippe and walked across to greet them, her husband somewhat reluctantly joining her.

'You look lovely, my dear,' Angela said as she came up to greet them.

The unexpected compliment raised Julia's spirits. Any small scrap of encouragement made her feel more confident.

'There is sad news for the Lester family, I'm afraid,' Angela said, trying to think just how to tell them what had happened.

'Not Kate and her baby?' Philippe asked, suddenly alarmed that something terrible had happened.

Angela shook her head and proceeded to tell them what had happened. When she had finished, she turned to Julia.

'You must tell Pippa tomorrow,' she said. 'She'll be wondering what's happened to Nancy.'

'I will,' Julia said, clearly shaken by the terrible news. 'And to think he will never get to meet his daughter. That's so dreadful. Kate must be heartbroken.'

What followed was a silence no one could think how to fill. In the end it was Ian Dixon who drew Philippe aside.

'This is a very awkward situation, Philippe,' he said. 'I'm probably breaking a confidence but you would have your suspicions as to who the father of Kate's baby actually is, I'm sure. But it seems his sister is totally unaware of it.'

Philippe nodded slightly. No one had ever confirmed it to him but he had guessed. He guessed too that Kate had told Richard of her condition at his and Julia's wedding.

'Does Richard know about Gerald Lester's death and the baby being born?' Philippe asked, in a voice barely above a whisper.

'Yes,' Ian said quietly. 'Angela telephoned him this afternoon, at Kate's request.'

'I hope he's not planning on coming down to the funeral,' Philippe said. 'That would be awkward to say the least.'

Ian shook his head.

'No, he said he won't come down for a couple of months, but I think you should tell Julia.'

Philippe considered this advice for a few moments and then nodded.

'I'll tell her when I get a chance,' he said. 'I think it will come as a shock to her.'

Philippe had been concentrating so hard on what Ian had been saying he did not see Karen until she was almost right in front of him.

'You two are in deep conversation here,' she said brightly.

He looked up and just for a fleeting moment, their eyes met. Then he looked away quickly.

She leant forward and greeted Ian with a quick kiss on the cheek. Just as Julia turned to look for Philippe, she saw Karen place her hand on his arm and greet him too, only this time she lingered over the kiss on the cheek. She noticed too how Philippe very briefly put his arm around her.

'Lovely to see you again,' she murmured.

Then he moved away from her slightly, yet he could not ignore the slight quickening of his pulse at the sight of her after so long. But he was all too aware that Julia had been watching the exchange closely.

'You remember my wife Julia,' he said, forcing Karen to turn her attention away from him.

She smiled and held out her hand to Julia, who took it reluctantly.

'He's mine, Karen,' Julia wanted to say. 'He's my husband now so keep your hands to yourself.' But she did not. Instead she smiled politely.

Karen couldn't help but notice the effort Julia had taken with her dress.

'Not bad,' she thought, 'but it needs to be a slightly different colour to suit her blonde hair. Philippe clearly adores her. But he's still attracted to me. I can see it in his eyes. I could feel it in his touch.'

'I'm assuming Angela just told you about Kate Lester?' Karen asked conversationally.

She had noticed the four of them in earnest discussion and guessed Angela would have been the source of the news that she herself had just heard from her uncle.

Julia nodded.

'It's terribly sad,' Julia replied, 'her husband being killed like that. To think he will never get to meet his daughter.'

Julia was stunned when Karen let out a sudden laugh. It seemed like a totally inappropriate response to the tragedy.

'His daughter?' she exclaimed.

And then the realisation hit her. Julia doesn't know.

'That wasn't her husband's baby she had, Julia,' Karen retorted.

She paused for breath. She was about to reveal the shocking truth about Kate Lester's baby. But Philippe drew in a deep breath and shot a warning glance at Karen, shaking his head slightly.

'Not her husband's baby?' Julia asked, her confusion obvious to everyone. 'What do you mean? Whose baby is it?'

She was suddenly aware then she was in the midst of a group of people who knew something important that she did not.

'Karen,' Philippe said. She could not miss the anger in his voice. 'I don't think this is the time or place for what you are about to say.'

She shrugged and smiled. It was a smile of delicious triumph.

'Then I'll leave you to tell your wife, Philippe,' she said as she turned and walked off.

Julia looked at him then and saw a mixture of exasperation and anger on his face. How was Karen so sure, Philippe wondered? She's been away for the greater part of the year. And then he remembered. Of course, she had lunch with Richard in London. Someone must have written to her to tell her Kate was pregnant and she's put Richard on the spot and he couldn't deny it.

'That woman is just plain trouble,' Ian lamented.

'Trouble is right,' Philippe agreed. 'She just couldn't resist making mischief.'

'Well, you would know, Philippe,' Ian wanted to say but he refrained.

Julia looked from one man to the other, but it was Angela who came to the rescue.

'My dear girl,' Angela said, as she slipped her arm through Julia's and guided her to a quiet space, 'this is going to come as something of a shock. How do I tell you this?'

'Tell me what?' Julia replied, still bewildered by the whole conversation.

Angela let out a deep sigh.

'Your brother Richard is the father of Kate's baby,' she said as calmly as she could.

Julia's face registered shock and disbelief in equal measure. How could this be, she wanted to ask? How could I not know? When? How?

But then she remembered. Richard had taken his son Paul to visit the Lester family around New Year. And she remembered how insistent he was that he be the one to accompany Pippa back to Sydney at the end of January. Was he seeing Kate Lester then? He must have been.

'Does he know about the baby being born?' Julia asked. 'Has somebody told him?'

Angela nodded.

'Yes, I called him this afternoon to tell him everything,' Angela replied. 'I think when the dust settles, you'll find Kate Lester will become your sister-in-law.'

She could see Julia was still struggling with the news as the two men joined them.

'Did you know, Philippe?' Julia asked, her face still registering the shock of the news.

'I suspected,' he said, as he put his arm around her, 'but I didn't know for sure.'

'Did you see them together?' Julia asked. 'You must have done to suspect my brother of having an affair with her.'

Memories of the dinner at Robert and Patricia Clarke's house came flooding back to him. And to Ian and Angela Dixon too.

Again, Angela came to the rescue. She knew Philippe would hardly want to recall that evening. It was dangerous ground for him. He would not want his own conduct at the dinner being discussed. Nor would he want Karen's name to be mentioned.

'We were all there, Julia,' she explained. 'At a dinner at the Clarke's house. We saw them together. Your brother came with his friend John Bertram. Kate came with us as she was visiting with her daughter to go to the ballet matinee that afternoon. It was mere coincidence that she was there without her husband.'

'But how would my brother know Robert Clarke?' Julia asked.

But she answered her own question.

'Through you, Philippe, I assume,' she said, struggling to get all the pieces in place in her mind.

'Well, actually, it was through Pippa and Anita,' Philippe explained. 'He brought the Clarke's daughter back from Bowral and when he dropped her off, he met the Clarkes then. Robert Clarke is very keen on war history so he was keen to have Richard come to dinner the next evening.'

Once again, he carefully avoided any mention of Karen.

Julia nodded then as if she finally understood. She remembered that Richard had told her briefly about his trip to Bowral and what he had done in Sydney but he had clearly omitted any reference to Kate Lester.

'He never mentioned Kate Lester except in passing,' she said. 'Nor Karen Clarke. I assume she saw them together too?'

Both Ian and Angela noticed Philippe's very slight intake of breath but he simply nodded to indicate she was right.

'There are some things about his life he would be very keen to keep from his new wife,' Angela whispered to her husband, who murmured his agreement.

They all followed Julia's gaze to where Karen was having an animated discussion with a group of people.

'I hope she's not spreading gossip about Richard,' Julia said, with a sense of alarm.

'So do I,' Philippe said. 'So do I.'

He guessed she had done it just to annoy him and to unsettle Julia. If that was the case, he thought, she's succeeded spectacularly.

CHAPTER 35

December 1960

The boardroom at Curtis Transport emptied quickly after the final meeting of the year until only three men remained. Evelyn Passmore, Sid Curtis's long-serving secretary, began to clear the table. Richard helped her collect the used coffee cups and water glasses. She mumbled her thanks. Such a courtesy was unusual and unexpected. It had almost never happened in her thirty years of service to the company.

But he waved away her thanks. It seemed such a small thing. Besides he had his motives too. He did not particularly want to walk out with David Clarke so he hung back but, in the end, he could not avoid the encounter. He looked up just as David Clarke motioned to him to join him and the chairman Sid Curtis. He held his hand out towards Richard, who could do nothing but reciprocate the gesture.

'That was a good suggestion,' David Clarke said, 'to split the company into operations and property holding. We can then consider that offer to take over the transport side without giving up the property assets.'

To Richard, it has seemed simple. The property assets had been wildly undervalued on the balance sheet and he had spotted it. As it stood, he believed the takeover bid currently being supported by Roger Fairholm would not see the shareholders get full value for the company. He suspected Roger Fairholm of having a secret stake in the bid.

'Well, our chairman wants to take life a bit easier,' Richard observed. 'Managing a property portfolio would surely be easier than managing a transport company.'

Sid Curtis managed a rare smile.

'I think it's time though for a younger man to step up to be chairman,' he said, looking pointedly in Richard's direction.

But Richard shook his head.

'I just wouldn't have the time,' he replied.

He could have added 'nor the inclination' but he did not. It was David Clarke who offered up an excuse for his reluctance.

'Sid, you probably don't know that young Mr Belleville is getting married again, I believe.'

Richard received hearty congratulations from Sid Curtis but said nothing beyond a simple 'thank you'. He held his breath for what might be coming next. It had, after all, been David Clarke's daughter who had forced others to tell his sister about his involvement with Kate Lester before he himself had the chance.

He recalled Julia's telephone call early the next morning. She had been very annoyed with him for not having told her. She had only calmed down when he had pointed out that the turn of events had been totally unexpected. Except for Kate becoming a widow, he would never have been able to claim the child as his own. He had not wanted to risk her being gossiped about.

'Anyone I know?' Sid Curtis asked out of politeness.

He liked Richard and was genuinely interested. In the corner of the boardroom, Evelyn Passmore, who had almost finished clearing the meeting table, was also keen to hear the reply. Such a nice man, she thought. He deserves a good woman. Please let it not be Karen Clarke. She hadn't forgotten Richard's gallant defence of Karen Clarke earlier in the year.

Again, it was David Clarke, not Richard, who provided the answer.

'If I'm not mistaken,' he said to Sid Curtis, 'it's Kate Lester. She was widowed quite recently. Her husband was Gerald Lester, killed in a horse-riding accident. You've probably met him at some time or another.'

'Yes, of course,' Sid Curtis replied. 'We've transported cattle for the Lesters for years. I heard about the accident. Terrible thing to happen.

She's just had a baby, as I recall. I'm sure someone told me that.'

Horrified, Richard noticed a strange knowing smile crease David Clarke's ruddy face.

'Well, I'm sure Richard will be a good father to the little girl,' David Clarke said looking at Richard and grinning all the more at the relief he saw in his face.

'I will indeed,' Richard said, as he edged towards the door in the hope of bringing the conversation to an end.

But he was still not to be free of David Clarke, who clapped him on the shoulder.

'Let's go down to that little Italian place for lunch,' he said. 'My daughter was hoping to catch up with you.'

They both turned to shake Sid Curtis's hand and Richard lifted his hand in farewell to Evelyn Passmore, who smiled her thanks. How lucky is the young widow to have him, she thought? Their families are probably old friends.

As the two men headed down in the lift together, it was Richard who broke the silence. He had been reluctant to accompany David Clarke but he had seen no way out without causing unnecessary offence.

'Your daughter is not in my good books right now,' Richard said, without wanting to explain why.

David Clarke inclined his head slightly.

'I can understand why,' he replied. 'I was there at the dinner and I saw her go up to your sister and her husband. It was the very day Kate Lester had her baby.'

Richard noted his reluctance to mention Philippe by name. He knew then that David Clarke was fully aware of what his daughter had done.

'Well, as you can imagine,' Richard said, 'I had my sister on the phone to me next morning. She was pretty upset, upset that Karen, of all people, was the one to break the news to her – or at least force others to tell her the news that would have been better coming from me.'

David Clarke nodded.

'I understand why you are annoyed with her,' he said, looking sideways at Richard to gauge his mood.

'I'm sorry my daughter did that,' he continued, 'but I suspect she just couldn't resist stirring up a bit of mischief. I don't think she's quite got that bloody American out of her system yet. He was sleeping with her you know. Our cleaning lady found one of his cufflinks under her bed when we got back. In fact, it was the day I came upon you and Karen having lunch together. I wished it had been your cufflink and not Duval's.'

They had been walking side by side heading towards the harbour. It was a warm day and Richard had slipped his jacket off. He did not relish the rehashing of old scandal concerning Philippe.

'I think that part of his life is best not spoken of,' Richard said tersely. 'He's married my sister as he said he would and they are making a life together. I hope Karen gives him a wide berth from now on.'

David Clarke nodded, this time he was in full agreement with Richard.

'I hope so too,' he said. And he meant it sincerely. 'Karen told me she had lunch with you in London in May. That was very nice of you. She found it all very interesting over there but she was lonely at times.'

That admission surprised Richard. Karen did not strike him as the type of girl to spend time alone.

'My friend John Bertram told me she had returned home when I saw him in October,' Richard said. 'He's a Qantas pilot and apparently she was on his flight back from London. He mentioned she was still keen on setting up a fashion business with her friend Bianca.'

David Clarke smiled. This time it was a smile of genuine pleasure. He admired his daughter's initiative even if he didn't have much faith in the business prospects of their venture.

'Oh, yes,' he said. 'The two of them are planning to launch with a winter range next year, whatever that means. I've been prevailed upon to lease them one of my small commercial properties for a rent-free period.'

Richard laughed then. He sympathised with David Clarke for once. Women's fashion was not something either man could get very enthused about.

'Just before we go across to meet her, though,' David Clarke said, putting a restraining hand on Richard's arm, 'there's one thing I would like you to know. I'm the only person, apart from Bianca, who knows this. Not even her mother knows.'

Richard stopped suddenly. He had a strong suspicion then of what was coming. For some reason he felt David Clarke had the urge to confide in him. He wondered idly what he had done to justify the older man's confidence in him.

'Karen had a miscarriage in London in April,' David Clarke said, with a deep sigh. 'I think she's only just recovered her spirits fully now.'

Richard didn't need to ask who the father had been. And it all fitted. She had expected to be away a full year, time enough to have a baby.

'You knew before she went, I take it?' Richard asked.

'I did,' he said. 'She needed money of course. In fact, she wasn't absolutely sure of her condition when she left but she wasn't taking any chances.'

Richard looked at him, trying to understand why he had felt compelled to mention it. It hardly made any sense at all.

'Why tell me now?' he asked, his face distorted by a deep frown. 'I didn't need to know. I didn't want to know.'

David Clarke turned towards him then.

'You've been kind to Karen,' he said. 'You're a decent man and I want you to know my daughter is really a decent girl.'

He paused, as if uncertain how much more he should say. But in the end, he wanted Richard to understand everything.

'She told me she did not want to ruin your sister's happiness', he explained. 'She did not want to force Duval to give up your sister and marry her. She did not want him on those terms. She felt he would have resented her in the end.'

Richard was momentarily lost for words. He hadn't expected to hear that about her and yet, thinking about it, he found himself believing it.

'And if she had gone on to have the baby?'

It was a question Richard wasn't sure he should ask. But he was curious. If she had come back to Sydney with a baby, everyone would have known, including Philippe. His marriage to Julia might well have collapsed.

'She was going to come back but to Melbourne, where she wasn't well known,' he said. 'She'd planned it all but then it didn't happen.'

Richard was silent for a minute or two, trying to understand what he had just been told.

'I'm shocked,' Richard said eventually. 'She seemed bright and her usual self when I saw her in May. I had no idea. Not the slightest inkling.'

'In a way I think she was relieved to be honest,' David Clarke admitted. 'But Duval must never know. And she must never know I've told you. I just don't want you to think badly of her. She's been through this by herself. With no support. Perhaps she brings some things on herself, I admit that. But Duval should have known better.'

Her father was right. Philippe should have known better. But then Richard felt he was hardly in a position to stand in judgement on another man's behaviour. And Karen? She's not blameless. He doubted Philippe would have forced himself on her.

'Thanks for telling me,' Richard said. 'Rest assured I won't be telling anyone.'

'Good man,' David Clarke said, as they spotted Karen and crossed the road to greet her.

It was mid-afternoon and Kate Lester couldn't settle. She would sit for a few moments and then she would get up and walk to the window. She would sit down again and pretend to read a magazine before repeating the whole thing again. Fortunately, none of this agitation was having any impact on her baby, who slept soundly in her carry cot in the corner of Angela Dixon's living room.

Finally, Angela lowered the book she was reading and looked at her friend.

'He will be here soon, Kate,' she said, with just a hint of exasperation.

Kate smiled apologetically.

'I'm sorry,' she said. 'I'm just nervous about seeing him. But I'm so grateful you've made it possible for me to meet him here.'

Angela got up then and came to sit beside her friend on the sofa. She put her arm around Kate's shoulders.

'You don't have to say a word of thanks,' she said. 'I'm always happy to help you.'

Kate smiled. Angela had been the best of friends to her.

'It's easier not to have the older children around when he sees Susan for the first time,' Kate said.

But her friend had already guessed that. The children were still grieving the loss of their father. They knew Richard but only as a family friend. They both knew the children would feel hurt to think someone was already trying to usurp their father's role in the family.

'Hopefully, he will bring something small, bright and expensive for you,' Angela said, which made Kate smile.

The sound of the doorbell cut across their conversation and Angela got up quickly to answer it. She ushered Richard into the living room and then headed to the kitchen to make coffee. Richard went straight across to Kate and kissed her tenderly.

'You've been through a lot, my darling,' he said, as he turned towards the baby girl who had woken up at the sound of his voice.

'It looks like I've disturbed her,' he apologised, as he walked across to her cot and lifted the baby into his arms.

The baby smiled for him and he was immediately captivated. His first daughter. Not quite planned, but welcome anyway. At that moment, he wondered if it was too late to try for a sister for her. The other children are so much older, he thought. He didn't want her to be a lonely child.

He handed the baby to Kate and then he plunged his hand into his pocket. He withdrew a small box and opened it.

Kate gasped and then smiled. He had brought something small, bright and expensive for me, as Angela had predicted, she thought.

'Will you marry me, Kate? he asked, as he slipped the emerald and diamond cluster ring on her finger.

She nodded and smiled happily.

'Oh, yes please,' she said, as she reached up to kiss him.

'When?' he asked. 'How long will I have to wait for you?'

She sat back on the sofa, a slight frown creasing her face.

'It would be unseemly for me to rush into another marriage,' she said. 'I have to think of the children. I don't want people gossiping.'

But he shook his head.

'They will gossip anyway when I claim Susan as mine,' he said. 'I don't accept that as an excuse.'

She had known he would say that, so she had already thought about a possible date.

'What about Easter Saturday?' she suggested. 'Unless you think the first of April is not a propitious day?'

It was sooner than he had hoped. In a little over three months, they would be married.

'First of April it is,' he said, smiling broadly.

Angela pushed open the living room door and he rushed to help her with the tray loaded with cups of coffee.

'You're the first to know, Angela,' Richard said. 'We are getting married on the first of April.'

She put the tray down on the coffee table and kissed each of them in turn, admiring the engagement ring Kate now wore in place of her previous rings.

'Well, something good has come from a tragedy,' she said, as she handed the coffee around. 'When will you tell your children, Kate? And your children will have to be told too, Richard.'

'After Christmas,' they said in unison. 'After Christmas will be soon enough.'

'In fact, I'm due to meet my younger son and his mother tomorrow and travel with them back home,' he said.

Kate already knew that. They had been in touch constantly by telephone. But it was news to Angela and she looked at her friend to gauge her reaction. But she need not have worried.

Kate was smiling happily. She knew Richard would be a happier man with both his sons living in Australia. To feel jealous of his first wife would be pointless, she had told herself repeatedly.

She was simply delighted she was going to be Richard's wife. She had not thought it would ever be possible. But fate had intervened. She already looked forward to their future together.

'And where will you live?' Angela asked.

It seemed an obvious question yet there were blank looks from both of them. And then they laughed.

'We haven't quite got that far yet, Angela,' Richard said, 'but if it's any help, I do have my private pilot's licence so it may be that we travel between homes.'

'Anyway, it's Tim who has inherited Berrima Park,' Kate explained. 'I have the right to live there and I am his trustee until he turns twenty-five but it will belong to him.'

She had already told Richard about the provisions of her husband's will.

'And Nancy?' Angela asked.

Why is it, she wondered, girls always seem to take second place to boys when it comes to family inheritances.

'She has a share in the family trust that draws income from all the properties and business interests as I do,' she explained, 'but it is Tim who has inherited the actual properties.'

'And Susan?' Angela asked.

But Richard intervened.

'I'll take care of Susan's future,' he said.

He did not expect his daughter to benefit from Gerald Lester's estate.

Kate nodded contentedly and turned her attention to baby Susan who had gone back to sleep but would very soon wake again demanding to be fed.

Anthony Belleville had been a mere five years old when he had travelled with his father to the other side of the world to visit his mother. And he had not returned to the home he had known since he was born. Until today.

He felt a simmering sense of excitement as his father drove them through the town, past funny timber houses set high up off the ground on posts, and eventually out into the countryside. He was forcing himself to remember. Everything was so different from what he had become used to. Fields of brownish green grass stretched interminably towards the horizon. Here and there on the fringes of the fields, tall straight trees with scanty leaves, some with bark separating from the trunks, offered scant shade. Eventually, the smooth road surface gave way to hard packed dirt but he noticed how easily his father negotiated the change.

His strongest memory was of the big house in which he had felt safe and protected from the world outside. But he knew not to expect to see it.

In the front seat, his mother was revisiting the same familiar world. He looked at his parents sitting side by side and for a moment he could imagine they were together again. But he knew it could never happen now. They would never be together again as a family. It was a momentary illusion.

He looked at his father. Will I look like him when I am older, he wondered? Does my brother already look like him?

The car slowed then as his father avoided the kangaroo that had hopped into the middle of the road and paused, before going on its way. Anthony sat up to catch a glimpse of the animal disappearing through the undergrowth.

A little while later, he felt the car slow again and his father turn into the Prior Park driveway.

'I remember this part,' he thought, 'and then it opens out to a circular driveway in front of the big house.'

But his father did not stop as Anthony remembered. Instead he kept going past a pile of old bricks onto a new road. He brought the car to a halt to the side of a large timber home with wide verandahs on three sides.

And there they all were to greet him and his mother. Aunt Alice. Marianne. His brother Paul And Uncle William. And Mrs Duffy and Charles Brockman. They were all there, welcoming him back. And welcoming his mother too.

But he knew there was one person missing whom he would never see again. His grandmother.

'Paul, you've grown so much,' his mother exclaimed as she enveloped him in a warm embrace. 'You're looking more and more like your father every day.'

He smiled. That suited him very well. He admired everything about his father. One day he expected to be the same kind of man as his father.

'What about me?' Anthony complained.

His mother put her arms around him to reassure him.

'I think perhaps you look like me,' she said, much to his disappointment. He wanted to look tall and strong like his father. Like his older brother.

Catherine looked around her. How is it possible to create a garden in such a place, she wondered? This must be Alice's doing.

'You've done wonders with the garden, Alice,' Catherine said, as she admired the expanse of improbably green lawn and the rose garden that had defied the extremes of climate to flourish.

'It's a battle,' Alice said, as they mounted the front stairs together. 'But I insisted on having a separate water supply for it, otherwise it would be dust by now.'

'And your new home is everything you hoped it would be?' Catherine asked.

'It is very comfortable,' Alice said, as she began to show Catherine around the house. 'Not as grand, but much easier to live in.'

Behind them, the men were left to bring in the luggage.

'Did you see Julia and Philippe in Sydney?' William asked Richard.

'Yes,' Richard replied. 'And Pippa too. We all had dinner together last night.'

'Do they seem settled together?

Richard nodded. William looked relieved.

'No sign of the other girl?'

Richard lowered his voice.

'I had lunch with her and her father two days ago,' he said. 'She never mentioned Philippe's name once.'

'That must have been a bit tough for you,' William said. 'Wasn't she the one who let on to Julia about Kate's baby? How is she by the way?'

'Kate is fine. My new daughter is beautiful,' he said, but William caught the warning in his voice.

'You haven't told Catherine you're getting married again, have you?'

He shook his head. He had forewarned Julia and Philippe not to speak about it.

'It didn't seem the right time somehow,' he said. 'But we've set a wedding date. First of April.'

William nodded but made no comment.

'Women never travel light, do they?' William grumbled, as he and Richard struggled under the weight of Catherine's heavy suitcases.

'You're right, brother,' he replied. 'They do not.'

They had all gathered on the verandah where tea had been drunk and cake had been eaten. Anthony had been fussed over, which he enjoyed, but which made the older children jealous.

As Mrs Duffy and Alice began clearing the tea things, Richard stood up and beckoned to his younger son.

'I want to show Anthony what remains of the old house,' Richard said, 'before it gets fully dark.'

'We'll all go and have a look, shall we?' Catherine suggested, 'unless Alice needs my help?'

But Alice waved her away. Richard held out his hand to Anthony, who took it happily. His mother and his brother fell in behind the pair as they walked the short distance down the shallow slope to where their grand home had once stood.

It still puzzled Anthony why anyone would hate his family so much that he would do such a terrible thing.

Anthony stood looking at the charred broken remains, partly covered now by vines and weeds, and then looked at his brother who saw the shock on his face and came to stand alongside him.

'When I'm in charge,' he said quietly, 'we're going to rebuild it.'

'Why didn't our father and Uncle William rebuild it?' he asked.

But his father heard the question too and provided the answer.

'That big house belonged to the past,' he said. 'Your uncle and I felt we couldn't recapture that past.'

The two boys watched as their mother and father walked across to two graves, one recent, one not so recent.

'How do you feel,' Richard asked, 'returning to Prior Park?'

'It feels strange,' Catherine replied. 'Very strange. And tragic too.'

'Because the house is no longer here?' he asked.

'Because the house is no longer here,' she said, 'and because I no longer belong here. It all belongs to my past now. It's not part of my future.'

'It could have been part of your future,' Richard said, 'only you chose for it not to be.'

She nodded. More than three years ago she had left, knowing then in her heart she would never return, or at least never return as his wife.

She looked at him. He still stirred something in her. There was a safe predictability in her life now with Edward. But with Richard, there had been a sense of unpredictability. She missed that in her life. Am I admitting I still miss him, she wondered?

For his part, he had not told her he had met someone else. Standing alongside her, he still felt the familiar urge to be with her. Would he always feel that way, he wondered? Would she always hold some power over him?

'Have you told Anthony he is staying on with me?' Richard asked.

She nodded.

'I have and he's very excited, I think,' she said, 'but I think he's also afraid.'

'Of missing you too much?' Richard asked.

She nodded again.

'It will be a big change for him,' she said.

'But you do know why I'm doing it?' Richard said. 'It's not just for my sake.'

'For his sake, do you mean?'

'I do,' he said. 'He belongs here at Prior Park. Your new son will inherit Haldon Hall. Anthony wouldn't belong at all in that world once you are gone.'

She couldn't disagree with him. He was right. Richard's children belonged in Australia. They belonged at Prior Park. Unfortunately, they were her children too. She fully excepted Richard would want Anthony to remain indefinitely. She had not been deceived by his promises to return him.

For Paul and Anthony's sake she knew she must make the sacrifice. But it was no easy sacrifice for a mother to be deprived of her children. He must know that. He put his arm around her then.

'Don't worry, I'll look after them,' he said. 'It will make it easier for you and Edward too I imagine.'

He did not explain further what he meant but she knew. Anthony was a constant reminder to Edward of her first marriage and her first husband.

'I remember when you first brought me here,' she said. 'It was all so strange. So foreign. It seems like a lifetime ago. But it's only fifteen years ago. Yet so much has happened.'

'Yes, so much has happened,' he agreed. 'But that's life. In another fifteen years, our children will be adults, making their own way in the world.'

'Yes, they will,' she said, as she turned to walk back to the house.

He followed her and the boys fell into step beside their father.

'It's good to be home,' Anthony said quietly. 'I feel like I belong here. But I wish we still had the big house and grandmother was still here.'

Richard heard him and turned and gave him a quick hug.

'I'm sorry your grandmother isn't here too,' he said. 'But you belong here, son. You and Paul both belong here. Maybe we'll have to rebuild the big house one day.'

'We will, Dad,' Paul said confidently. 'We will. Prior Park without the grand house doesn't seem right.'

Richard smiled as Marianne came to join her cousins.

'She's the leader,' Richard thought, except Paul doesn't know it yet. And now there's another one to add to the next generation.

Susan Belleville.

There'll be a new chapter for the family soon, he thought, as he joined William and Charles on the verandah where glasses of cold beer had already been poured for them.

Paul. Marianne. Anthony. Susan.

The future of Prior Park. The future of the Belleville family.

For the first time in years, he felt content.

Made in the USA
Middletown, DE
05 March 2020